midnight mover

™

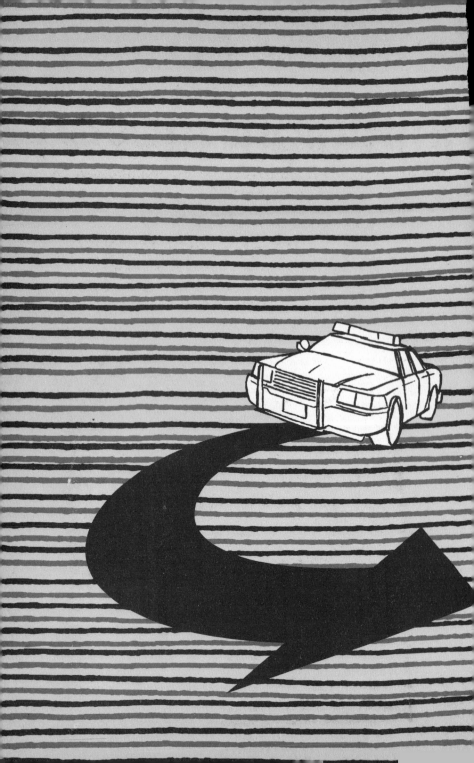

midnight mover ™

written by **GARY PHILLIPS**
pencilled by **JEREMY LOVE**
inked by **JEFF WASSON**

cover & chapter breaks by **MIKE HUDDLESTON**
lettered by **JEREMY LOVE &**
GETTOSAKE PRODUCTIONS

designed by **STEVEN BIRCH @ SERVO**
edited by **JAMES LUCAS JONES**

Published by ONI PRESS, INC.
JOE NOZEMACK publisher
JAMIE S. RICH editor in chief

This collects issues 1-4 of the
miniseries *Midnight Mover*.

ONI PRESS, INC.
6336 SE Milwaukie Avenue, PMB 30
Portland, OR 97202
USA

www.onipress.com
www.gdphillips.com
www.gettosake.com

First edition: January 2004
ISBN 1-929998-77-5

1 3 5 7 9 10 8 6 4 2
PRINTED IN CANADA.

the movers and shakers

Danny Shaw

Ginger Sweet

Remy

Sgt. Cynthia Oh

Det. Francisco Padilla

"Skull" Fuentes

Marc St. Mark

chapter one

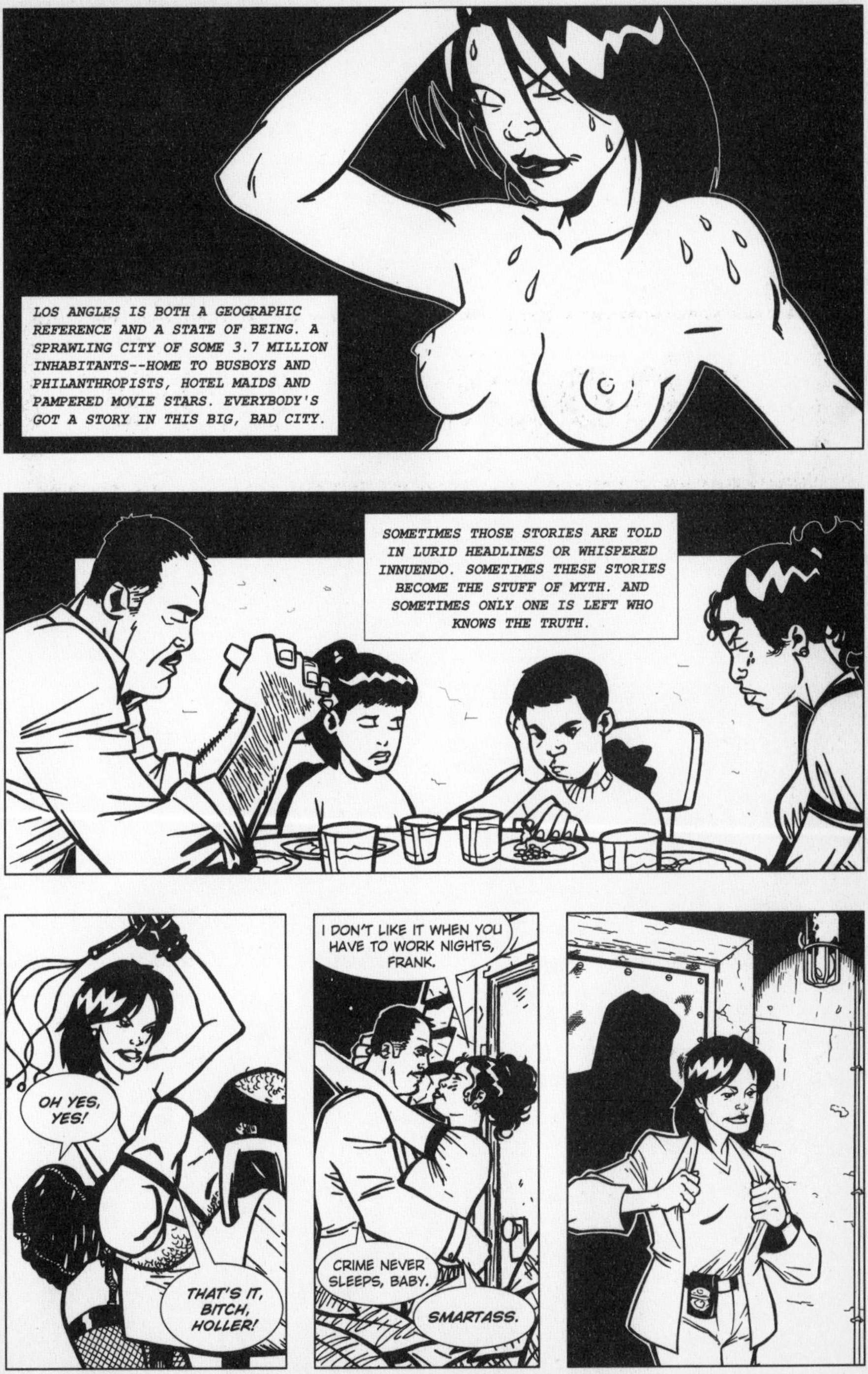
LOS ANGLES IS BOTH A GEOGRAPHIC REFERENCE AND A STATE OF BEING. A SPRAWLING CITY OF SOME 3.7 MILLION INHABITANTS--HOME TO BUSBOYS AND PHILANTHROPISTS, HOTEL MAIDS AND PAMPERED MOVIE STARS. EVERYBODY'S GOT A STORY IN THIS BIG, BAD CITY.
SOMETIMES THOSE STORIES ARE TOLD IN LURID HEADLINES OR WHISPERED INNUENDO. SOMETIMES THESE STORIES BECOME THE STUFF OF MYTH. AND SOMETIMES ONLY ONE IS LEFT WHO KNOWS THE TRUTH.
OH YES, YES!
THAT'S IT, BITCH, HOLLER!
I DON'T LIKE IT WHEN YOU HAVE TO WORK NIGHTS, FRANK.
CRIME NEVER SLEEPS, BABY.
SMARTASS.

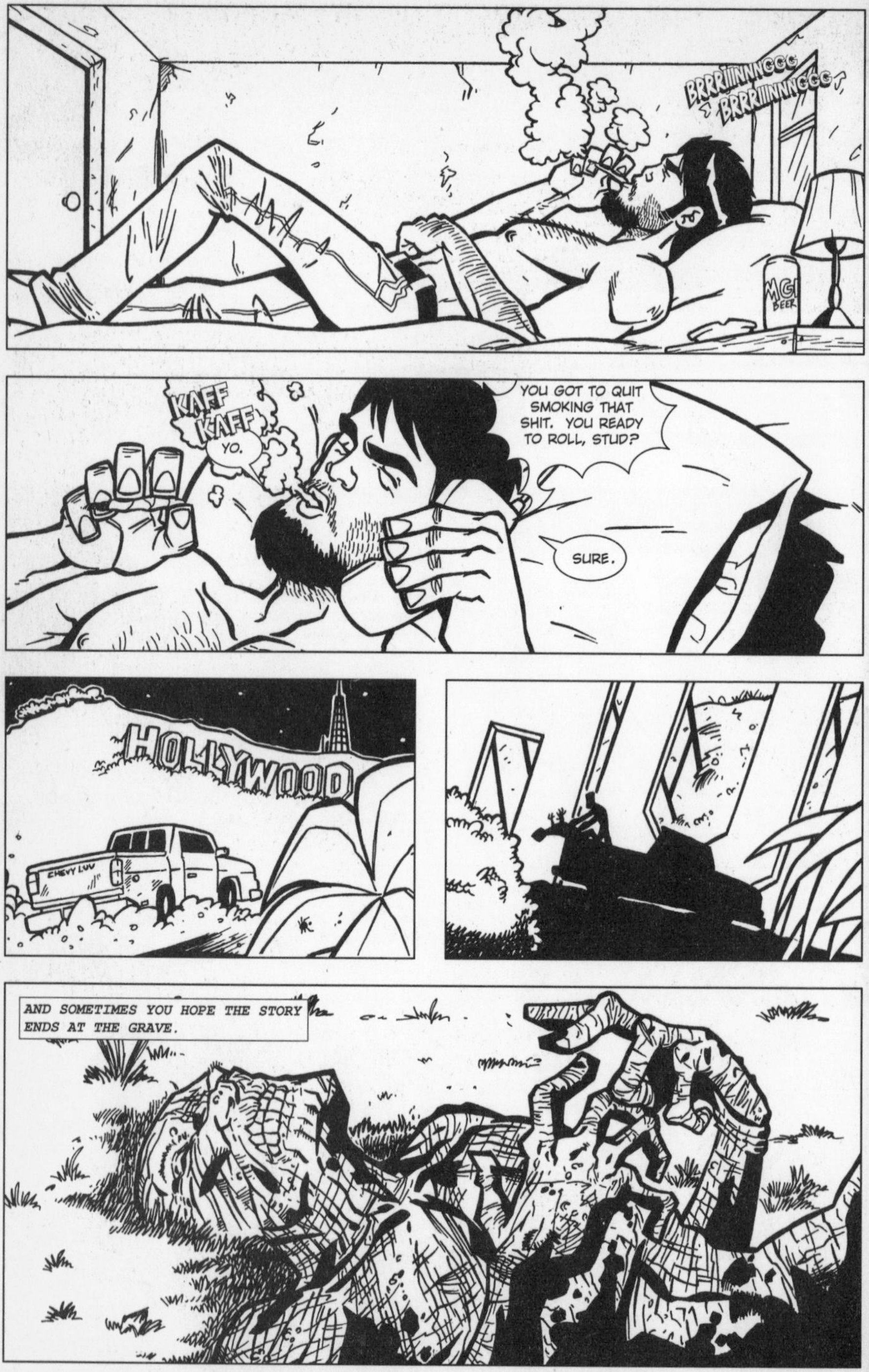
BRRRIIINNNGGG
BRRRIIINNNGGG
MGI BEER
KAFF KAFF
YO.
YOU GOT TO QUIT SMOKING THAT SHIT. YOU READY TO ROLL, STUD?
SURE.
HOLLYWOOD
CHEVY LUV
AND SOMETIMES YOU HOPE THE STORY ENDS AT THE GRAVE.

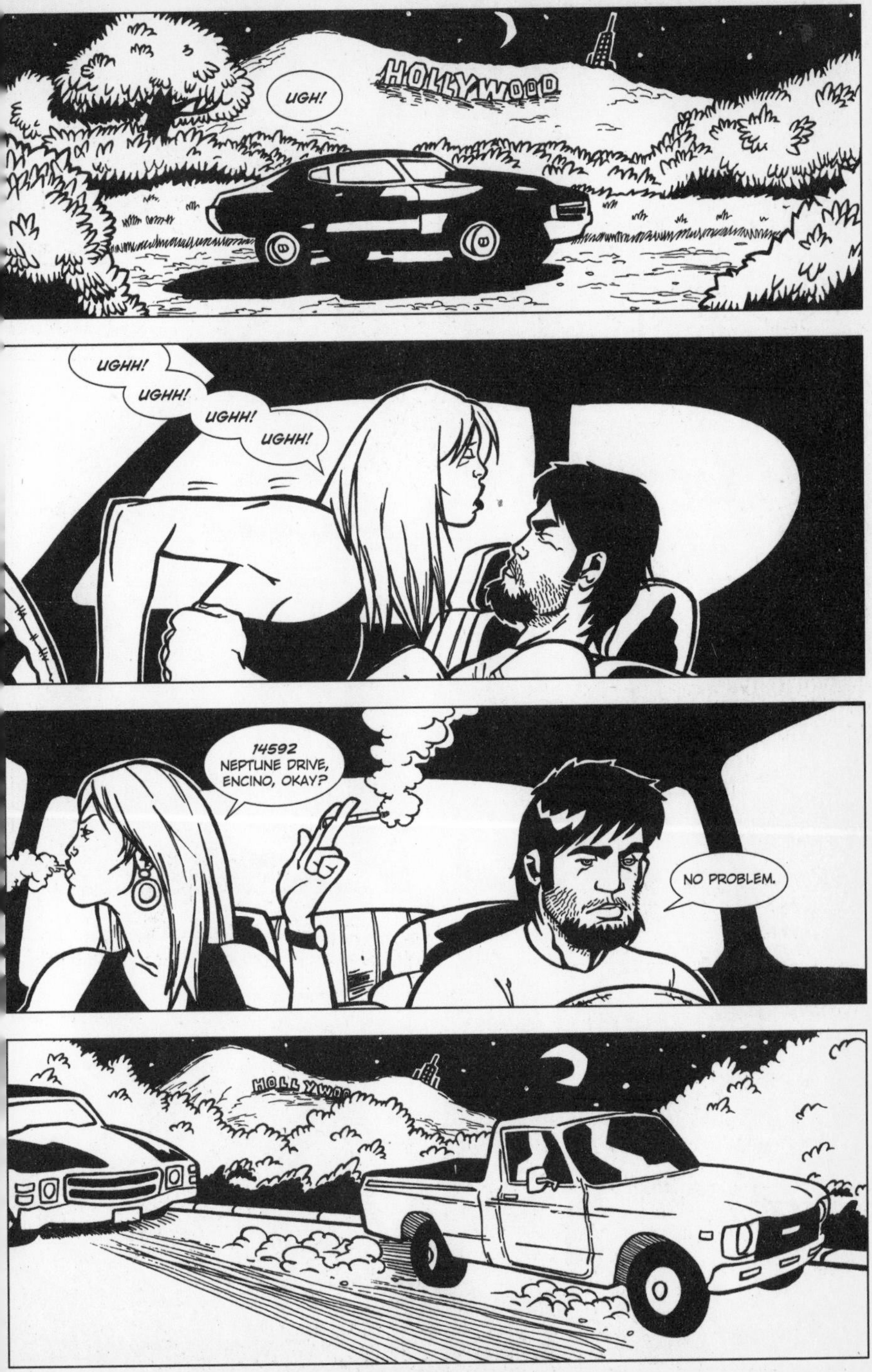
UGH!
UGHH!
UGHH!
UGHH!
UGHH!
14592 NEPTUNE DRIVE, ENCINO, OKAY?
NO PROBLEM.

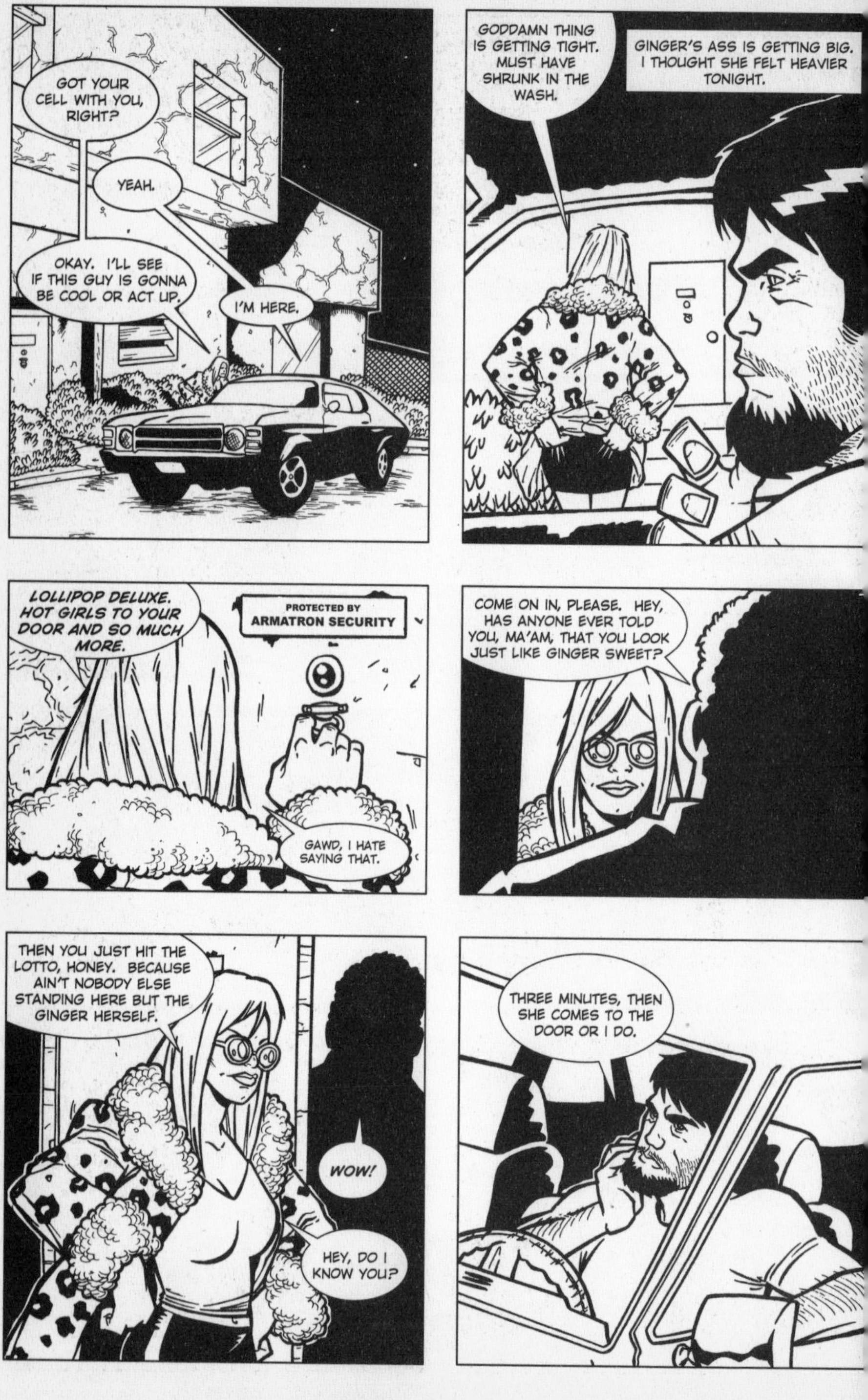
GOT YOUR CELL WITH YOU, RIGHT?
YEAH.
OKAY. I'LL SEE IF THIS GUY IS GONNA BE COOL OR ACT UP.
I'M HERE.
GODDAMN THING IS GETTING TIGHT. MUST HAVE SHRUNK IN THE WASH.
GINGER'S ASS IS GETTING BIG. I THOUGHT SHE FELT HEAVIER TONIGHT.
LOLLIPOP DELUXE. HOT GIRLS TO YOUR DOOR AND SO MUCH MORE.
PROTECTED BY ARMATRON SECURITY
GAWD, I HATE SAYING THAT.
COME ON IN, PLEASE. HEY, HAS ANYONE EVER TOLD YOU, MA'AM, THAT YOU LOOK JUST LIKE GINGER SWEET?
THEN YOU JUST HIT THE LOTTO, HONEY. BECAUSE AIN'T NOBODY ELSE STANDING HERE BUT THE GINGER HERSELF.
WOW!
HEY, DO I KNOW YOU?
THREE MINUTES, THEN SHE COMES TO THE DOOR OR I DO.

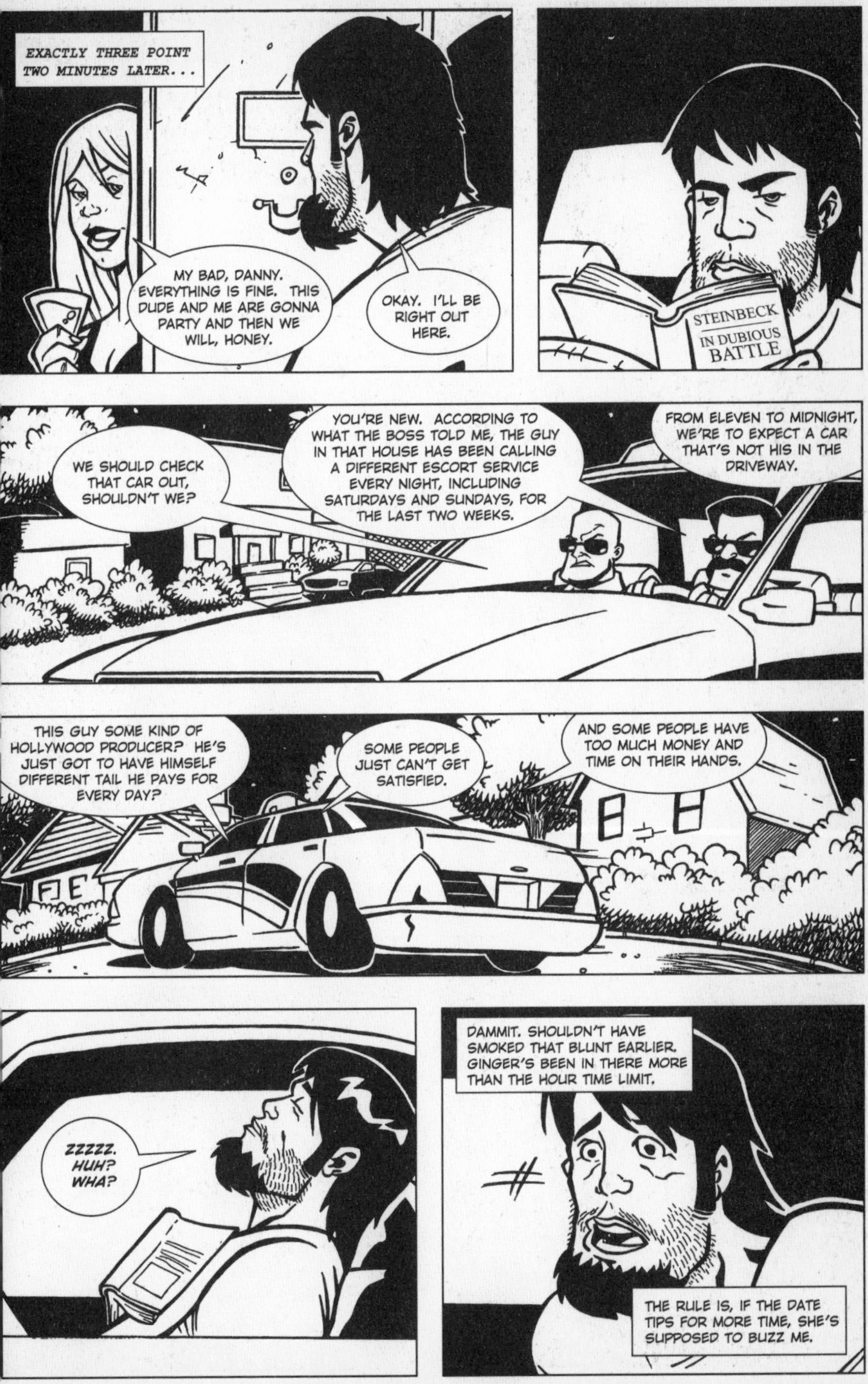
EXACTLY THREE POINT TWO MINUTES LATER...
MY BAD, DANNY. EVERYTHING IS FINE. THIS DUDE AND ME ARE GONNA PARTY AND THEN WE WILL, HONEY.
OKAY. I'LL BE RIGHT OUT HERE.
STEINBECK
IN DUBIOUS BATTLE
WE SHOULD CHECK THAT CAR OUT, SHOULDN'T WE?
YOU'RE NEW. ACCORDING TO WHAT THE BOSS TOLD ME, THE GUY IN THAT HOUSE HAS BEEN CALLING A DIFFERENT ESCORT SERVICE EVERY NIGHT, INCLUDING SATURDAYS AND SUNDAYS, FOR THE LAST TWO WEEKS.
FROM ELEVEN TO MIDNIGHT, WE'RE TO EXPECT A CAR THAT'S NOT HIS IN THE DRIVEWAY.
THIS GUY SOME KIND OF HOLLYWOOD PRODUCER? HE'S JUST GOT TO HAVE HIMSELF DIFFERENT TAIL HE PAYS FOR EVERY DAY?
SOME PEOPLE JUST CAN'T GET SATISFIED.
AND SOME PEOPLE HAVE TOO MUCH MONEY AND TIME ON THEIR HANDS.
ZZZZZ. HUH? WHA?
DAMMIT. SHOULDN'T HAVE SMOKED THAT BLUNT EARLIER. GINGER'S BEEN IN THERE MORE THAN THE HOUR TIME LIMIT.
THE RULE IS, IF THE DATE TIPS FOR MORE TIME, SHE'S SUPPOSED TO BUZZ ME.

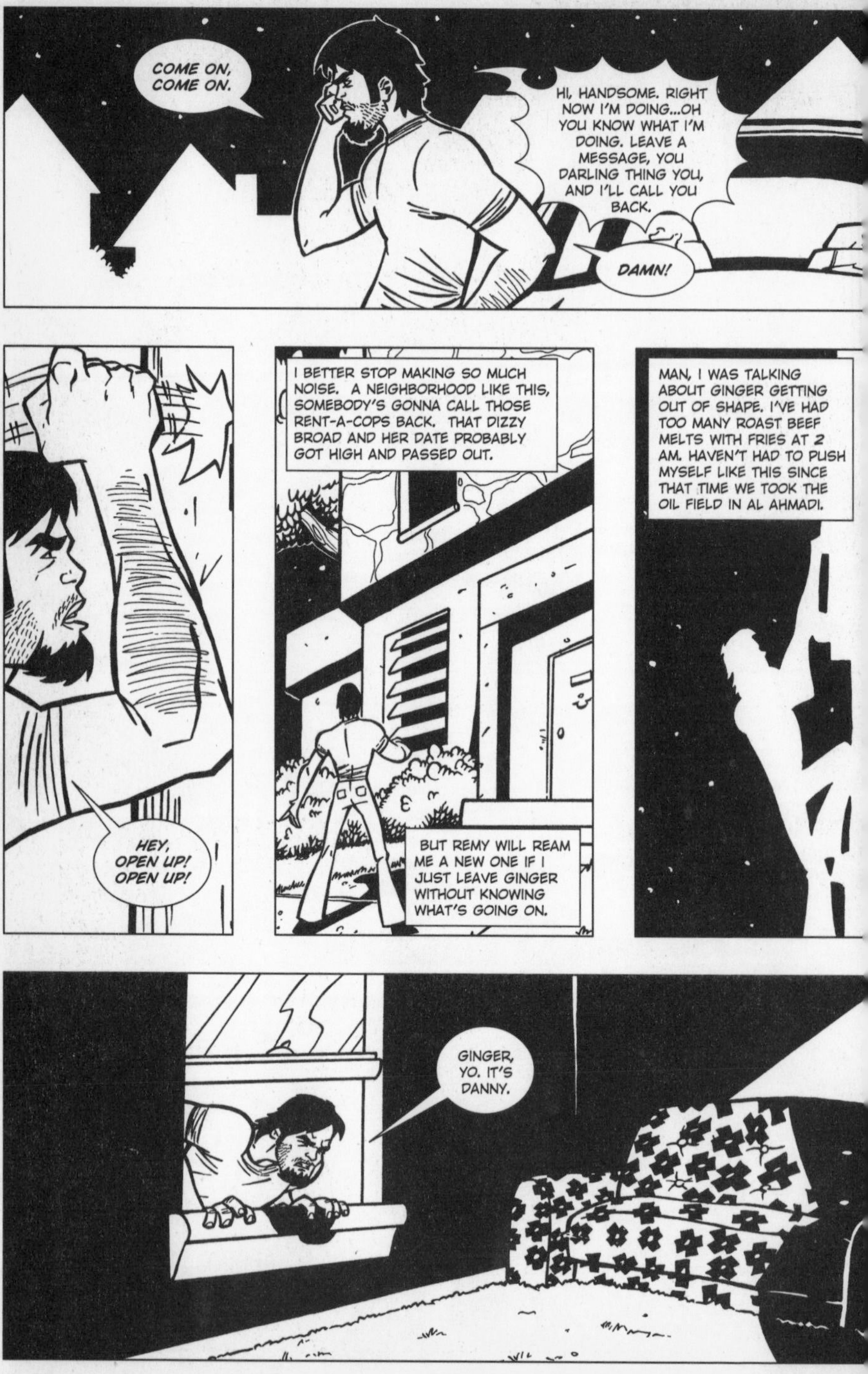
COME ON, COME ON.
HI, HANDSOME. RIGHT NOW I'M DOING...OH YOU KNOW WHAT I'M DOING. LEAVE A MESSAGE, YOU DARLING THING YOU, AND I'LL CALL YOU BACK.
DAMN!
HEY, OPEN UP! OPEN UP!
I BETTER STOP MAKING SO MUCH NOISE. A NEIGHBORHOOD LIKE THIS, SOMEBODY'S GONNA CALL THOSE RENT-A-COPS BACK. THAT DIZZY BROAD AND HER DATE PROBABLY GOT HIGH AND PASSED OUT.
BUT REMY WILL REAM ME A NEW ONE IF I JUST LEAVE GINGER WITHOUT KNOWING WHAT'S GOING ON.
MAN, I WAS TALKING ABOUT GINGER GETTING OUT OF SHAPE. I'VE HAD TOO MANY ROAST BEEF MELTS WITH FRIES AT 2 AM. HAVEN'T HAD TO PUSH MYSELF LIKE THIS SINCE THAT TIME WE TOOK THE OIL FIELD IN AL AHMADI.
GINGER, YO. IT'S DANNY.

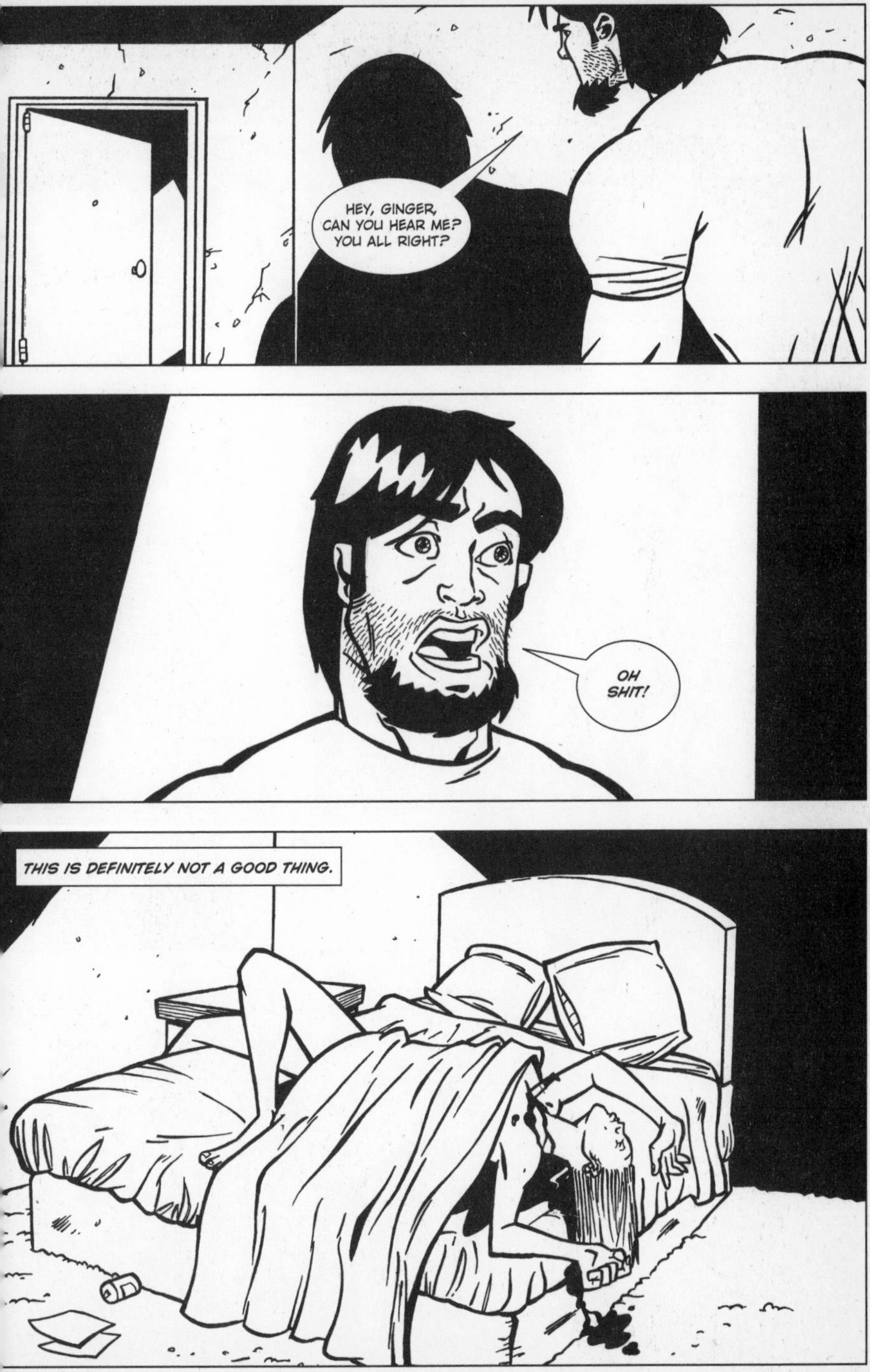
HEY, GINGER,
CAN YOU HEAR ME?
YOU ALL RIGHT?
OH
SHIT!
THIS IS DEFINITELY NOT A GOOD THING.

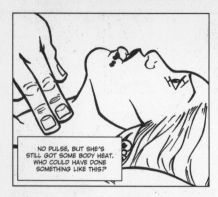

NO PULSE, BUT SHE'S STILL GOT SOME BODY HEAT. WHO COULD HAVE DONE SOMETHING LIKE THIS?

AND THIS IS A K-BAR LIKE THE ONES WE WERE TRAINED TO USE IN THE SERVICE. WHAT KIND OF COINCIDENCE IS THAT?

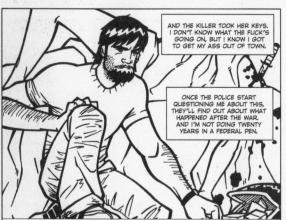

AND THE KILLER TOOK HER KEYS. I DON'T KNOW WHAT THE FLICK'S GOING ON, BUT I KNOW I GOT TO GET MY ASS OUT OF TOWN.

ONCE THE POLICE START QUESTIONING ME ABOUT THIS, THEY'LL FIND OUT ABOUT WHAT HAPPENED AFTER THE WAR. AND I'M NOT DOING TWENTY YEARS IN A FEDERAL PEN.

NO SENSE MAKING IT TOO EASY FOR THE COPS. I'LL WIPE MY PRINTS OFF OF ANYTHING I TOUCHED.

I'M SORRY, GINGER. WE HAD OUR FUN.

OKAY, TOOK CARE OF MY PRINTS ON THE WINDOW UPSTAIRS. NOW TO...

...GREAT, THESE CLOWNS ARE BACK.

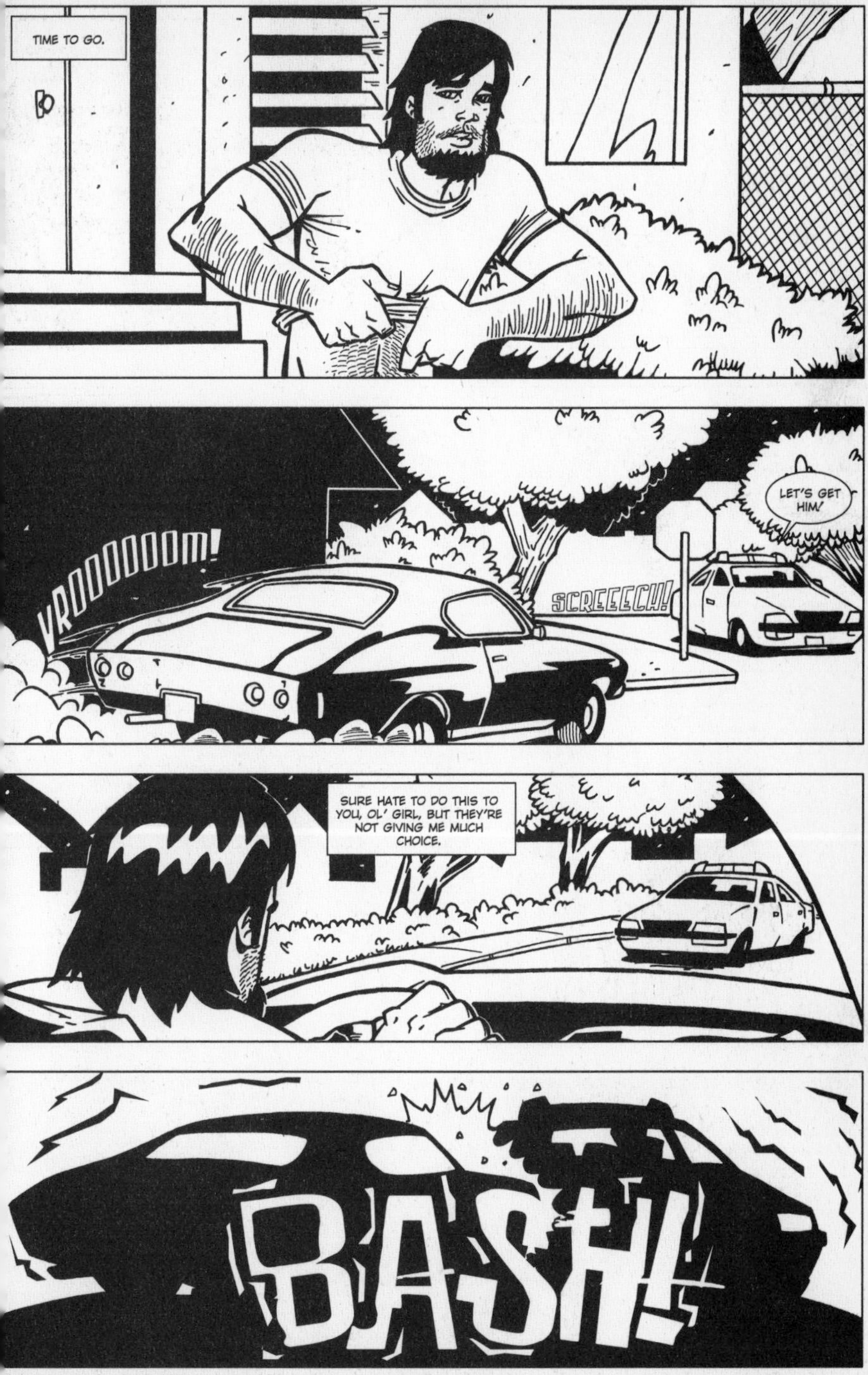

TIME TO GO.
VROOOOOOOM!
SCREEEECH!
LET'S GET HIM!
SURE HATE TO DO THIS TO YOU, OL' GIRL, BUT THEY'RE NOT GIVING ME MUCH CHOICE.
BASH!

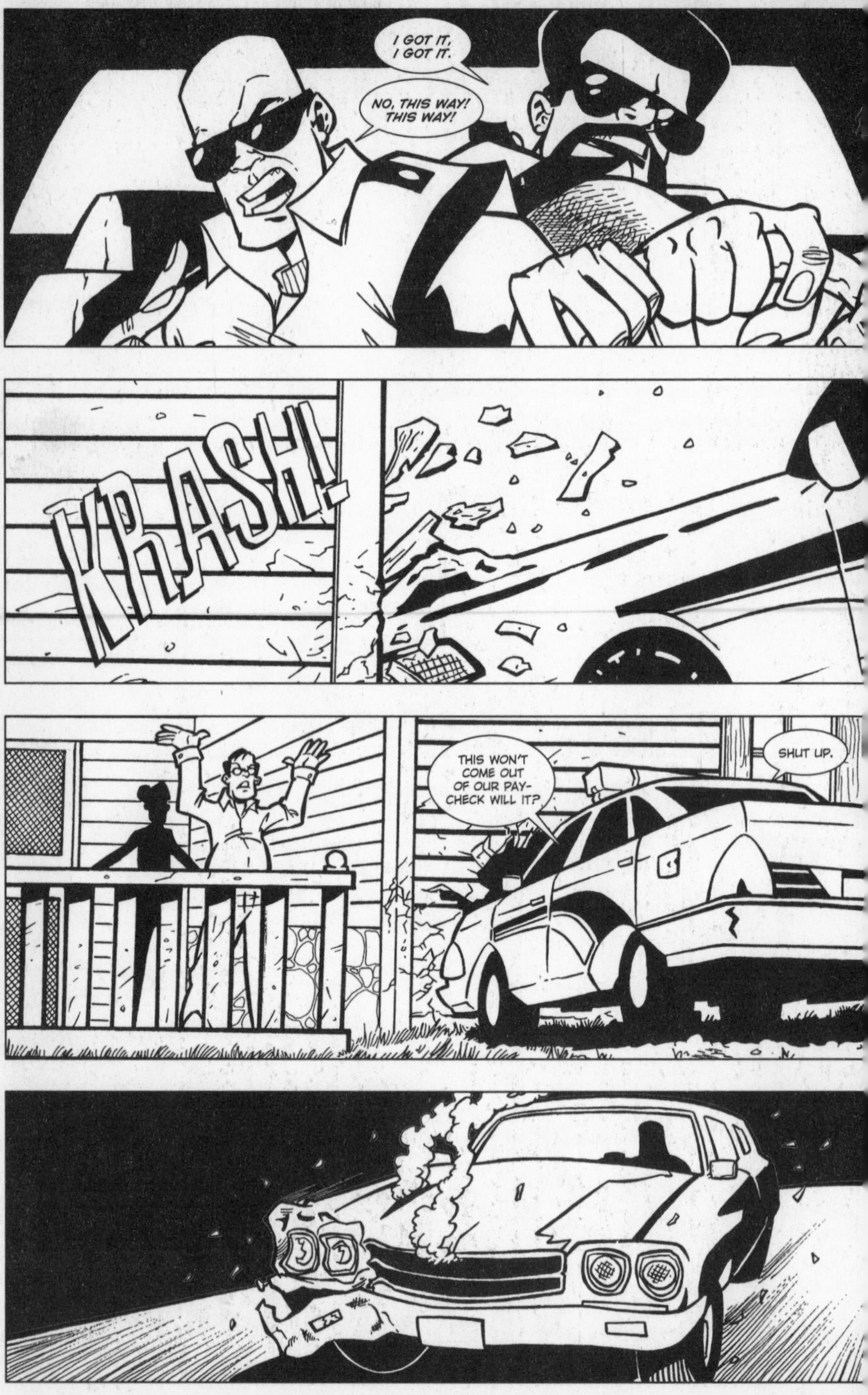
I GOT IT, I GOT IT.
NO, THIS WAY! THIS WAY!
KRASH!
THIS WON'T COME OUT OF OUR PAY-CHECK WILL IT?
SHUT UP.

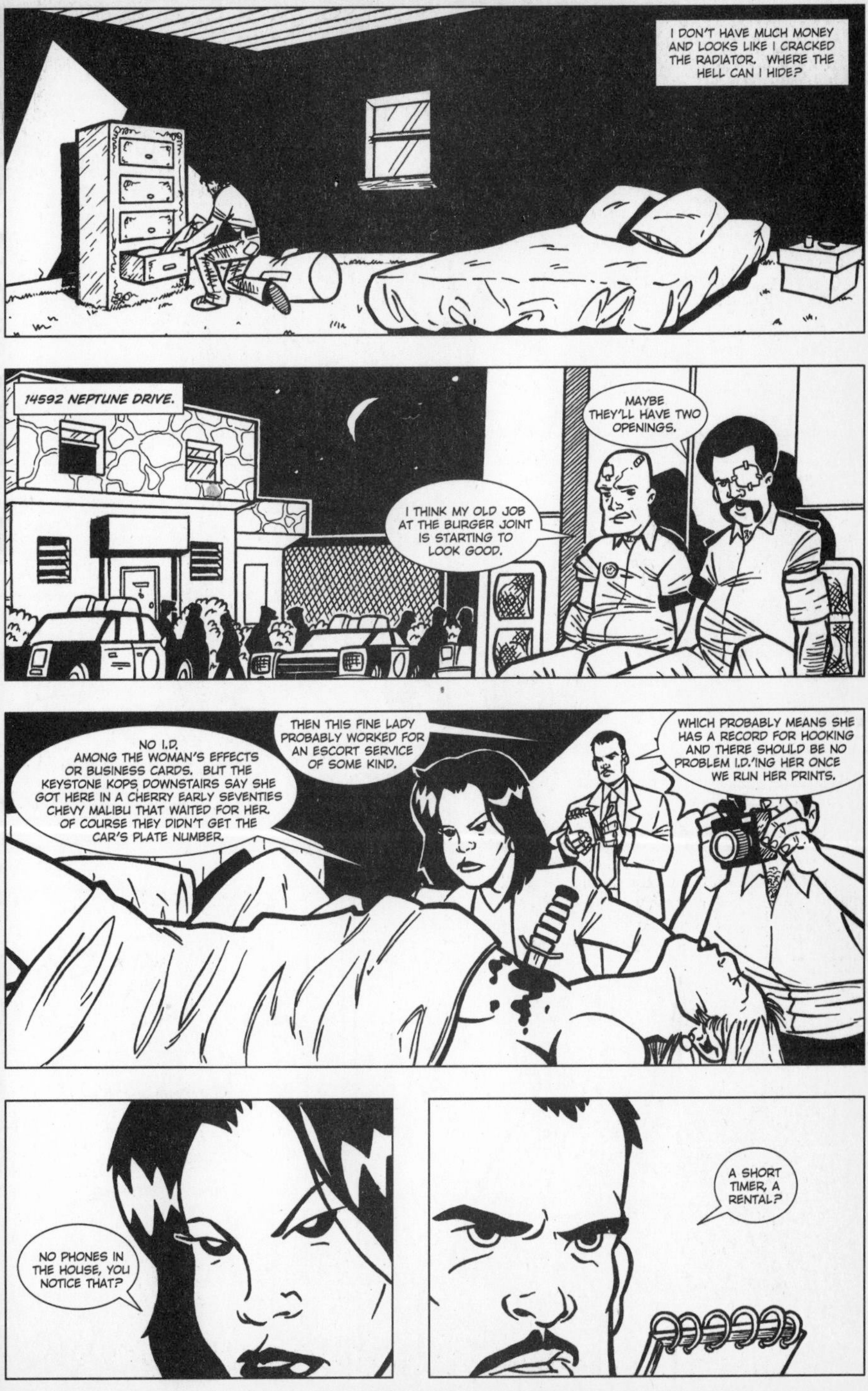
I DON'T HAVE MUCH MONEY AND LOOKS LIKE I CRACKED THE RADIATOR. WHERE THE HELL CAN I HIDE?
14592 NEPTUNE DRIVE.
MAYBE THEY'LL HAVE TWO OPENINGS.
I THINK MY OLD JOB AT THE BURGER JOINT IS STARTING TO LOOK GOOD.
NO I.D. AMONG THE WOMAN'S EFFECTS OR BUSINESS CARDS. BUT THE KEYSTONE KOPS DOWNSTAIRS SAY SHE GOT HERE IN A CHERRY EARLY SEVENTIES CHEVY MALIBU THAT WAITED FOR HER. OF COURSE THEY DIDN'T GET THE CAR'S PLATE NUMBER.
THEN THIS FINE LADY PROBABLY WORKED FOR AN ESCORT SERVICE OF SOME KIND.
WHICH PROBABLY MEANS SHE HAS A RECORD FOR HOOKING AND THERE SHOULD BE NO PROBLEM I.D.'ING HER ONCE WE RUN HER PRINTS.
NO PHONES IN THE HOUSE, YOU NOTICE THAT?
A SHORT TIMER, A RENTAL?

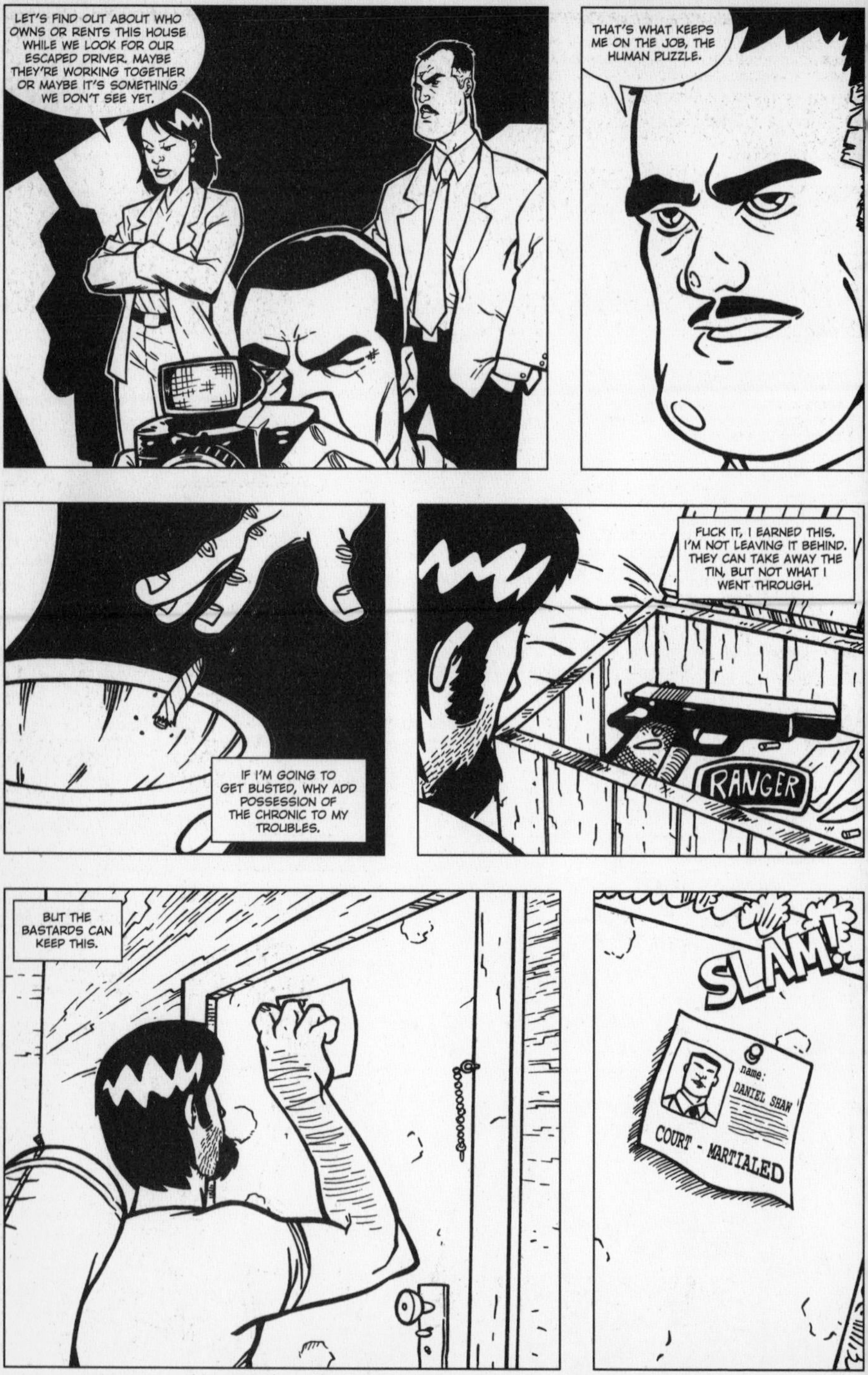
LET'S FIND OUT ABOUT WHO OWNS OR RENTS THIS HOUSE WHILE WE LOOK FOR OUR ESCAPED DRIVER. MAYBE THEY'RE WORKING TOGETHER OR MAYBE IT'S SOMETHING WE DON'T SEE YET.
THAT'S WHAT KEEPS ME ON THE JOB, THE HUMAN PUZZLE.
IF I'M GOING TO GET BUSTED, WHY ADD POSSESSION OF THE CHRONIC TO MY TROUBLES.
FUCK IT, I EARNED THIS. I'M NOT LEAVING IT BEHIND. THEY CAN TAKE AWAY THE TIN, BUT NOT WHAT I WENT THROUGH.
RANGER
BUT THE BASTARDS CAN KEEP THIS.
SLAM!
name:
DANIEL SHAW
COURT - MARTIALED

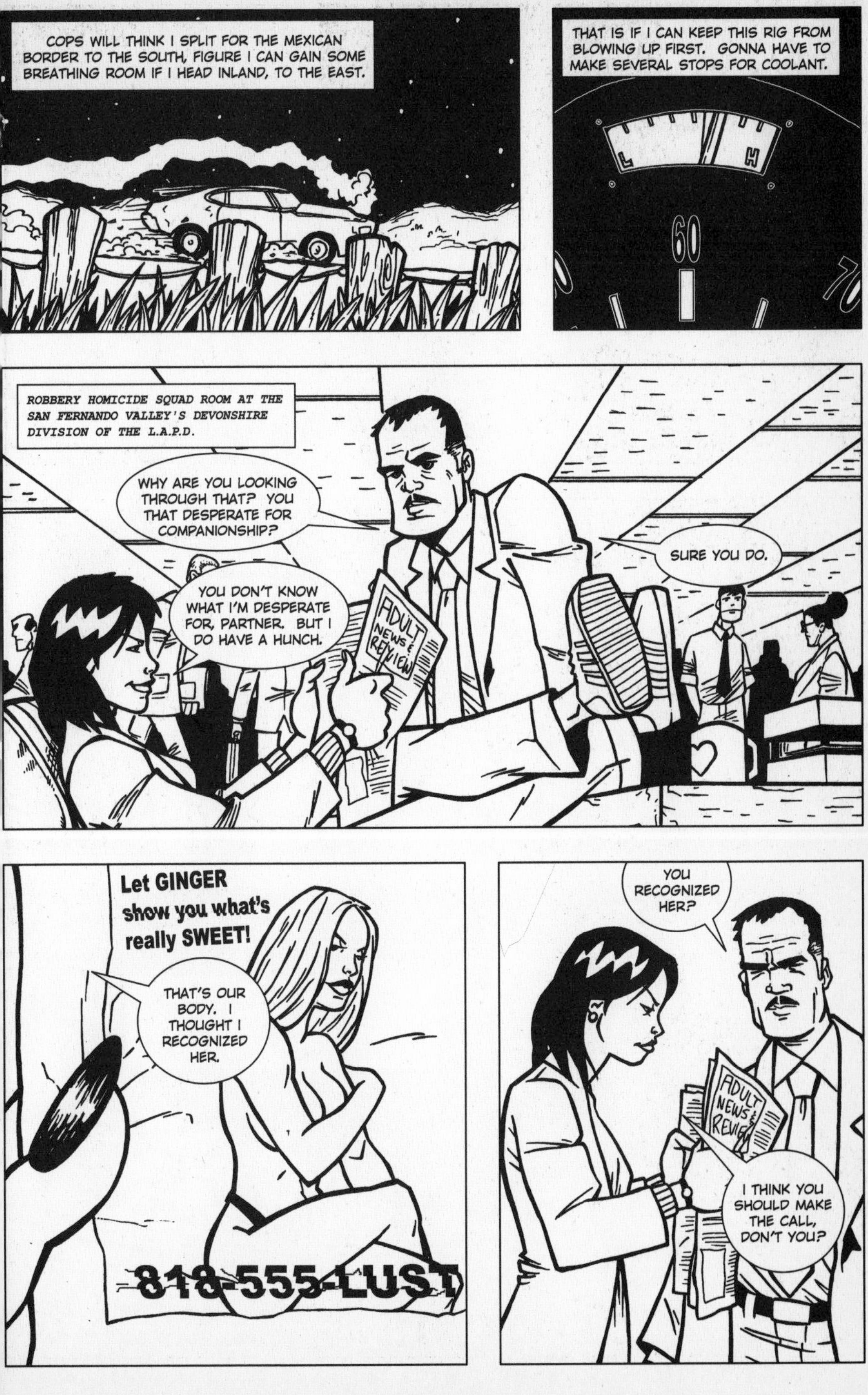
COPS WILL THINK I SPLIT FOR THE MEXICAN BORDER TO THE SOUTH, FIGURE I CAN GAIN SOME BREATHING ROOM IF I HEAD INLAND, TO THE EAST.
THAT IS IF I CAN KEEP THIS RIG FROM BLOWING UP FIRST. GONNA HAVE TO MAKE SEVERAL STOPS FOR COOLANT.
L
H
60
ROBBERY HOMICIDE SQUAD ROOM AT THE SAN FERNANDO VALLEY'S DEVONSHIRE DIVISION OF THE L.A.P.D.
WHY ARE YOU LOOKING THROUGH THAT? YOU THAT DESPERATE FOR COMPANIONSHIP?
YOU DON'T KNOW WHAT I'M DESPERATE FOR, PARTNER. BUT I DO HAVE A HUNCH.
SURE YOU DO.
ADULT NEWS & REVIEW
Let GINGER show you what's really SWEET!
THAT'S OUR BODY. I THOUGHT I RECOGNIZED HER.
818-555-LUST
YOU RECOGNIZED HER?
I THINK YOU SHOULD MAKE THE CALL, DON'T YOU?

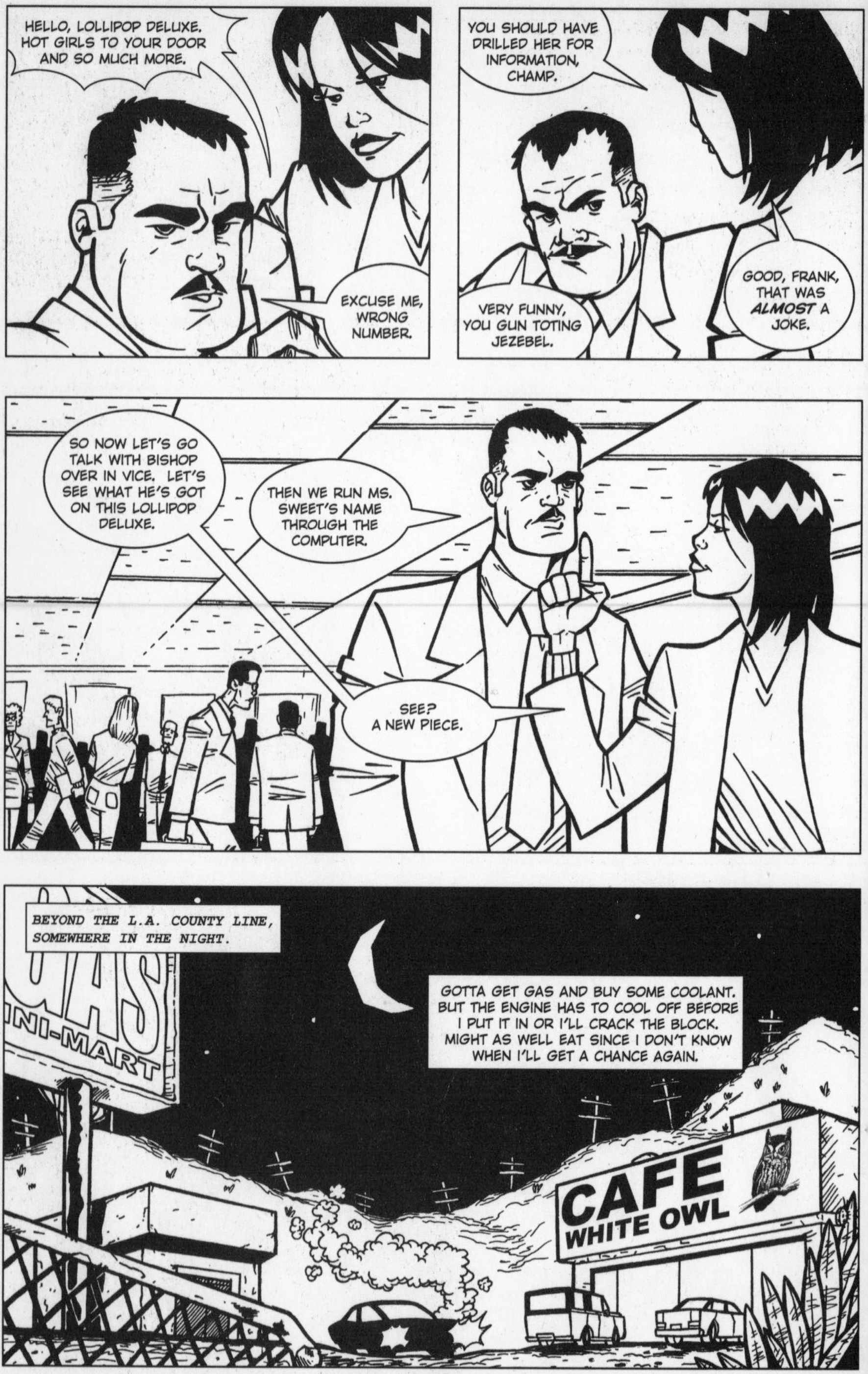
HELLO, LOLLIPOP DELUXE. HOT GIRLS TO YOUR DOOR AND SO MUCH MORE.
EXCUSE ME, WRONG NUMBER.
YOU SHOULD HAVE DRILLED HER FOR INFORMATION, CHAMP.
VERY FUNNY, YOU GUN TOTING JEZEBEL.
GOOD, FRANK, THAT WAS *ALMOST* A JOKE.
SO NOW LET'S GO TALK WITH BISHOP OVER IN VICE. LET'S SEE WHAT HE'S GOT ON THIS LOLLIPOP DELUXE.
THEN WE RUN MS. SWEET'S NAME THROUGH THE COMPUTER.
SEE? A NEW PIECE.
BEYOND THE L.A. COUNTY LINE, SOMEWHERE IN THE NIGHT.
GOTTA GET GAS AND BUY SOME COOLANT. BUT THE ENGINE HAS TO COOL OFF BEFORE I PUT IT IN OR I'LL CRACK THE BLOCK. MIGHT AS WELL EAT SINCE I DON'T KNOW WHEN I'LL GET A CHANCE AGAIN.
CAFE WHITE OWL

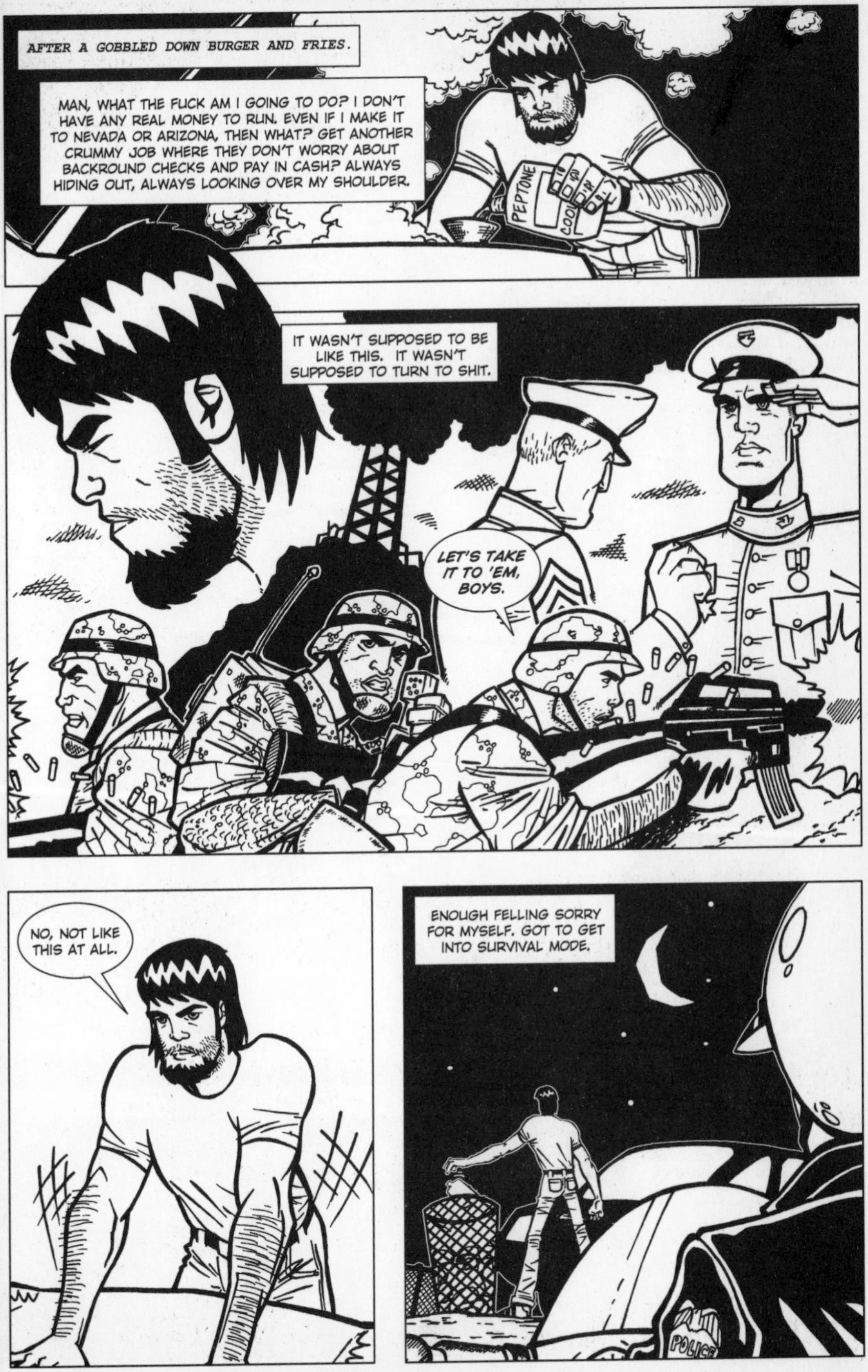
AFTER A GOBBLED DOWN BURGER AND FRIES.
MAN, WHAT THE FUCK AM I GOING TO DO? I DON'T HAVE ANY REAL MONEY TO RUN. EVEN IF I MAKE IT TO NEVADA OR ARIZONA, THEN WHAT? GET ANOTHER CRUMMY JOB WHERE THEY DON'T WORRY ABOUT BACKROUND CHECKS AND PAY IN CASH? ALWAYS HIDING OUT, ALWAYS LOOKING OVER MY SHOULDER.
PEPTONE
IT WASN'T SUPPOSED TO BE LIKE THIS. IT WASN'T SUPPOSED TO TURN TO SHIT.
LET'S TAKE IT TO 'EM, BOYS.
NO, NOT LIKE THIS AT ALL.
ENOUGH FELLING SORRY FOR MYSELF. GOT TO GET INTO SURVIVAL MODE.
POLICE

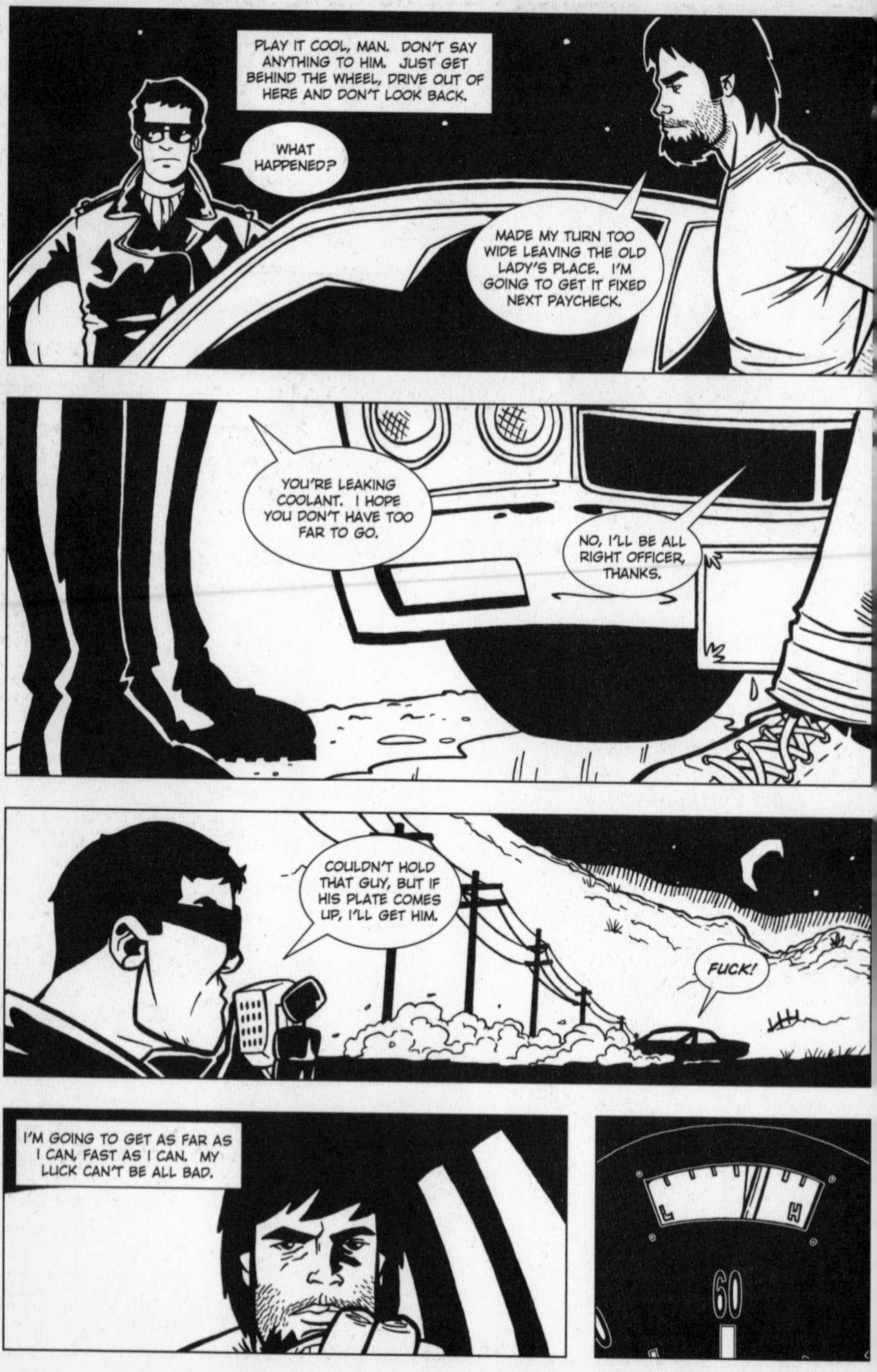
PLAY IT COOL, MAN. DON'T SAY ANYTHING TO HIM. JUST GET BEHIND THE WHEEL, DRIVE OUT OF HERE AND DON'T LOOK BACK.
WHAT HAPPENED?
MADE MY TURN TOO WIDE LEAVING THE OLD LADY'S PLACE. I'M GOING TO GET IT FIXED NEXT PAYCHECK.
YOU'RE LEAKING COOLANT. I HOPE YOU DON'T HAVE TOO FAR TO GO.
NO, I'LL BE ALL RIGHT OFFICER, THANKS.
COULDN'T HOLD THAT GUY, BUT IF HIS PLATE COMES UP, I'LL GET HIM.
FUCK!
I'M GOING TO GET AS FAR AS I CAN, FAST AS I CAN. MY LUCK CAN'T BE ALL BAD.
L
H
60

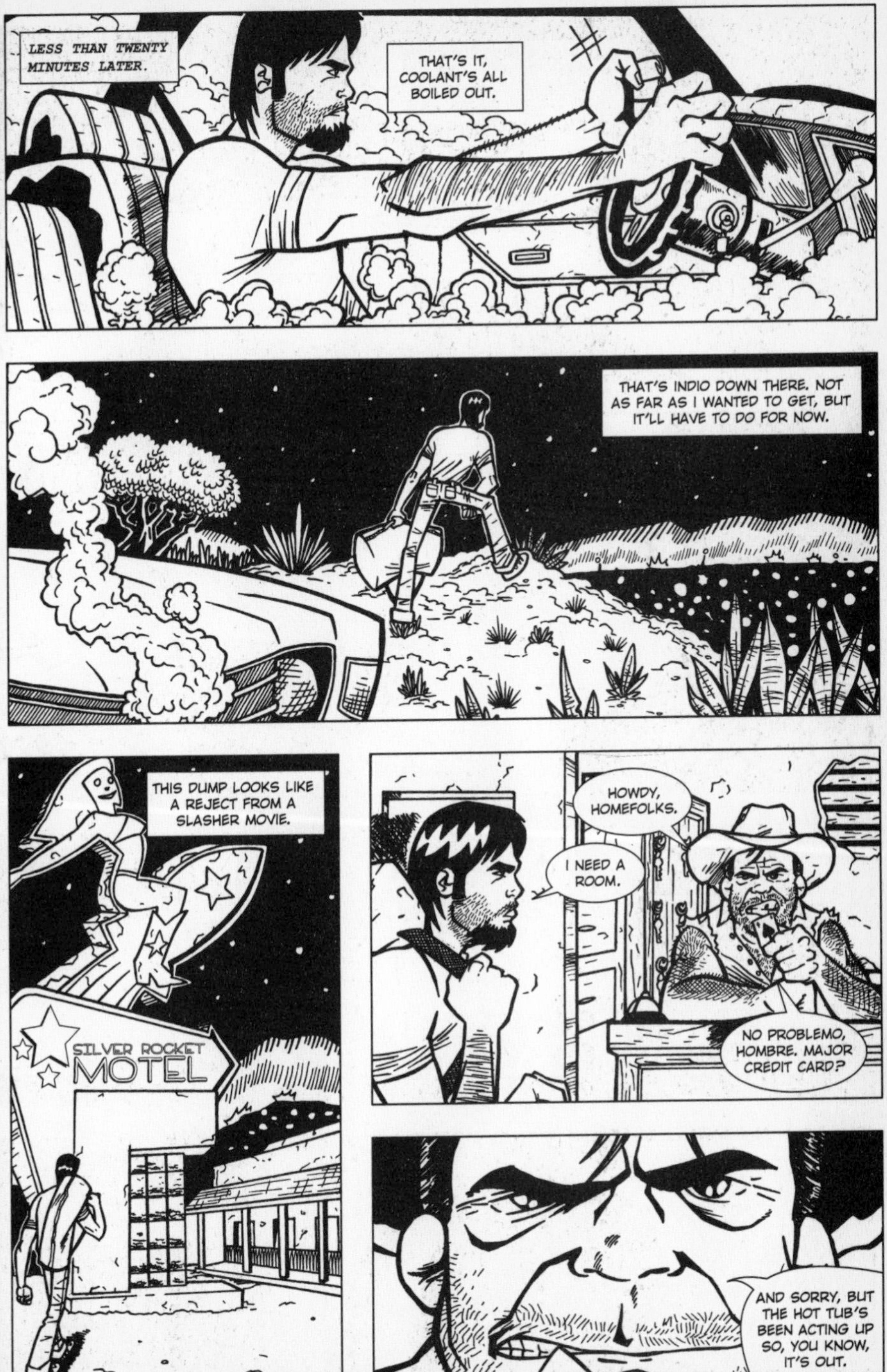
LESS THAN TWENTY MINUTES LATER.
THAT'S IT, COOLANT'S ALL BOILED OUT.
THAT'S INDIO DOWN THERE. NOT AS FAR AS I WANTED TO GET, BUT IT'LL HAVE TO DO FOR NOW.
THIS DUMP LOOKS LIKE A REJECT FROM A SLASHER MOVIE.
SILVER ROCKET MOTEL
HOWDY, HOMEFOLKS.
I NEED A ROOM.
NO PROBLEMO, HOMBRE. MAJOR CREDIT CARD?
AND SORRY, BUT THE HOT TUB'S BEEN ACTING UP SO, YOU KNOW, IT'S OUT.

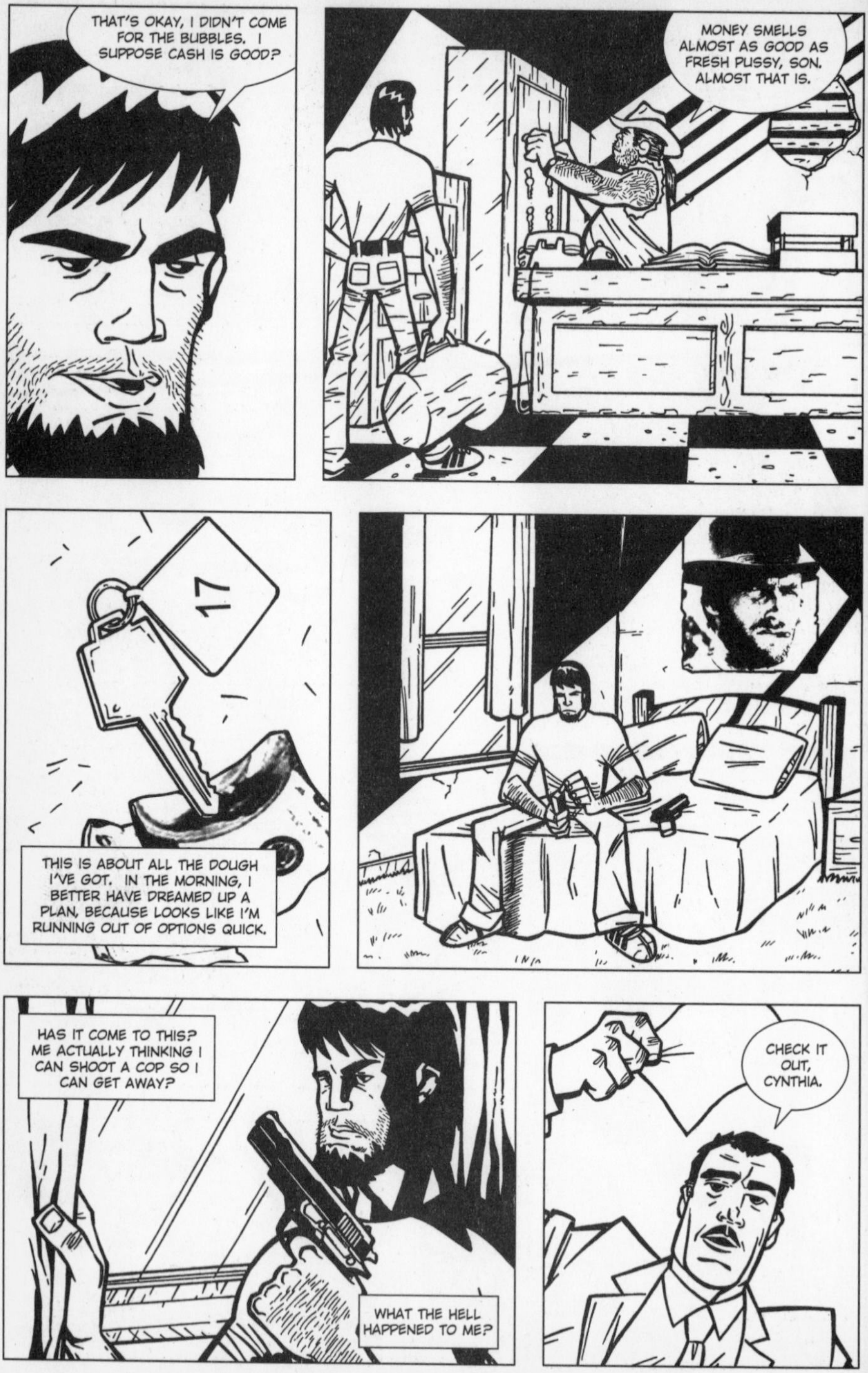
THAT'S OKAY, I DIDN'T COME FOR THE BUBBLES. I SUPPOSE CASH IS GOOD?
MONEY SMELLS ALMOST AS GOOD AS FRESH PUSSY, SON. ALMOST THAT IS.
17
THIS IS ABOUT ALL THE DOUGH I'VE GOT. IN THE MORNING, I BETTER HAVE DREAMED UP A PLAN, BECAUSE LOOKS LIKE I'M RUNNING OUT OF OPTIONS QUICK.
HAS IT COME TO THIS? ME ACTUALLY THINKING I CAN SHOOT A COP SO I CAN GET AWAY?
WHAT THE HELL HAPPENED TO ME?
CHECK IT OUT, CYNTHIA.

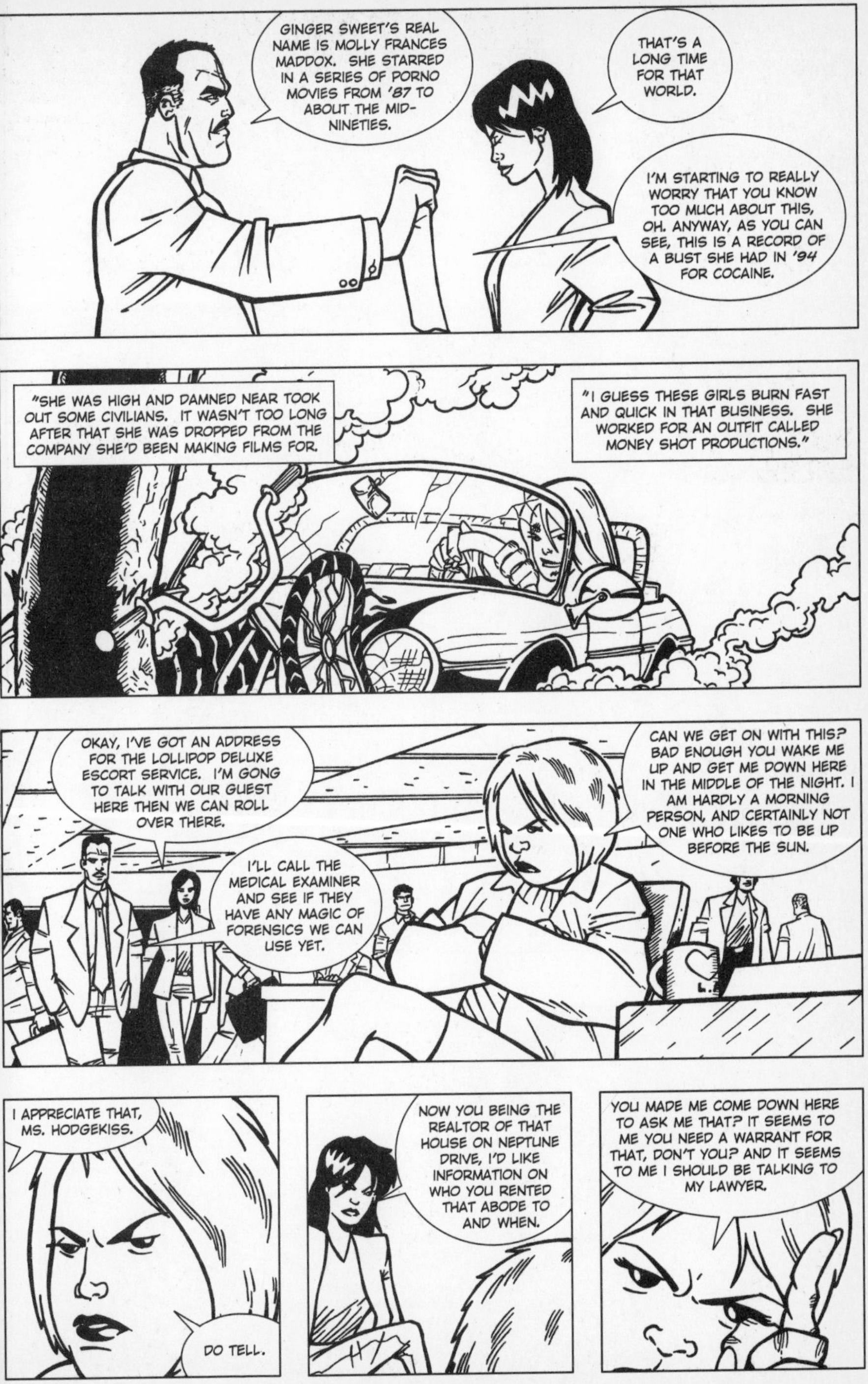
GINGER SWEET'S REAL NAME IS MOLLY FRANCES MADDOX. SHE STARRED IN A SERIES OF PORNO MOVIES FROM '87 TO ABOUT THE MID-NINETIES.
THAT'S A LONG TIME FOR THAT WORLD.
I'M STARTING TO REALLY WORRY THAT YOU KNOW TOO MUCH ABOUT THIS, OH. ANYWAY, AS YOU CAN SEE, THIS IS A RECORD OF A BUST SHE HAD IN '94 FOR COCAINE.
"SHE WAS HIGH AND DAMNED NEAR TOOK OUT SOME CIVILIANS. IT WASN'T TOO LONG AFTER THAT SHE WAS DROPPED FROM THE COMPANY SHE'D BEEN MAKING FILMS FOR.
"I GUESS THESE GIRLS BURN FAST AND QUICK IN THAT BUSINESS. SHE WORKED FOR AN OUTFIT CALLED MONEY SHOT PRODUCTIONS."
OKAY, I'VE GOT AN ADDRESS FOR THE LOLLIPOP DELUXE ESCORT SERVICE. I'M GONG TO TALK WITH OUR GUEST HERE THEN WE CAN ROLL OVER THERE.
I'LL CALL THE MEDICAL EXAMINER AND SEE IF THEY HAVE ANY MAGIC OF FORENSICS WE CAN USE YET.
CAN WE GET ON WITH THIS? BAD ENOUGH YOU WAKE ME UP AND GET ME DOWN HERE IN THE MIDDLE OF THE NIGHT. I AM HARDLY A MORNING PERSON, AND CERTAINLY NOT ONE WHO LIKES TO BE UP BEFORE THE SUN.
I APPRECIATE THAT, MS. HODGEKISS.
DO TELL.
NOW YOU BEING THE REALTOR OF THAT HOUSE ON NEPTUNE DRIVE, I'D LIKE INFORMATION ON WHO YOU RENTED THAT ABODE TO AND WHEN.
YOU MADE ME COME DOWN HERE TO ASK ME THAT? IT SEEMS TO ME YOU NEED A WARRANT FOR THAT, DON'T YOU? AND IT SEEMS TO ME I SHOULD BE TALKING TO MY LAWYER.

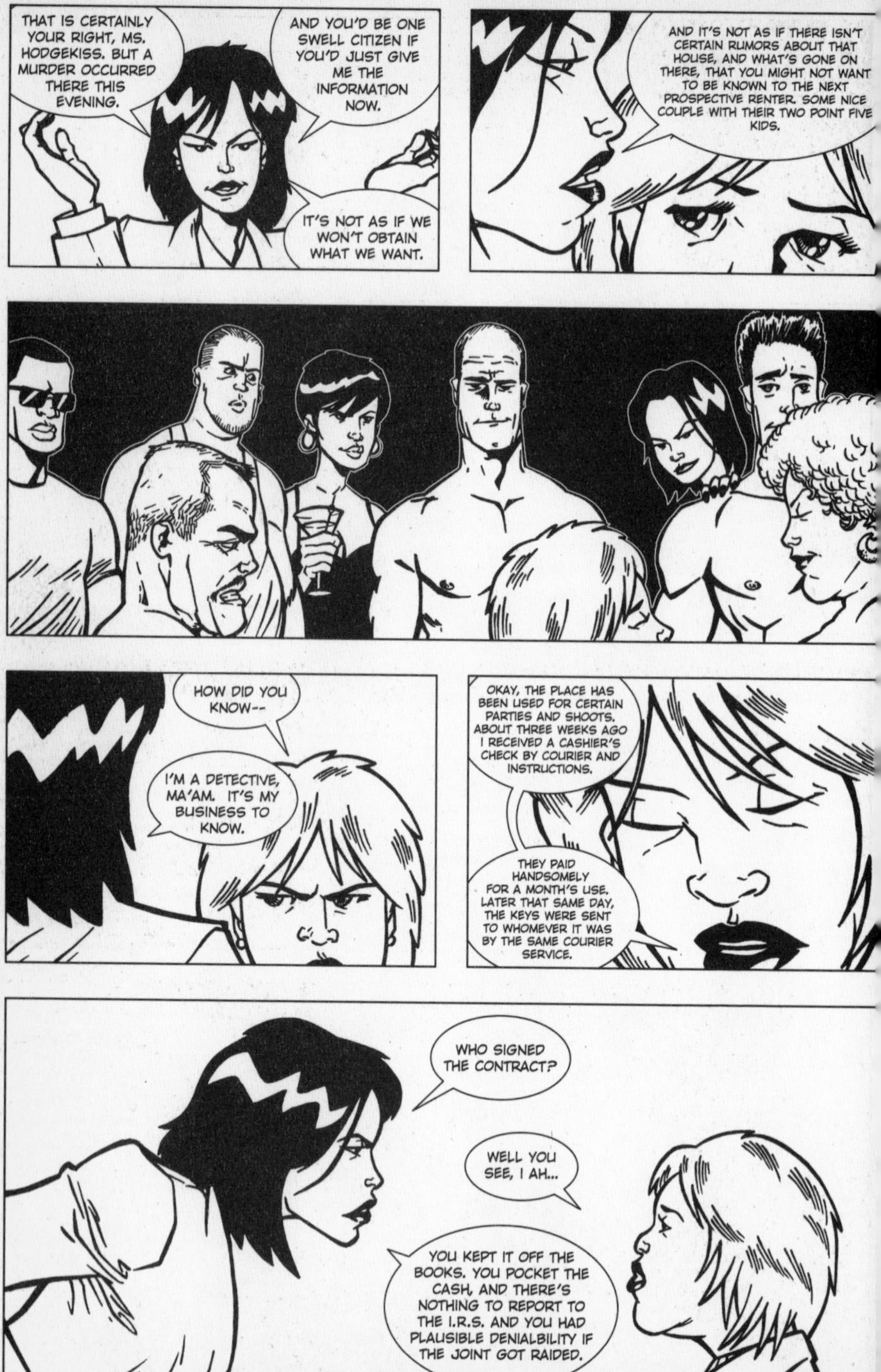
THAT IS CERTAINLY YOUR RIGHT, MS. HODGEKISS. BUT A MURDER OCCURRED THERE THIS EVENING.
AND YOU'D BE ONE SWELL CITIZEN IF YOU'D JUST GIVE ME THE INFORMATION NOW.
IT'S NOT AS IF WE WON'T OBTAIN WHAT WE WANT.
AND IT'S NOT AS IF THERE ISN'T CERTAIN RUMORS ABOUT THAT HOUSE, AND WHAT'S GONE ON THERE, THAT YOU MIGHT NOT WANT TO BE KNOWN TO THE NEXT PROSPECTIVE RENTER. SOME NICE COUPLE WITH THEIR TWO POINT FIVE KIDS.
HOW DID YOU KNOW--
I'M A DETECTIVE, MA'AM. IT'S MY BUSINESS TO KNOW.
OKAY, THE PLACE HAS BEEN USED FOR CERTAIN PARTIES AND SHOOTS. ABOUT THREE WEEKS AGO I RECEIVED A CASHIER'S CHECK BY COURIER AND INSTRUCTIONS.
THEY PAID HANDSOMELY FOR A MONTH'S USE. LATER THAT SAME DAY, THE KEYS WERE SENT TO WHOMEVER IT WAS BY THE SAME COURIER SERVICE.
WHO SIGNED THE CONTRACT?
WELL YOU SEE, I AH...
YOU KEPT IT OFF THE BOOKS. YOU POCKET THE CASH, AND THERE'S NOTHING TO REPORT TO THE I.R.S. AND YOU HAD PLAUSIBLE DENIALBILITY IF THE JOINT GOT RAIDED.

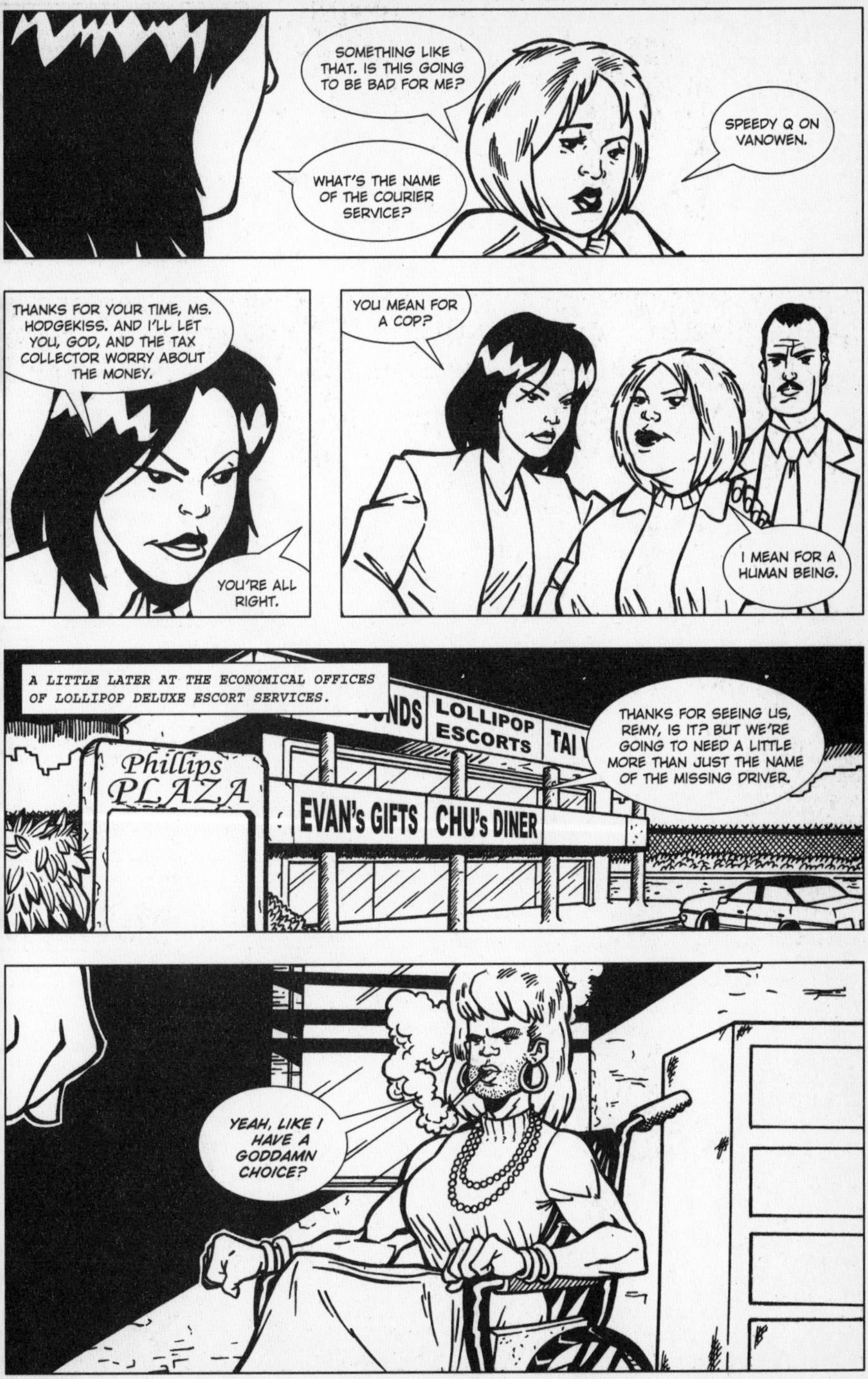
SOMETHING LIKE THAT. IS THIS GOING TO BE BAD FOR ME?
WHAT'S THE NAME OF THE COURIER SERVICE?
SPEEDY Q ON VANOWEN.
THANKS FOR YOUR TIME, MS. HODGEKISS. AND I'LL LET YOU, GOD, AND THE TAX COLLECTOR WORRY ABOUT THE MONEY.
YOU'RE ALL RIGHT.
YOU MEAN FOR A COP?
I MEAN FOR A HUMAN BEING.
A LITTLE LATER AT THE ECONOMICAL OFFICES OF LOLLIPOP DELUXE ESCORT SERVICES.
LOLLIPOP ESCORTS
Phillips PLAZA
EVAN's GIFTS
CHU's DINER
THANKS FOR SEEING US, REMY, IS IT? BUT WE'RE GOING TO NEED A LITTLE MORE THAN JUST THE NAME OF THE MISSING DRIVER.
YEAH, LIKE I HAVE A GODDAMN CHOICE?

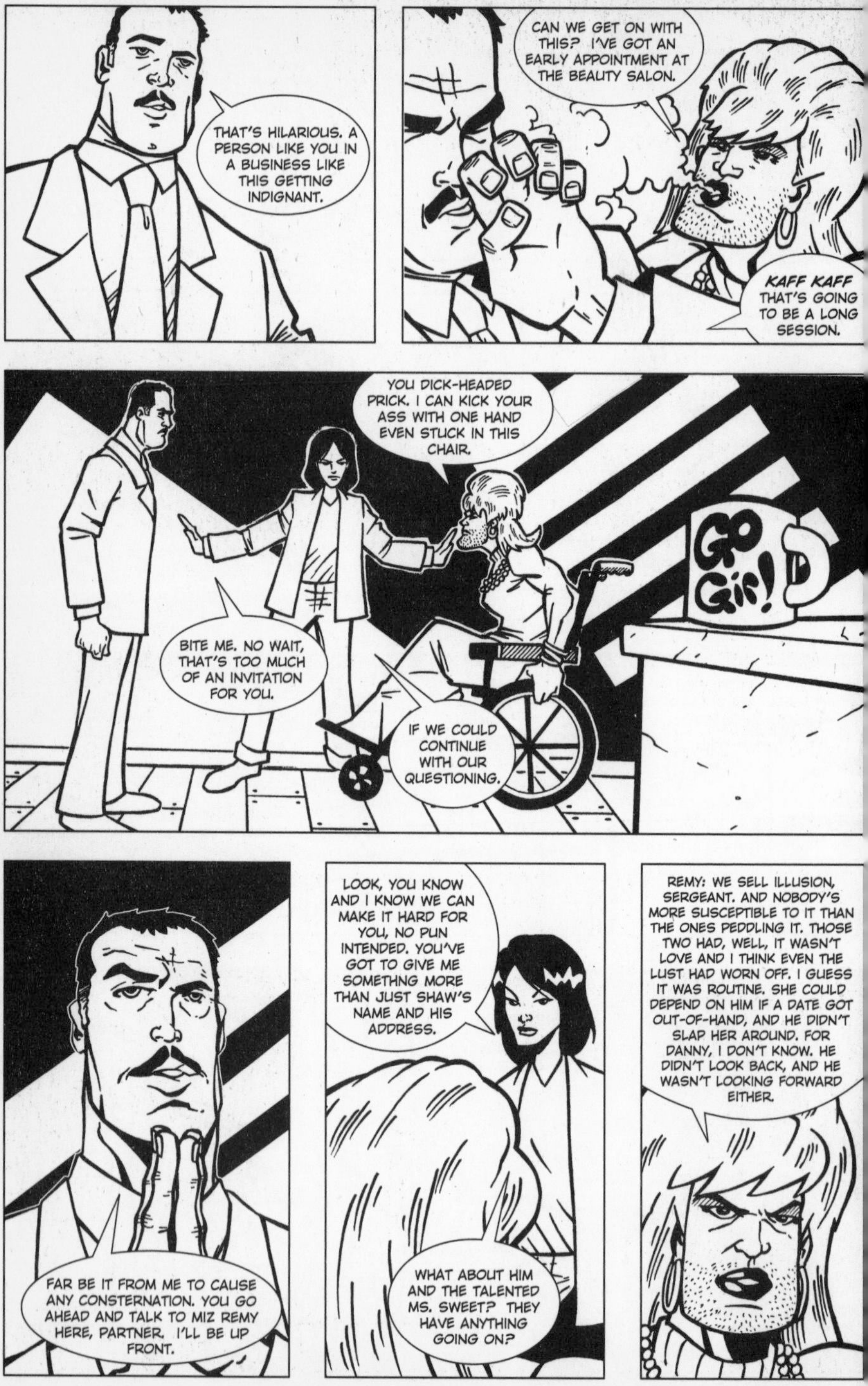
THAT'S HILARIOUS. A PERSON LIKE YOU IN A BUSINESS LIKE THIS GETTING INDIGNANT.
CAN WE GET ON WITH THIS? I'VE GOT AN EARLY APPOINTMENT AT THE BEAUTY SALON.
KAFF KAFF THAT'S GOING TO BE A LONG SESSION.
YOU DICK-HEADED PRICK. I CAN KICK YOUR ASS WITH ONE HAND EVEN STUCK IN THIS CHAIR.
BITE ME. NO WAIT, THAT'S TOO MUCH OF AN INVITATION FOR YOU.
IF WE COULD CONTINUE WITH OUR QUESTIONING.
GO Girl!
FAR BE IT FROM ME TO CAUSE ANY CONSTERNATION. YOU GO AHEAD AND TALK TO MIZ REMY HERE, PARTNER. I'LL BE UP FRONT.
LOOK, YOU KNOW AND I KNOW WE CAN MAKE IT HARD FOR YOU, NO PUN INTENDED. YOU'VE GOT TO GIVE ME SOMETHNG MORE THAN JUST SHAW'S NAME AND HIS ADDRESS.
WHAT ABOUT HIM AND THE TALENTED MS. SWEET? THEY HAVE ANYTHING GOING ON?
REMY: WE SELL ILLUSION, SERGEANT. AND NOBODY'S MORE SUSCEPTIBLE TO IT THAN THE ONES PEDDLING IT. THOSE TWO HAD, WELL, IT WASN'T LOVE AND I THINK EVEN THE LUST HAD WORN OFF. I GUESS IT WAS ROUTINE. SHE COULD DEPEND ON HIM IF A DATE GOT OUT-OF-HAND, AND HE DIDN'T SLAP HER AROUND. FOR DANNY, I DON'T KNOW. HE DIDN'T LOOK BACK, AND HE WASN'T LOOKING FORWARD EITHER.

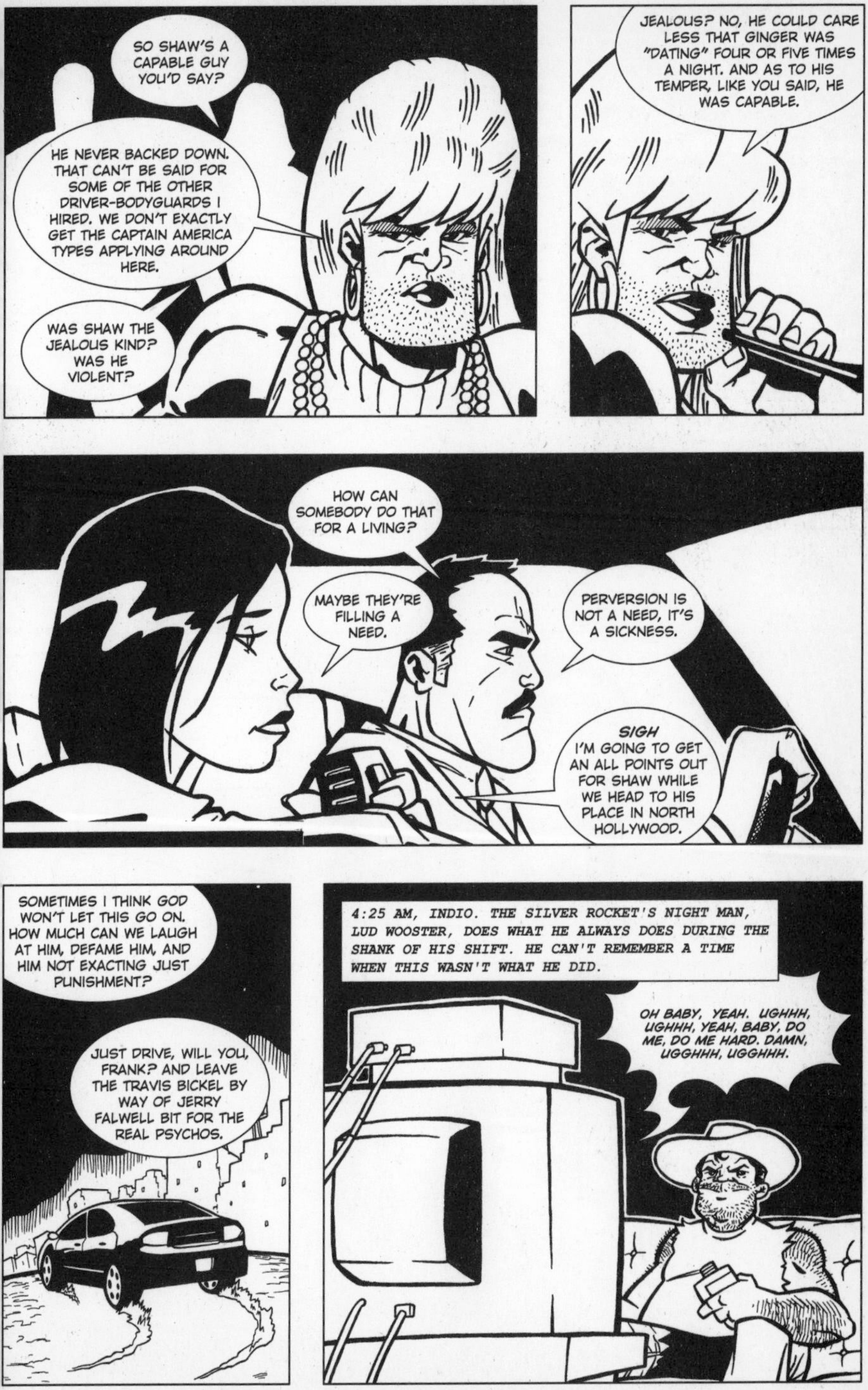
SO SHAW'S A CAPABLE GUY YOU'D SAY?
HE NEVER BACKED DOWN. THAT CAN'T BE SAID FOR SOME OF THE OTHER DRIVER-BODYGUARDS I HIRED. WE DON'T EXACTLY GET THE CAPTAIN AMERICA TYPES APPLYING AROUND HERE.
WAS SHAW THE JEALOUS KIND? WAS HE VIOLENT?
JEALOUS? NO, HE COULD CARE LESS THAT GINGER WAS "DATING" FOUR OR FIVE TIMES A NIGHT. AND AS TO HIS TEMPER, LIKE YOU SAID, HE WAS CAPABLE.
HOW CAN SOMEBODY DO THAT FOR A LIVING?
MAYBE THEY'RE FILLING A NEED.
PERVERSION IS NOT A NEED, IT'S A SICKNESS.
SIGH I'M GOING TO GET AN ALL POINTS OUT FOR SHAW WHILE WE HEAD TO HIS PLACE IN NORTH HOLLYWOOD.
SOMETIMES I THINK GOD WON'T LET THIS GO ON. HOW MUCH CAN WE LAUGH AT HIM, DEFAME HIM, AND HIM NOT EXACTING JUST PUNISHMENT?
JUST DRIVE, WILL YOU, FRANK? AND LEAVE THE TRAVIS BICKEL BY WAY OF JERRY FALWELL BIT FOR THE REAL PSYCHOS.
4:25 AM, INDIO. THE SILVER ROCKET'S NIGHT MAN, LUD WOOSTER, DOES WHAT HE ALWAYS DOES DURING THE SHANK OF HIS SHIFT. HE CAN'T REMEMBER A TIME WHEN THIS WASN'T WHAT HE DID.
OH BABY, YEAH. UGHHH, UGHHH, YEAH, BABY, DO ME, DO ME HARD. DAMN, UGGHHH, UGGHHH.

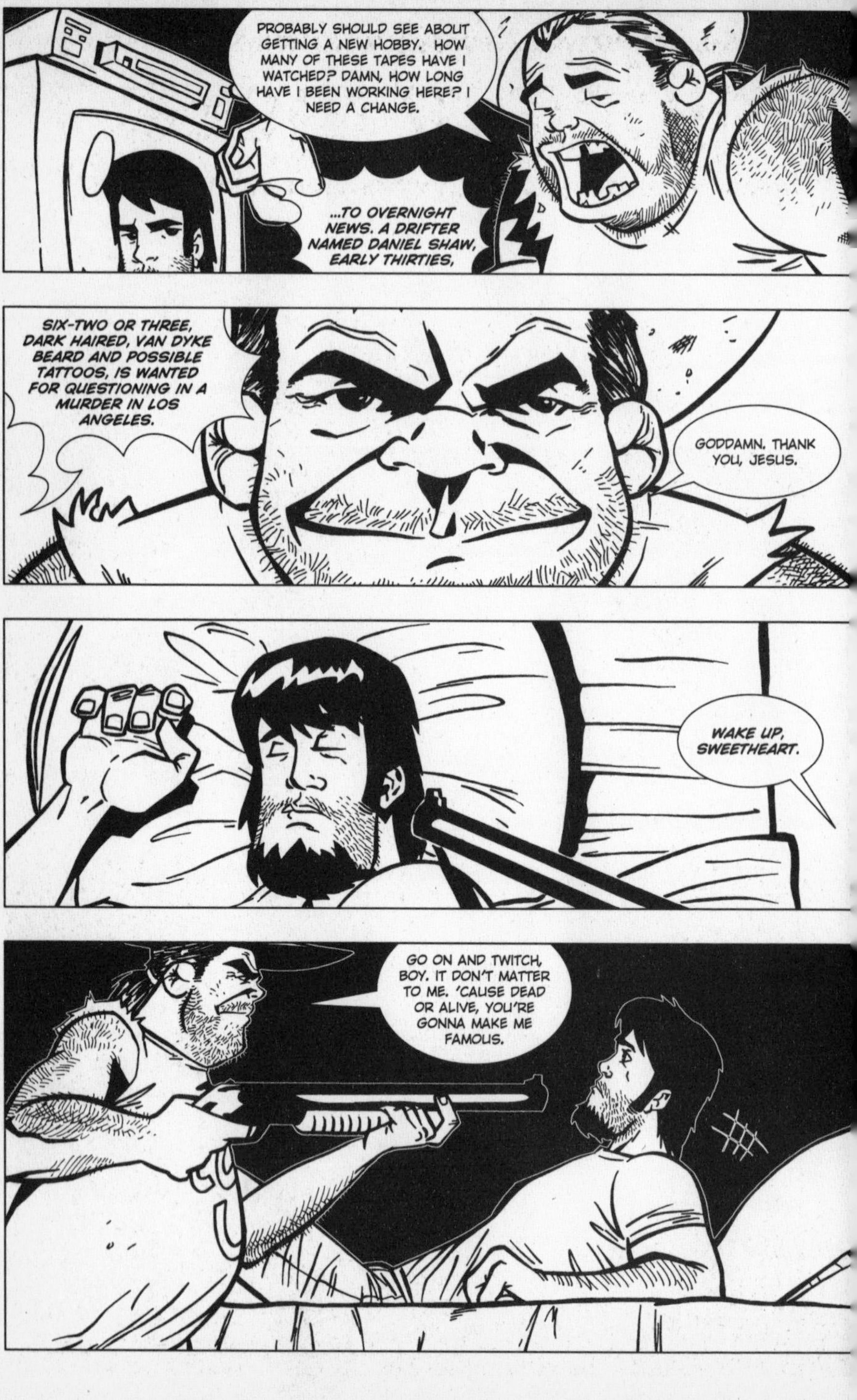
PROBABLY SHOULD SEE ABOUT GETTING A NEW HOBBY. HOW MANY OF THESE TAPES HAVE I WATCHED? DAMN, HOW LONG HAVE I BEEN WORKING HERE? I NEED A CHANGE.
...TO OVERNIGHT NEWS. A DRIFTER NAMED DANIEL SHAW, EARLY THIRTIES,
SIX-TWO OR THREE, DARK HAIRED, VAN DYKE BEARD AND POSSIBLE TATTOOS, IS WANTED FOR QUESTIONING IN A MURDER IN LOS ANGELES.
GODDAMN. THANK YOU, JESUS.
WAKE UP, SWEETHEART.
GO ON AND TWITCH, BOY. IT DON'T MATTER TO ME. 'CAUSE DEAD OR ALIVE, YOU'RE GONNA MAKE ME FAMOUS.

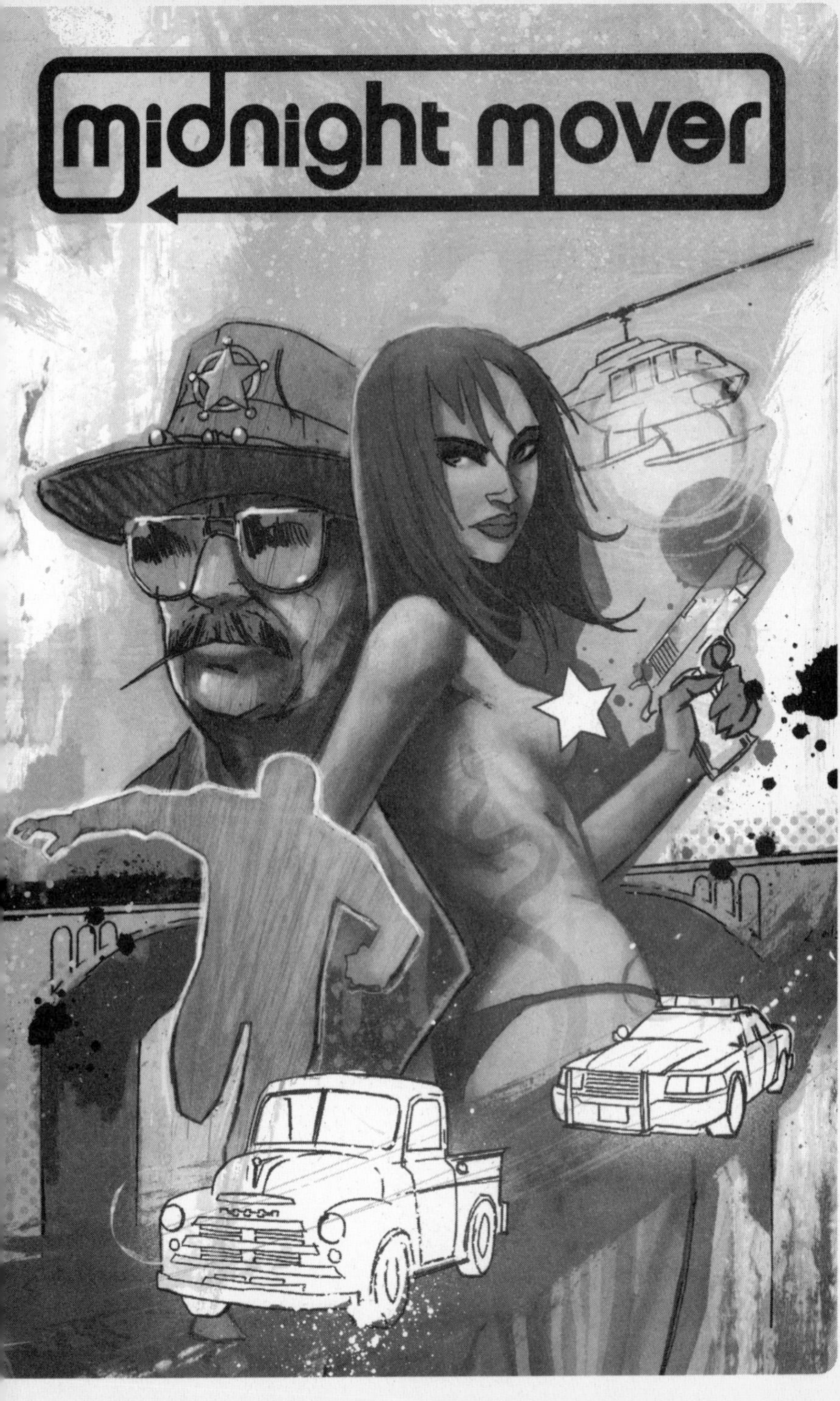
midnight mover

chapter two

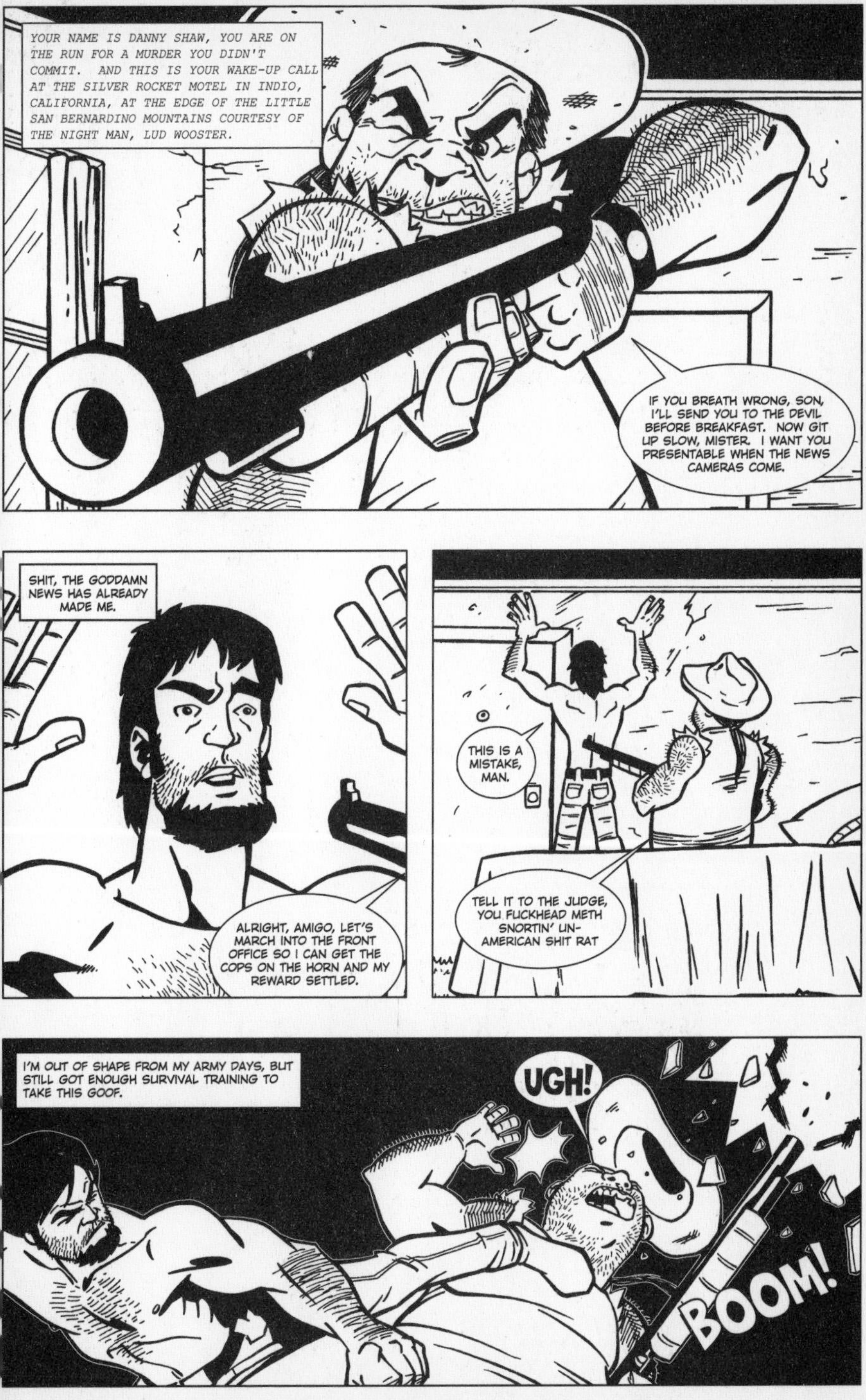
YOUR NAME IS DANNY SHAW, YOU ARE ON THE RUN FOR A MURDER YOU DIDN'T COMMIT. AND THIS IS YOUR WAKE-UP CALL AT THE SILVER ROCKET MOTEL IN INDIO, CALIFORNIA, AT THE EDGE OF THE LITTLE SAN BERNARDINO MOUNTAINS COURTESY OF THE NIGHT MAN, LUD WOOSTER.
IF YOU BREATH WRONG, SON, I'LL SEND YOU TO THE DEVIL BEFORE BREAKFAST. NOW GIT UP SLOW, MISTER. I WANT YOU PRESENTABLE WHEN THE NEWS CAMERAS COME.
SHIT, THE GODDAMN NEWS HAS ALREADY MADE ME.
ALRIGHT, AMIGO, LET'S MARCH INTO THE FRONT OFFICE SO I CAN GET THE COPS ON THE HORN AND MY REWARD SETTLED.
THIS IS A MISTAKE, MAN.
TELL IT TO THE JUDGE, YOU FUCKHEAD METH SNORTIN' UN-AMERICAN SHIT RAT
I'M OUT OF SHAPE FROM MY ARMY DAYS, BUT STILL GOT ENOUGH SURVIVAL TRAINING TO TAKE THIS GOOF.
UGH!
BOOM!

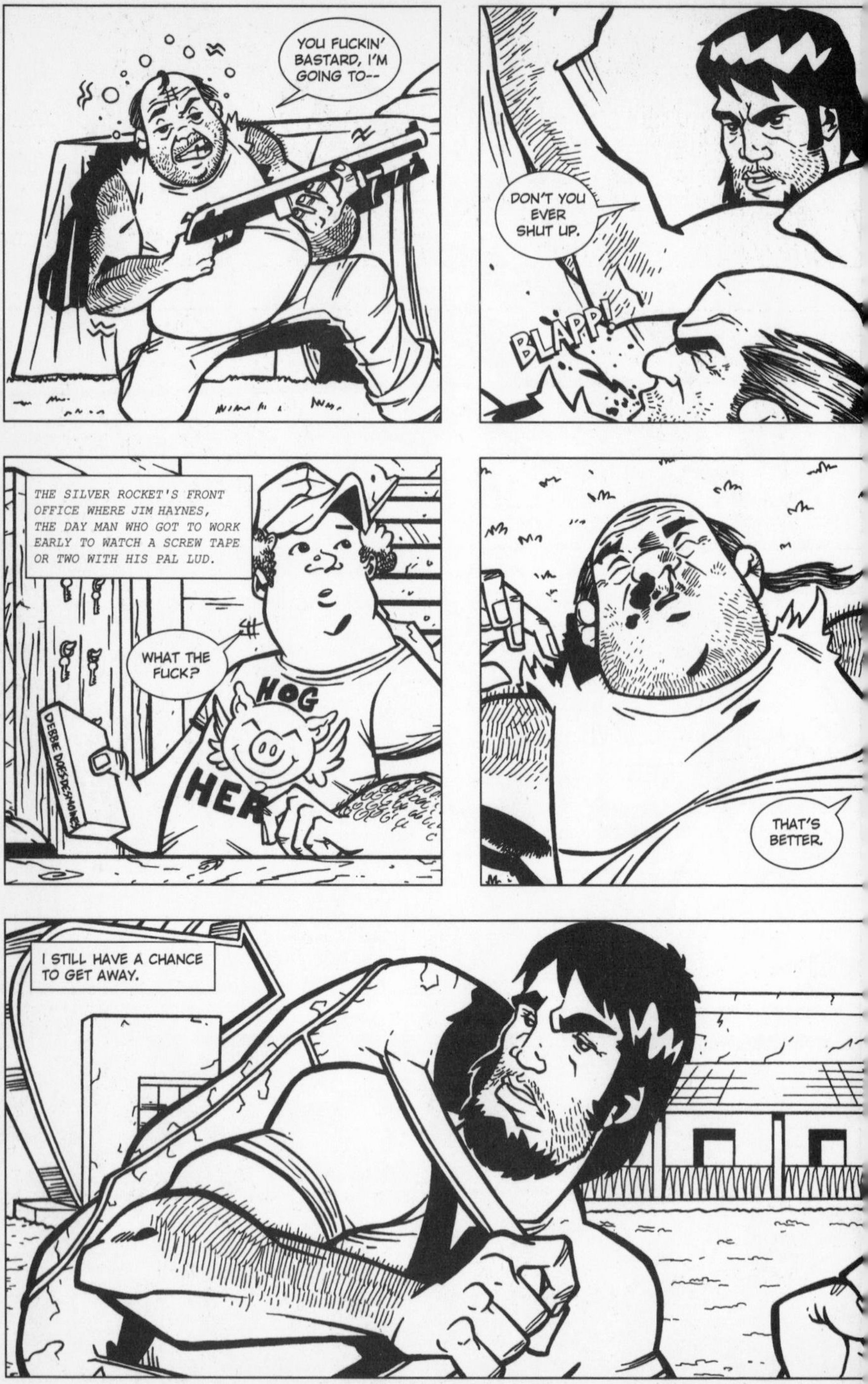
YOU FUCKIN' BASTARD, I'M GOING TO--
DON'T YOU EVER SHUT UP.
BLAPP!
THE SILVER ROCKET'S FRONT OFFICE WHERE JIM HAYNES, THE DAY MAN WHO GOT TO WORK EARLY TO WATCH A SCREW TAPE OR TWO WITH HIS PAL LUD.
WHAT THE FUCK?
HOG HER
DEBBIE DOES DES MOINES
THAT'S BETTER.
I STILL HAVE A CHANCE TO GET AWAY.

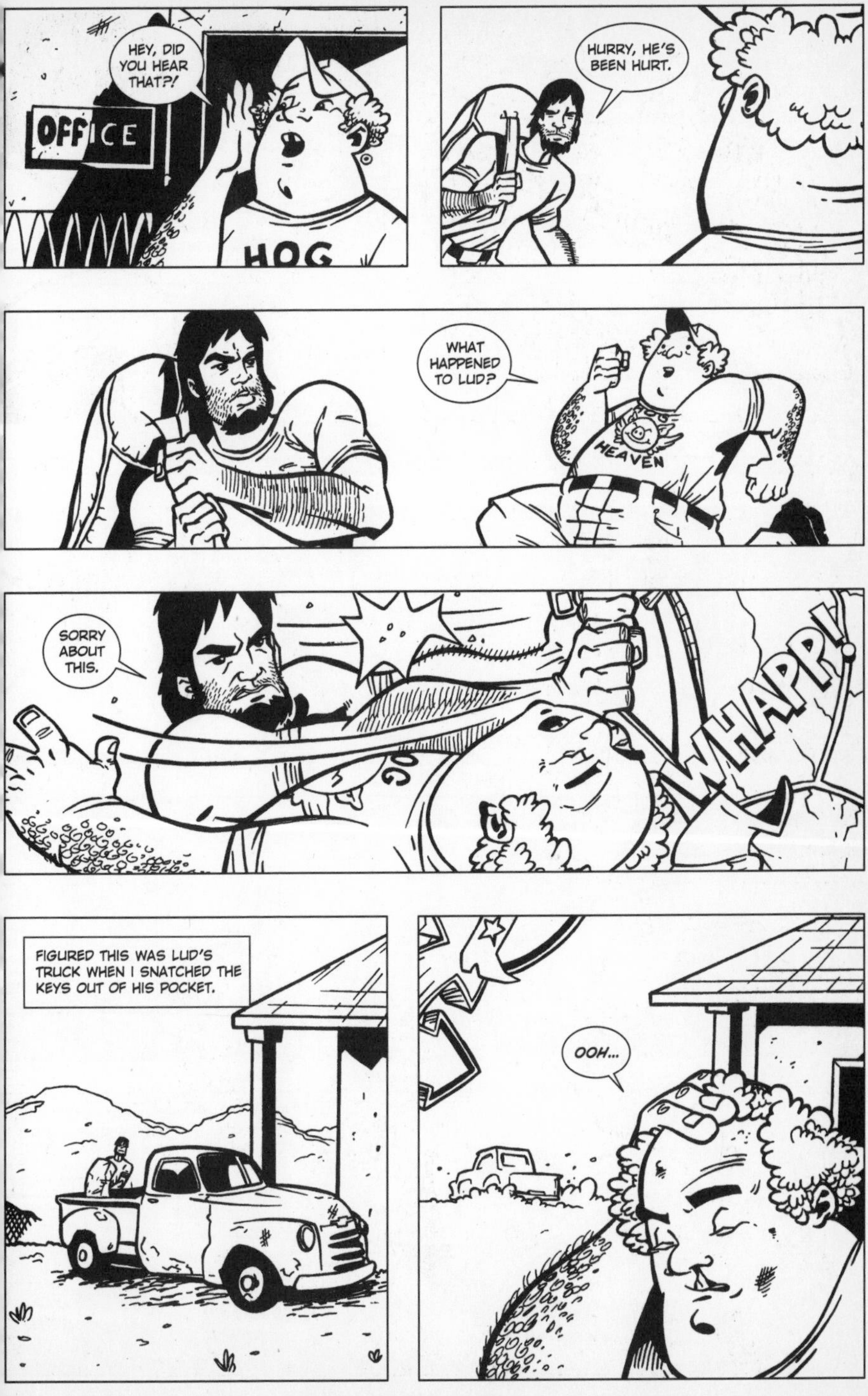
OFFICE
HEY, DID YOU HEAR THAT?!
HOG
HURRY, HE'S BEEN HURT.
WHAT HAPPENED TO LUD?
HEAVEN
SORRY ABOUT THIS.
WHAPP!
FIGURED THIS WAS LUD'S TRUCK WHEN I SNATCHED THE KEYS OUT OF HIS POCKET.
OOH...

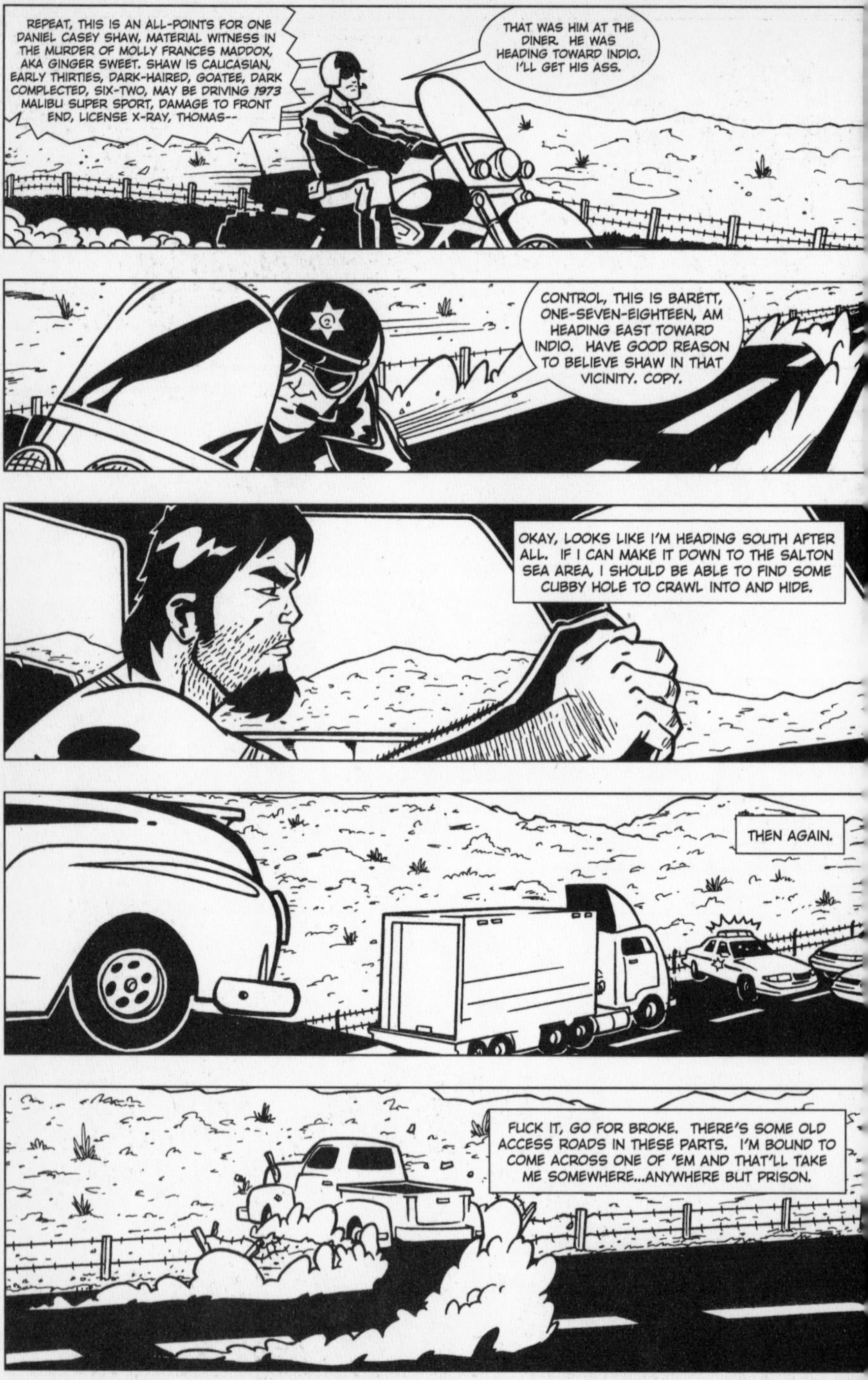
REPEAT, THIS IS AN ALL-POINTS FOR ONE DANIEL CASEY SHAW, MATERIAL WITNESS IN THE MURDER OF MOLLY FRANCES MADDOX, AKA GINGER SWEET. SHAW IS CAUCASIAN, EARLY THIRTIES, DARK-HAIRED, GOATEE, DARK COMPLECTED, SIX-TWO, MAY BE DRIVING 1973 MALIBU SUPER SPORT, DAMAGE TO FRONT END, LICENSE X-RAY, THOMAS--
THAT WAS HIM AT THE DINER. HE WAS HEADING TOWARD INDIO. I'LL GET HIS ASS.
CONTROL, THIS IS BARETT, ONE-SEVEN-EIGHTEEN, AM HEADING EAST TOWARD INDIO. HAVE GOOD REASON TO BELIEVE SHAW IN THAT VICINITY. COPY.
OKAY, LOOKS LIKE I'M HEADING SOUTH AFTER ALL. IF I CAN MAKE IT DOWN TO THE SALTON SEA AREA, I SHOULD BE ABLE TO FIND SOME CUBBY HOLE TO CRAWL INTO AND HIDE.
THEN AGAIN.
FUCK IT, GO FOR BROKE. THERE'S SOME OLD ACCESS ROADS IN THESE PARTS. I'M BOUND TO COME ACROSS ONE OF 'EM AND THAT'LL TAKE ME SOMEWHERE...ANYWHERE BUT PRISON.

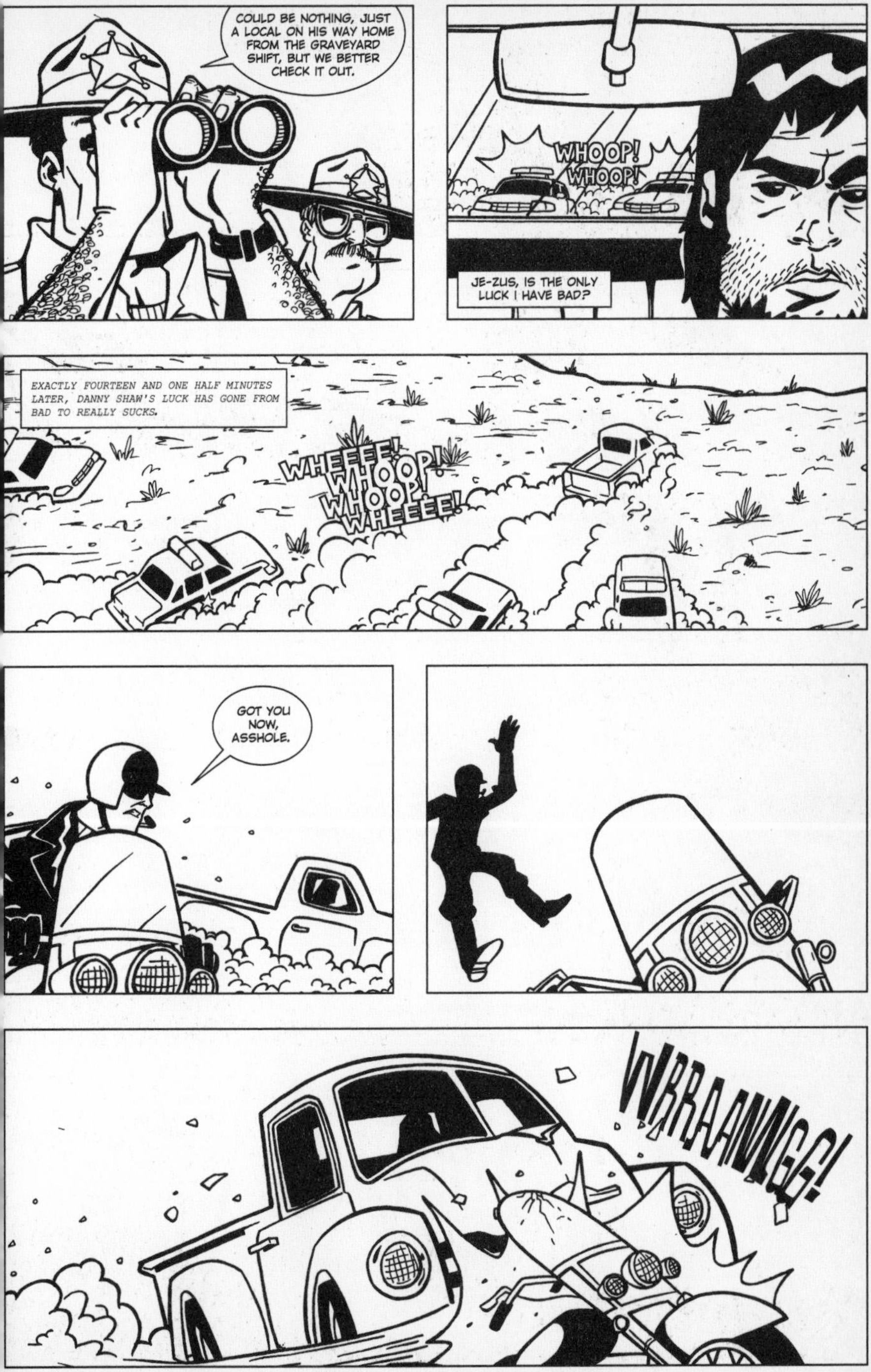
COULD BE NOTHING, JUST A LOCAL ON HIS WAY HOME FROM THE GRAVEYARD SHIFT, BUT WE BETTER CHECK IT OUT.
WHOOP! WHOOP!
JE-ZUS, IS THE ONLY LUCK I HAVE BAD?
EXACTLY FOURTEEN AND ONE HALF MINUTES LATER, DANNY SHAW'S LUCK HAS GONE FROM BAD TO REALLY SUCKS.
WHEEEE! WHOOP! WHOOP! WHEEEEE!
GOT YOU NOW, ASSHOLE.
WRRAANNGG!

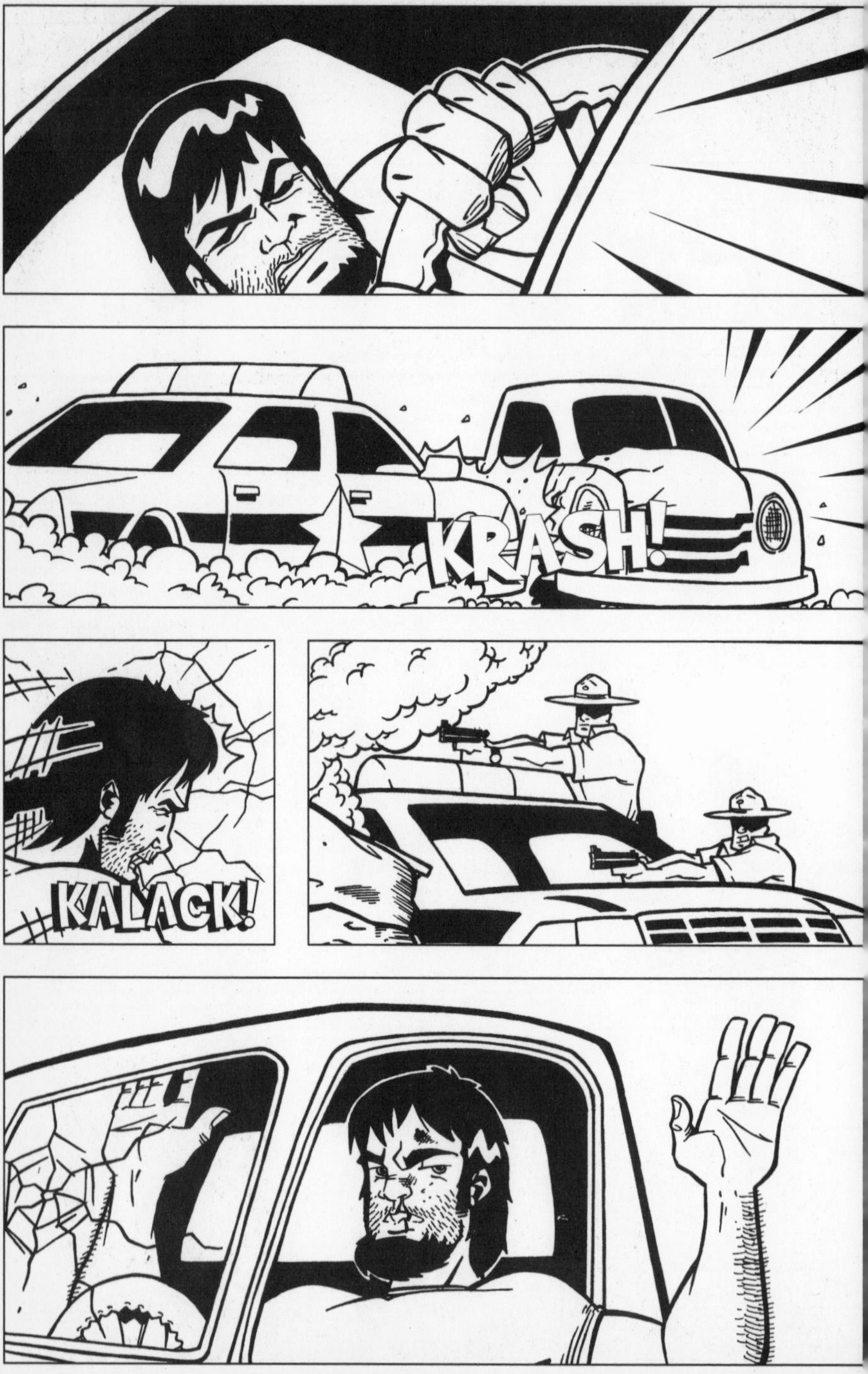
KRASH!
KALACK!

EVERY TIME YOU TELL IT, DANNY, IT JUST SOUNDS WORSE AND WORSE, YOU KNOW THAT?

I CAN'T HELP THAT, SERGEANT. GINGER WAS DEAD WHEN I CLIMBED INTO THE BEDROOM. I PANICKED AND THAT'S WHY I RAN.

YOU DON'T HAVE MY PRINTS ON THAT KNIFE, AND YOU KNOW IT.

MID-MORNING, DEVONSHIRE DIVISION.

BY YOUR OWN ADMISSION, SLICK, YOU WIPED DOWN YOUR PRINTS IN THE HOUSE BEFORE LEAVING. YOU COULD HAVE DONE THE SAME WITH THAT BLADE.

AND THEN THERE'S THAT MATTER OF YOUR DOWNHILL SLIDE FROM WHEN YOU WERE AN ARMY RANGER IN THE GULF WAR. A SLIDE YOU'VE YET TO RECOVER FROM IT SEEMS, DANNY BOY.

ACCORDING TO YOUR FILE, YOU HAVE A TALENT FOR KILLING, DANNY. BIG MEDALS. BIG HERO. BUT YOU ALSO HAD A TALENT FOR FUCKING UP.

MAYBE IT FINALLY GOT TO YOU, MAN. YOU AND GINGER HAD A THING GOING AND YET SHE WAS WITH ALL THESE MEN, NIGHT AFTER NIGHT.

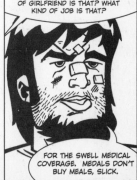

MEN YOU HAD TO DRIVE HER TO SEE, DOING ALL SORTS OF VILE THINGS WITH HER FOR MONEY. WHAT KIND OF GIRLFRIEND IS THAT? WHAT KIND OF JOB IS THAT?

FOR THE SWELL MEDICAL COVERAGE. MEDALS DON'T BUY MEALS, SLICK.

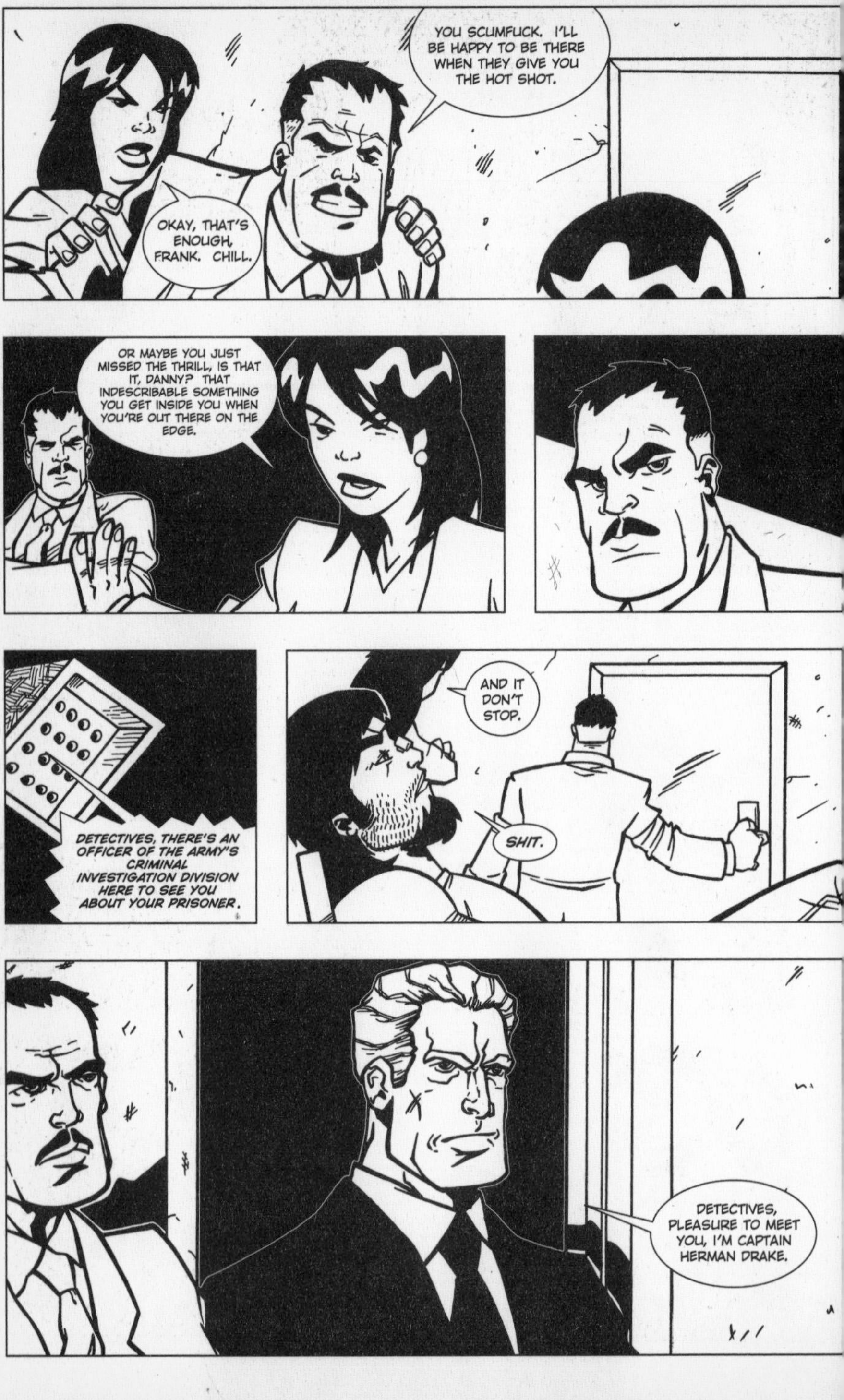
YOU SCUMFUCK. I'LL BE HAPPY TO BE THERE WHEN THEY GIVE YOU THE HOT SHOT.
OKAY, THAT'S ENOUGH, FRANK. CHILL.
OR MAYBE YOU JUST MISSED THE THRILL, IS THAT IT, DANNY? THAT INDESCRIBABLE SOMETHING YOU GET INSIDE YOU WHEN YOU'RE OUT THERE ON THE EDGE.
DETECTIVES, THERE'S AN OFFICER OF THE ARMY'S CRIMINAL INVESTIGATION DIVISION HERE TO SEE YOU ABOUT YOUR PRISONER.
AND IT DON'T STOP.
SHIT.
DETECTIVES, PLEASURE TO MEET YOU, I'M CAPTAIN HERMAN DRAKE.

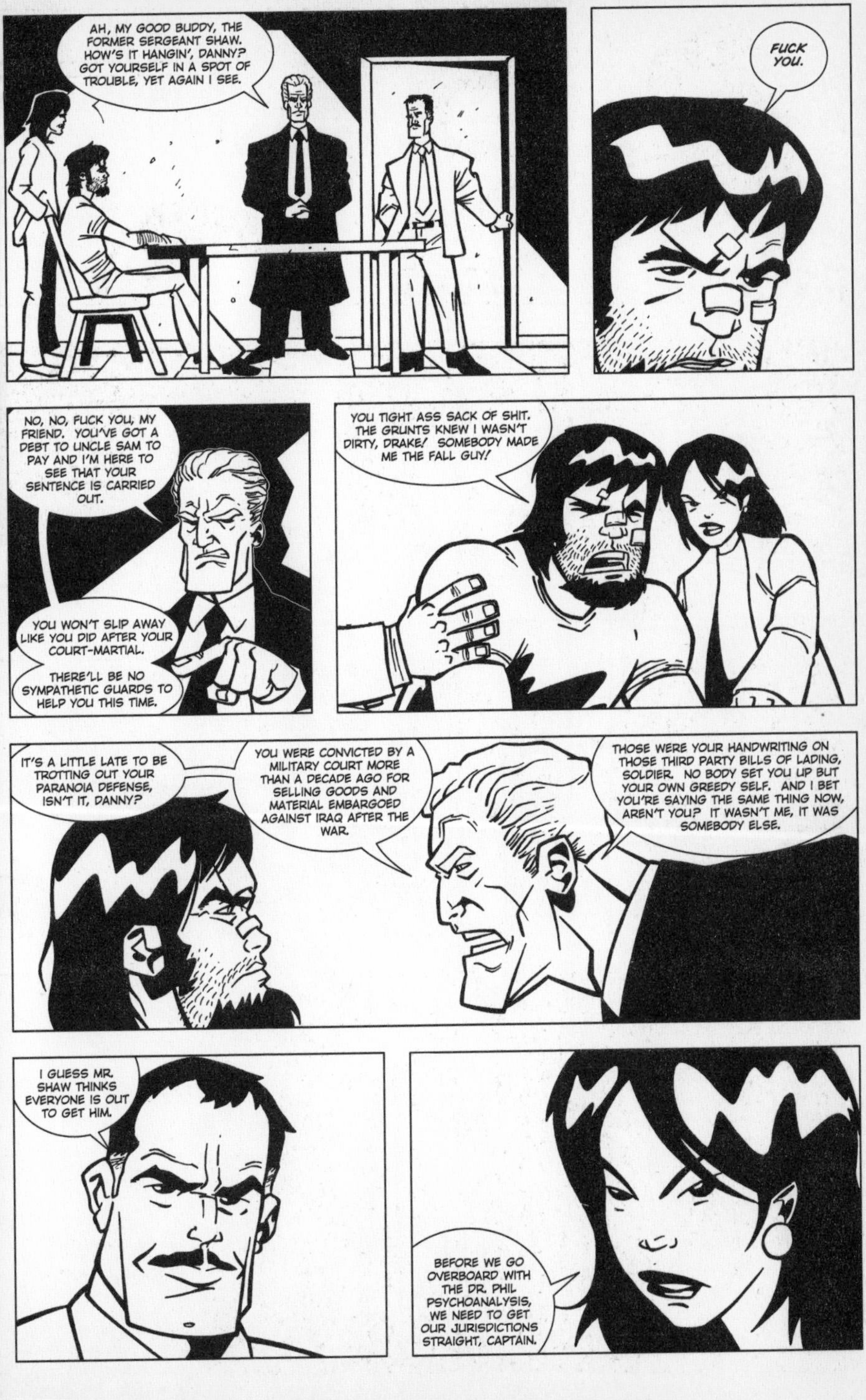
AH, MY GOOD BUDDY, THE FORMER SERGEANT SHAW. HOW'S IT HANGIN', DANNY? GOT YOURSELF IN A SPOT OF TROUBLE, YET AGAIN I SEE.
FUCK YOU.
NO, NO, FUCK YOU, MY FRIEND. YOU'VE GOT A DEBT TO UNCLE SAM TO PAY AND I'M HERE TO SEE THAT YOUR SENTENCE IS CARRIED OUT.
YOU WON'T SLIP AWAY LIKE YOU DID AFTER YOUR COURT-MARTIAL.
THERE'LL BE NO SYMPATHETIC GUARDS TO HELP YOU THIS TIME.
YOU TIGHT ASS SACK OF SHIT. THE GRUNTS KNEW I WASN'T DIRTY, DRAKE! SOMEBODY MADE ME THE FALL GUY!
IT'S A LITTLE LATE TO BE TROTTING OUT YOUR PARANOIA DEFENSE, ISN'T IT, DANNY?
YOU WERE CONVICTED BY A MILITARY COURT MORE THAN A DECADE AGO FOR SELLING GOODS AND MATERIAL EMBARGOED AGAINST IRAQ AFTER THE WAR.
THOSE WERE YOUR HANDWRITING ON THOSE THIRD PARTY BILLS OF LADING, SOLDIER. NO BODY SET YOU UP BUT YOUR OWN GREEDY SELF. AND I BET YOU'RE SAYING THE SAME THING NOW, AREN'T YOU? IT WASN'T ME, IT WAS SOMEBODY ELSE.
I GUESS MR. SHAW THINKS EVERYONE IS OUT TO GET HIM.
BEFORE WE GO OVERBOARD WITH THE DR. PHIL PSYCHOANALYSIS, WE NEED TO GET OUR JURISDICTIONS STRAIGHT, CAPTAIN.

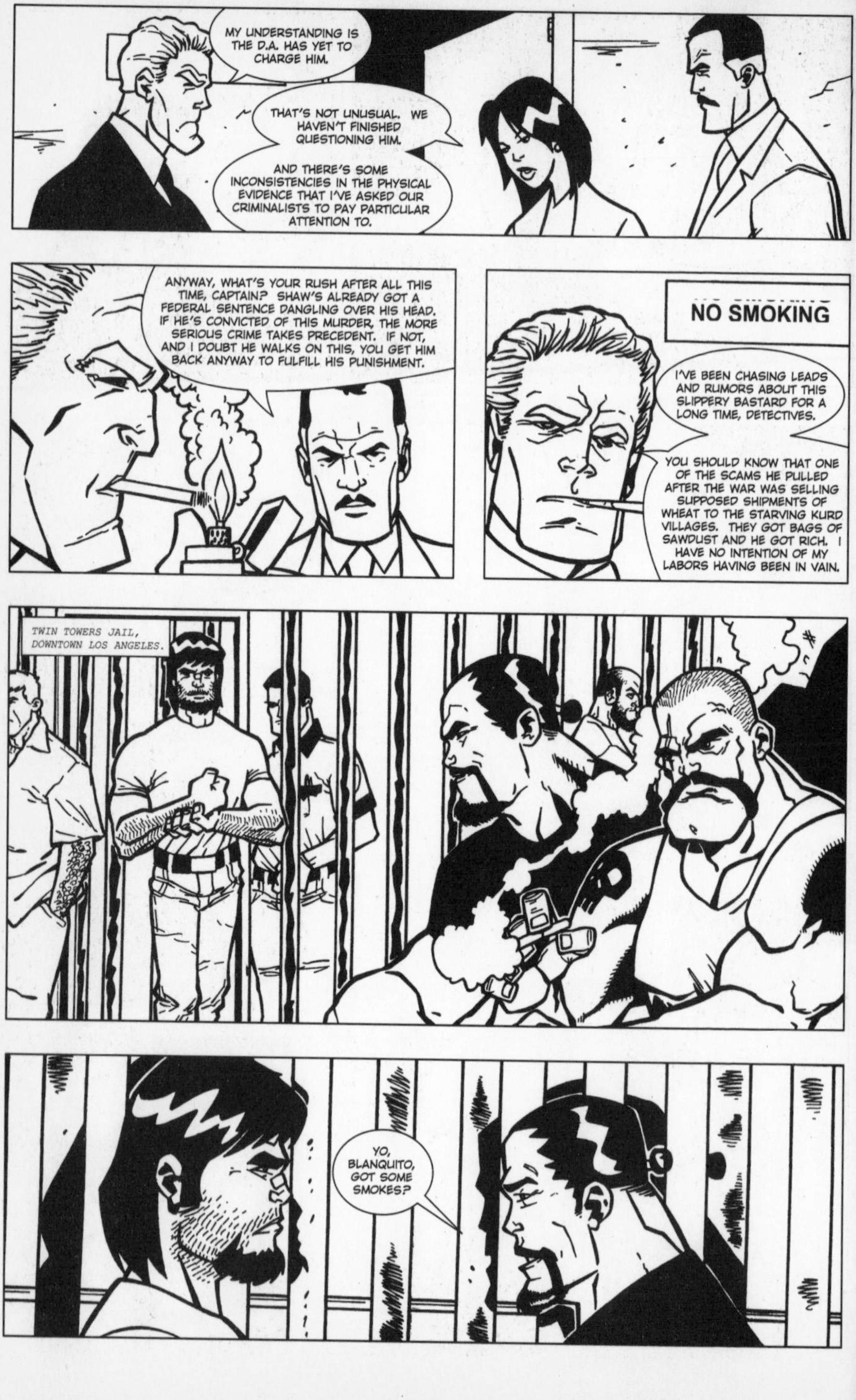
MY UNDERSTANDING IS THE D.A. HAS YET TO CHARGE HIM.
THAT'S NOT UNUSUAL. WE HAVEN'T FINISHED QUESTIONING HIM.
AND THERE'S SOME INCONSISTENCIES IN THE PHYSICAL EVIDENCE THAT I'VE ASKED OUR CRIMINALISTS TO PAY PARTICULAR ATTENTION TO.
ANYWAY, WHAT'S YOUR RUSH AFTER ALL THIS TIME, CAPTAIN? SHAW'S ALREADY GOT A FEDERAL SENTENCE DANGLING OVER HIS HEAD. IF HE'S CONVICTED OF THIS MURDER, THE MORE SERIOUS CRIME TAKES PRECEDENT. IF NOT, AND I DOUBT HE WALKS ON THIS, YOU GET HIM BACK ANYWAY TO FULFILL HIS PUNISHMENT.
NO SMOKING
I'VE BEEN CHASING LEADS AND RUMORS ABOUT THIS SLIPPERY BASTARD FOR A LONG TIME, DETECTIVES.
YOU SHOULD KNOW THAT ONE OF THE SCAMS HE PULLED AFTER THE WAR WAS SELLING SUPPOSED SHIPMENTS OF WHEAT TO THE STARVING KURD VILLAGES. THEY GOT BAGS OF SAWDUST AND HE GOT RICH. I HAVE NO INTENTION OF MY LABORS HAVING BEEN IN VAIN.
TWIN TOWERS JAIL, DOWNTOWN LOS ANGELES.
YO, BLANQUITO, GOT SOME SMOKES?

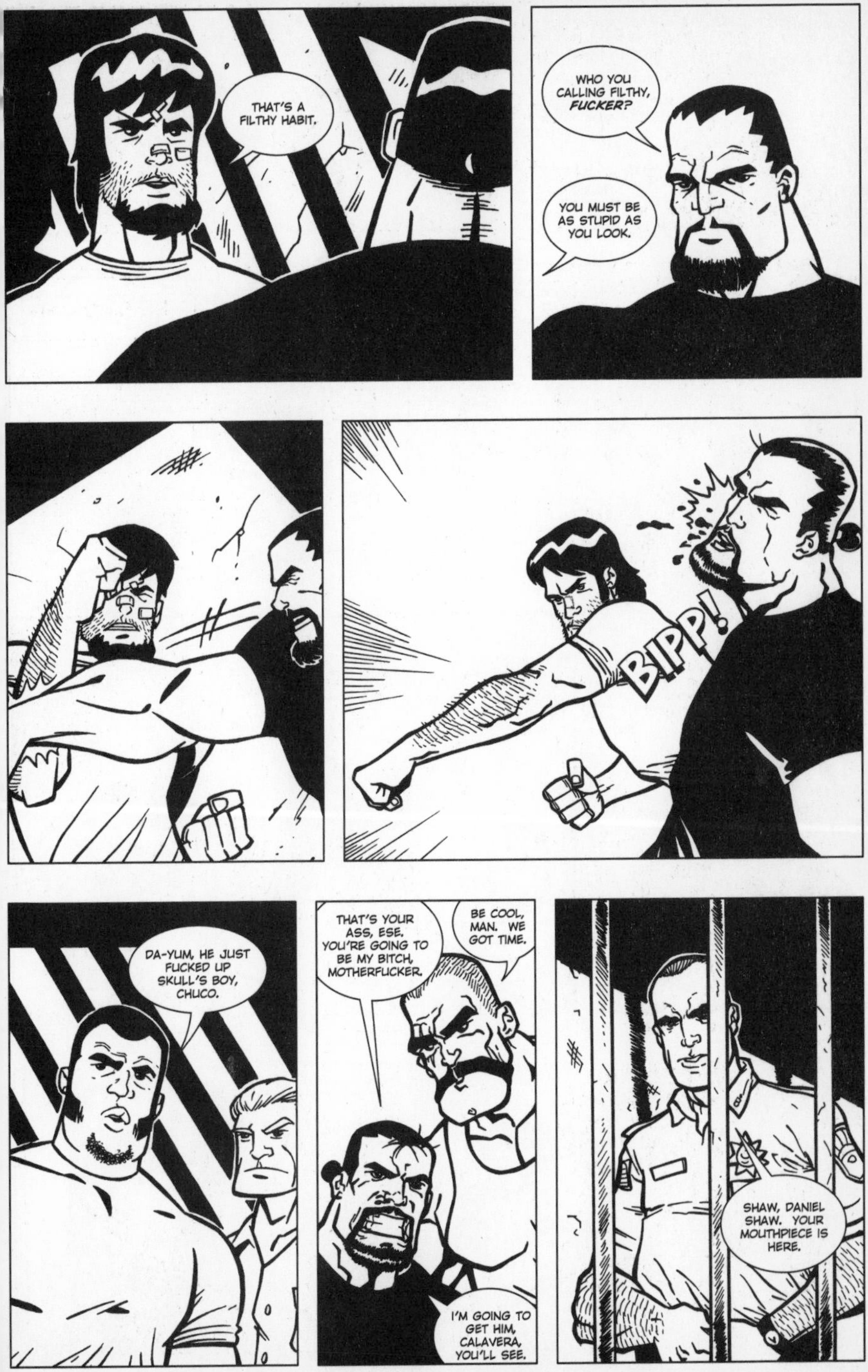
THAT'S A FILTHY HABIT.
WHO YOU CALLING FILTHY, *FUCKER?*
YOU MUST BE AS STUPID AS YOU LOOK.
BIPP!
DA-YUM, HE JUST FUCKED UP SKULL'S BOY, CHUCO.
THAT'S YOUR ASS, ESE. YOU'RE GOING TO BE MY BITCH, MOTHERFUCKER.
BE COOL, MAN. WE GOT TIME.
I'M GOING TO GET HIM, CALAVERA, YOU'LL SEE.
SHAW, DANIEL SHAW. YOUR MOUTHPIECE IS HERE.

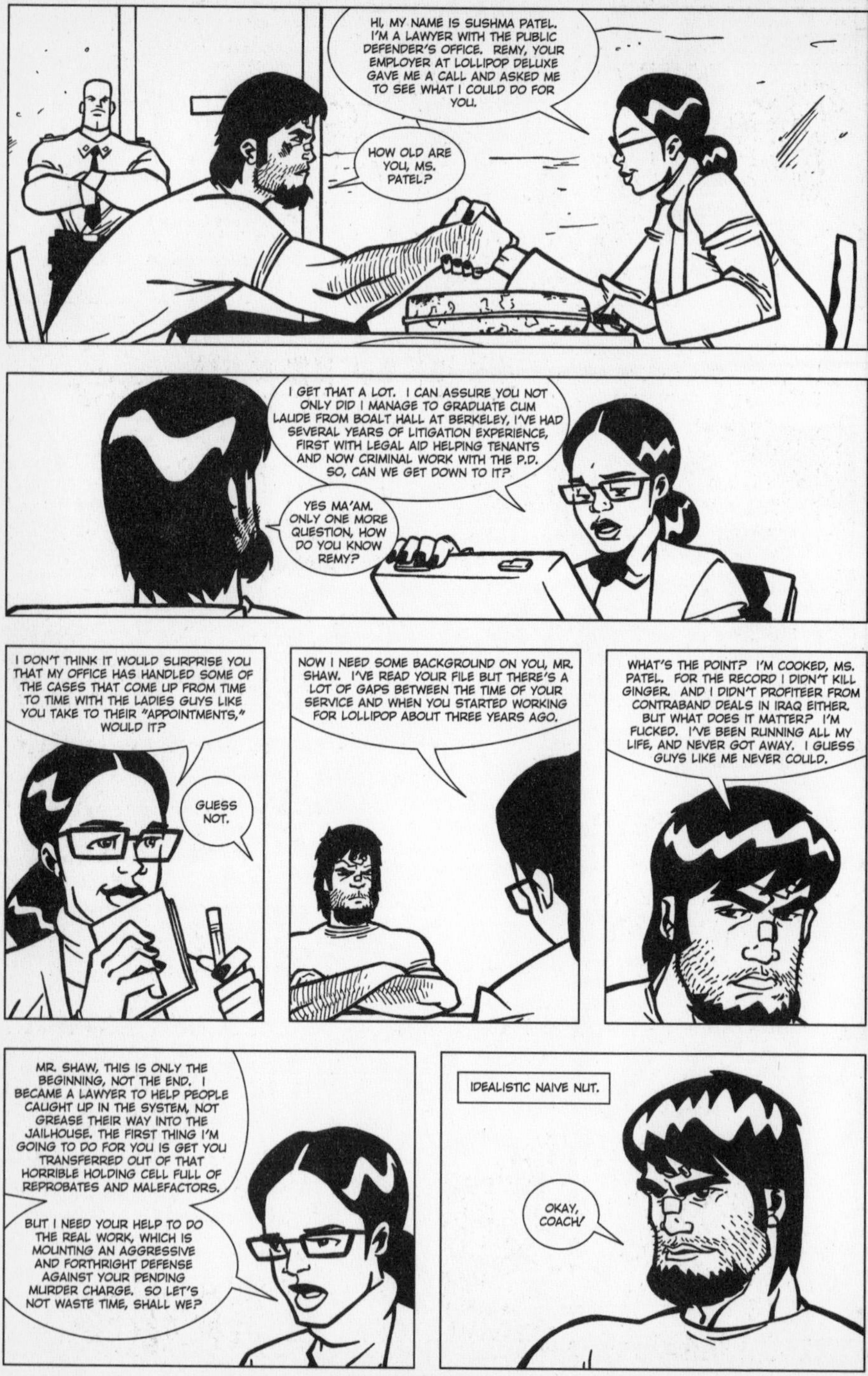
HI, MY NAME IS SUSHMA PATEL. I'M A LAWYER WITH THE PUBLIC DEFENDER'S OFFICE. REMY, YOUR EMPLOYER AT LOLLIPOP DELUXE GAVE ME A CALL AND ASKED ME TO SEE WHAT I COULD DO FOR YOU.
HOW OLD ARE YOU, MS. PATEL?
I GET THAT A LOT. I CAN ASSURE YOU NOT ONLY DID I MANAGE TO GRADUATE CUM LAUDE FROM BOALT HALL AT BERKELEY, I'VE HAD SEVERAL YEARS OF LITIGATION EXPERIENCE, FIRST WITH LEGAL AID HELPING TENANTS AND NOW CRIMINAL WORK WITH THE P.D. SO, CAN WE GET DOWN TO IT?
YES MA'AM. ONLY ONE MORE QUESTION, HOW DO YOU KNOW REMY?
I DON'T THINK IT WOULD SURPRISE YOU THAT MY OFFICE HAS HANDLED SOME OF THE CASES THAT COME UP FROM TIME TO TIME WITH THE LADIES GUYS LIKE YOU TAKE TO THEIR "APPOINTMENTS," WOULD IT?
GUESS NOT.
NOW I NEED SOME BACKGROUND ON YOU, MR. SHAW. I'VE READ YOUR FILE BUT THERE'S A LOT OF GAPS BETWEEN THE TIME OF YOUR SERVICE AND WHEN YOU STARTED WORKING FOR LOLLIPOP ABOUT THREE YEARS AGO.
WHAT'S THE POINT? I'M COOKED, MS. PATEL. FOR THE RECORD I DIDN'T KILL GINGER. AND I DIDN'T PROFITEER FROM CONTRABAND DEALS IN IRAQ EITHER. BUT WHAT DOES IT MATTER? I'M FUCKED. I'VE BEEN RUNNING ALL MY LIFE, AND NEVER GOT AWAY. I GUESS GUYS LIKE ME NEVER COULD.
MR. SHAW, THIS IS ONLY THE BEGINNING, NOT THE END. I BECAME A LAWYER TO HELP PEOPLE CAUGHT UP IN THE SYSTEM, NOT GREASE THEIR WAY INTO THE JAILHOUSE. THE FIRST THING I'M GOING TO DO FOR YOU IS GET YOU TRANSFERRED OUT OF THAT HORRIBLE HOLDING CELL FULL OF REPROBATES AND MALEFACTORS.
BUT I NEED YOUR HELP TO DO THE REAL WORK, WHICH IS MOUNTING AN AGGRESSIVE AND FORTHRIGHT DEFENSE AGAINST YOUR PENDING MURDER CHARGE. SO LET'S NOT WASTE TIME, SHALL WE?
IDEALISTIC NAIVE NUT.
OKAY, COACH!

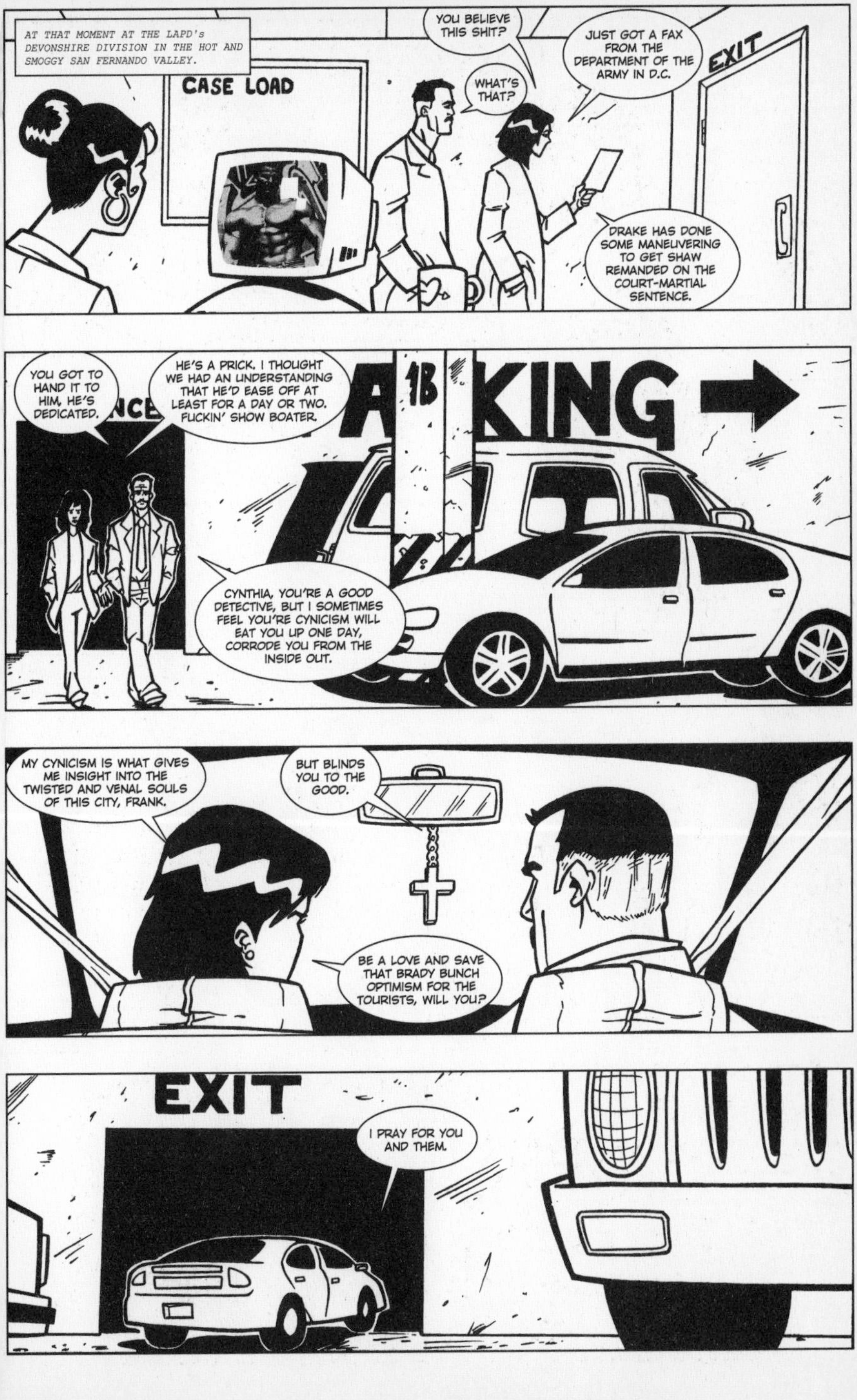
AT THAT MOMENT AT THE LAPD's DEVONSHIRE DIVISION IN THE HOT AND SMOGGY SAN FERNANDO VALLEY.
CASE LOAD
YOU BELIEVE THIS SHIT?
WHAT'S THAT?
JUST GOT A FAX FROM THE DEPARTMENT OF THE ARMY IN D.C.
EXIT
DRAKE HAS DONE SOME MANEUVERING TO GET SHAW REMANDED ON THE COURT-MARTIAL SENTENCE.
YOU GOT TO HAND IT TO HIM, HE'S DEDICATED.
HE'S A PRICK. I THOUGHT WE HAD AN UNDERSTANDING THAT HE'D EASE OFF AT LEAST FOR A DAY OR TWO. FUCKIN' SHOW BOATER.
CYNTHIA, YOU'RE A GOOD DETECTIVE, BUT I SOMETIMES FEEL YOU'RE CYNICISM WILL EAT YOU UP ONE DAY, CORRODE YOU FROM THE INSIDE OUT.
MY CYNICISM IS WHAT GIVES ME INSIGHT INTO THE TWISTED AND VENAL SOULS OF THIS CITY, FRANK.
BUT BLINDS YOU TO THE GOOD.
BE A LOVE AND SAVE THAT BRADY BUNCH OPTIMISM FOR THE TOURISTS, WILL YOU?
EXIT
I PRAY FOR YOU AND THEM.

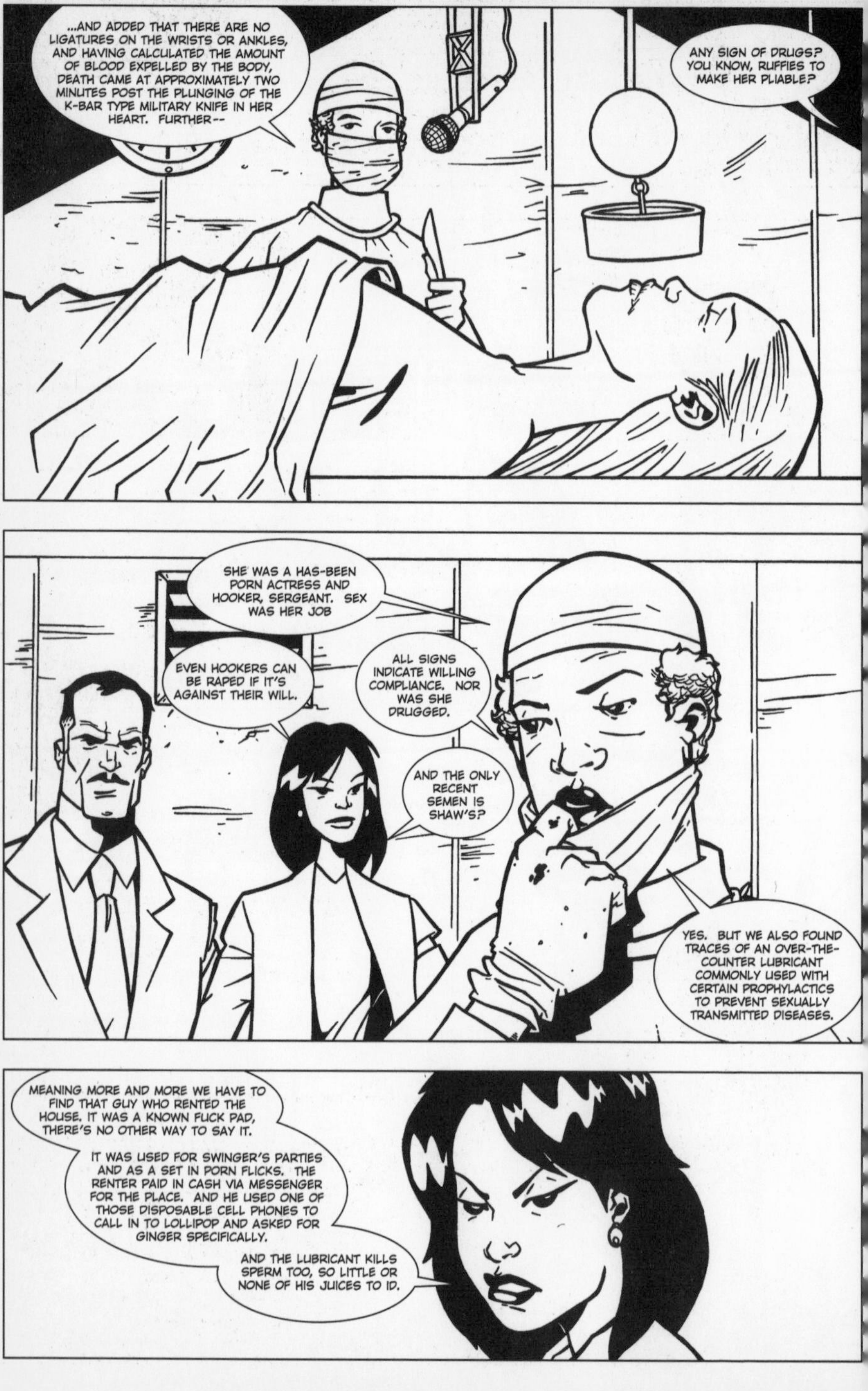
...AND ADDED THAT THERE ARE NO LIGATURES ON THE WRISTS OR ANKLES, AND HAVING CALCULATED THE AMOUNT OF BLOOD EXPELLED BY THE BODY, DEATH CAME AT APPROXIMATELY TWO MINUTES POST THE PLUNGING OF THE K-BAR TYPE MILITARY KNIFE IN HER HEART. FURTHER--
ANY SIGN OF DRUGS? YOU KNOW, RUFFIES TO MAKE HER PLIABLE?
SHE WAS A HAS-BEEN PORN ACTRESS AND HOOKER, SERGEANT. SEX WAS HER JOB
EVEN HOOKERS CAN BE RAPED IF IT'S AGAINST THEIR WILL.
ALL SIGNS INDICATE WILLING COMPLIANCE. NOR WAS SHE DRUGGED.
AND THE ONLY RECENT SEMEN IS SHAW'S?
YES. BUT WE ALSO FOUND TRACES OF AN OVER-THE-COUNTER LUBRICANT COMMONLY USED WITH CERTAIN PROPHYLACTICS TO PREVENT SEXUALLY TRANSMITTED DISEASES.
MEANING MORE AND MORE WE HAVE TO FIND THAT GUY WHO RENTED THE HOUSE. IT WAS A KNOWN FUCK PAD, THERE'S NO OTHER WAY TO SAY IT.
IT WAS USED FOR SWINGER'S PARTIES AND AS A SET IN PORN FLICKS. THE RENTER PAID IN CASH VIA MESSENGER FOR THE PLACE. AND HE USED ONE OF THOSE DISPOSABLE CELL PHONES TO CALL IN TO LOLLIPOP AND ASKED FOR GINGER SPECIFICALLY.
AND THE LUBRICANT KILLS SPERM TOO, SO LITTLE OR NONE OF HIS JUICES TO ID.

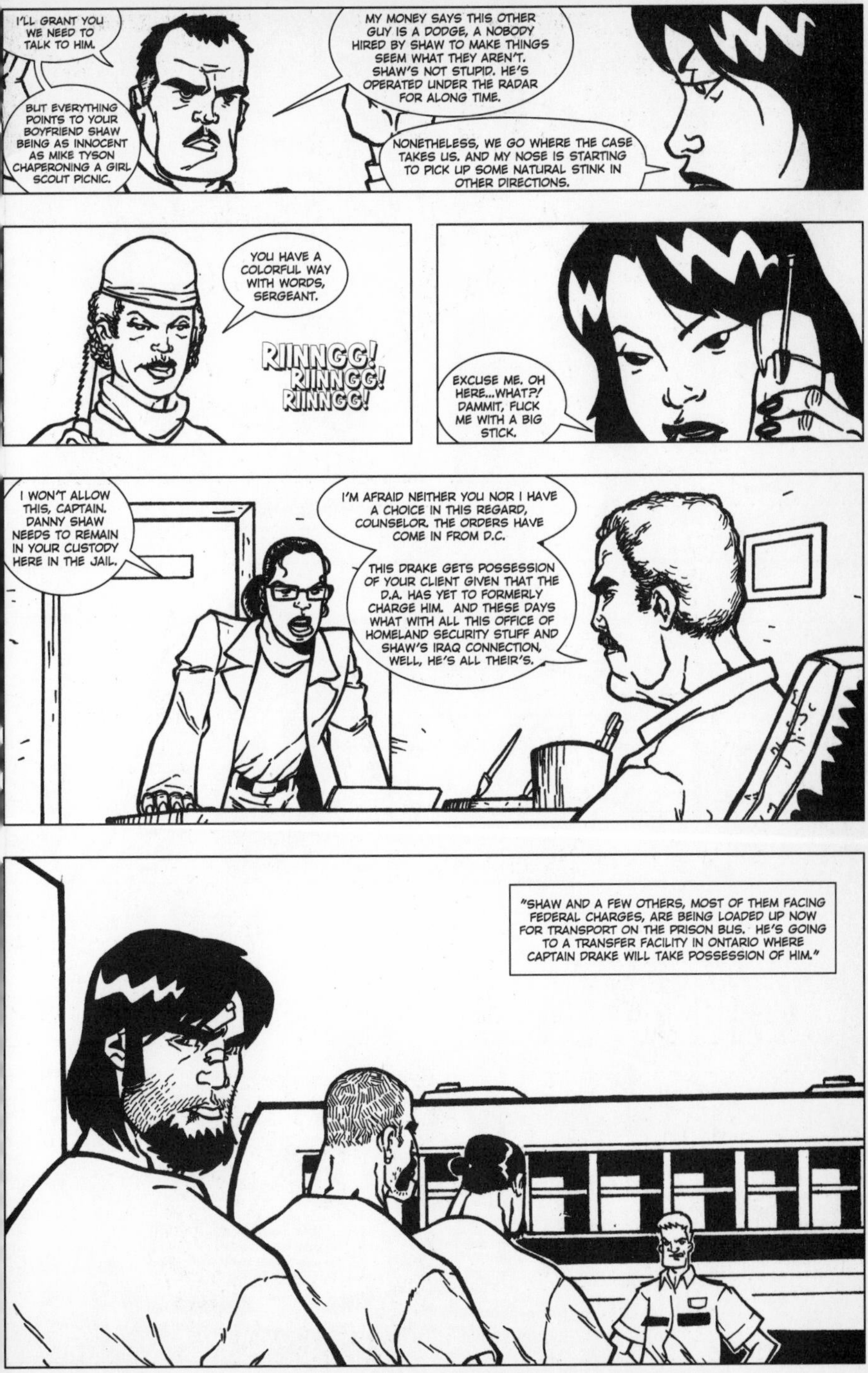
I'LL GRANT YOU WE NEED TO TALK TO HIM.
BUT EVERYTHING POINTS TO YOUR BOYFRIEND SHAW BEING AS INNOCENT AS MIKE TYSON CHAPERONING A GIRL SCOUT PICNIC.
MY MONEY SAYS THIS OTHER GUY IS A DODGE, A NOBODY HIRED BY SHAW TO MAKE THINGS SEEM WHAT THEY AREN'T. SHAW'S NOT STUPID. HE'S OPERATED UNDER THE RADAR FOR ALONG TIME.
NONETHELESS, WE GO WHERE THE CASE TAKES US. AND MY NOSE IS STARTING TO PICK UP SOME NATURAL STINK IN OTHER DIRECTIONS.
YOU HAVE A COLORFUL WAY WITH WORDS, SERGEANT.
RIINNGG! RIINNGG! RIINNGG!
EXCUSE ME. OH HERE...WHAT?! DAMMIT, FUCK ME WITH A BIG STICK.
I WON'T ALLOW THIS, CAPTAIN. DANNY SHAW NEEDS TO REMAIN IN YOUR CUSTODY HERE IN THE JAIL.
I'M AFRAID NEITHER YOU NOR I HAVE A CHOICE IN THIS REGARD, COUNSELOR. THE ORDERS HAVE COME IN FROM D.C.
THIS DRAKE GETS POSSESSION OF YOUR CLIENT GIVEN THAT THE D.A. HAS YET TO FORMERLY CHARGE HIM. AND THESE DAYS WHAT WITH ALL THIS OFFICE OF HOMELAND SECURITY STUFF AND SHAW'S IRAQ CONNECTION, WELL, HE'S ALL THEIR'S.
"SHAW AND A FEW OTHERS, MOST OF THEM FACING FEDERAL CHARGES, ARE BEING LOADED UP NOW FOR TRANSPORT ON THE PRISON BUS. HE'S GOING TO A TRANSFER FACILITY IN ONTARIO WHERE CAPTAIN DRAKE WILL TAKE POSSESSION OF HIM."

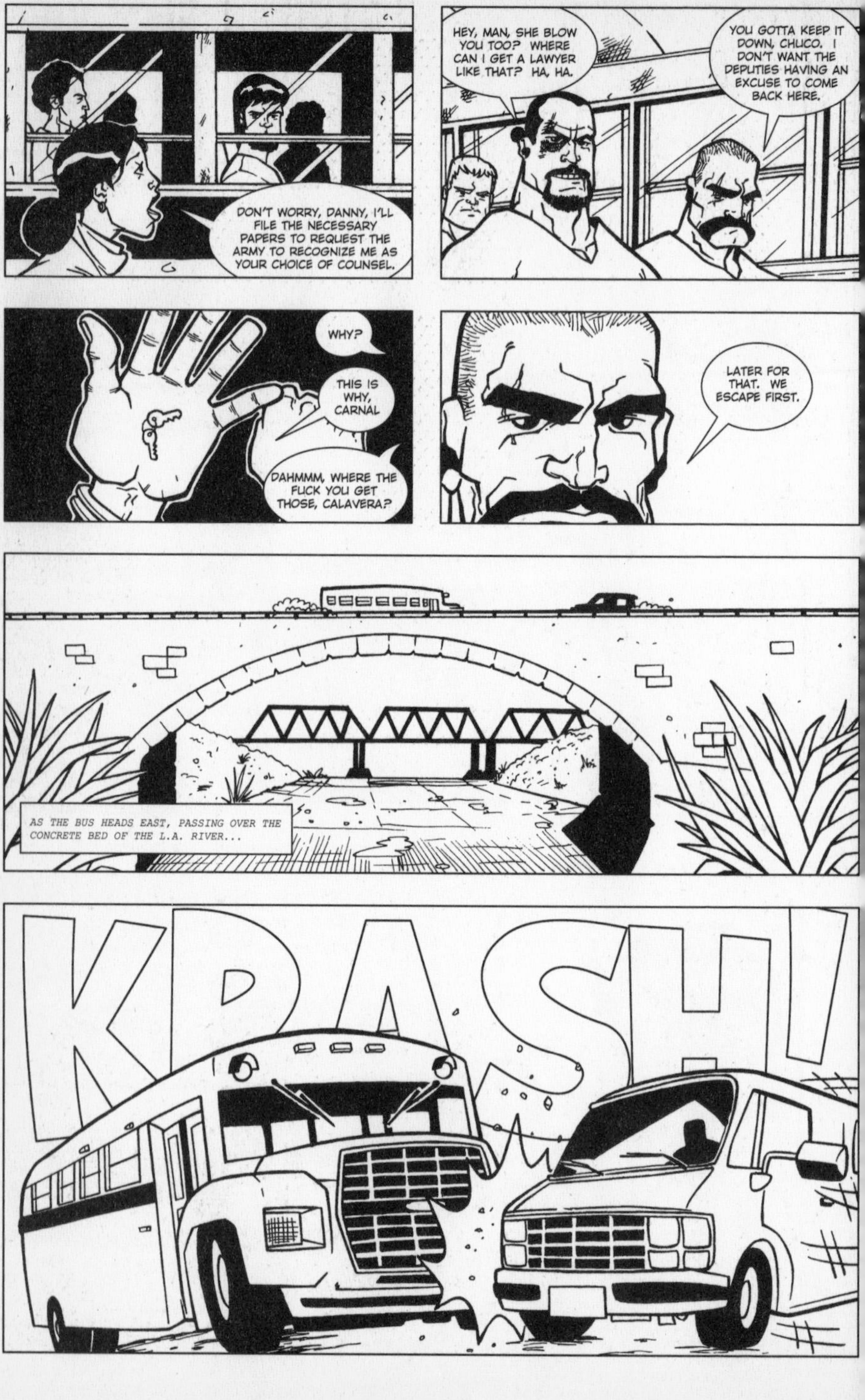
DON'T WORRY, DANNY, I'LL FILE THE NECESSARY PAPERS TO REQUEST THE ARMY TO RECOGNIZE ME AS YOUR CHOICE OF COUNSEL.
HEY, MAN, SHE BLOW YOU TOO? WHERE CAN I GET A LAWYER LIKE THAT? HA, HA.
YOU GOTTA KEEP IT DOWN, CHUCO. I DON'T WANT THE DEPUTIES HAVING AN EXCUSE TO COME BACK HERE.
WHY?
THIS IS WHY, CARNAL
DAHMMM, WHERE THE FUCK YOU GET THOSE, CALAVERA?
LATER FOR THAT. WE ESCAPE FIRST.
AS THE BUS HEADS EAST, PASSING OVER THE CONCRETE BED OF THE L.A. RIVER...
KRASH!

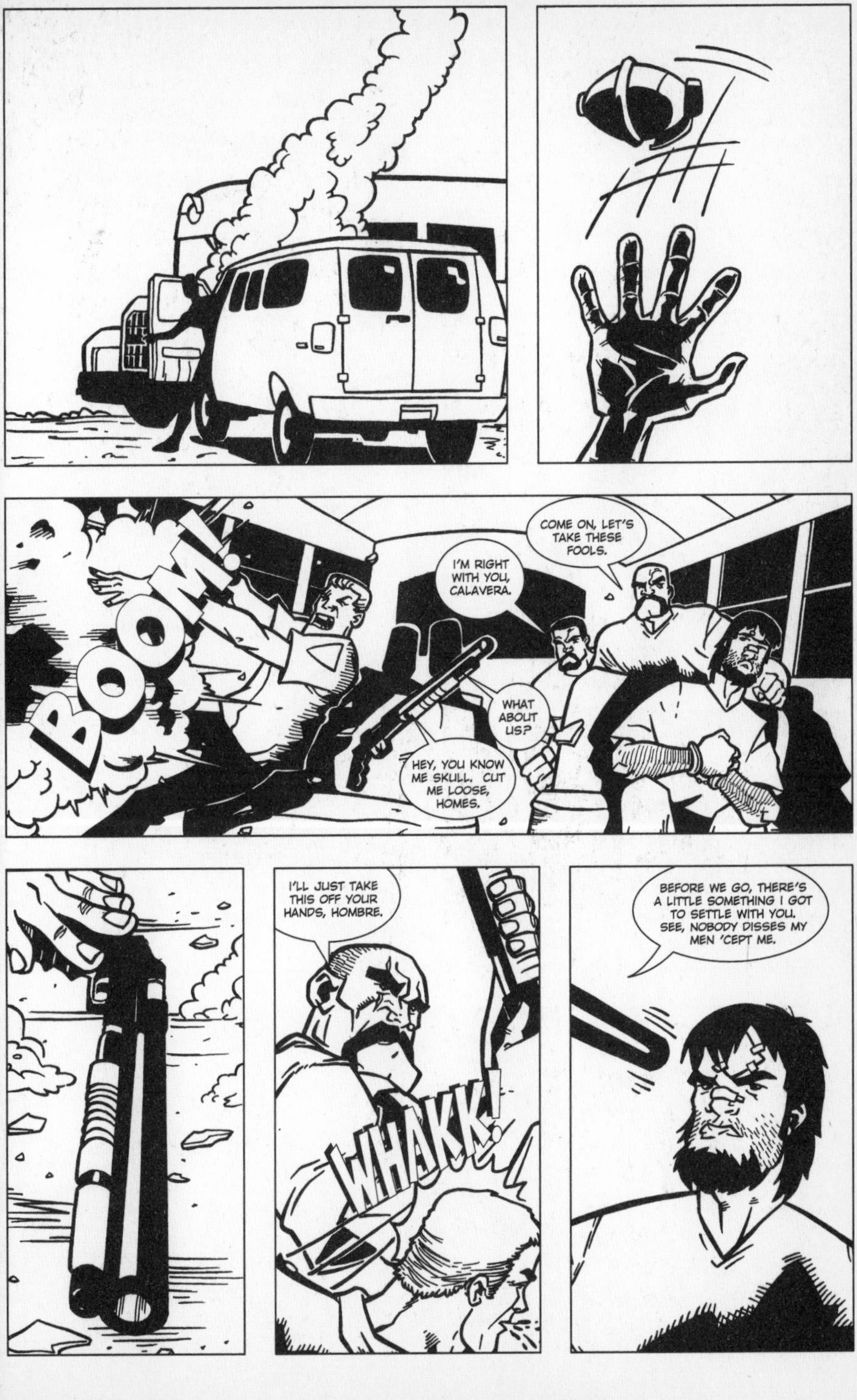
BOOOM!
COME ON, LET'S TAKE THESE FOOLS.
I'M RIGHT WITH YOU, CALAVERA.
WHAT ABOUT US?
HEY, YOU KNOW ME SKULL. CUT ME LOOSE, HOMES.
I'LL JUST TAKE THIS OFF YOUR HANDS, HOMBRE.
WHAKK!
BEFORE WE GO, THERE'S A LITTLE SOMETHING I GOT TO SETTLE WITH YOU. SEE, NOBODY DISSES MY MEN 'CEPT ME.

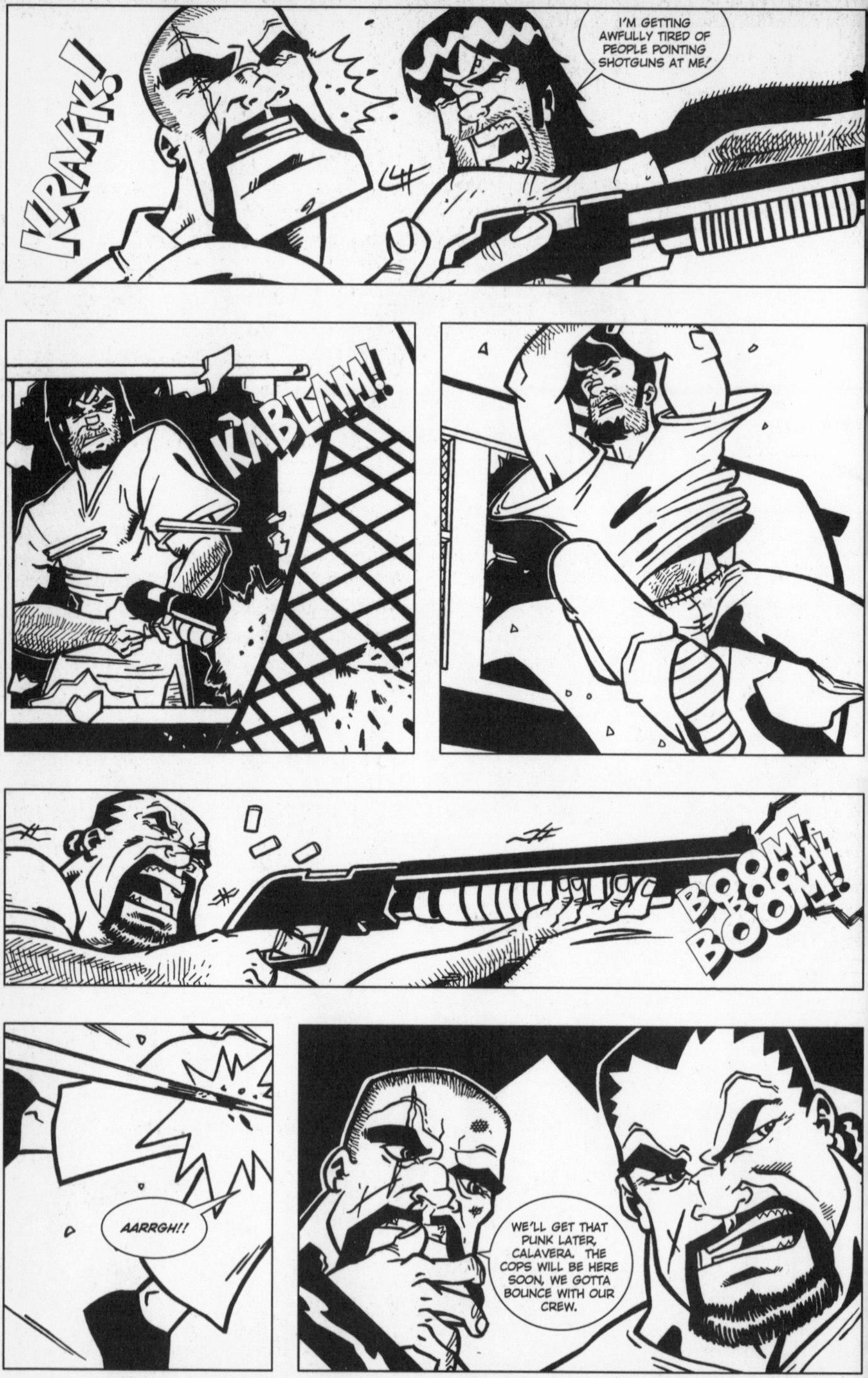

KRAKK!
I'M GETTING AWFULLY TIRED OF PEOPLE POINTING SHOTGUNS AT ME!
KABLAM!
BOOM! BOOM! BOOM!
AARRGH!!
WE'LL GET THAT PUNK LATER, CALAVERA. THE COPS WILL BE HERE SOON, WE GOTTA BOUNCE WITH OUR CREW.

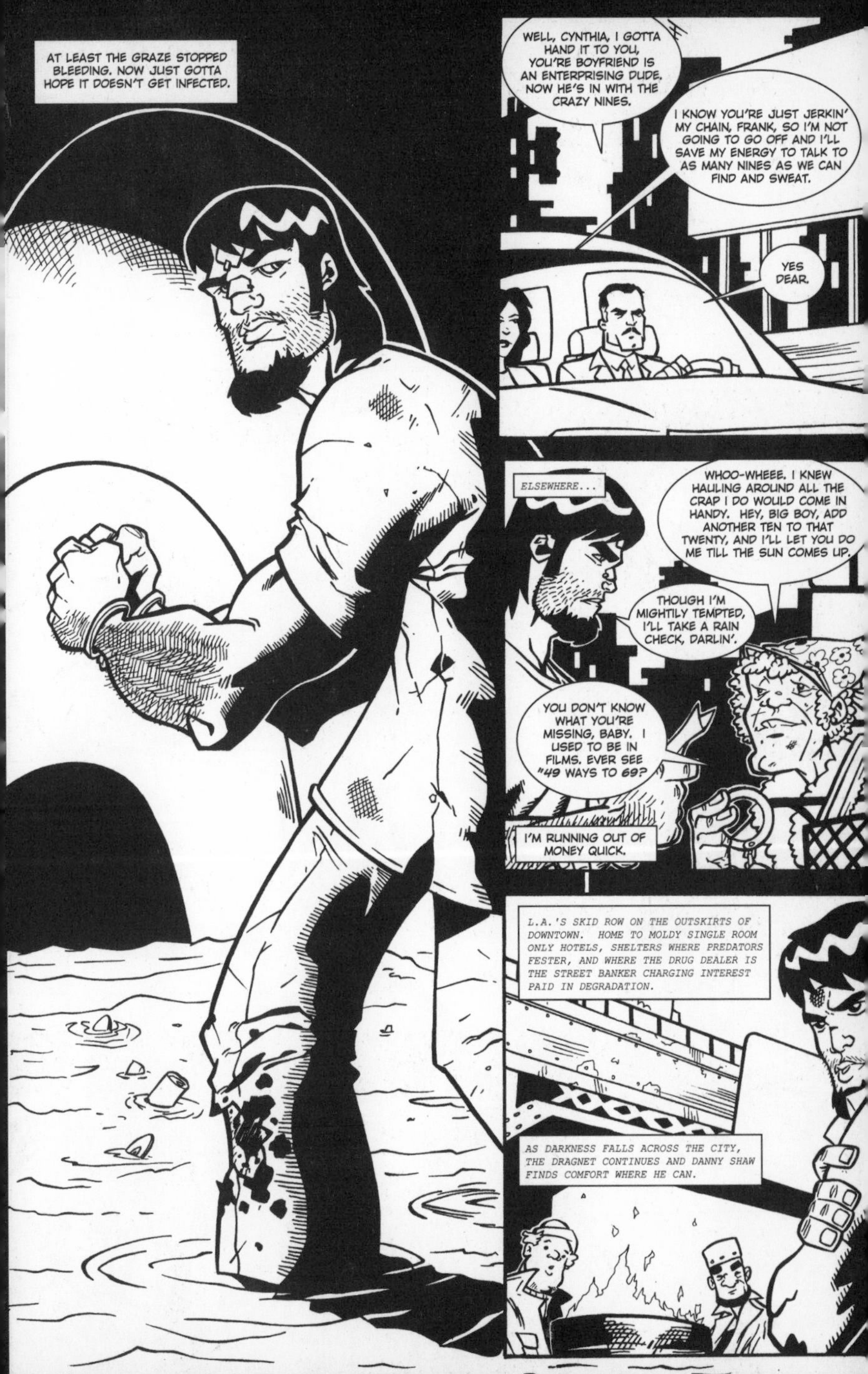
AT LEAST THE GRAZE STOPPED BLEEDING. NOW JUST GOTTA HOPE IT DOESN'T GET INFECTED.
WELL, CYNTHIA, I GOTTA HAND IT TO YOU, YOU'RE BOYFRIEND IS AN ENTERPRISING DUDE. NOW HE'S IN WITH THE CRAZY NINES.
I KNOW YOU'RE JUST JERKIN' MY CHAIN, FRANK, SO I'M NOT GOING TO GO OFF AND I'LL SAVE MY ENERGY TO TALK TO AS MANY NINES AS WE CAN FIND AND SWEAT.
YES DEAR.
ELSEWHERE...
WHOO-WHEEE. I KNEW HAULING AROUND ALL THE CRAP I DO WOULD COME IN HANDY. HEY, BIG BOY, ADD ANOTHER TEN TO THAT TWENTY, AND I'LL LET YOU DO ME TILL THE SUN COMES UP.
THOUGH I'M MIGHTILY TEMPTED, I'LL TAKE A RAIN CHECK, DARLIN'.
YOU DON'T KNOW WHAT YOU'RE MISSING, BABY. I USED TO BE IN FILMS. EVER SEE "49 WAYS TO 69?
I'M RUNNING OUT OF MONEY QUICK.
L.A.'S SKID ROW ON THE OUTSKIRTS OF DOWNTOWN. HOME TO MOLDY SINGLE ROOM ONLY HOTELS, SHELTERS WHERE PREDATORS FESTER, AND WHERE THE DRUG DEALER IS THE STREET BANKER CHARGING INTEREST PAID IN DEGRADATION.
AS DARKNESS FALLS ACROSS THE CITY, THE DRAGNET CONTINUES AND DANNY SHAW FINDS COMFORT WHERE HE CAN.

WHILE SOME 25 MILES TO THE SOUTH IN THE PORT CITY OF LONG BEACH, CALAVERA FUENTES, CHUCO VALDEZ AND THEIR FELLOW CRAZY NINES GANG MEMBERS WHO SPRUNG THEM FIND COMFORT IN A MUCH DIFFERENT FASHION.

LIFE IS GOOD WHEN YOU ESCAPE JAIL, HOMES.

GODDAMN GOOD.

AS THE PARTIERS CONTINUE EXPLORING THE CLIFF'S NOTES VERSION OF THE KAMA SUTRA, AN UNINVITED GUEST ARRIVES.

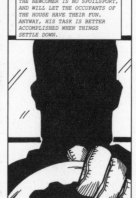

THE NEWCOMER IS NO SPOILSPORT, AND WILL LET THE OCCUPANTS OF THE HOUSE HAVE THEIR FUN. ANYWAY, HIS TASK IS BETTER ACCOMPLISHED WHEN THINGS SETTLE DOWN.

LATER THAT NIGHT THE EXHAUSTED FINALLY JOURNEY TO THE LAND OF NOD...

...NO MATTER WHERE THEY MAY LAY THEIR HEAD.

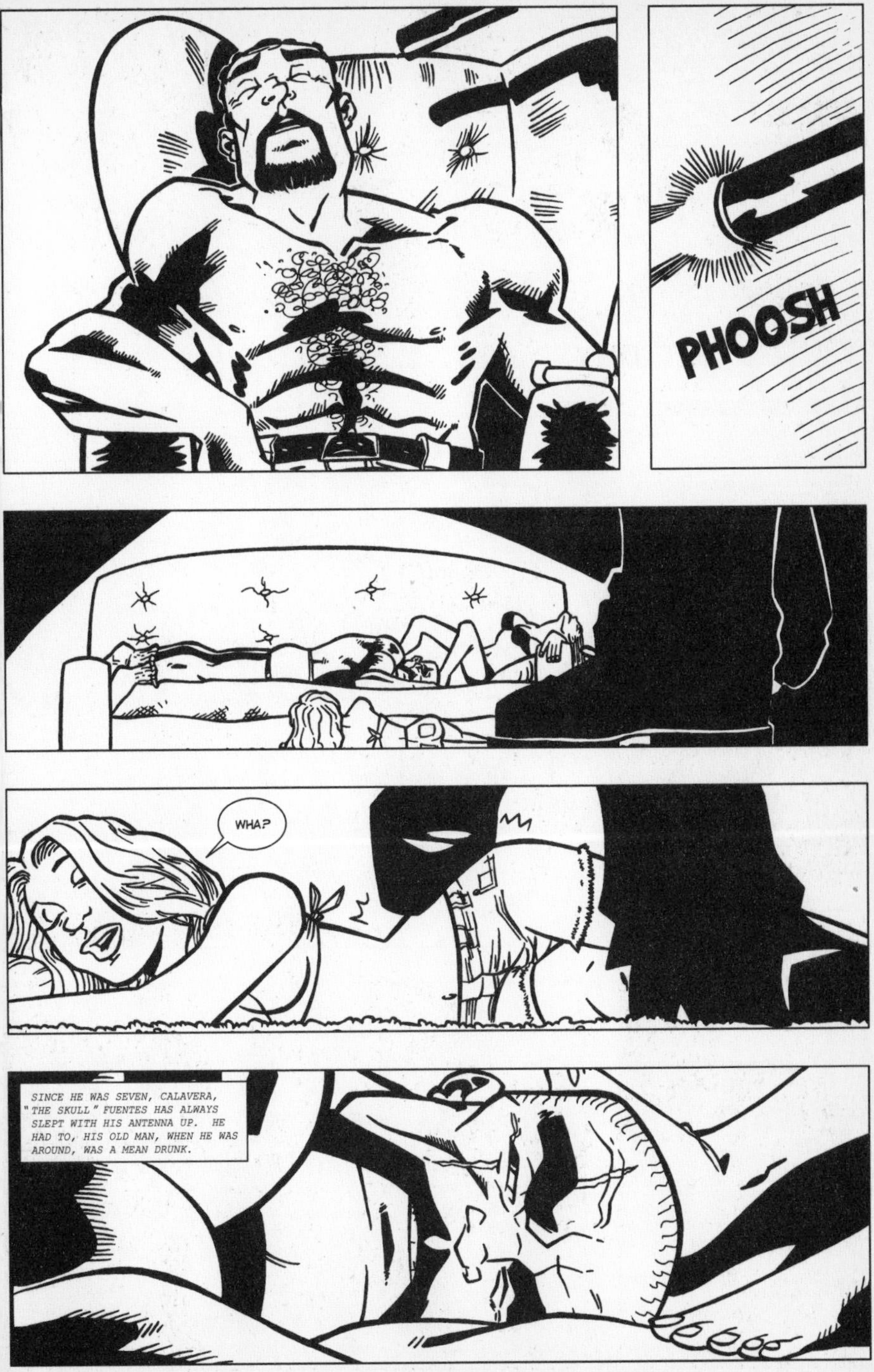
PHOOSH
WHA?
SINCE HE WAS SEVEN, CALAVERA, "THE SKULL" FUENTES HAS ALWAYS SLEPT WITH HIS ANTENNA UP. HE HAD TO, HIS OLD MAN, WHEN HE WAS AROUND, WAS A MEAN DRUNK.

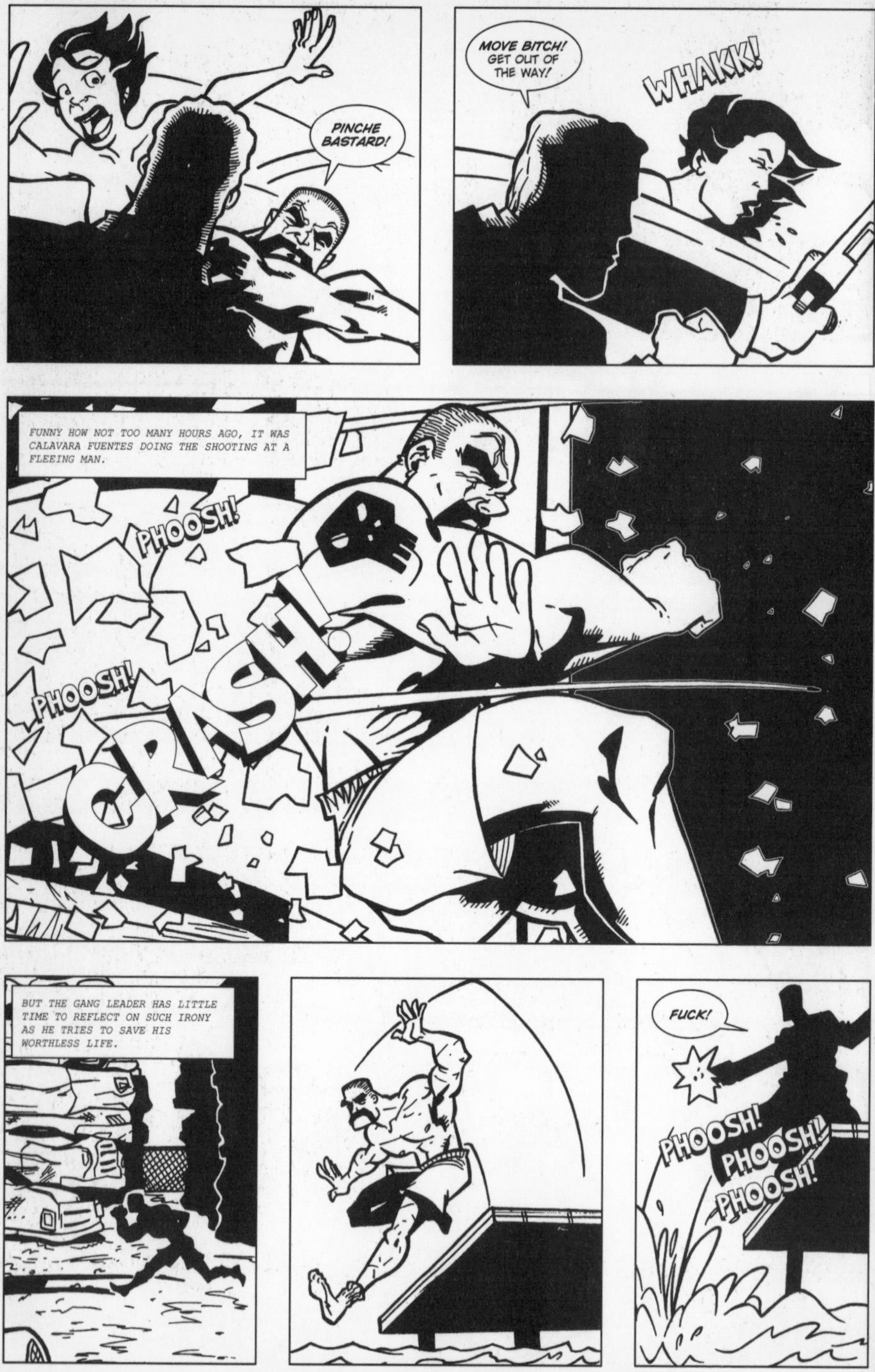
PINCHE BASTARD!
MOVE BITCH! GET OUT OF THE WAY!
WHAKK!
FUNNY HOW NOT TOO MANY HOURS AGO, IT WAS CALAVARA FUENTES DOING THE SHOOTING AT A FLEEING MAN.
PHOOSH!
PHOOSH!
CRASH!
BUT THE GANG LEADER HAS LITTLE TIME TO REFLECT ON SUCH IRONY AS HE TRIES TO SAVE HIS WORTHLESS LIFE.
FUCK!
PHOOSH!
PHOOSH!
PHOOSH!

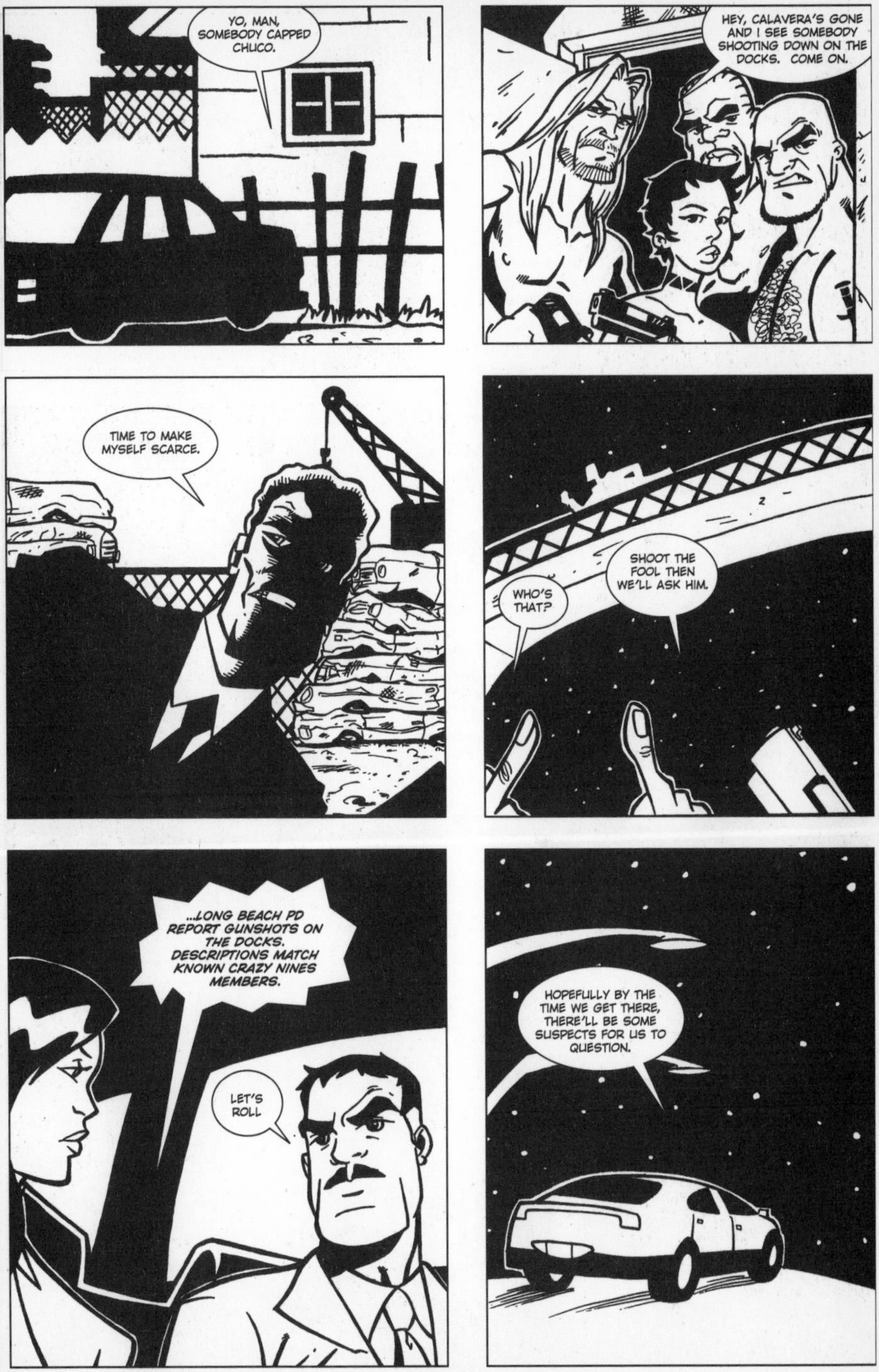
YO, MAN, SOMEBODY CAPPED CHUCO.
HEY, CALAVERA'S GONE AND I SEE SOMEBODY SHOOTING DOWN ON THE DOCKS. COME ON.
TIME TO MAKE MYSELF SCARCE.
WHO'S THAT?
SHOOT THE FOOL THEN WE'LL ASK HIM.
...LONG BEACH PD REPORT GUNSHOTS ON THE DOCKS. DESCRIPTIONS MATCH KNOWN CRAZY NINES MEMBERS.
LET'S ROLL
HOPEFULLY BY THE TIME WE GET THERE, THERE'LL BE SOME SUSPECTS FOR US TO QUESTION.

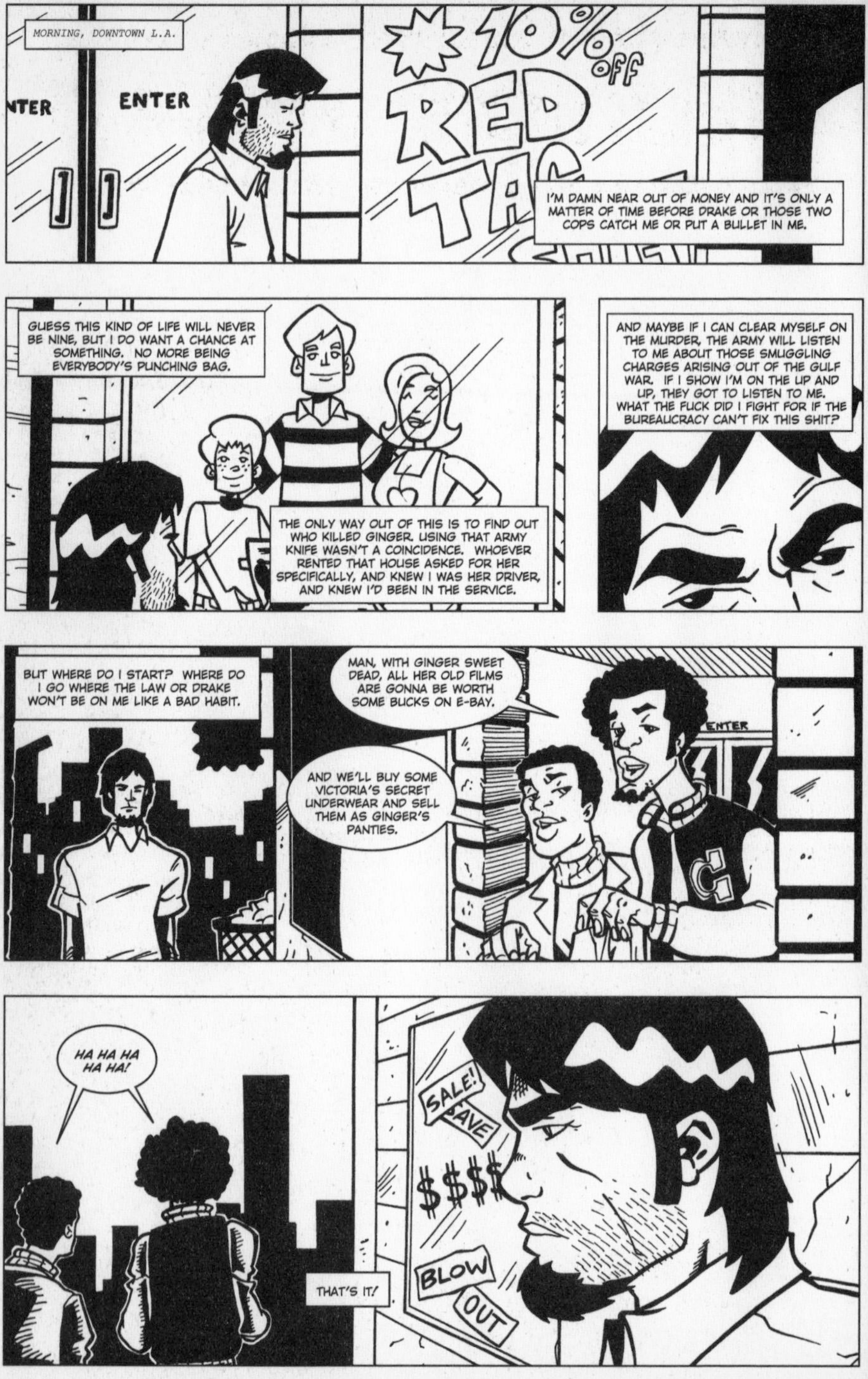
MORNING, DOWNTOWN L.A.
NTER
ENTER
10% off
RED TAG
I'M DAMN NEAR OUT OF MONEY AND IT'S ONLY A MATTER OF TIME BEFORE DRAKE OR THOSE TWO COPS CATCH ME OR PUT A BULLET IN ME.
GUESS THIS KIND OF LIFE WILL NEVER BE NINE, BUT I DO WANT A CHANCE AT SOMETHING. NO MORE BEING EVERYBODY'S PUNCHING BAG.
THE ONLY WAY OUT OF THIS IS TO FIND OUT WHO KILLED GINGER. USING THAT ARMY KNIFE WASN'T A COINCIDENCE. WHOEVER RENTED THAT HOUSE ASKED FOR HER SPECIFICALLY, AND KNEW I WAS HER DRIVER, AND KNEW I'D BEEN IN THE SERVICE.
AND MAYBE IF I CAN CLEAR MYSELF ON THE MURDER, THE ARMY WILL LISTEN TO ME ABOUT THOSE SMUGGLING CHARGES ARISING OUT OF THE GULF WAR. IF I SHOW I'M ON THE UP AND UP, THEY GOT TO LISTEN TO ME. WHAT THE FUCK DID I FIGHT FOR IF THE BUREAUCRACY CAN'T FIX THIS SHIT?
BUT WHERE DO I START? WHERE DO I GO WHERE THE LAW OR DRAKE WON'T BE ON ME LIKE A BAD HABIT.
MAN, WITH GINGER SWEET DEAD, ALL HER OLD FILMS ARE GONNA BE WORTH SOME BUCKS ON E-BAY.
AND WE'LL BUY SOME VICTORIA'S SECRET UNDERWEAR AND SELL THEM AS GINGER'S PANTIES.
ENTER
HA HA HA HA HA!
SALE!
SAVE
$$$$
THAT'S IT!
BLOW
OUT

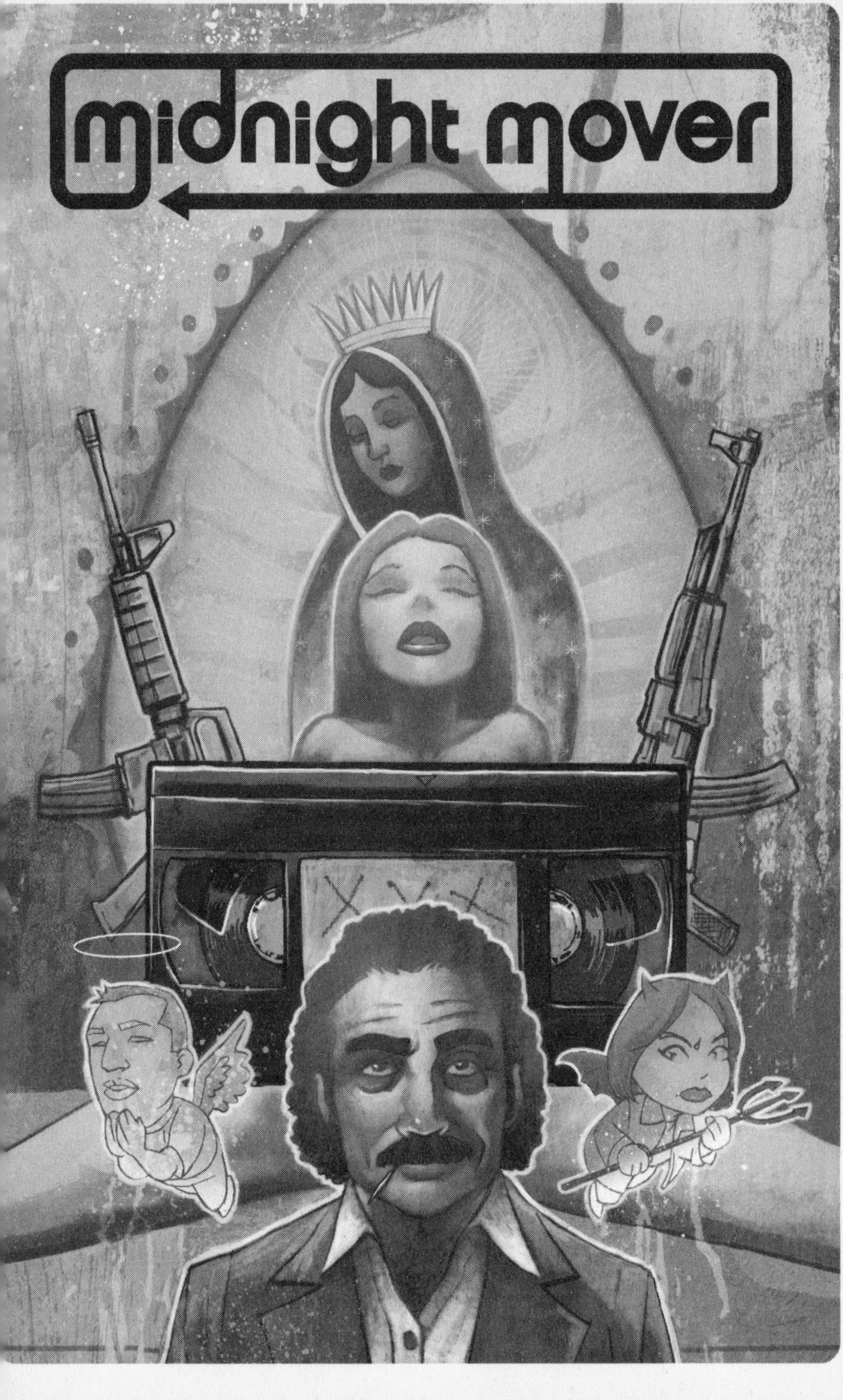
midnight mover
XXX

chapter three

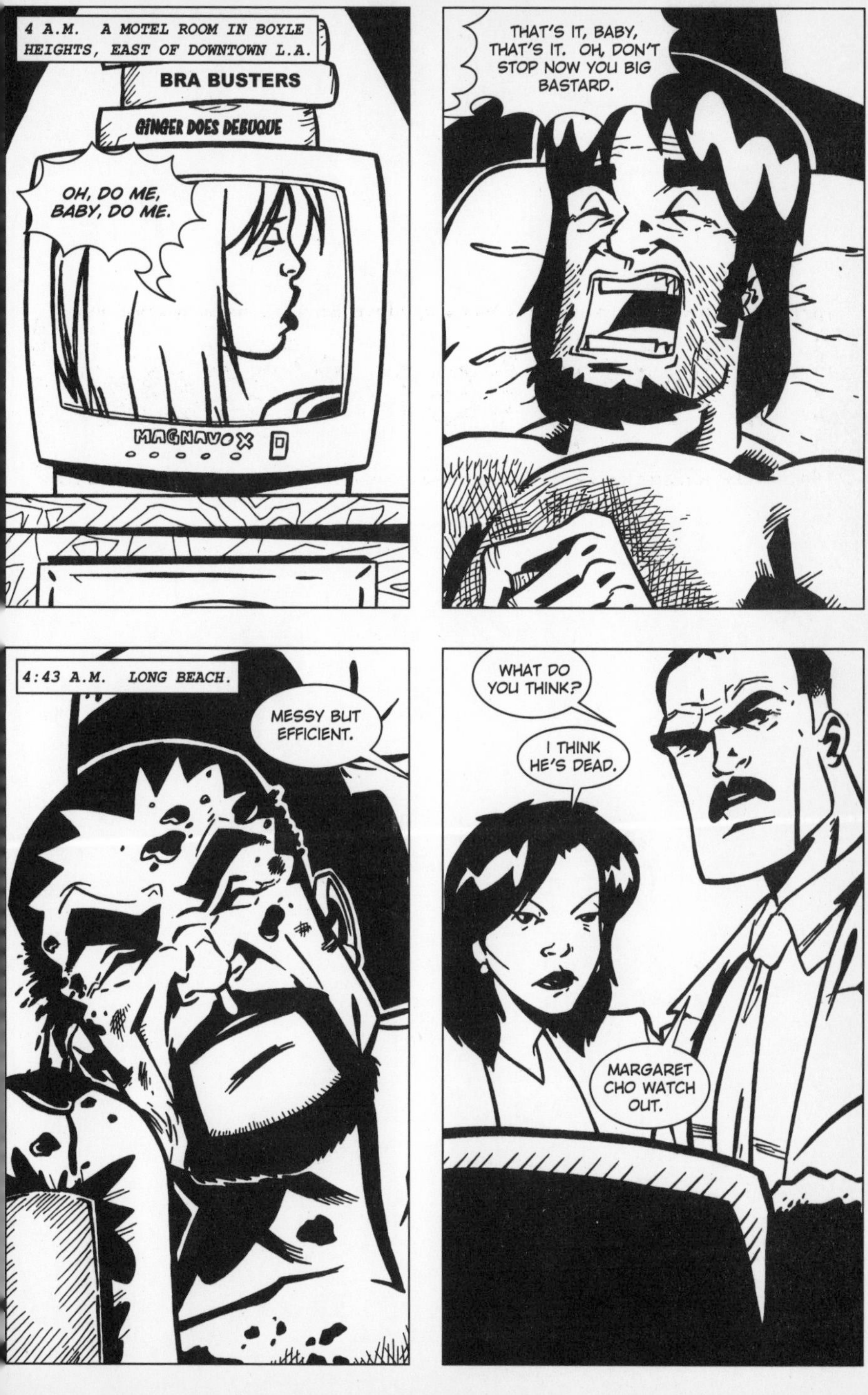

4 A.M. A MOTEL ROOM IN BOYLE HEIGHTS, EAST OF DOWNTOWN L.A.
BRA BUSTERS
GINGER DOES DEBUQUE
OH, DO ME, BABY, DO ME.
MAGNAVOX
THAT'S IT, BABY, THAT'S IT. OH, DON'T STOP NOW YOU BIG BASTARD.
4:43 A.M. LONG BEACH.
MESSY BUT EFFICIENT.
WHAT DO YOU THINK?
I THINK HE'S DEAD.
MARGARET CHO WATCH OUT.

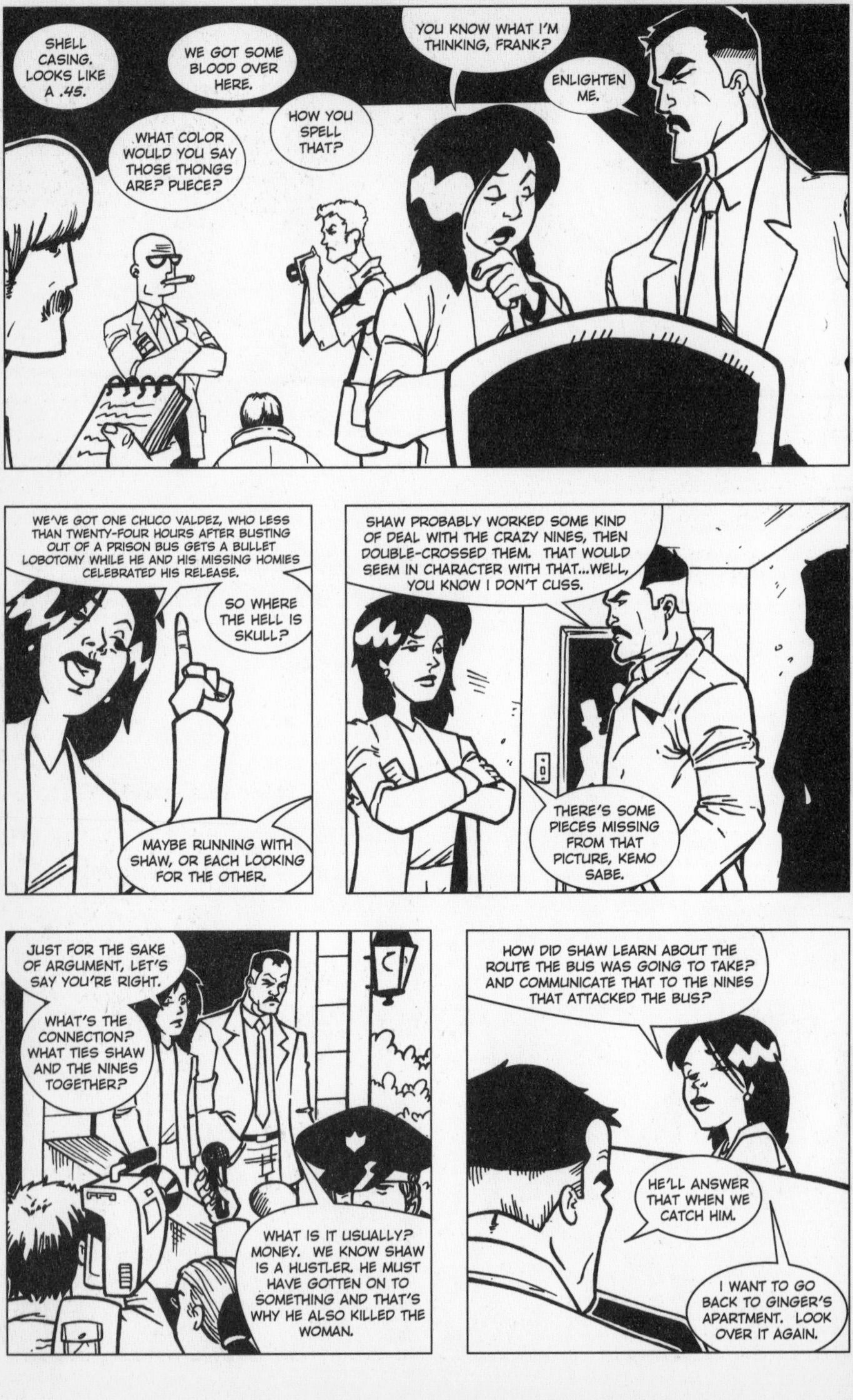
SHELL CASING. LOOKS LIKE A .45.
WE GOT SOME BLOOD OVER HERE.
WHAT COLOR WOULD YOU SAY THOSE THONGS ARE? PUECE?
HOW YOU SPELL THAT?
YOU KNOW WHAT I'M THINKING, FRANK?
ENLIGHTEN ME.
WE'VE GOT ONE CHUCO VALDEZ, WHO LESS THAN TWENTY-FOUR HOURS AFTER BUSTING OUT OF A PRISON BUS GETS A BULLET LOBOTOMY WHILE HE AND HIS MISSING HOMIES CELEBRATED HIS RELEASE.
SO WHERE THE HELL IS SKULL?
MAYBE RUNNING WITH SHAW, OR EACH LOOKING FOR THE OTHER.
SHAW PROBABLY WORKED SOME KIND OF DEAL WITH THE CRAZY NINES, THEN DOUBLE-CROSSED THEM. THAT WOULD SEEM IN CHARACTER WITH THAT...WELL, YOU KNOW I DON'T CUSS.
THERE'S SOME PIECES MISSING FROM THAT PICTURE, KEMO SABE.
JUST FOR THE SAKE OF ARGUMENT, LET'S SAY YOU'RE RIGHT.
WHAT'S THE CONNECTION? WHAT TIES SHAW AND THE NINES TOGETHER?
WHAT IS IT USUALLY? MONEY. WE KNOW SHAW IS A HUSTLER. HE MUST HAVE GOTTEN ON TO SOMETHING AND THAT'S WHY HE ALSO KILLED THE WOMAN.
HOW DID SHAW LEARN ABOUT THE ROUTE THE BUS WAS GOING TO TAKE? AND COMMUNICATE THAT TO THE NINES THAT ATTACKED THE BUS?
HE'LL ANSWER THAT WHEN WE CATCH HIM.
I WANT TO GO BACK TO GINGER'S APARTMENT. LOOK OVER IT AGAIN.

WHAT FOR?

HMMM, GOT A MESSAGE FROM MY BUDDY BLAIR AT HOLLYWOOD DIVISION.

IT WAS GONE OVER LAST TIME FOR EVIDENCE CONNECTING HER TO SHAW. THIS TIME I'M CURIOUS ABOUT HER AND WHO SHE WAS.

SHE WAS A FLESH PEDDLER. WHAT ELSE IS THERE TO KNOW?

EVEN *FLESH PEDDLERS* HAVE LIVES, FRANK.

AND I'VE GOT AN ITCH THAT THERE WAS SOMETHING IN GINGER'S THAT FINALLY CAUGHT UP TO HER. MAYBE SHAW WAS PART OF IT, OR HE JUST HAPPENED TO BE AROUND WHEN THINGS WENT BAD.

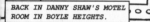

BACK IN DANNY SHAW'S MOTEL ROOM IN BOYLE HEIGHTS.

BUT VANESSA DIDN'T LAST TOO LONG 'CAUSE SHE LIKED THAT METH NOSE DIVING TOO MUCH. SHE GOT TOO UNRELIABLE FOR REMY TO KEEP HER ON WHEN SHE KEPT MISSING APPOINTMENTS.

Snif

I THOUGHT THAT CHICK LOOKED FAMILIAR. THAT'S VANESSA. SHE USED TO WORK AT LOLLIPOP RIGHT BEFORE GINGER CAME ON BOARD. AND I REMEMBER TAKING THE TWO OF THEM ON A COUPLE OF CALLS TOGETHER.

IT'S NOT MUCH TO GO ON, BUT MAYBE SHE AND GINGER KEPT IN TOUCH. OF COURSE THERE'S THE PROBLEM OF HOW THE HELL DO I FIND HER. THIS TAPE LIKE A COUPLE OF THE OTHERS WAS DONE BY AN OUTFIT CALLED EXPOSURE.

THERE'S ONLY A POST OFFICE BOX LISTED FOR THE ADDRESS, SO THAT'S NO HELP.

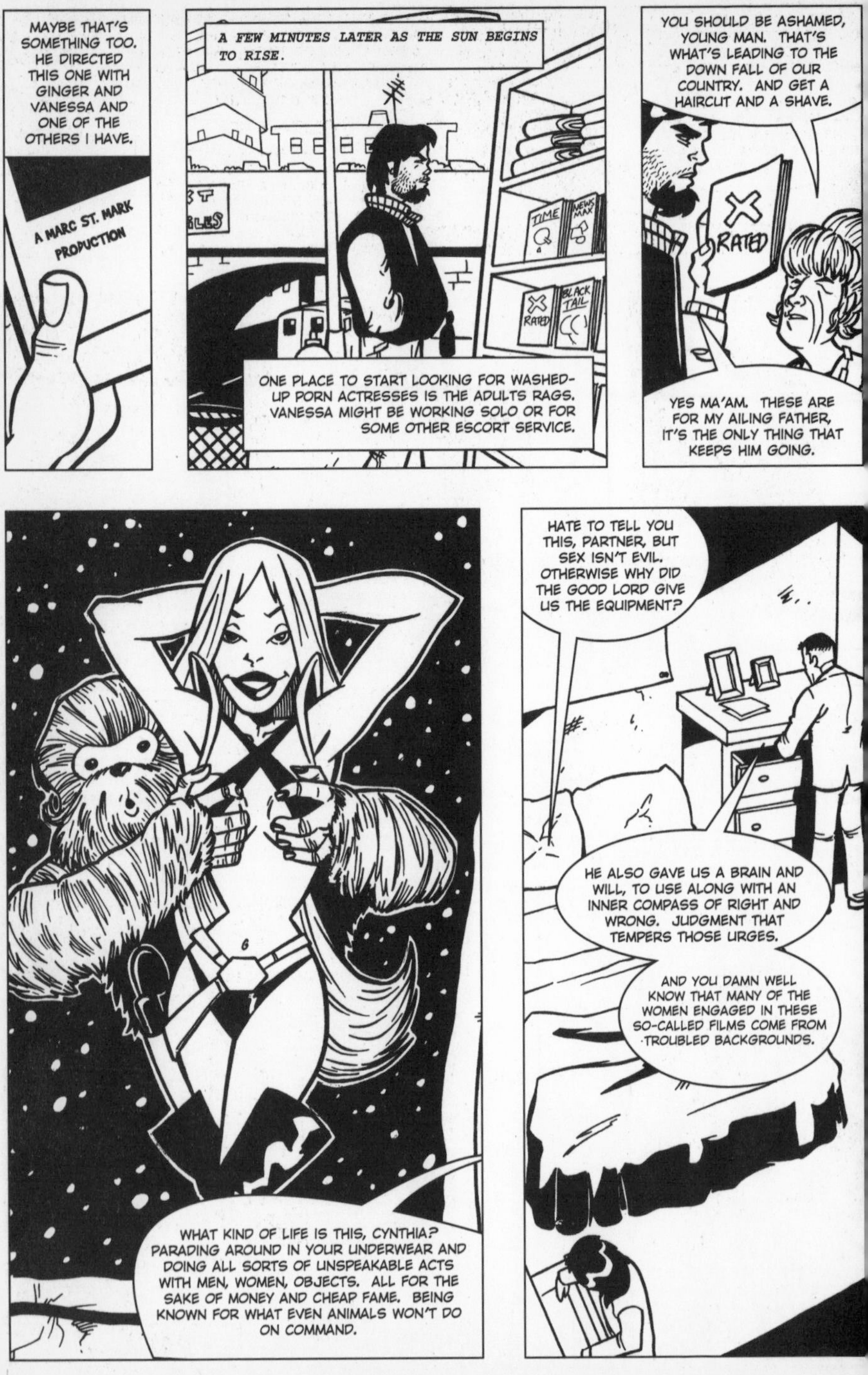
MAYBE THAT'S SOMETHING TOO. HE DIRECTED THIS ONE WITH GINGER AND VANESSA AND ONE OF THE OTHERS I HAVE.
A MARC ST. MARK PRODUCTION
A FEW MINUTES LATER AS THE SUN BEGINS TO RISE.
TIME
NEWS MAX
X RATED
BLACK TAIL
ONE PLACE TO START LOOKING FOR WASHED-UP PORN ACTRESSES IS THE ADULTS RAGS. VANESSA MIGHT BE WORKING SOLO OR FOR SOME OTHER ESCORT SERVICE.
YOU SHOULD BE ASHAMED, YOUNG MAN. THAT'S WHAT'S LEADING TO THE DOWN FALL OF OUR COUNTRY. AND GET A HAIRCUT AND A SHAVE.
X RATED
YES MA'AM. THESE ARE FOR MY AILING FATHER, IT'S THE ONLY THING THAT KEEPS HIM GOING.
WHAT KIND OF LIFE IS THIS, CYNTHIA? PARADING AROUND IN YOUR UNDERWEAR AND DOING ALL SORTS OF UNSPEAKABLE ACTS WITH MEN, WOMEN, OBJECTS. ALL FOR THE SAKE OF MONEY AND CHEAP FAME. BEING KNOWN FOR WHAT EVEN ANIMALS WON'T DO ON COMMAND.
HATE TO TELL YOU THIS, PARTNER, BUT SEX ISN'T EVIL. OTHERWISE WHY DID THE GOOD LORD GIVE US THE EQUIPMENT?
HE ALSO GAVE US A BRAIN AND WILL, TO USE ALONG WITH AN INNER COMPASS OF RIGHT AND WRONG. JUDGMENT THAT TEMPERS THOSE URGES.
AND YOU DAMN WELL KNOW THAT MANY OF THE WOMEN ENGAGED IN THESE SO-CALLED FILMS COME FROM TROUBLED BACKGROUNDS.

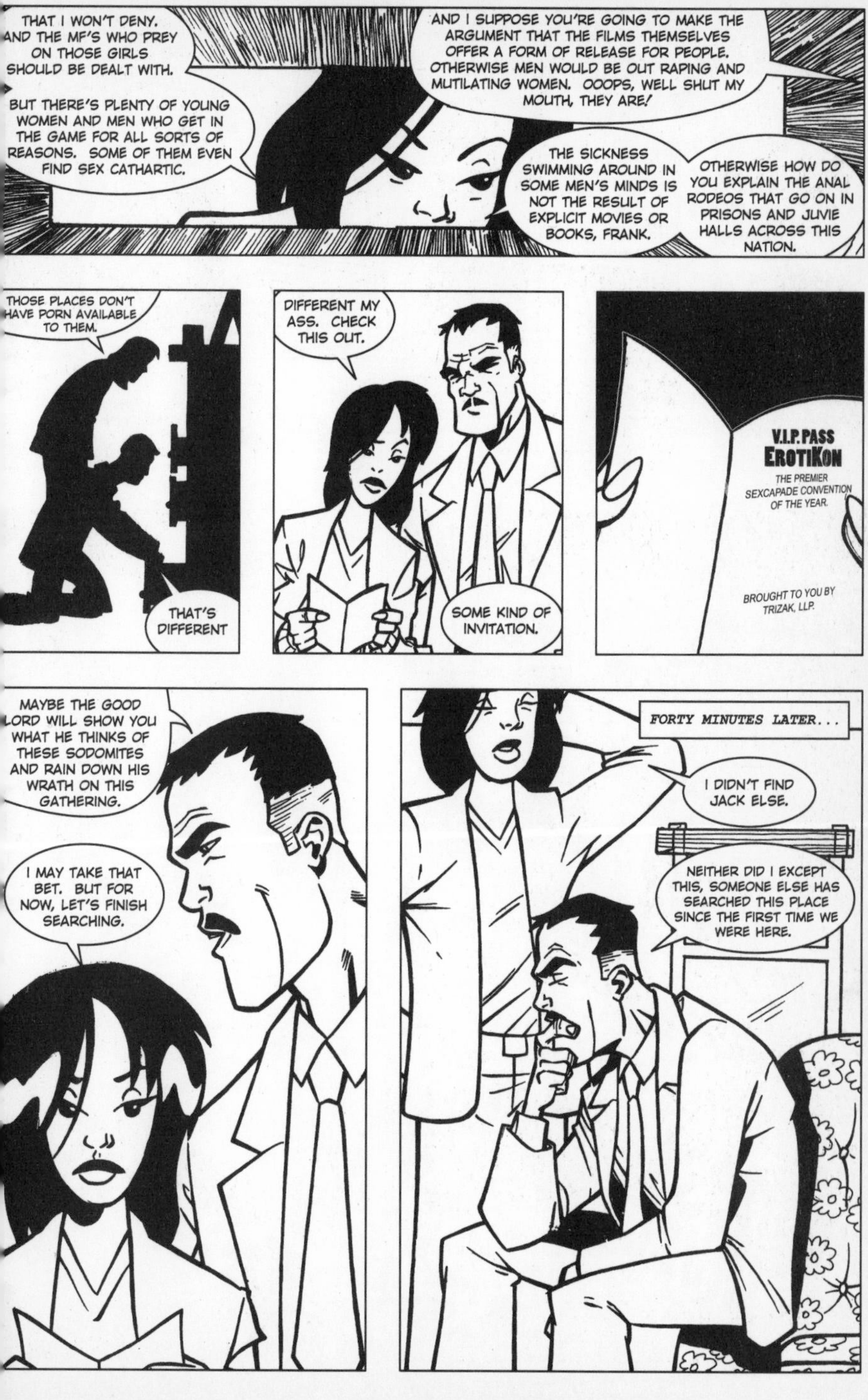
THAT I WON'T DENY. AND THE MF'S WHO PREY ON THOSE GIRLS SHOULD BE DEALT WITH.
BUT THERE'S PLENTY OF YOUNG WOMEN AND MEN WHO GET IN THE GAME FOR ALL SORTS OF REASONS. SOME OF THEM EVEN FIND SEX CATHARTIC.
AND I SUPPOSE YOU'RE GOING TO MAKE THE ARGUMENT THAT THE FILMS THEMSELVES OFFER A FORM OF RELEASE FOR PEOPLE. OTHERWISE MEN WOULD BE OUT RAPING AND MUTILATING WOMEN. OOOPS, WELL SHUT MY MOUTH, THEY ARE!
THE SICKNESS SWIMMING AROUND IN SOME MEN'S MINDS IS NOT THE RESULT OF EXPLICIT MOVIES OR BOOKS, FRANK.
OTHERWISE HOW DO YOU EXPLAIN THE ANAL RODEOS THAT GO ON IN PRISONS AND JUVIE HALLS ACROSS THIS NATION.
THOSE PLACES DON'T HAVE PORN AVAILABLE TO THEM.
THAT'S DIFFERENT
DIFFERENT MY ASS. CHECK THIS OUT.
SOME KIND OF INVITATION.
V.I.P. PASS
EROTIKON
THE PREMIER SEXCAPADE CONVENTION OF THE YEAR.
BROUGHT TO YOU BY TRIZAK, LLP.
MAYBE THE GOOD LORD WILL SHOW YOU WHAT HE THINKS OF THESE SODOMITES AND RAIN DOWN HIS WRATH ON THIS GATHERING.
I MAY TAKE THAT BET. BUT FOR NOW, LET'S FINISH SEARCHING.
FORTY MINUTES LATER...
I DIDN'T FIND JACK ELSE.
NEITHER DID I EXCEPT THIS, SOMEONE ELSE HAS SEARCHED THIS PLACE SINCE THE FIRST TIME WE WERE HERE.

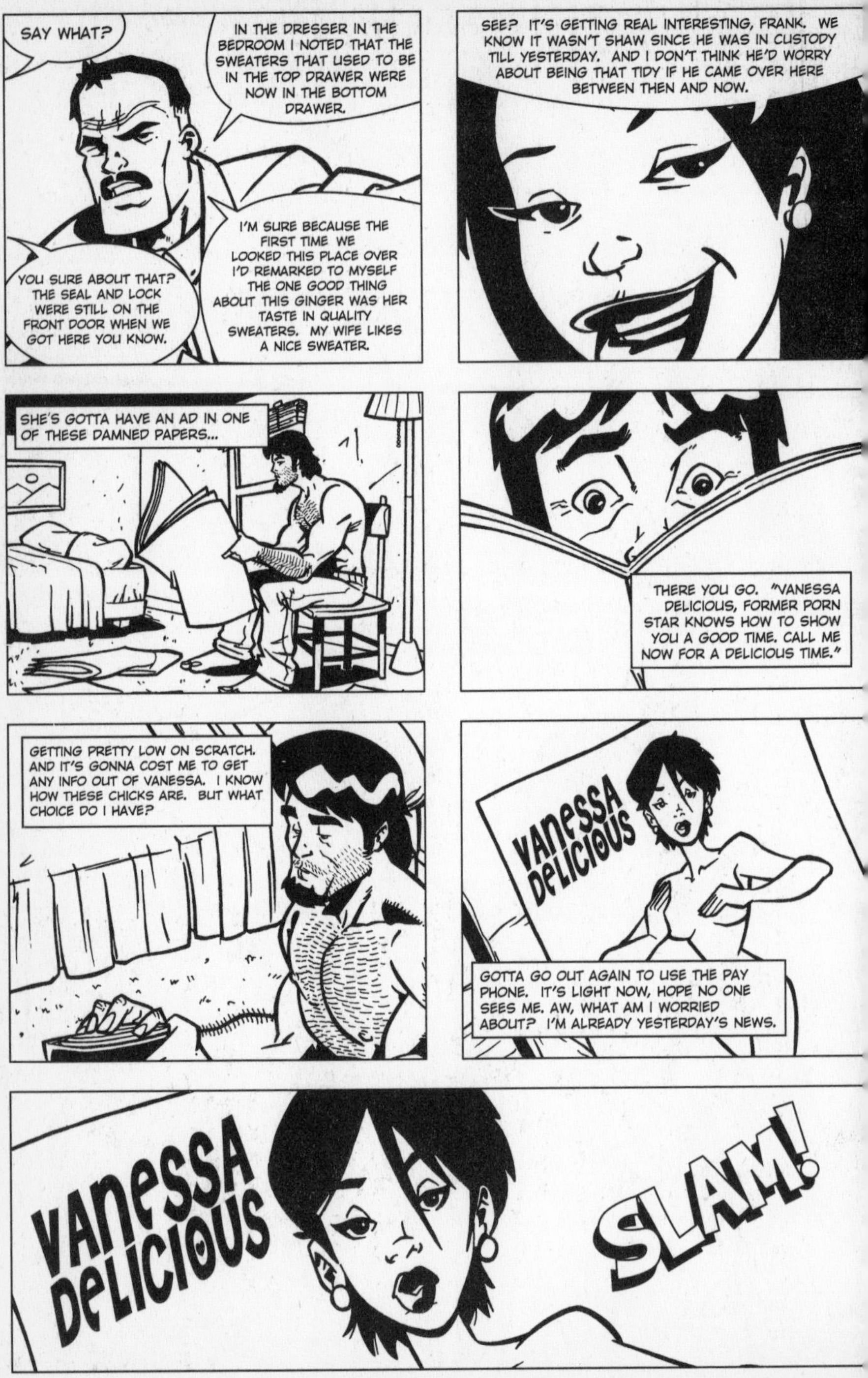
SAY WHAT?
IN THE DRESSER IN THE BEDROOM I NOTED THAT THE SWEATERS THAT USED TO BE IN THE TOP DRAWER WERE NOW IN THE BOTTOM DRAWER.
YOU SURE ABOUT THAT? THE SEAL AND LOCK WERE STILL ON THE FRONT DOOR WHEN WE GOT HERE YOU KNOW.
I'M SURE BECAUSE THE FIRST TIME WE LOOKED THIS PLACE OVER I'D REMARKED TO MYSELF THE ONE GOOD THING ABOUT THIS GINGER WAS HER TASTE IN QUALITY SWEATERS. MY WIFE LIKES A NICE SWEATER.
SEE? IT'S GETTING REAL INTERESTING, FRANK. WE KNOW IT WASN'T SHAW SINCE HE WAS IN CUSTODY TILL YESTERDAY. AND I DON'T THINK HE'D WORRY ABOUT BEING THAT TIDY IF HE CAME OVER HERE BETWEEN THEN AND NOW.
SHE'S GOTTA HAVE AN AD IN ONE OF THESE DAMNED PAPERS...
THERE YOU GO. "VANESSA DELICIOUS, FORMER PORN STAR KNOWS HOW TO SHOW YOU A GOOD TIME. CALL ME NOW FOR A DELICIOUS TIME."
GETTING PRETTY LOW ON SCRATCH. AND IT'S GONNA COST ME TO GET ANY INFO OUT OF VANESSA. I KNOW HOW THESE CHICKS ARE. BUT WHAT CHOICE DO I HAVE?
VANESSA DELICIOUS
GOTTA GO OUT AGAIN TO USE THE PAY PHONE. IT'S LIGHT NOW, HOPE NO ONE SEES ME. AW, WHAT AM I WORRIED ABOUT? I'M ALREADY YESTERDAY'S NEWS.
VANESSA DELICIOUS
SLAM!

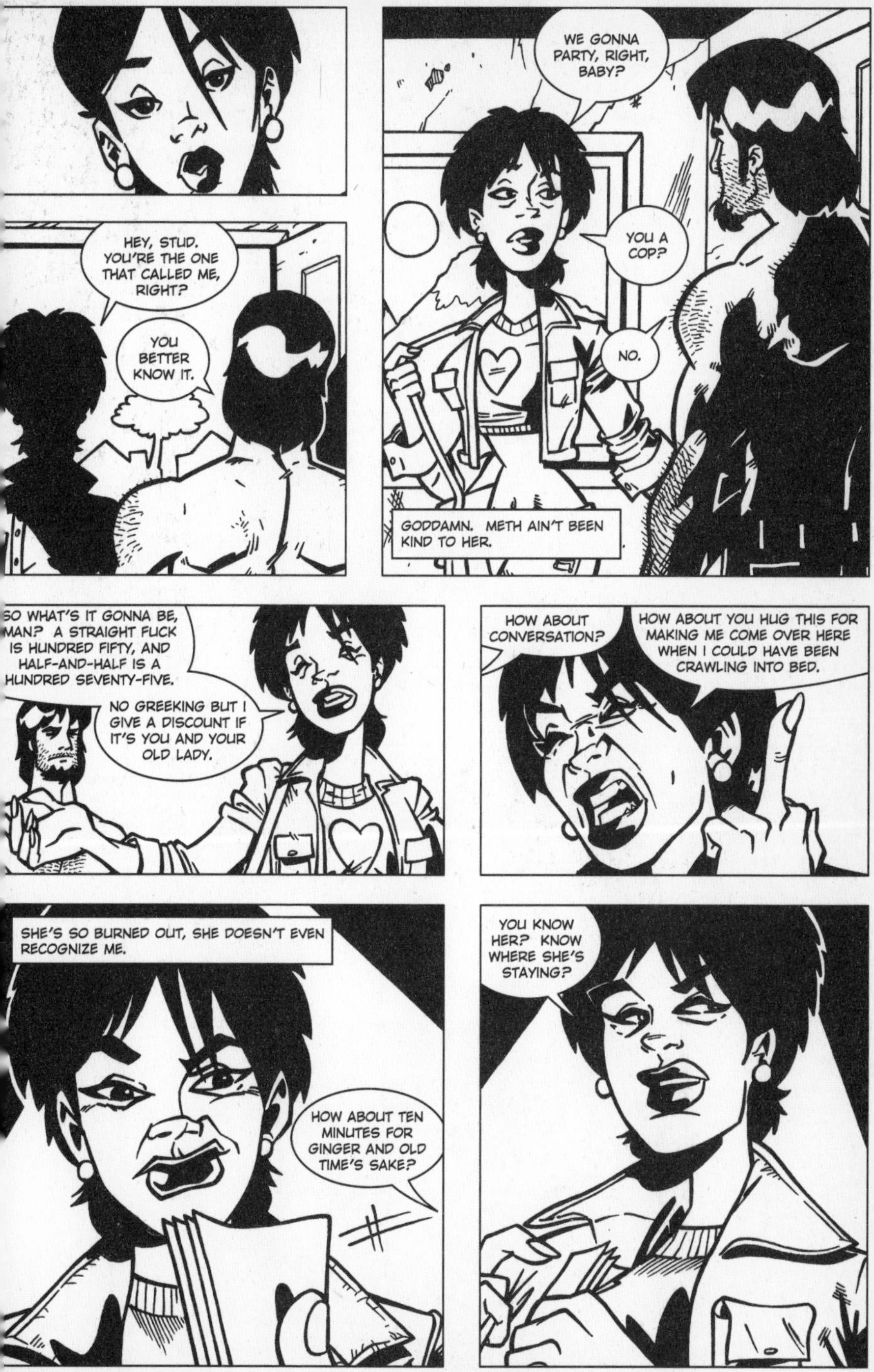

WE GONNA PARTY, RIGHT, BABY?
HEY, STUD. YOU'RE THE ONE THAT CALLED ME, RIGHT?
YOU BETTER KNOW IT.
YOU A COP?
NO.
GODDAMN. METH AIN'T BEEN KIND TO HER.
SO WHAT'S IT GONNA BE, MAN? A STRAIGHT FUCK IS HUNDRED FIFTY, AND HALF-AND-HALF IS A HUNDRED SEVENTY-FIVE.
NO GREEKING BUT I GIVE A DISCOUNT IF IT'S YOU AND YOUR OLD LADY.
HOW ABOUT CONVERSATION?
HOW ABOUT YOU HUG THIS FOR MAKING ME COME OVER HERE WHEN I COULD HAVE BEEN CRAWLING INTO BED.
SHE'S SO BURNED OUT, SHE DOESN'T EVEN RECOGNIZE ME.
HOW ABOUT TEN MINUTES FOR GINGER AND OLD TIME'S SAKE?
YOU KNOW HER? KNOW WHERE SHE'S STAYING?

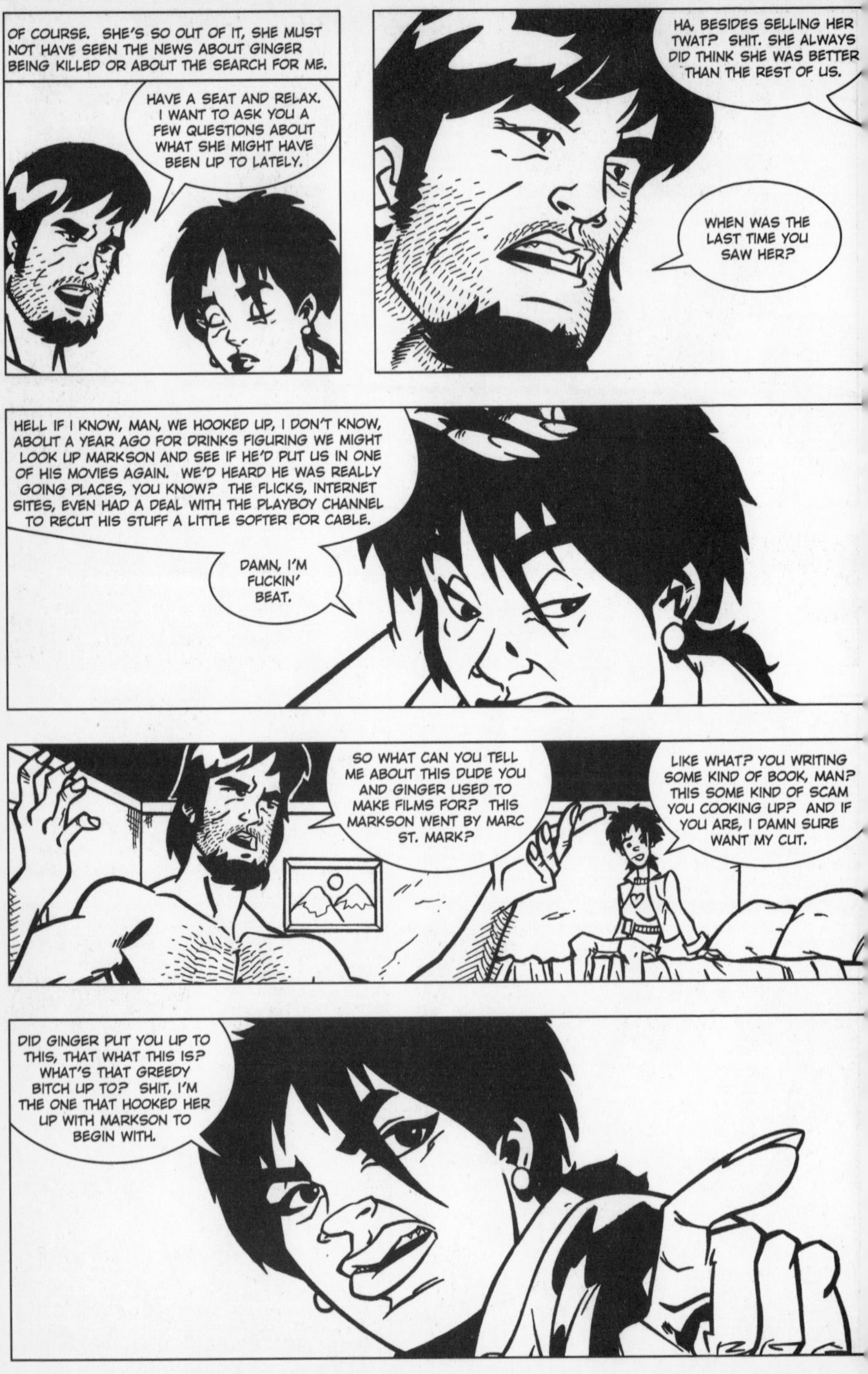

OF COURSE. SHE'S SO OUT OF IT, SHE MUST NOT HAVE SEEN THE NEWS ABOUT GINGER BEING KILLED OR ABOUT THE SEARCH FOR ME.
HAVE A SEAT AND RELAX. I WANT TO ASK YOU A FEW QUESTIONS ABOUT WHAT SHE MIGHT HAVE BEEN UP TO LATELY.
HA, BESIDES SELLING HER TWAT? SHIT. SHE ALWAYS DID THINK SHE WAS BETTER THAN THE REST OF US.
WHEN WAS THE LAST TIME YOU SAW HER?
HELL IF I KNOW, MAN, WE HOOKED UP, I DON'T KNOW, ABOUT A YEAR AGO FOR DRINKS FIGURING WE MIGHT LOOK UP MARKSON AND SEE IF HE'D PUT US IN ONE OF HIS MOVIES AGAIN. WE'D HEARD HE WAS REALLY GOING PLACES, YOU KNOW? THE FLICKS, INTERNET SITES, EVEN HAD A DEAL WITH THE PLAYBOY CHANNEL TO RECUT HIS STUFF A LITTLE SOFTER FOR CABLE.
DAMN, I'M FUCKIN' BEAT.
SO WHAT CAN YOU TELL ME ABOUT THIS DUDE YOU AND GINGER USED TO MAKE FILMS FOR? THIS MARKSON WENT BY MARC ST. MARK?
LIKE WHAT? YOU WRITING SOME KIND OF BOOK, MAN? THIS SOME KIND OF SCAM YOU COOKING UP? AND IF YOU ARE, I DAMN SURE WANT MY CUT.
DID GINGER PUT YOU UP TO THIS, THAT WHAT THIS IS? WHAT'S THAT GREEDY BITCH UP TO? SHIT, I'M THE ONE THAT HOOKED HER UP WITH MARKSON TO BEGIN WITH.

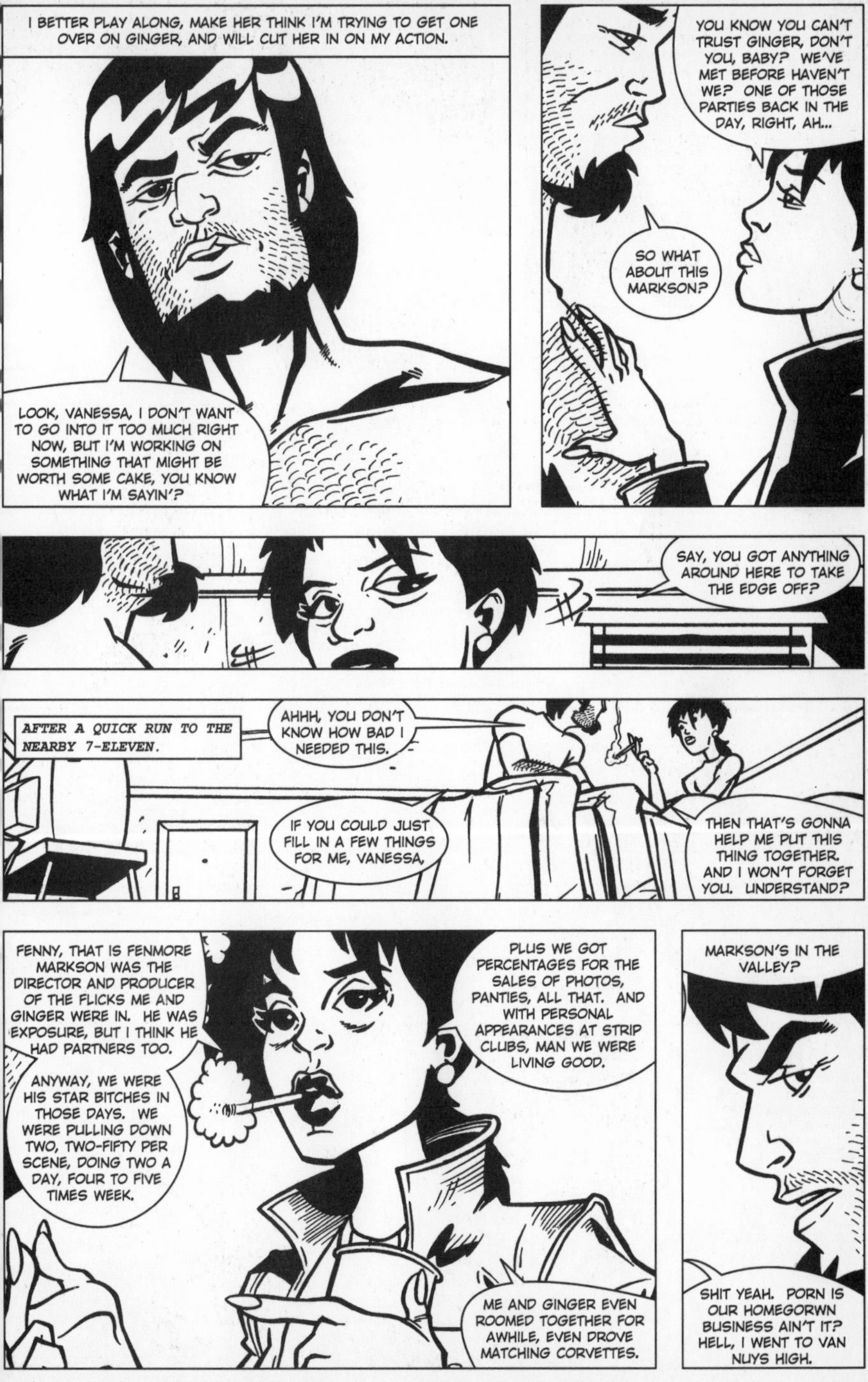
I BETTER PLAY ALONG, MAKE HER THINK I'M TRYING TO GET ONE OVER ON GINGER, AND WILL CUT HER IN ON MY ACTION.
LOOK, VANESSA, I DON'T WANT TO GO INTO IT TOO MUCH RIGHT NOW, BUT I'M WORKING ON SOMETHING THAT MIGHT BE WORTH SOME CAKE, YOU KNOW WHAT I'M SAYIN'?
YOU KNOW YOU CAN'T TRUST GINGER, DON'T YOU, BABY? WE'VE MET BEFORE HAVEN'T WE? ONE OF THOSE PARTIES BACK IN THE DAY, RIGHT, AH...
SO WHAT ABOUT THIS MARKSON?
SAY, YOU GOT ANYTHING AROUND HERE TO TAKE THE EDGE OFF?
AFTER A QUICK RUN TO THE NEARBY 7-ELEVEN.
AHHH, YOU DON'T KNOW HOW BAD I NEEDED THIS.
IF YOU COULD JUST FILL IN A FEW THINGS FOR ME, VANESSA,
THEN THAT'S GONNA HELP ME PUT THIS THING TOGETHER. AND I WON'T FORGET YOU. UNDERSTAND?
FENNY, THAT IS FENMORE MARKSON WAS THE DIRECTOR AND PRODUCER OF THE FLICKS ME AND GINGER WERE IN. HE WAS EXPOSURE, BUT I THINK HE HAD PARTNERS TOO.
ANYWAY, WE WERE HIS STAR BITCHES IN THOSE DAYS. WE WERE PULLING DOWN TWO, TWO-FIFTY PER SCENE, DOING TWO A DAY, FOUR TO FIVE TIMES WEEK.
PLUS WE GOT PERCENTAGES FOR THE SALES OF PHOTOS, PANTIES, ALL THAT. AND WITH PERSONAL APPEARANCES AT STRIP CLUBS, MAN WE WERE LIVING GOOD.
ME AND GINGER EVEN ROOMED TOGETHER FOR AWHILE, EVEN DROVE MATCHING CORVETTES.
MARKSON'S IN THE VALLEY?
SHIT YEAH. PORN IS OUR HOMEGORWN BUSINESS AIN'T IT? HELL, I WENT TO VAN NUYS HIGH.

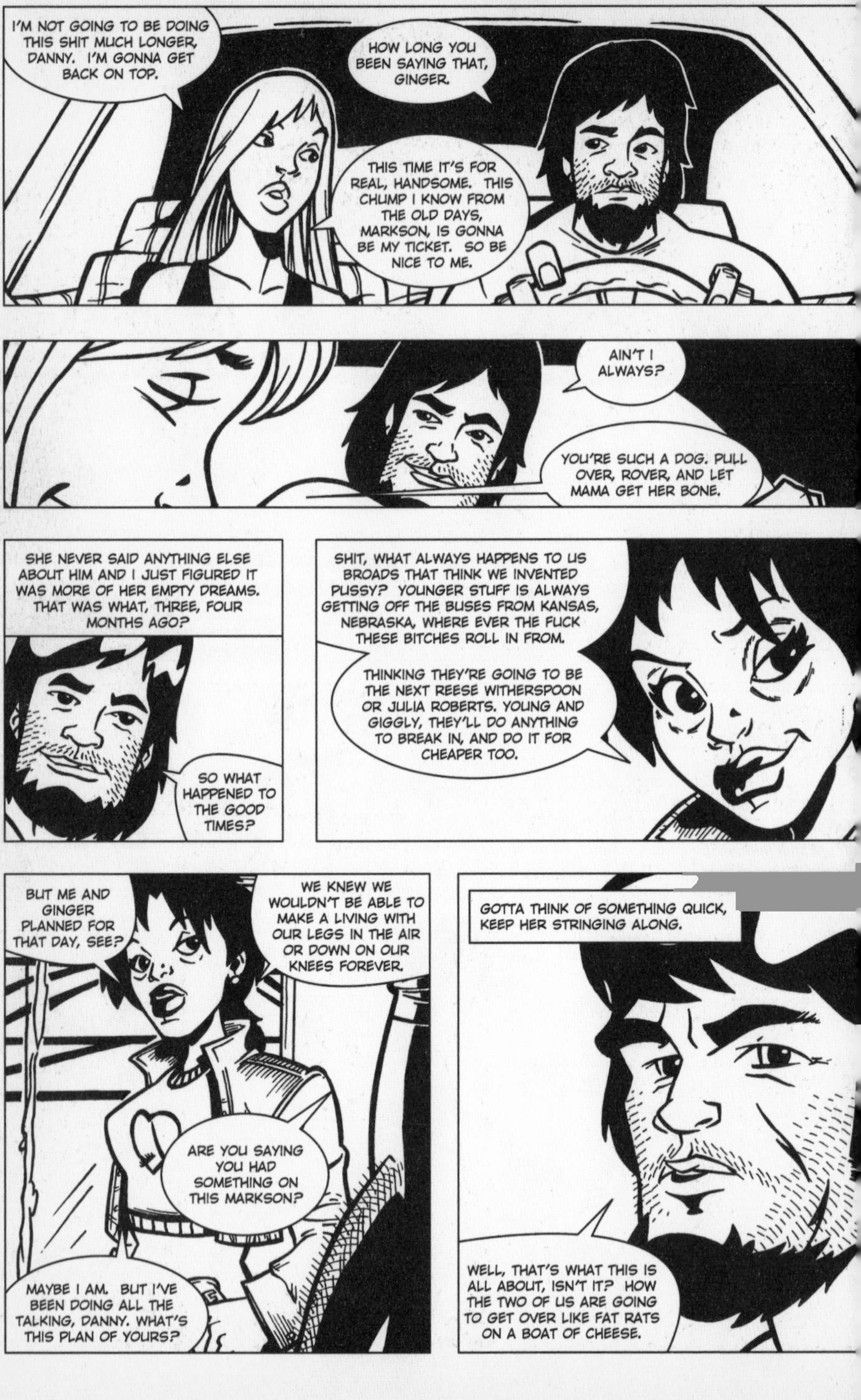
I'M NOT GOING TO BE DOING THIS SHIT MUCH LONGER, DANNY. I'M GONNA GET BACK ON TOP.
HOW LONG YOU BEEN SAYING THAT, GINGER.
THIS TIME IT'S FOR REAL, HANDSOME. THIS CHUMP I KNOW FROM THE OLD DAYS, MARKSON, IS GONNA BE MY TICKET. SO BE NICE TO ME.
AIN'T I ALWAYS?
YOU'RE SUCH A DOG. PULL OVER, ROVER, AND LET MAMA GET HER BONE.
SHE NEVER SAID ANYTHING ELSE ABOUT HIM AND I JUST FIGURED IT WAS MORE OF HER EMPTY DREAMS. THAT WAS WHAT, THREE, FOUR MONTHS AGO?
SO WHAT HAPPENED TO THE GOOD TIMES?
SHIT, WHAT ALWAYS HAPPENS TO US BROADS THAT THINK WE INVENTED PUSSY? YOUNGER STUFF IS ALWAYS GETTING OFF THE BUSES FROM KANSAS, NEBRASKA, WHERE EVER THE FUCK THESE BITCHES ROLL IN FROM.
THINKING THEY'RE GOING TO BE THE NEXT REESE WITHERSPOON OR JULIA ROBERTS. YOUNG AND GIGGLY, THEY'LL DO ANYTHING TO BREAK IN, AND DO IT FOR CHEAPER TOO.
BUT ME AND GINGER PLANNED FOR THAT DAY, SEE?
WE KNEW WE WOULDN'T BE ABLE TO MAKE A LIVING WITH OUR LEGS IN THE AIR OR DOWN ON OUR KNEES FOREVER.
ARE YOU SAYING YOU HAD SOMETHING ON THIS MARKSON?
MAYBE I AM. BUT I'VE BEEN DOING ALL THE TALKING, DANNY. WHAT'S THIS PLAN OF YOURS?
GOTTA THINK OF SOMETHING QUICK, KEEP HER STRINGING ALONG.
WELL, THAT'S WHAT THIS IS ALL ABOUT, ISN'T IT? HOW THE TWO OF US ARE GOING TO GET OVER LIKE FAT RATS ON A BOAT OF CHEESE.

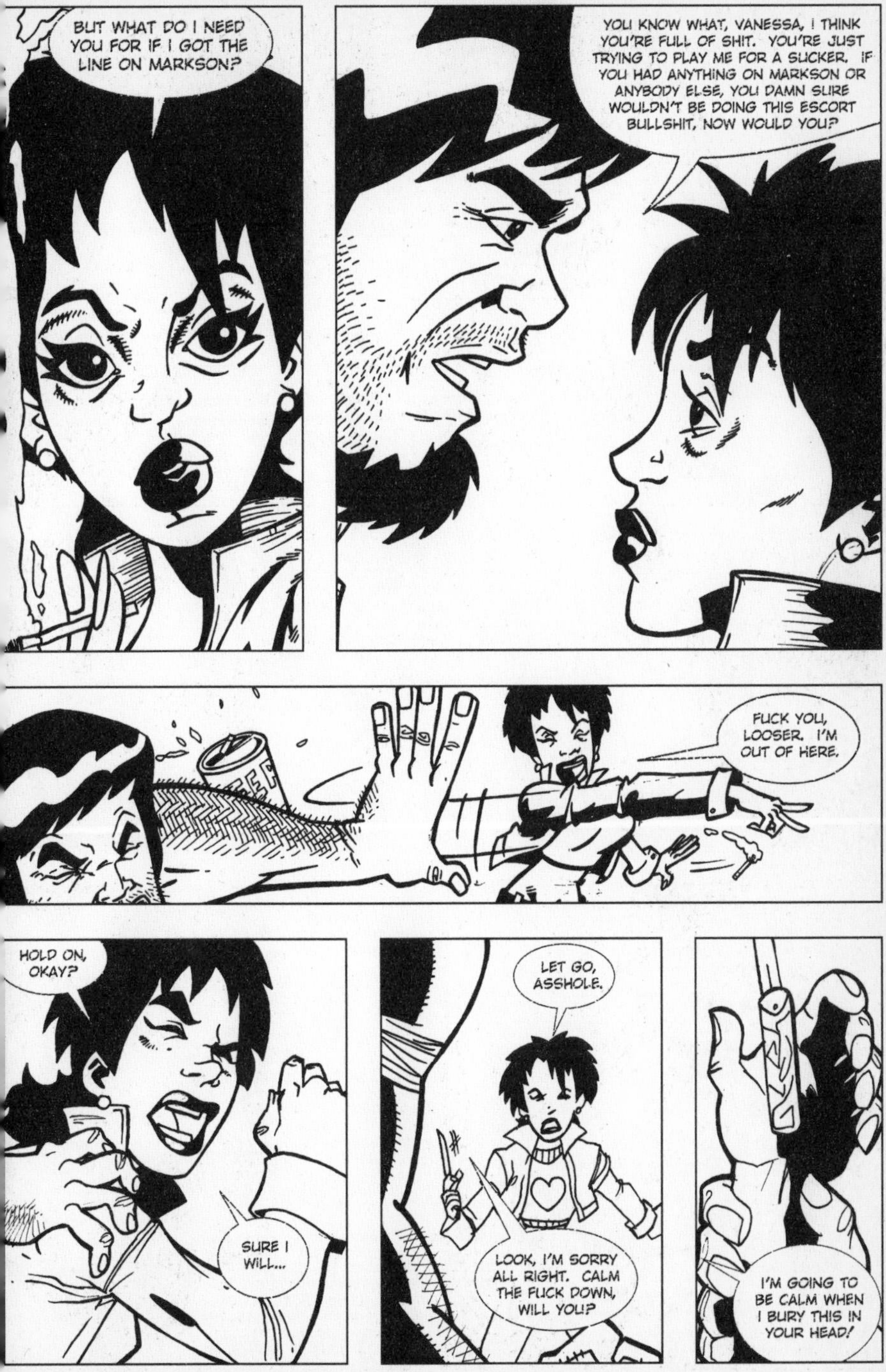
BUT WHAT DO I NEED YOU FOR IF I GOT THE LINE ON MARKSON?
YOU KNOW WHAT, VANESSA, I THINK YOU'RE FULL OF SHIT. YOU'RE JUST TRYING TO PLAY ME FOR A SUCKER. IF YOU HAD ANYTHING ON MARKSON OR ANYBODY ELSE, YOU DAMN SURE WOULDN'T BE DOING THIS ESCORT BULLSHIT, NOW WOULD YOU?
FUCK YOU, LOOSER. I'M OUT OF HERE.
HOLD ON, OKAY?
SURE I WILL...
LET GO, ASSHOLE.
LOOK, I'M SORRY ALL RIGHT. CALM THE FUCK DOWN, WILL YOU?
I'M GOING TO BE CALM WHEN I BURY THIS IN YOUR HEAD!

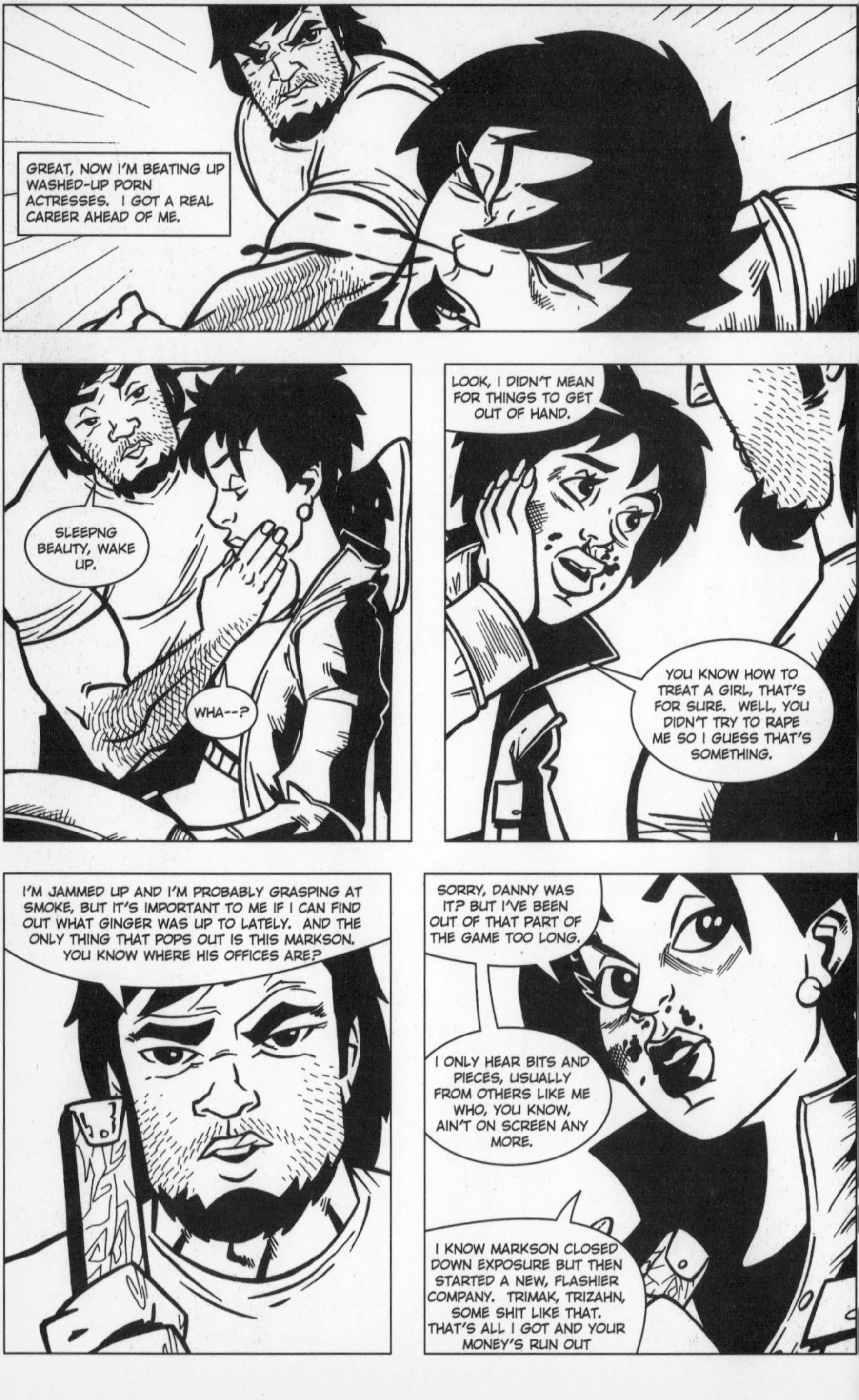

GREAT, NOW I'M BEATING UP WASHED-UP PORN ACTRESSES. I GOT A REAL CAREER AHEAD OF ME.
SLEEPNG BEAUTY, WAKE UP.
WHA--?
LOOK, I DIDN'T MEAN FOR THINGS TO GET OUT OF HAND.
YOU KNOW HOW TO TREAT A GIRL, THAT'S FOR SURE. WELL, YOU DIDN'T TRY TO RAPE ME SO I GUESS THAT'S SOMETHING.
I'M JAMMED UP AND I'M PROBABLY GRASPING AT SMOKE, BUT IT'S IMPORTANT TO ME IF I CAN FIND OUT WHAT GINGER WAS UP TO LATELY. AND THE ONLY THING THAT POPS OUT IS THIS MARKSON. YOU KNOW WHERE HIS OFFICES ARE?
SORRY, DANNY WAS IT? BUT I'VE BEEN OUT OF THAT PART OF THE GAME TOO LONG.
I ONLY HEAR BITS AND PIECES, USUALLY FROM OTHERS LIKE ME WHO, YOU KNOW, AIN'T ON SCREEN ANY MORE.
I KNOW MARKSON CLOSED DOWN EXPOSURE BUT THEN STARTED A NEW, FLASHIER COMPANY. TRIMAK, TRIZAHN, SOME SHIT LIKE THAT. THAT'S ALL I GOT AND YOUR MONEY'S RUN OUT

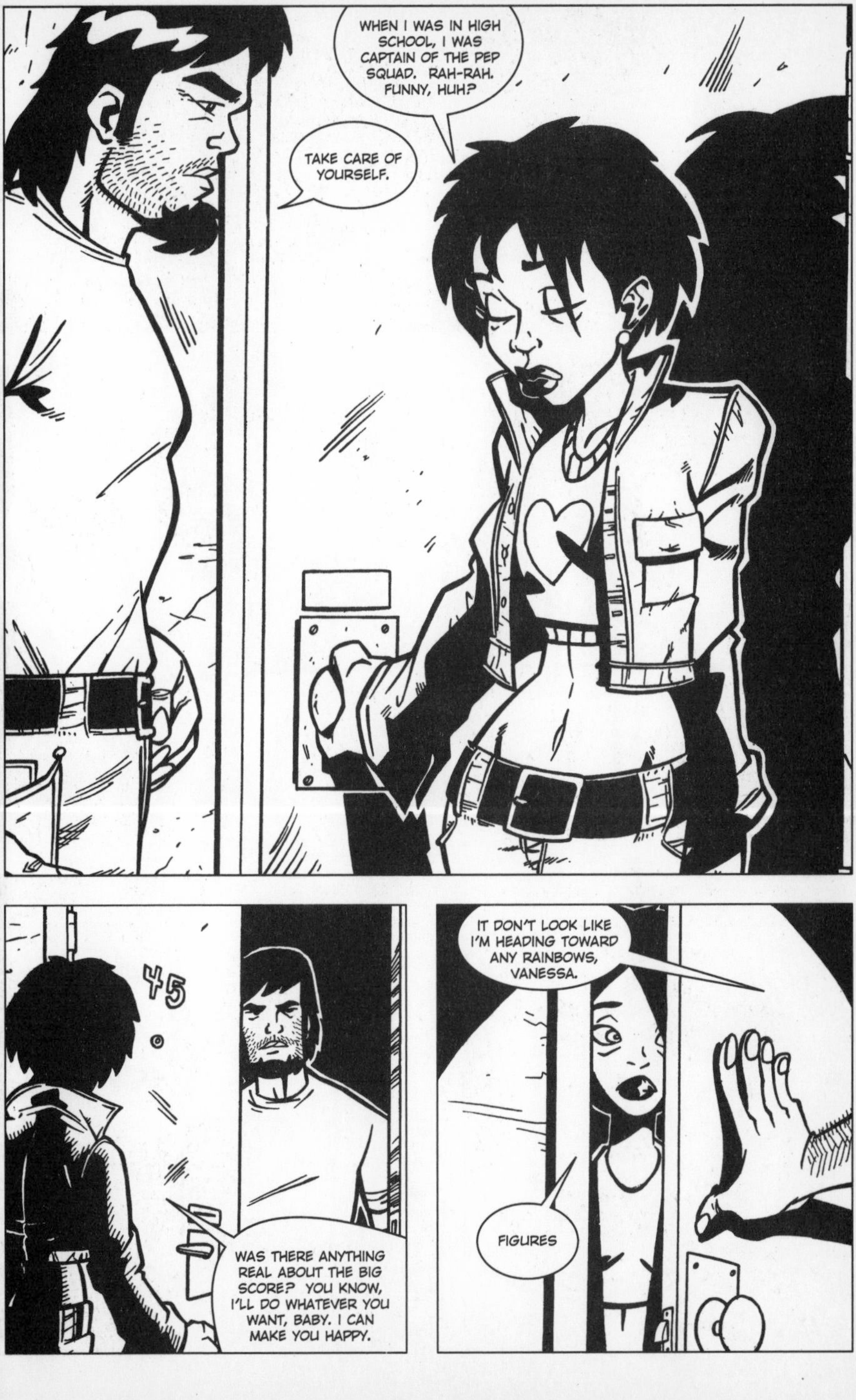
WHEN I WAS IN HIGH SCHOOL, I WAS CAPTAIN OF THE PEP SQUAD. RAH-RAH. FUNNY, HUH?
TAKE CARE OF YOURSELF.
45
WAS THERE ANYTHING REAL ABOUT THE BIG SCORE? YOU KNOW, I'LL DO WHATEVER YOU WANT, BABY. I CAN MAKE YOU HAPPY.
IT DON'T LOOK LIKE I'M HEADING TOWARD ANY RAINBOWS, VANESSA.
FIGURES

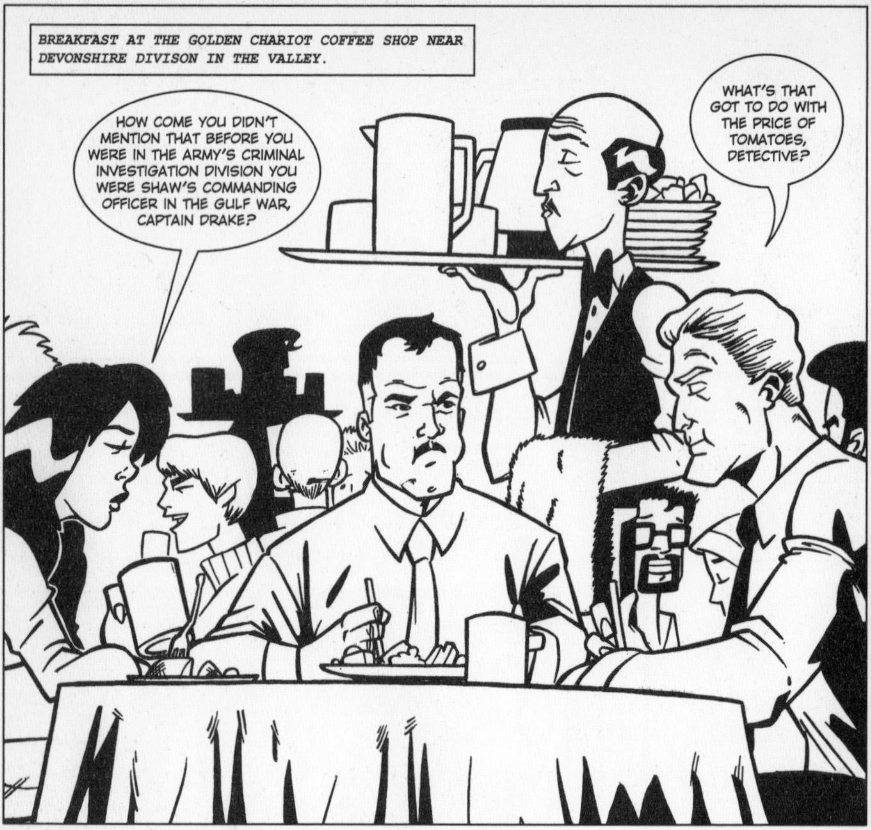
BREAKFAST AT THE GOLDEN CHARIOT COFFEE SHOP NEAR DEVONSHIRE DIVISON IN THE VALLEY.
HOW COME YOU DIDN'T MENTION THAT BEFORE YOU WERE IN THE ARMY'S CRIMINAL INVESTIGATION DIVISION YOU WERE SHAW'S COMMANDING OFFICER IN THE GULF WAR, CAPTAIN DRAKE?
WHAT'S THAT GOT TO DO WITH THE PRICE OF TOMATOES, DETECTIVE?

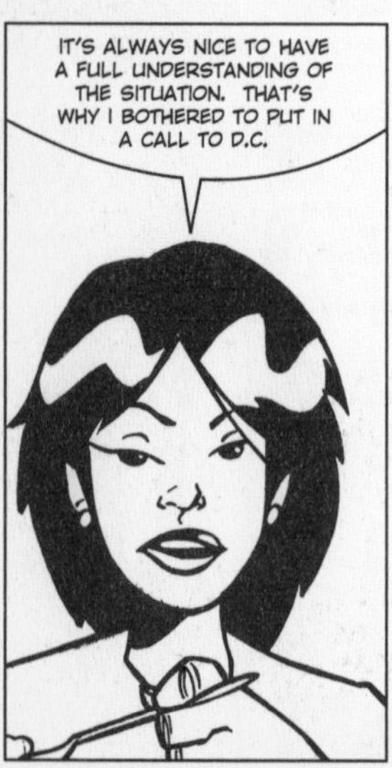
IT'S ALWAYS NICE TO HAVE A FULL UNDERSTANDING OF THE SITUATION. THAT'S WHY I BOTHERED TO PUT IN A CALL TO D.C.

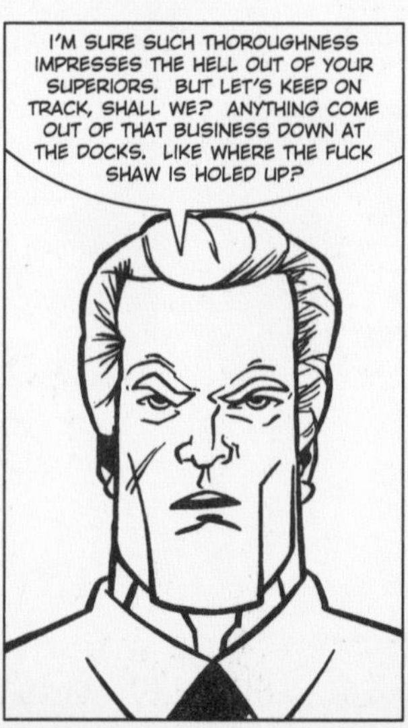
I'M SURE SUCH THOROUGHNESS IMPRESSES THE HELL OUT OF YOUR SUPERIORS. BUT LET'S KEEP ON TRACK, SHALL WE? ANYTHING COME OUT OF THAT BUSINESS DOWN AT THE DOCKS. LIKE WHERE THE FUCK SHAW IS HOLED UP?

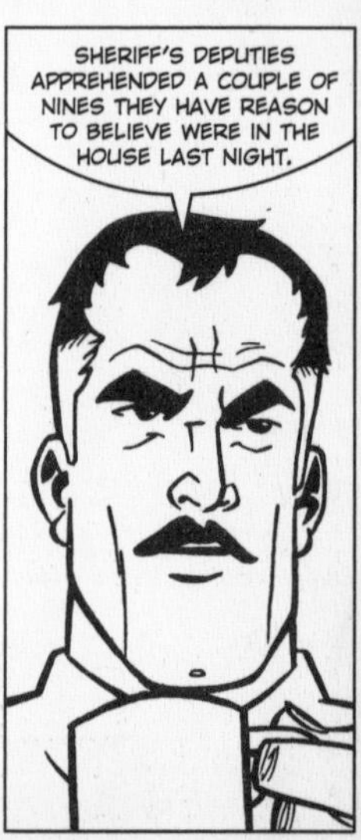
SHERIFF'S DEPUTIES APPREHENDED A COUPLE OF NINES THEY HAVE REASON TO BELIEVE WERE IN THE HOUSE LAST NIGHT.

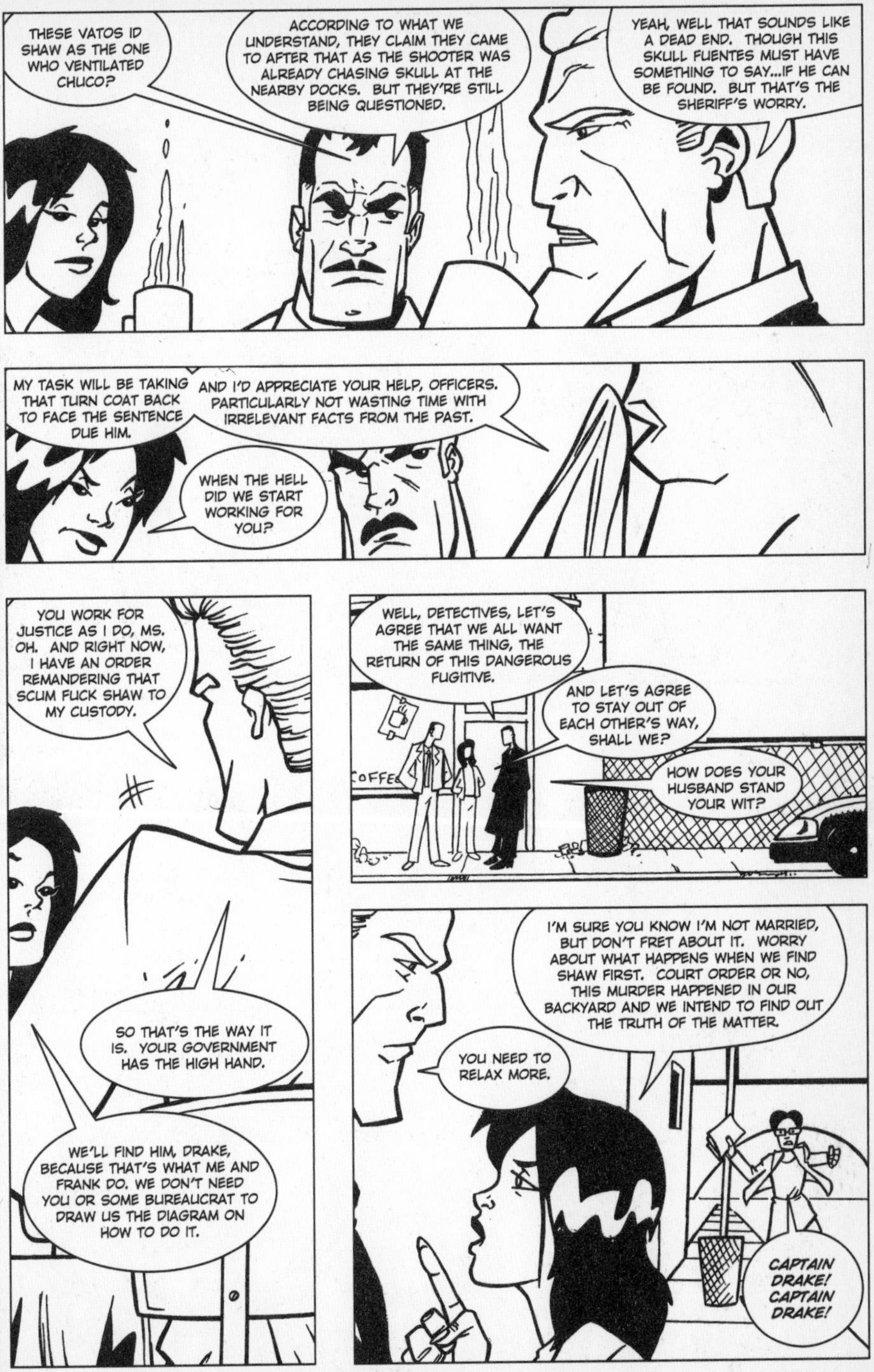
THESE VATOS ID SHAW AS THE ONE WHO VENTILATED CHUCO?
ACCORDING TO WHAT WE UNDERSTAND, THEY CLAIM THEY CAME TO AFTER THAT AS THE SHOOTER WAS ALREADY CHASING SKULL AT THE NEARBY DOCKS. BUT THEY'RE STILL BEING QUESTIONED.
YEAH, WELL THAT SOUNDS LIKE A DEAD END. THOUGH THIS SKULL FUENTES MUST HAVE SOMETHING TO SAY...IF HE CAN BE FOUND. BUT THAT'S THE SHERIFF'S WORRY.
MY TASK WILL BE TAKING THAT TURN COAT BACK TO FACE THE SENTENCE DUE HIM.
AND I'D APPRECIATE YOUR HELP, OFFICERS. PARTICULARLY NOT WASTING TIME WITH IRRELEVANT FACTS FROM THE PAST.
WHEN THE HELL DID WE START WORKING FOR YOU?
YOU WORK FOR JUSTICE AS I DO, MS. OH. AND RIGHT NOW, I HAVE AN ORDER REMANDERING THAT SCUM FUCK SHAW TO MY CUSTODY.
SO THAT'S THE WAY IT IS. YOUR GOVERNMENT HAS THE HIGH HAND.
WE'LL FIND HIM, DRAKE, BECAUSE THAT'S WHAT ME AND FRANK DO. WE DON'T NEED YOU OR SOME BUREAUCRAT TO DRAW US THE DIAGRAM ON HOW TO DO IT.
WELL, DETECTIVES, LET'S AGREE THAT WE ALL WANT THE SAME THING, THE RETURN OF THIS DANGEROUS FUGITIVE.
AND LET'S AGREE TO STAY OUT OF EACH OTHER'S WAY, SHALL WE?
HOW DOES YOUR HUSBAND STAND YOUR WIT?
COFFEE
I'M SURE YOU KNOW I'M NOT MARRIED, BUT DON'T FRET ABOUT IT. WORRY ABOUT WHAT HAPPENS WHEN WE FIND SHAW FIRST. COURT ORDER OR NO, THIS MURDER HAPPENED IN OUR BACKYARD AND WE INTEND TO FIND OUT THE TRUTH OF THE MATTER.
YOU NEED TO RELAX MORE.
CAPTAIN DRAKE! CAPTAIN DRAKE!

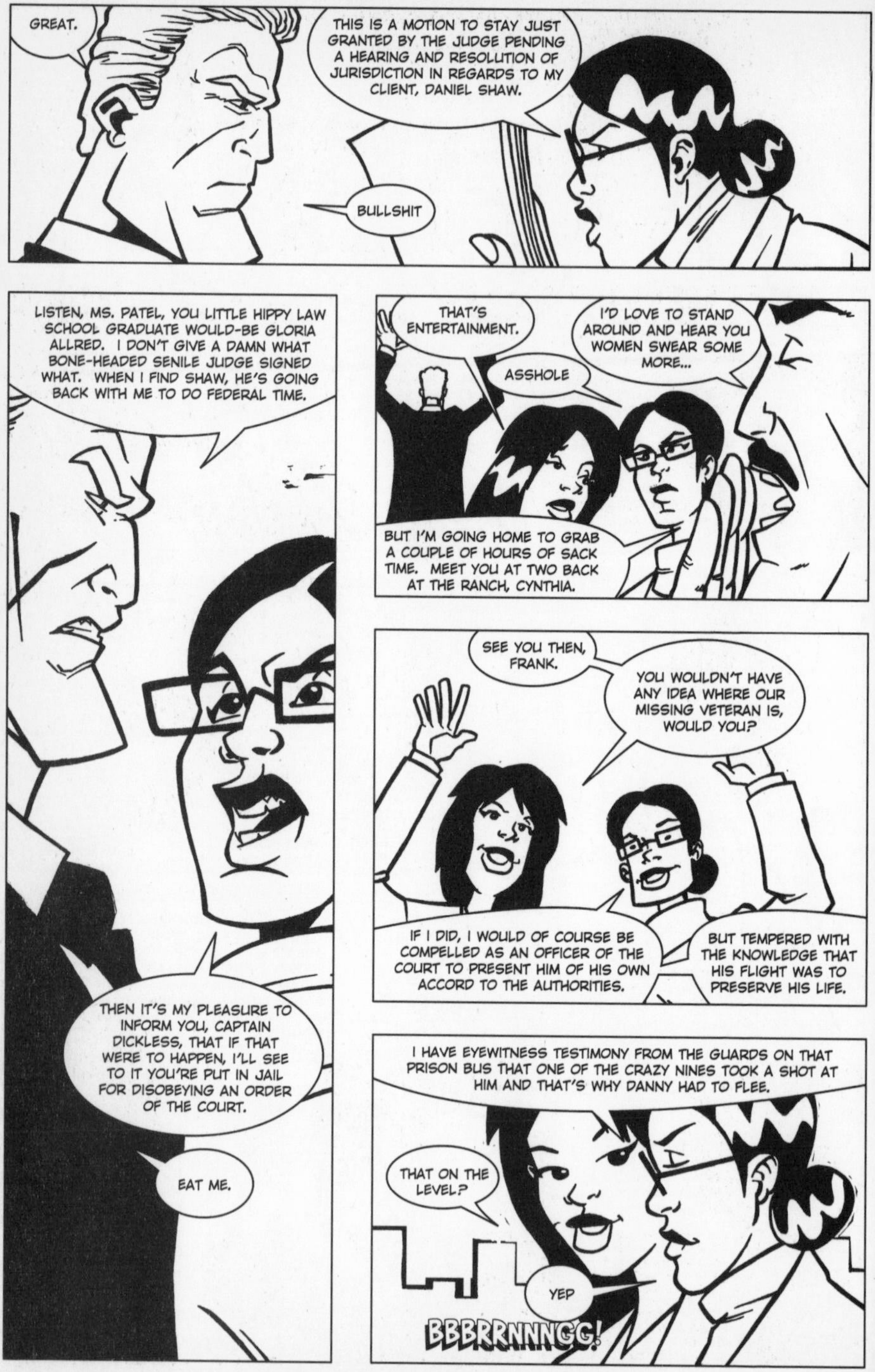
GREAT.
THIS IS A MOTION TO STAY JUST GRANTED BY THE JUDGE PENDING A HEARING AND RESOLUTION OF JURISDICTION IN REGARDS TO MY CLIENT, DANIEL SHAW.
BULLSHIT
LISTEN, MS. PATEL, YOU LITTLE HIPPY LAW SCHOOL GRADUATE WOULD-BE GLORIA ALLRED. I DON'T GIVE A DAMN WHAT BONE-HEADED SENILE JUDGE SIGNED WHAT. WHEN I FIND SHAW, HE'S GOING BACK WITH ME TO DO FEDERAL TIME.
THEN IT'S MY PLEASURE TO INFORM YOU, CAPTAIN DICKLESS, THAT IF THAT WERE TO HAPPEN, I'LL SEE TO IT YOU'RE PUT IN JAIL FOR DISOBEYING AN ORDER OF THE COURT.
EAT ME.
THAT'S ENTERTAINMENT.
ASSHOLE
I'D LOVE TO STAND AROUND AND HEAR YOU WOMEN SWEAR SOME MORE...
BUT I'M GOING HOME TO GRAB A COUPLE OF HOURS OF SACK TIME. MEET YOU AT TWO BACK AT THE RANCH, CYNTHIA.
SEE YOU THEN, FRANK.
YOU WOULDN'T HAVE ANY IDEA WHERE OUR MISSING VETERAN IS, WOULD YOU?
IF I DID, I WOULD OF COURSE BE COMPELLED AS AN OFFICER OF THE COURT TO PRESENT HIM OF HIS OWN ACCORD TO THE AUTHORITIES.
BUT TEMPERED WITH THE KNOWLEDGE THAT HIS FLIGHT WAS TO PRESERVE HIS LIFE.
I HAVE EYEWITNESS TESTIMONY FROM THE GUARDS ON THAT PRISON BUS THAT ONE OF THE CRAZY NINES TOOK A SHOT AT HIM AND THAT'S WHY DANNY HAD TO FLEE.
THAT ON THE LEVEL?
YEP
BBBRRNNNGG!

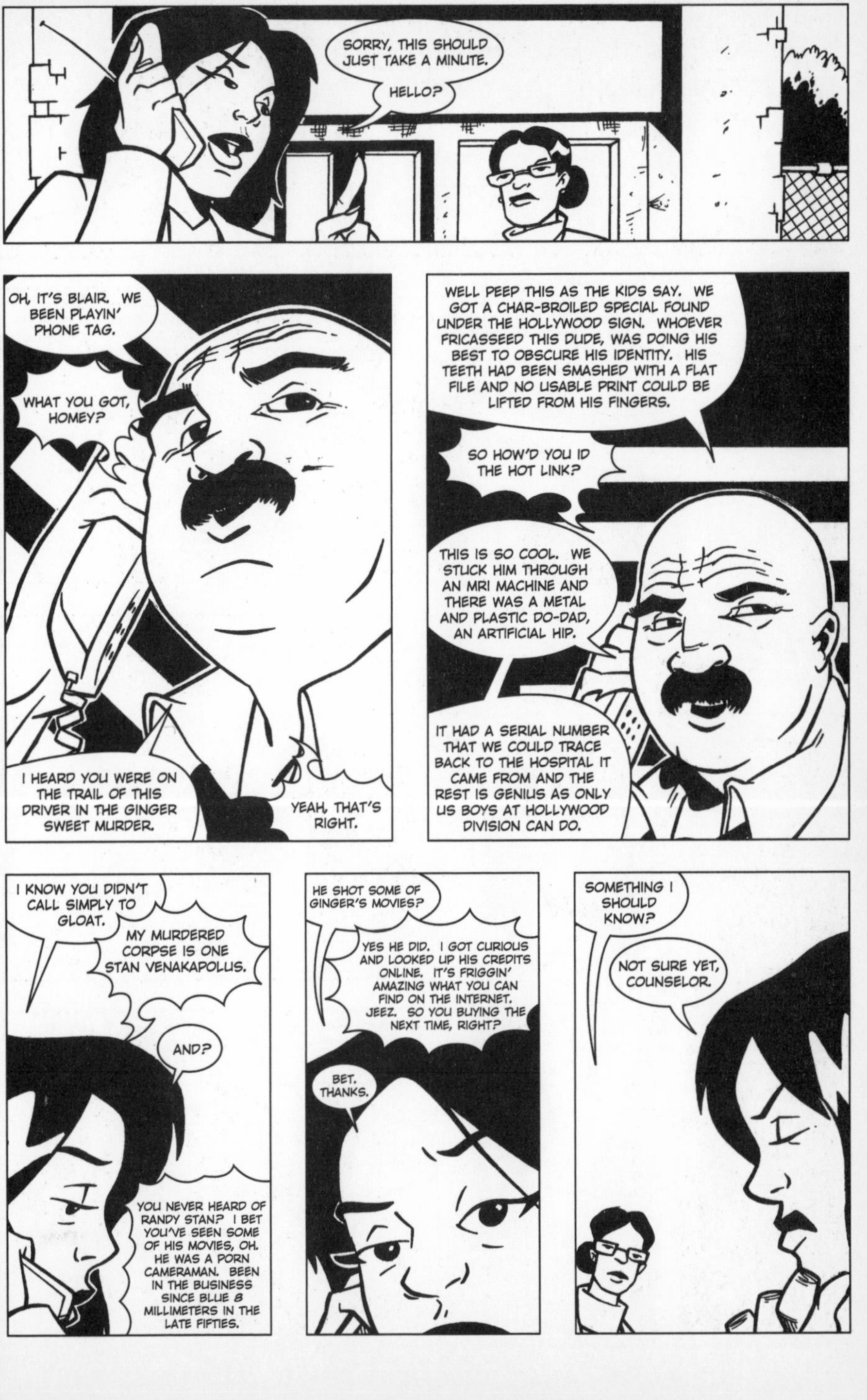
SORRY, THIS SHOULD JUST TAKE A MINUTE.
HELLO?
OH, IT'S BLAIR. WE BEEN PLAYIN' PHONE TAG.
WHAT YOU GOT, HOMEY?
I HEARD YOU WERE ON THE TRAIL OF THIS DRIVER IN THE GINGER SWEET MURDER.
YEAH, THAT'S RIGHT.
WELL PEEP THIS AS THE KIDS SAY. WE GOT A CHAR-BROILED SPECIAL FOUND UNDER THE HOLLYWOOD SIGN. WHOEVER FRICASSEED THIS DUDE, WAS DOING HIS BEST TO OBSCURE HIS IDENTITY. HIS TEETH HAD BEEN SMASHED WITH A FLAT FILE AND NO USABLE PRINT COULD BE LIFTED FROM HIS FINGERS.
SO HOW'D YOU ID THE HOT LINK?
THIS IS SO COOL. WE STUCK HIM THROUGH AN MRI MACHINE AND THERE WAS A METAL AND PLASTIC DO-DAD, AN ARTIFICIAL HIP.
IT HAD A SERIAL NUMBER THAT WE COULD TRACE BACK TO THE HOSPITAL IT CAME FROM AND THE REST IS GENIUS AS ONLY US BOYS AT HOLLYWOOD DIVISION CAN DO.
I KNOW YOU DIDN'T CALL SIMPLY TO GLOAT.
MY MURDERED CORPSE IS ONE STAN VENAKAPOLUS.
AND?
YOU NEVER HEARD OF RANDY STAN? I BET YOU'VE SEEN SOME OF HIS MOVIES, OH. HE WAS A PORN CAMERAMAN. BEEN IN THE BUSINESS SINCE BLUE 8 MILLIMETERS IN THE LATE FIFTIES.
HE SHOT SOME OF GINGER'S MOVIES?
YES HE DID. I GOT CURIOUS AND LOOKED UP HIS CREDITS ONLINE. IT'S FRIGGIN' AMAZING WHAT YOU CAN FIND ON THE INTERNET. JEEZ. SO YOU BUYING THE NEXT TIME, RIGHT?
BET. THANKS.
SOMETHING I SHOULD KNOW?
NOT SURE YET, COUNSELOR.

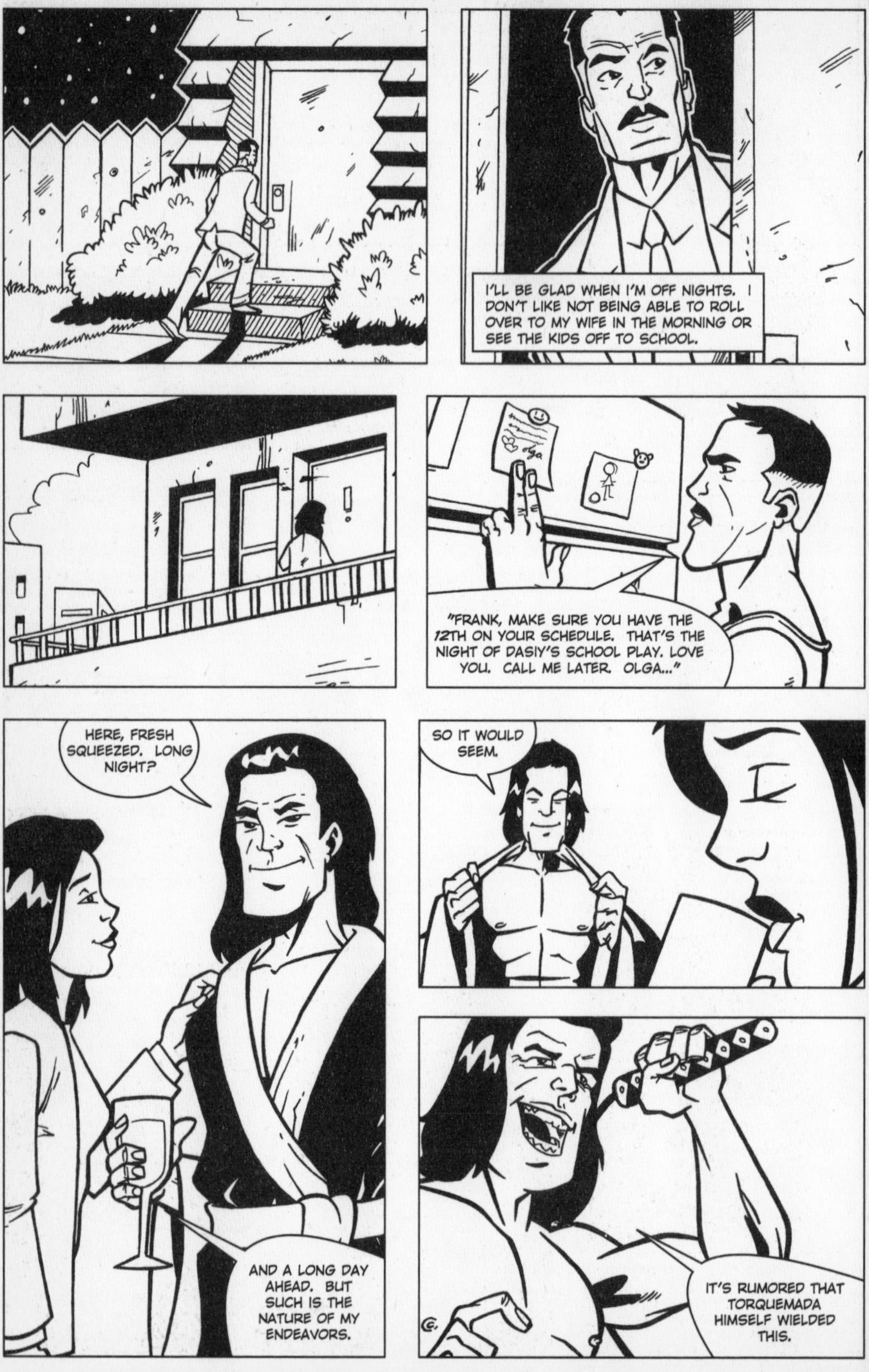
I'LL BE GLAD WHEN I'M OFF NIGHTS. I DON'T LIKE NOT BEING ABLE TO ROLL OVER TO MY WIFE IN THE MORNING OR SEE THE KIDS OFF TO SCHOOL.
"FRANK, MAKE SURE YOU HAVE THE 12TH ON YOUR SCHEDULE. THAT'S THE NIGHT OF DASIY'S SCHOOL PLAY. LOVE YOU. CALL ME LATER. OLGA..."
HERE, FRESH SQUEEZED. LONG NIGHT?
AND A LONG DAY AHEAD. BUT SUCH IS THE NATURE OF MY ENDEAVORS.
SO IT WOULD SEEM.
IT'S RUMORED THAT TORQUEMADA HIMSELF WIELDED THIS.

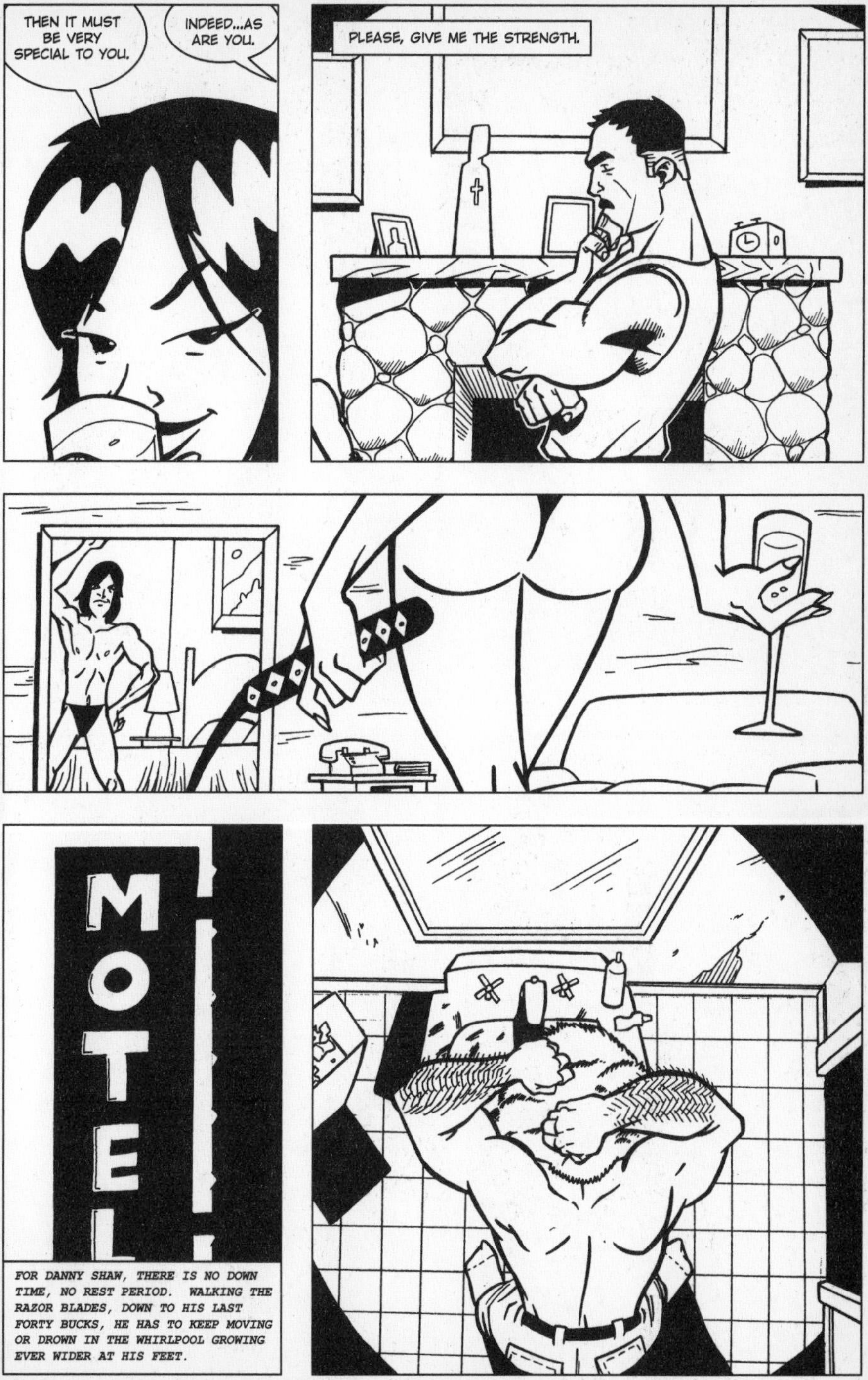
THEN IT MUST BE VERY SPECIAL TO YOU.
INDEED...AS ARE YOU.
PLEASE, GIVE ME THE STRENGTH.
MOTEL
FOR DANNY SHAW, THERE IS NO DOWN TIME, NO REST PERIOD. WALKING THE RAZOR BLADES, DOWN TO HIS LAST FORTY BUCKS, HE HAS TO KEEP MOVING OR DROWN IN THE WHIRLPOOL GROWING EVER WIDER AT HIS FEET.

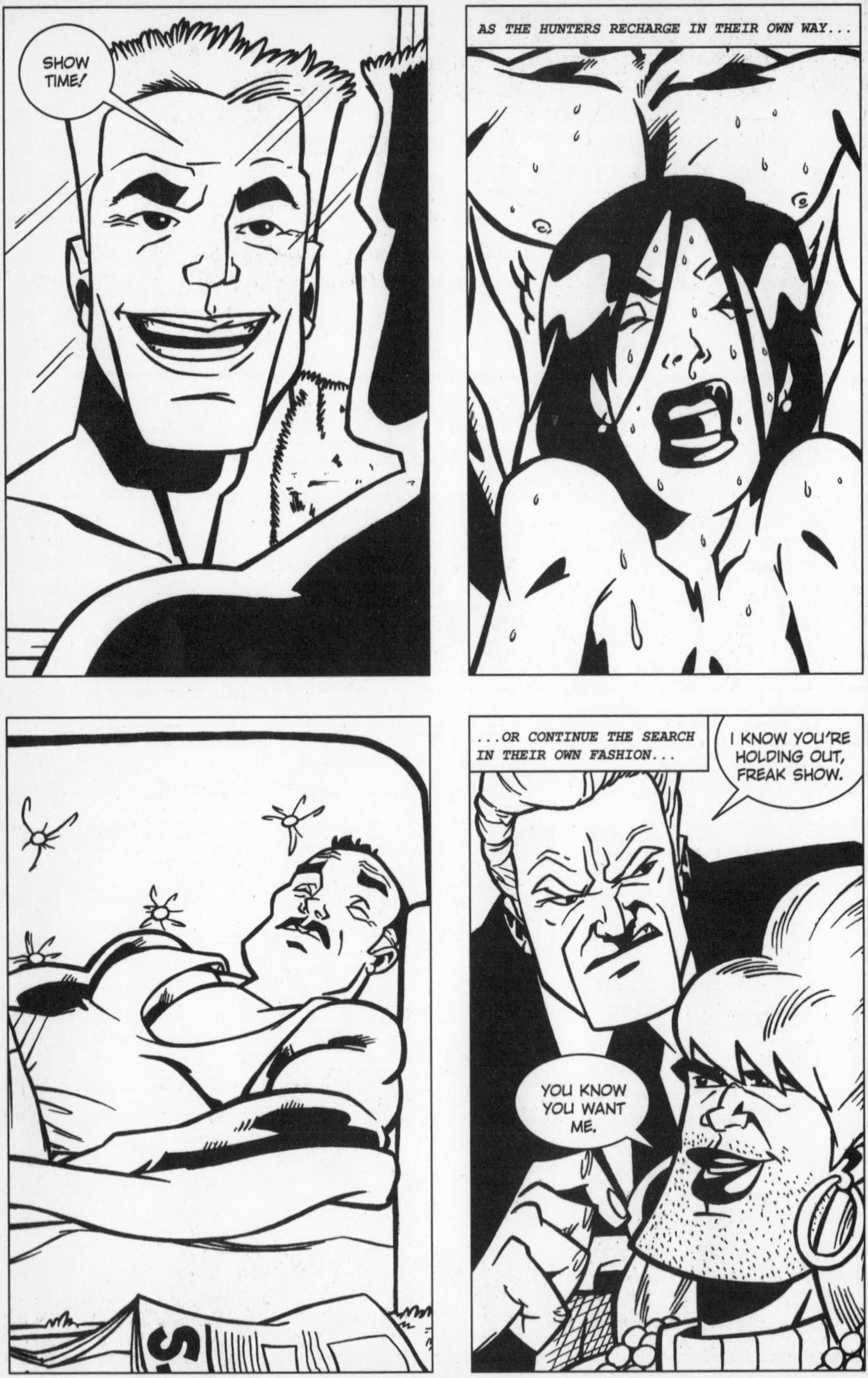
SHOW TIME!
AS THE HUNTERS RECHARGE IN THEIR OWN WAY...
...OR CONTINUE THE SEARCH IN THEIR OWN FASHION...
I KNOW YOU'RE HOLDING OUT, FREAK SHOW.
YOU KNOW YOU WANT ME.

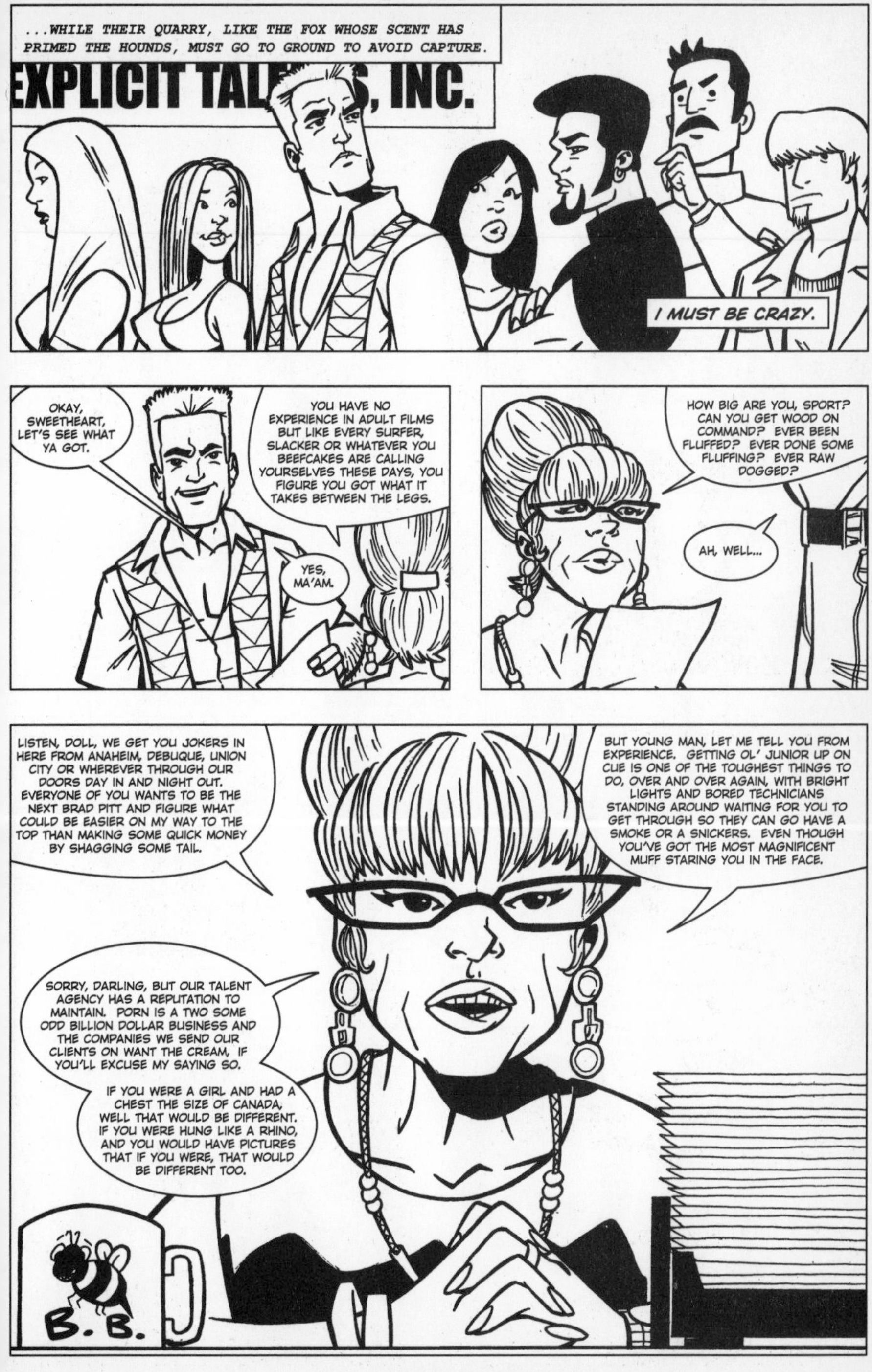
...WHILE THEIR QUARRY, LIKE THE FOX WHOSE SCENT HAS PRIMED THE HOUNDS, MUST GO TO GROUND TO AVOID CAPTURE.
EXPLICIT TAL S, INC.
I MUST BE CRAZY.
OKAY, SWEETHEART, LET'S SEE WHAT YA GOT.
YOU HAVE NO EXPERIENCE IN ADULT FILMS BUT LIKE EVERY SURFER, SLACKER OR WHATEVER YOU BEEFCAKES ARE CALLING YOURSELVES THESE DAYS, YOU FIGURE YOU GOT WHAT IT TAKES BETWEEN THE LEGS.
YES, MA'AM.
HOW BIG ARE YOU, SPORT? CAN YOU GET WOOD ON COMMAND? EVER BEEN FLUFFED? EVER DONE SOME FLUFFING? EVER RAW DOGGED?
AH, WELL...
LISTEN, DOLL, WE GET YOU JOKERS IN HERE FROM ANAHEIM, DEBUQUE, UNION CITY OR WHEREVER THROUGH OUR DOORS DAY IN AND NIGHT OUT. EVERYONE OF YOU WANTS TO BE THE NEXT BRAD PITT AND FIGURE WHAT COULD BE EASIER ON MY WAY TO THE TOP THAN MAKING SOME QUICK MONEY BY SHAGGING SOME TAIL.
BUT YOUNG MAN, LET ME TELL YOU FROM EXPERIENCE. GETTING OL' JUNIOR UP ON CUE IS ONE OF THE TOUGHEST THINGS TO DO, OVER AND OVER AGAIN, WITH BRIGHT LIGHTS AND BORED TECHNICIANS STANDING AROUND WAITING FOR YOU TO GET THROUGH SO THEY CAN GO HAVE A SMOKE OR A SNICKERS. EVEN THOUGH YOU'VE GOT THE MOST MAGNIFICENT MUFF STARING YOU IN THE FACE.
SORRY, DARLING, BUT OUR TALENT AGENCY HAS A REPUTATION TO MAINTAIN. PORN IS A TWO SOME ODD BILLION DOLLAR BUSINESS AND THE COMPANIES WE SEND OUR CLIENTS ON WANT THE CREAM, IF YOU'LL EXCUSE MY SAYING SO.
IF YOU WERE A GIRL AND HAD A CHEST THE SIZE OF CANADA, WELL THAT WOULD BE DIFFERENT. IF YOU WERE HUNG LIKE A RHINO, AND YOU WOULD HAVE PICTURES THAT IF YOU WERE, THAT WOULD BE DIFFERENT TOO.
B. B.

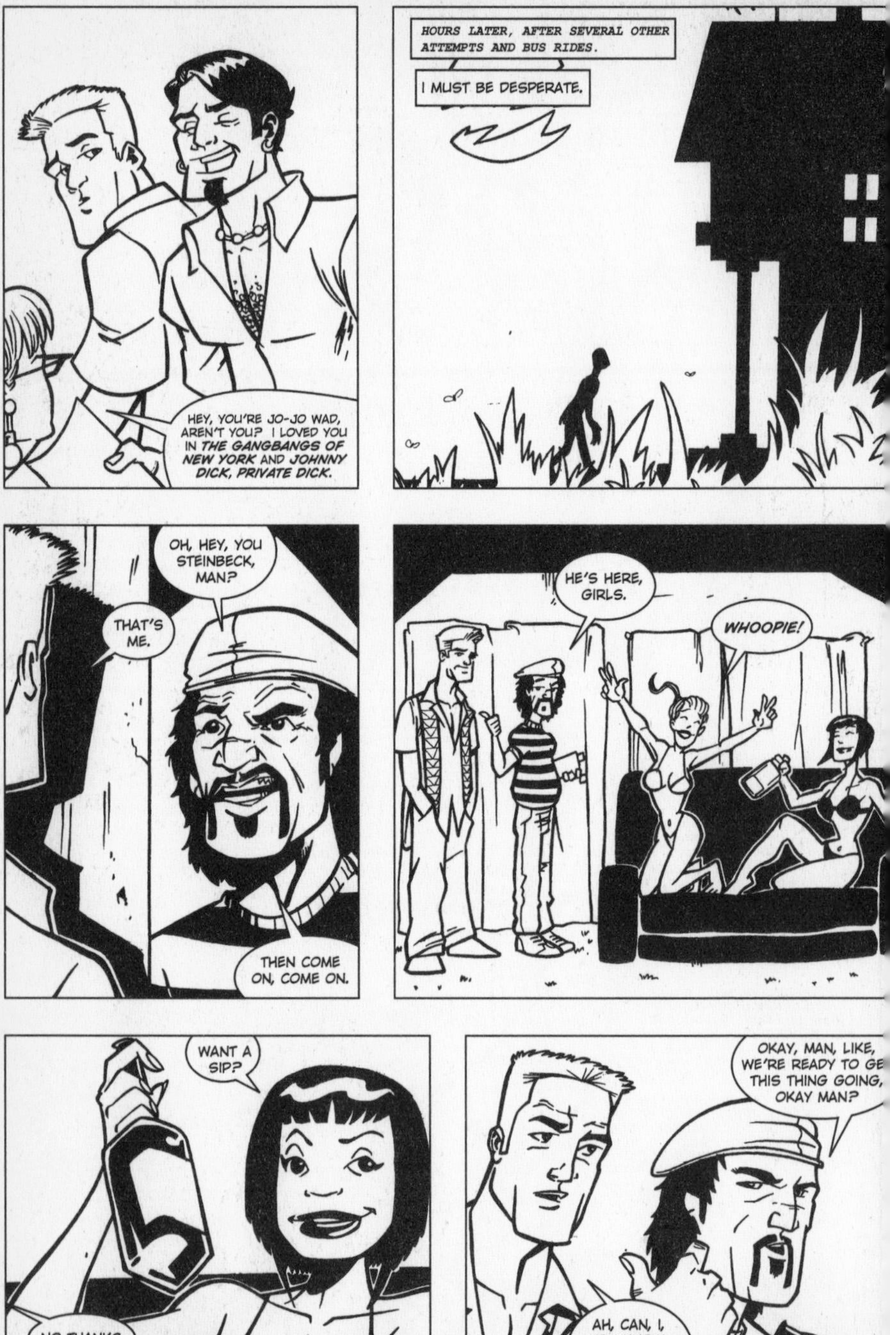
HEY, YOU'RE JO-JO WAD, AREN'T YOU? I LOVED YOU IN THE GANGBANGS OF NEW YORK AND JOHNNY DICK, PRIVATE DICK.
HOURS LATER, AFTER SEVERAL OTHER ATTEMPTS AND BUS RIDES.
I MUST BE DESPERATE.
OH, HEY, YOU STEINBECK, MAN?
THAT'S ME.
THEN COME ON, COME ON.
HE'S HERE, GIRLS.
WHOOPIE!
WANT A SIP?
NO THANKS.
OKAY, MAN, LIKE, WE'RE READY TO GE THIS THING GOING, OKAY MAN?
AH, CAN, I, YOU KNOW, GET READY?

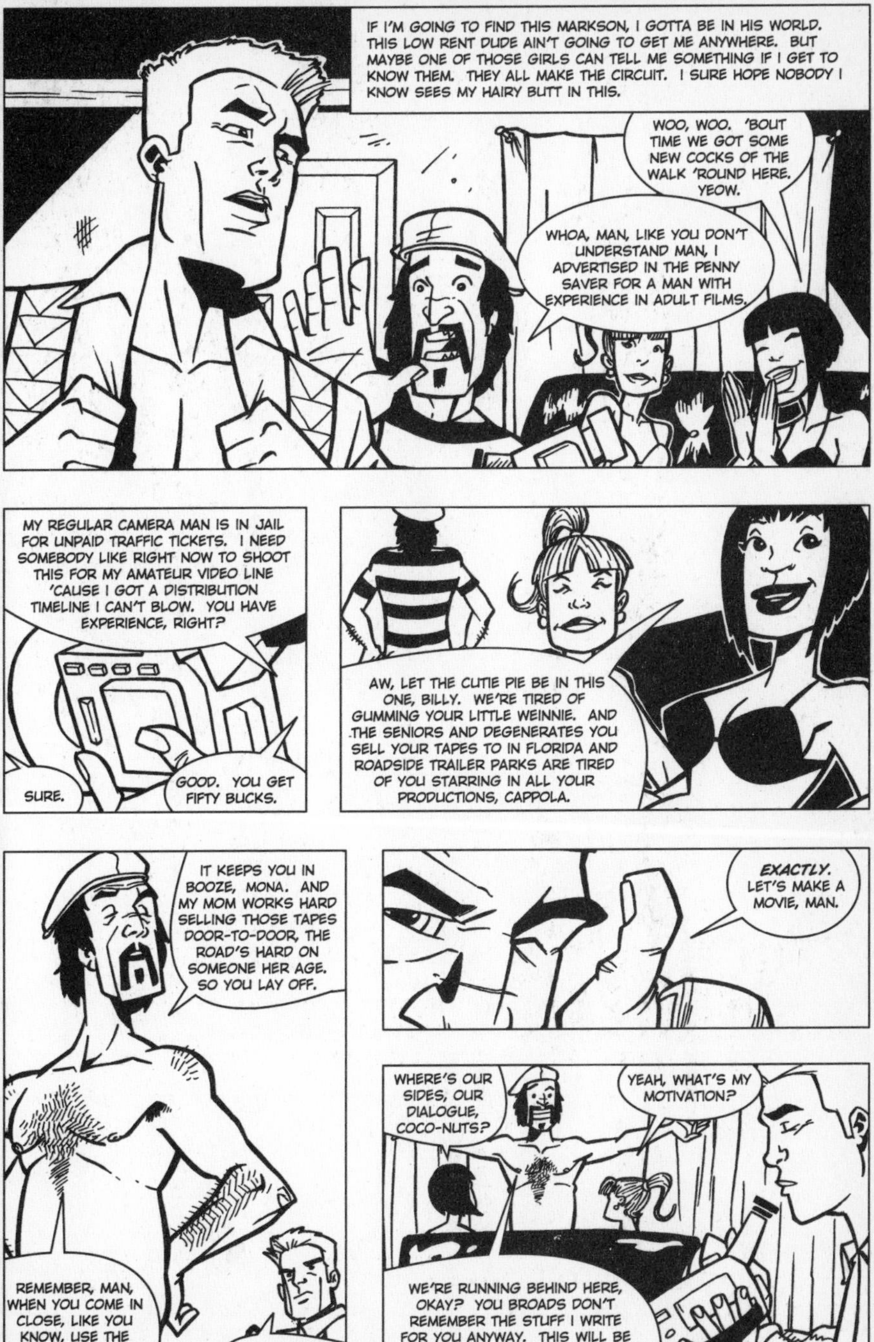

IF I'M GOING TO FIND THIS MARKSON, I GOTTA BE IN HIS WORLD. THIS LOW RENT DUDE AIN'T GOING TO GET ME ANYWHERE. BUT MAYBE ONE OF THOSE GIRLS CAN TELL ME SOMETHING IF I GET TO KNOW THEM. THEY ALL MAKE THE CIRCUIT. I SURE HOPE NOBODY I KNOW SEES MY HAIRY BUTT IN THIS.
WOO, WOO. 'BOUT TIME WE GOT SOME NEW COCKS OF THE WALK 'ROUND HERE. YEOW.
WHOA, MAN, LIKE YOU DON'T UNDERSTAND MAN, I ADVERTISED IN THE PENNY SAVER FOR A MAN WITH EXPERIENCE IN ADULT FILMS.
MY REGULAR CAMERA MAN IS IN JAIL FOR UNPAID TRAFFIC TICKETS. I NEED SOMEBODY LIKE RIGHT NOW TO SHOOT THIS FOR MY AMATEUR VIDEO LINE 'CAUSE I GOT A DISTRIBUTION TIMELINE I CAN'T BLOW. YOU HAVE EXPERIENCE, RIGHT?
SURE.
GOOD. YOU GET FIFTY BUCKS.
AW, LET THE CUTIE PIE BE IN THIS ONE, BILLY. WE'RE TIRED OF GUMMING YOUR LITTLE WEINNIE. AND THE SENIORS AND DEGENERATES YOU SELL YOUR TAPES TO IN FLORIDA AND ROADSIDE TRAILER PARKS ARE TIRED OF YOU STARRING IN ALL YOUR PRODUCTIONS, CAPPOLA.
IT KEEPS YOU IN BOOZE, MONA. AND MY MOM WORKS HARD SELLING THOSE TAPES DOOR-TO-DOOR, THE ROAD'S HARD ON SOMEONE HER AGE. SO YOU LAY OFF.
EXACTLY. LET'S MAKE A MOVIE, MAN.
REMEMBER, MAN, WHEN YOU COME IN CLOSE, LIKE YOU KNOW, USE THE ZOOM BECAUSE IT WILL, YOU KNOW...
MAKE YOU LOOK LARGER?
WHERE'S OUR SIDES, OUR DIALOGUE, COCO-NUTS?
YEAH, WHAT'S MY MOTIVATION?
WE'RE RUNNING BEHIND HERE, OKAY? YOU BROADS DON'T REMEMBER THE STUFF I WRITE FOR YOU ANYWAY. THIS WILL BE THE CABLE REPAIR MAN AND THE LONELY HOUSEWIVES.

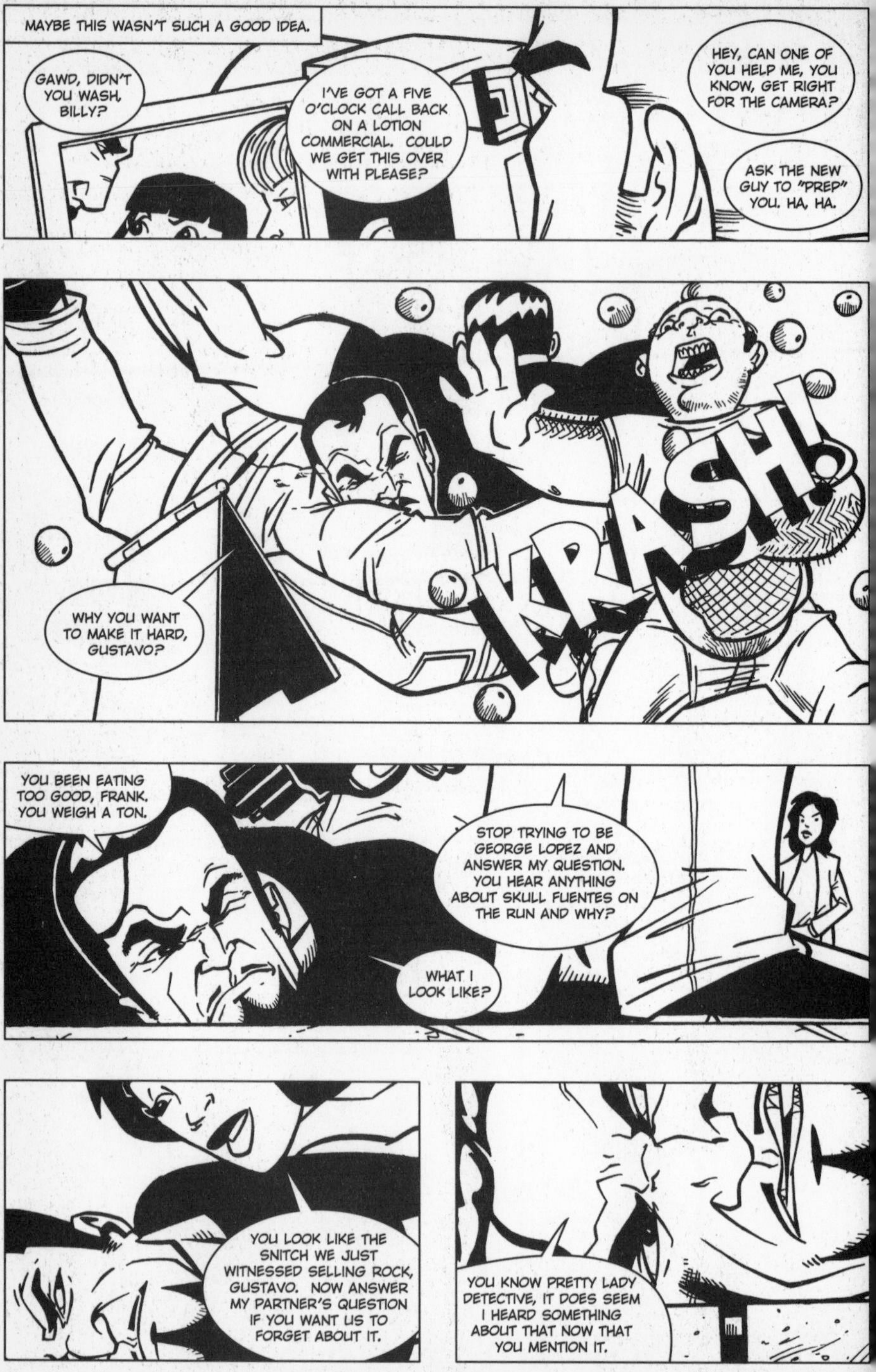
MAYBE THIS WASN'T SUCH A GOOD IDEA.
GAWD, DIDN'T YOU WASH, BILLY?
I'VE GOT A FIVE O'CLOCK CALL BACK ON A LOTION COMMERCIAL. COULD WE GET THIS OVER WITH PLEASE?
HEY, CAN ONE OF YOU HELP ME, YOU KNOW, GET RIGHT FOR THE CAMERA?
ASK THE NEW GUY TO "PREP" YOU. HA, HA.
KRASH!
WHY YOU WANT TO MAKE IT HARD, GUSTAVO?
YOU BEEN EATING TOO GOOD, FRANK. YOU WEIGH A TON.
STOP TRYING TO BE GEORGE LOPEZ AND ANSWER MY QUESTION. YOU HEAR ANYTHING ABOUT SKULL FUENTES ON THE RUN AND WHY?
WHAT I LOOK LIKE?
YOU LOOK LIKE THE SNITCH WE JUST WITNESSED SELLING ROCK, GUSTAVO. NOW ANSWER MY PARTNER'S QUESTION IF YOU WANT US TO FORGET ABOUT IT.
YOU KNOW PRETTY LADY DETECTIVE, IT DOES SEEM I HEARD SOMETHING ABOUT THAT NOW THAT YOU MENTION IT.

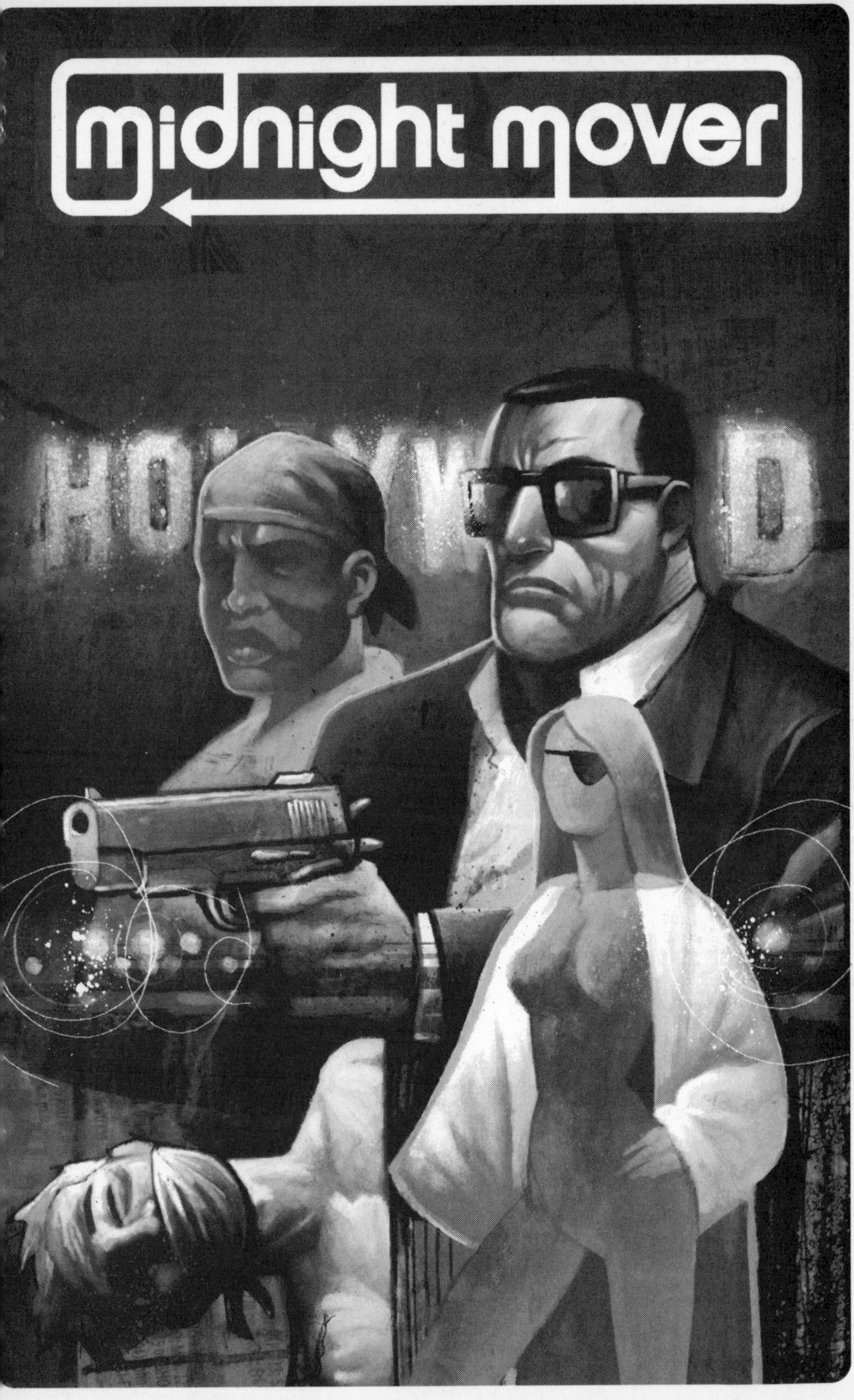
midnight mover

chapter four

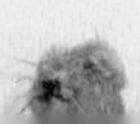

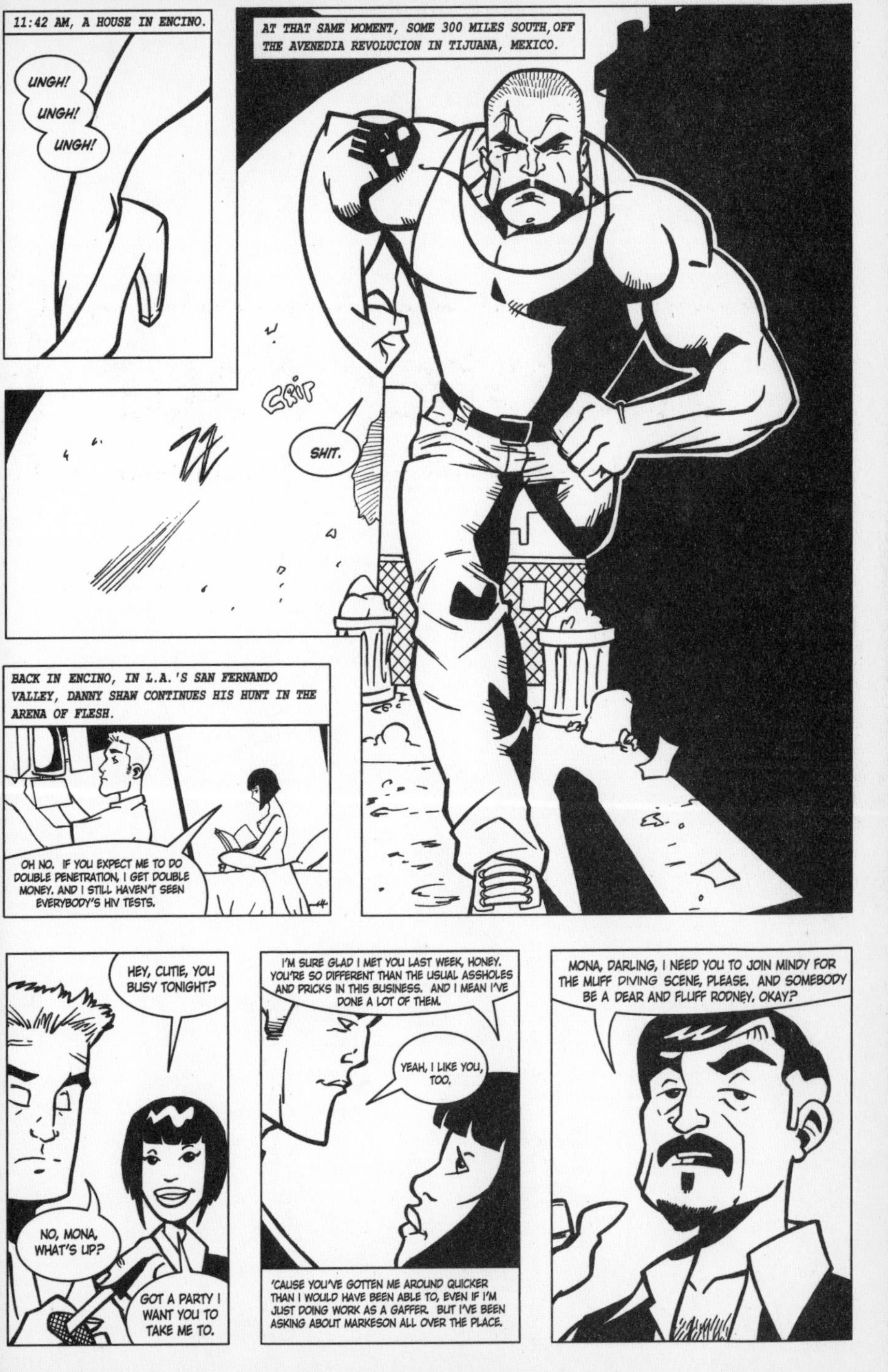
11:42 AM, A HOUSE IN ENCINO.
UNGH!
UNGH!
UNGH!
AT THAT SAME MOMENT, SOME 300 MILES SOUTH, OFF THE AVENEDIA REVOLUCION IN TIJUANA, MEXICO.
CRIP
SHIT.
BACK IN ENCINO, IN L.A.'S SAN FERNANDO VALLEY, DANNY SHAW CONTINUES HIS HUNT IN THE ARENA OF FLESH.
OH NO. IF YOU EXPECT ME TO DO DOUBLE PENETRATION, I GET DOUBLE MONEY. AND I STILL HAVEN'T SEEN EVERYBODY'S HIV TESTS.
HEY, CUTIE, YOU BUSY TONIGHT?
NO, MONA, WHAT'S UP?
GOT A PARTY I WANT YOU TO TAKE ME TO.
I'M SURE GLAD I MET YOU LAST WEEK, HONEY. YOU'RE SO DIFFERENT THAN THE USUAL ASSHOLES AND PRICKS IN THIS BUSINESS. AND I MEAN I'VE DONE A LOT OF THEM.
YEAH, I LIKE YOU, TOO.
'CAUSE YOU'VE GOTTEN ME AROUND QUICKER THAN I WOULD HAVE BEEN ABLE TO, EVEN IF I'M JUST DOING WORK AS A GAFFER. BUT I'VE BEEN ASKING ABOUT MARKESON ALL OVER THE PLACE.
MONA, DARLING, I NEED YOU TO JOIN MINDY FOR THE MUFF DIVING SCENE, PLEASE. AND SOMEBODY BE A DEAR AND FLUFF RODNEY. OKAY?

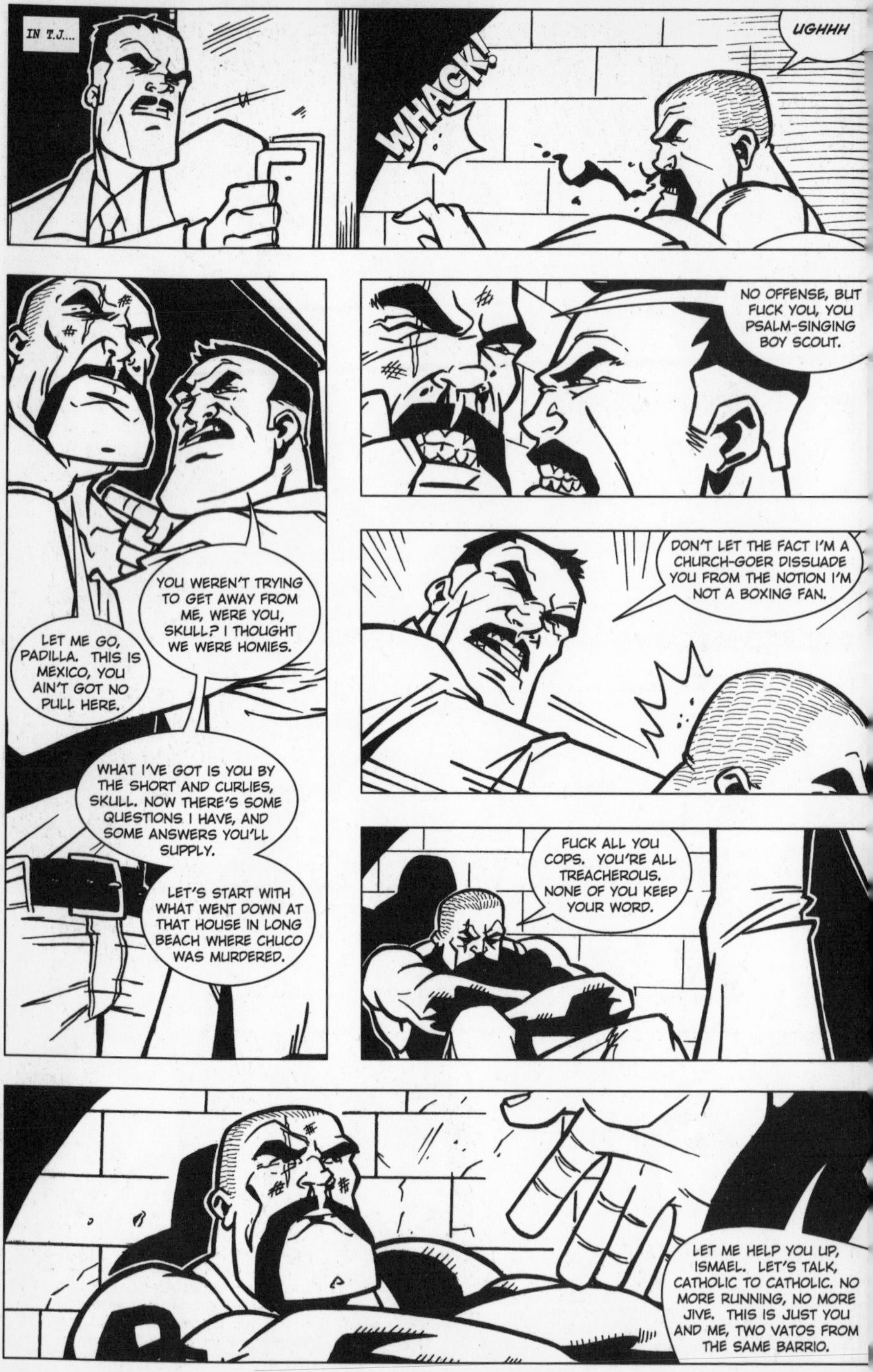
IN T.J....
WHACK!
UGHHH
NO OFFENSE, BUT FUCK YOU, YOU PSALM-SINGING BOY SCOUT.
YOU WEREN'T TRYING TO GET AWAY FROM ME, WERE YOU, SKULL? I THOUGHT WE WERE HOMIES.
LET ME GO, PADILLA. THIS IS MEXICO, YOU AIN'T GOT NO PULL HERE.
WHAT I'VE GOT IS YOU BY THE SHORT AND CURLIES, SKULL. NOW THERE'S SOME QUESTIONS I HAVE, AND SOME ANSWERS YOU'LL SUPPLY.
LET'S START WITH WHAT WENT DOWN AT THAT HOUSE IN LONG BEACH WHERE CHUCO WAS MURDERED.
DON'T LET THE FACT I'M A CHURCH-GOER DISSUADE YOU FROM THE NOTION I'M NOT A BOXING FAN.
FUCK ALL YOU COPS. YOU'RE ALL TREACHEROUS. NONE OF YOU KEEP YOUR WORD.
LET ME HELP YOU UP, ISMAEL. LET'S TALK, CATHOLIC TO CATHOLIC. NO MORE RUNNING, NO MORE JIVE. THIS IS JUST YOU AND ME, TWO VATOS FROM THE SAME BARRIO.

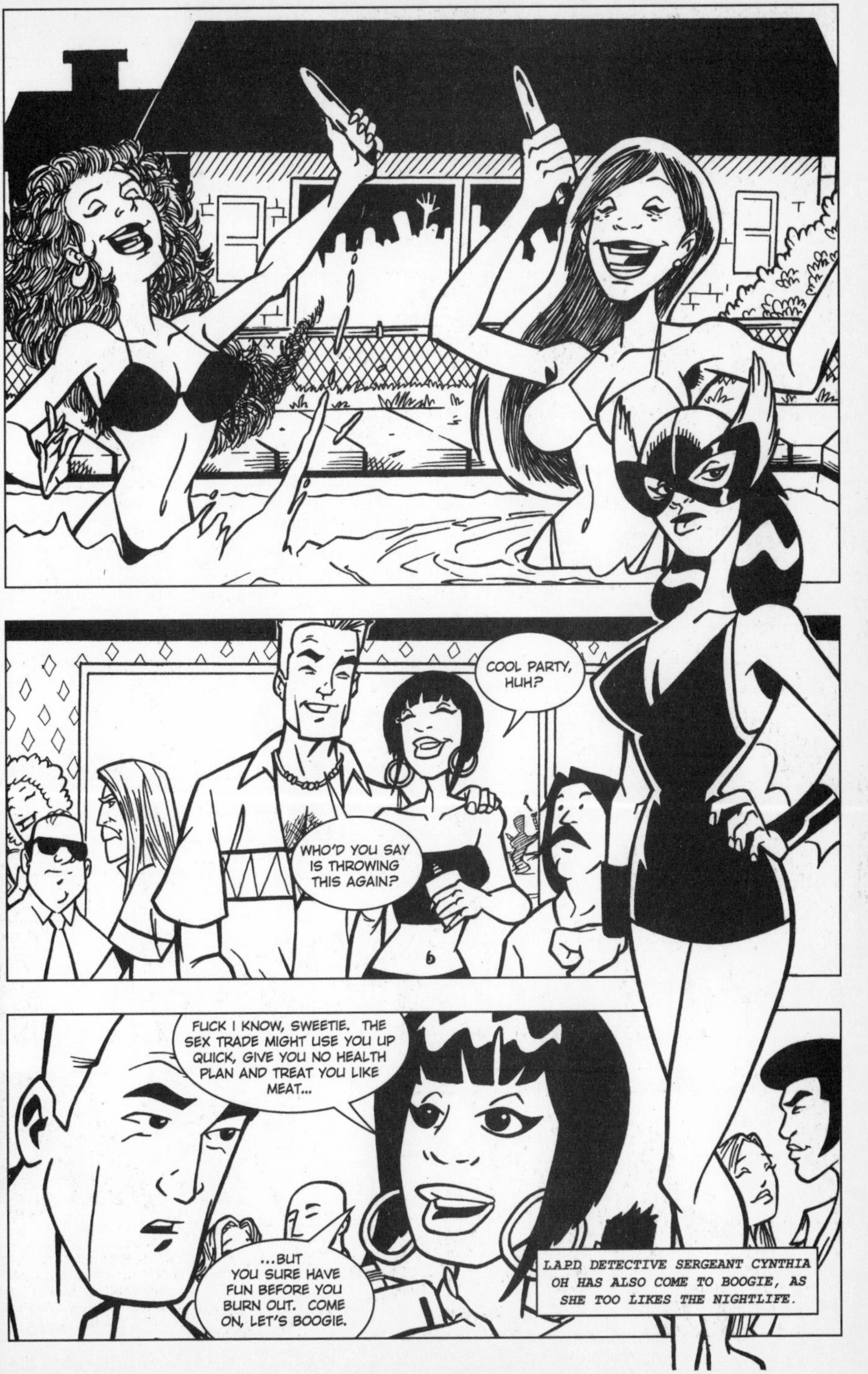
COOL PARTY, HUH?
WHO'D YOU SAY IS THROWING THIS AGAIN?
FUCK I KNOW, SWEETIE. THE SEX TRADE MIGHT USE YOU UP QUICK, GIVE YOU NO HEALTH PLAN AND TREAT YOU LIKE MEAT...
...BUT YOU SURE HAVE FUN BEFORE YOU BURN OUT. COME ON, LET'S BOOGIE.
L.A.P.D. DETECTIVE SERGEANT CYNTHIA OH HAS ALSO COME TO BOOGIE, AS SHE TOO LIKES THE NIGHTLIFE.

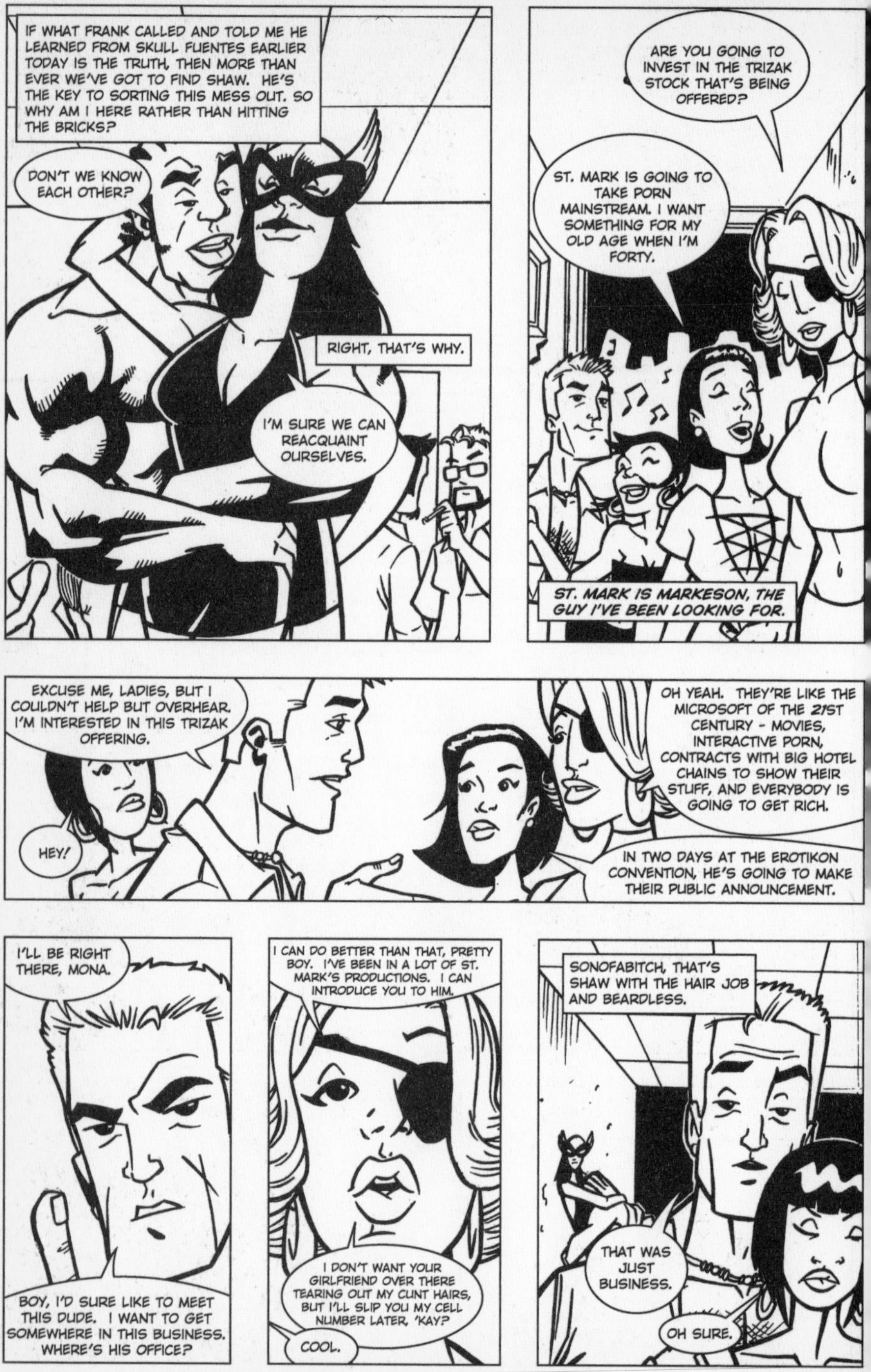
IF WHAT FRANK CALLED AND TOLD ME HE LEARNED FROM SKULL FUENTES EARLIER TODAY IS THE TRUTH, THEN MORE THAN EVER WE'VE GOT TO FIND SHAW. HE'S THE KEY TO SORTING THIS MESS OUT. SO WHY AM I HERE RATHER THAN HITTING THE BRICKS?
DON'T WE KNOW EACH OTHER?
RIGHT, THAT'S WHY.
I'M SURE WE CAN REACQUAINT OURSELVES.
ARE YOU GOING TO INVEST IN THE TRIZAK STOCK THAT'S BEING OFFERED?
ST. MARK IS GOING TO TAKE PORN MAINSTREAM. I WANT SOMETHING FOR MY OLD AGE WHEN I'M FORTY.
ST. MARK IS MARKESON, THE GUY I'VE BEEN LOOKING FOR.
EXCUSE ME, LADIES, BUT I COULDN'T HELP BUT OVERHEAR. I'M INTERESTED IN THIS TRIZAK OFFERING.
HEY!
OH YEAH. THEY'RE LIKE THE MICROSOFT OF THE 21ST CENTURY - MOVIES, INTERACTIVE PORN, CONTRACTS WITH BIG HOTEL CHAINS TO SHOW THEIR STUFF, AND EVERYBODY IS GOING TO GET RICH.
IN TWO DAYS AT THE EROTIKON CONVENTION, HE'S GOING TO MAKE THEIR PUBLIC ANNOUNCEMENT.
I'LL BE RIGHT THERE, MONA.
BOY, I'D SURE LIKE TO MEET THIS DUDE. I WANT TO GET SOMEWHERE IN THIS BUSINESS. WHERE'S HIS OFFICE?
I CAN DO BETTER THAN THAT, PRETTY BOY. I'VE BEEN IN A LOT OF ST. MARK'S PRODUCTIONS. I CAN INTRODUCE YOU TO HIM.
I DON'T WANT YOUR GIRLFRIEND OVER THERE TEARING OUT MY CUNT HAIRS, BUT I'LL SLIP YOU MY CELL NUMBER LATER, 'KAY?
COOL.
SONOFABITCH, THAT'S SHAW WITH THE HAIR JOB AND BEARDLESS.
THAT WAS JUST BUSINESS.
OH SURE.

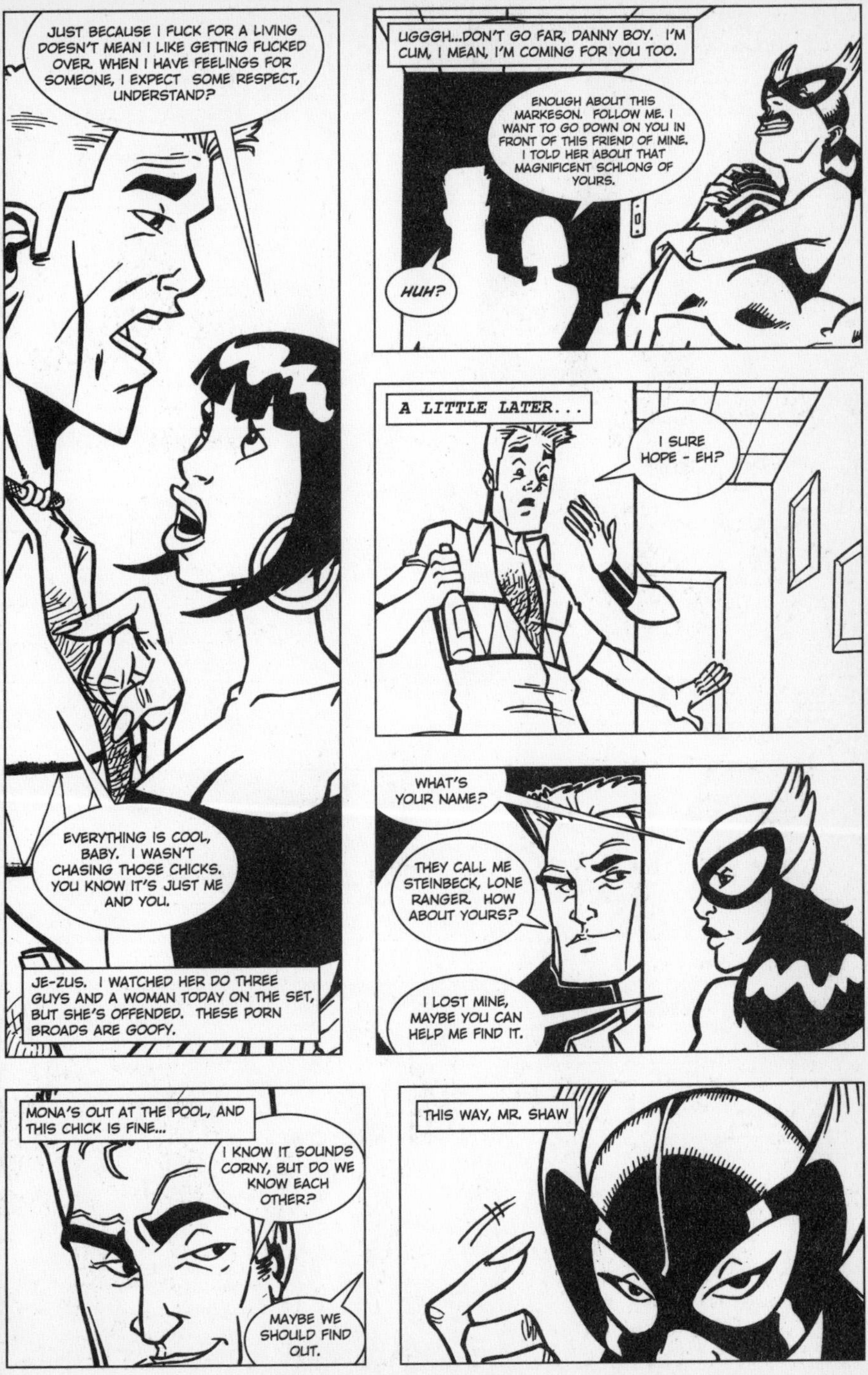
JUST BECAUSE I FUCK FOR A LIVING DOESN'T MEAN I LIKE GETTING FUCKED OVER. WHEN I HAVE FEELINGS FOR SOMEONE, I EXPECT SOME RESPECT, UNDERSTAND?
EVERYTHING IS COOL, BABY. I WASN'T CHASING THOSE CHICKS. YOU KNOW IT'S JUST ME AND YOU.
JE-ZUS. I WATCHED HER DO THREE GUYS AND A WOMAN TODAY ON THE SET, BUT SHE'S OFFENDED. THESE PORN BROADS ARE GOOFY.
UGGGH...DON'T GO FAR, DANNY BOY. I'M CUM, I MEAN, I'M COMING FOR YOU TOO.
ENOUGH ABOUT THIS MARKESON. FOLLOW ME. I WANT TO GO DOWN ON YOU IN FRONT OF THIS FRIEND OF MINE. I TOLD HER ABOUT THAT MAGNIFICENT SCHLONG OF YOURS.
HUH?
A LITTLE LATER...
I SURE HOPE - EH?
WHAT'S YOUR NAME?
THEY CALL ME STEINBECK, LONE RANGER. HOW ABOUT YOURS?
I LOST MINE, MAYBE YOU CAN HELP ME FIND IT.
MONA'S OUT AT THE POOL, AND THIS CHICK IS FINE...
I KNOW IT SOUNDS CORNY, BUT DO WE KNOW EACH OTHER?
MAYBE WE SHOULD FIND OUT.
THIS WAY, MR. SHAW

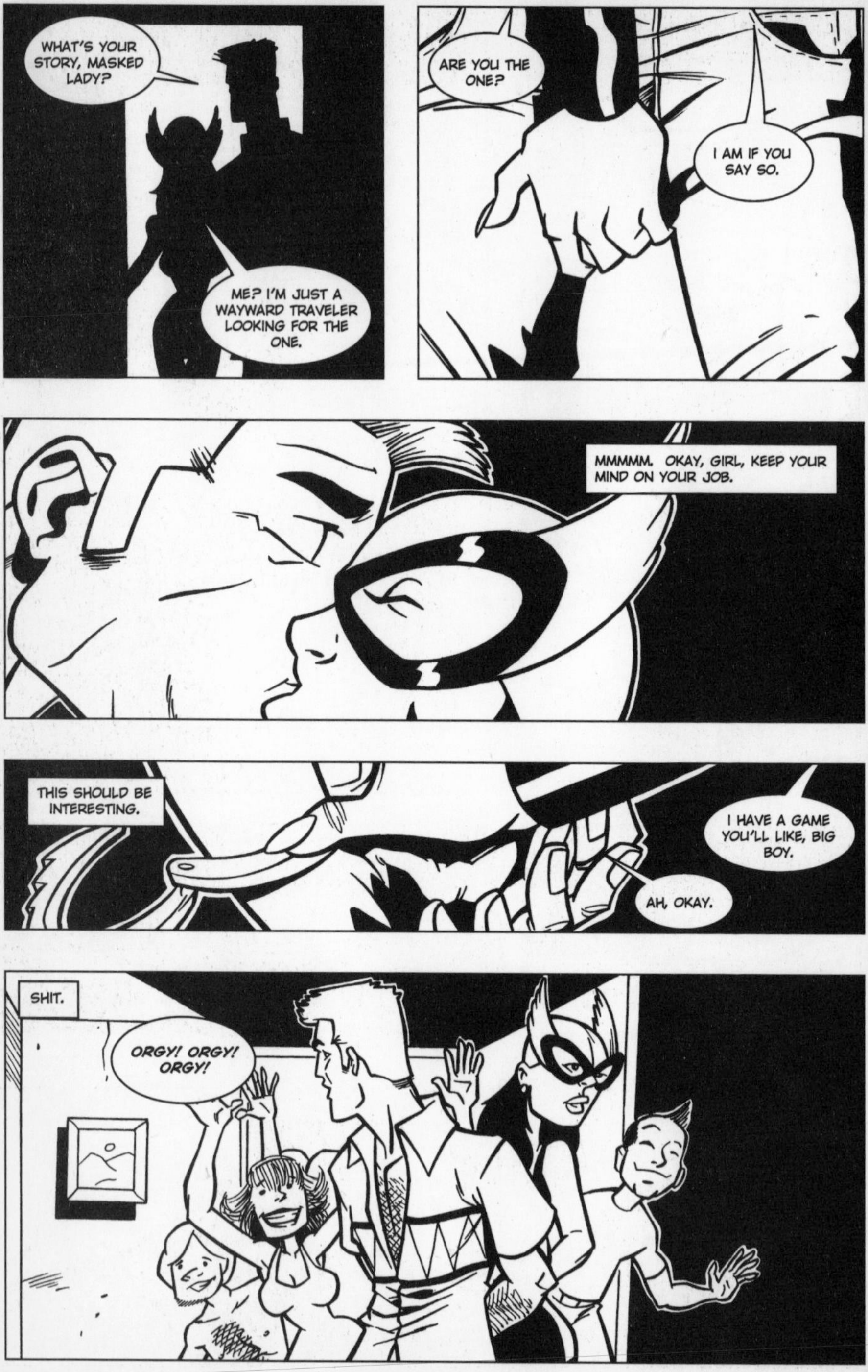
WHAT'S YOUR STORY, MASKED LADY?
ME? I'M JUST A WAYWARD TRAVELER LOOKING FOR THE ONE.
ARE YOU THE ONE?
I AM IF YOU SAY SO.
MMMMM. OKAY, GIRL, KEEP YOUR MIND ON YOUR JOB.
THIS SHOULD BE INTERESTING.
I HAVE A GAME YOU'LL LIKE, BIG BOY.
AH, OKAY.
SHIT.
ORGY! ORGY! ORGY!

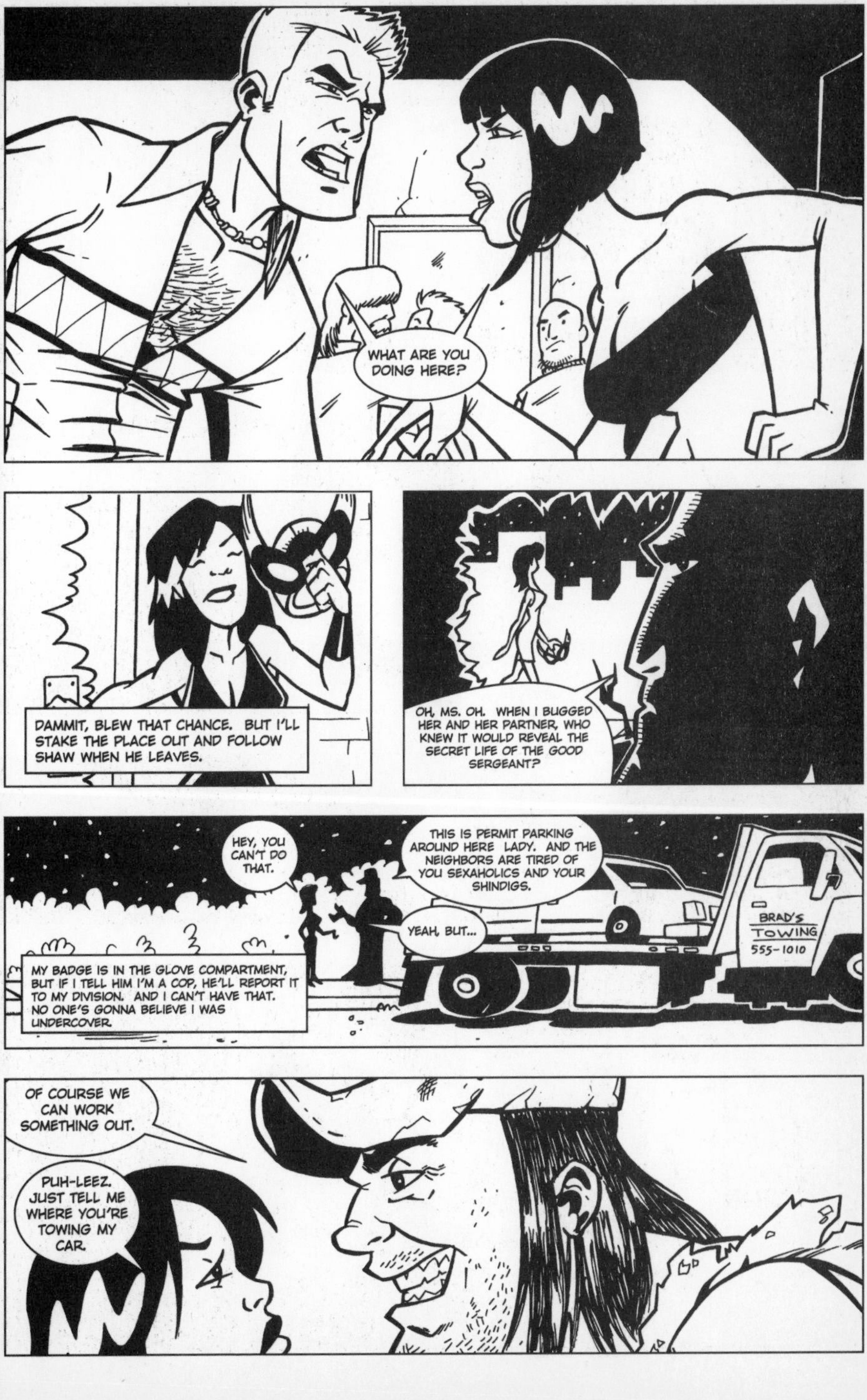
WHAT ARE YOU DOING HERE?
DAMMIT, BLEW THAT CHANCE. BUT I'LL STAKE THE PLACE OUT AND FOLLOW SHAW WHEN HE LEAVES.
OH, MS. OH. WHEN I BUGGED HER AND HER PARTNER, WHO KNEW IT WOULD REVEAL THE SECRET LIFE OF THE GOOD SERGEANT?
HEY, YOU CAN'T DO THAT.
THIS IS PERMIT PARKING AROUND HERE LADY. AND THE NEIGHBORS ARE TIRED OF YOU SEXAHOLICS AND YOUR SHINDIGS.
YEAH, BUT...
BRAD'S TOWING 555-1010
MY BADGE IS IN THE GLOVE COMPARTMENT, BUT IF I TELL HIM I'M A COP, HE'LL REPORT IT TO MY DIVISION. AND I CAN'T HAVE THAT. NO ONE'S GONNA BELIEVE I WAS UNDERCOVER.
OF COURSE WE CAN WORK SOMETHING OUT.
PUH-LEEZ. JUST TELL ME WHERE YOU'RE TOWING MY CAR.

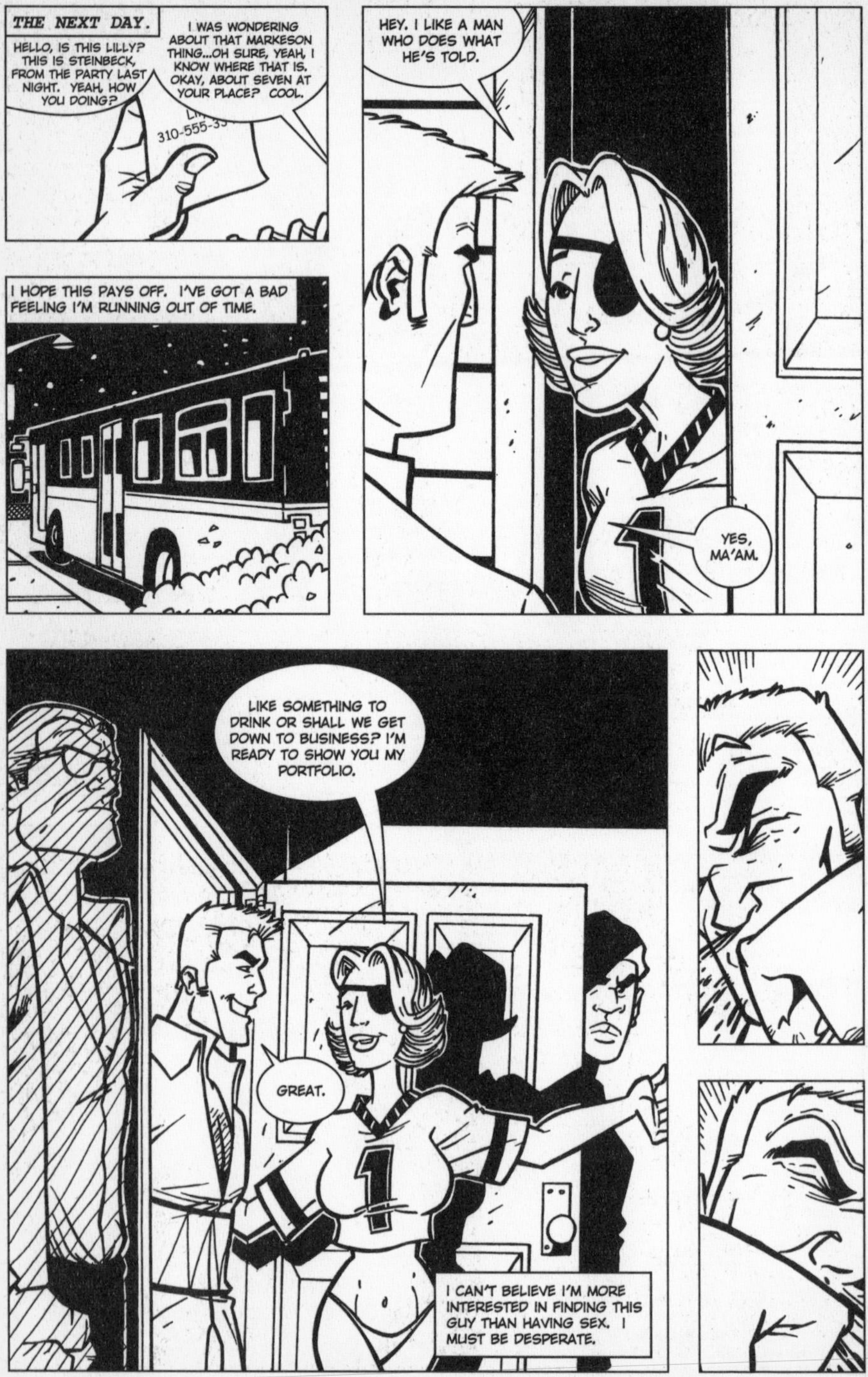
THE NEXT DAY.
HELLO, IS THIS LILLY? THIS IS STEINBECK, FROM THE PARTY LAST NIGHT. YEAH, HOW YOU DOING?
I WAS WONDERING ABOUT THAT MARKESON THING...OH SURE, YEAH, I KNOW WHERE THAT IS. OKAY, ABOUT SEVEN AT YOUR PLACE? COOL.
HEY. I LIKE A MAN WHO DOES WHAT HE'S TOLD.
YES, MA'AM.
I HOPE THIS PAYS OFF. I'VE GOT A BAD FEELING I'M RUNNING OUT OF TIME.
LIKE SOMETHING TO DRINK OR SHALL WE GET DOWN TO BUSINESS? I'M READY TO SHOW YOU MY PORTFOLIO.
GREAT.
I CAN'T BELIEVE I'M MORE INTERESTED IN FINDING THIS GUY THAN HAVING SEX. I MUST BE DESPERATE.

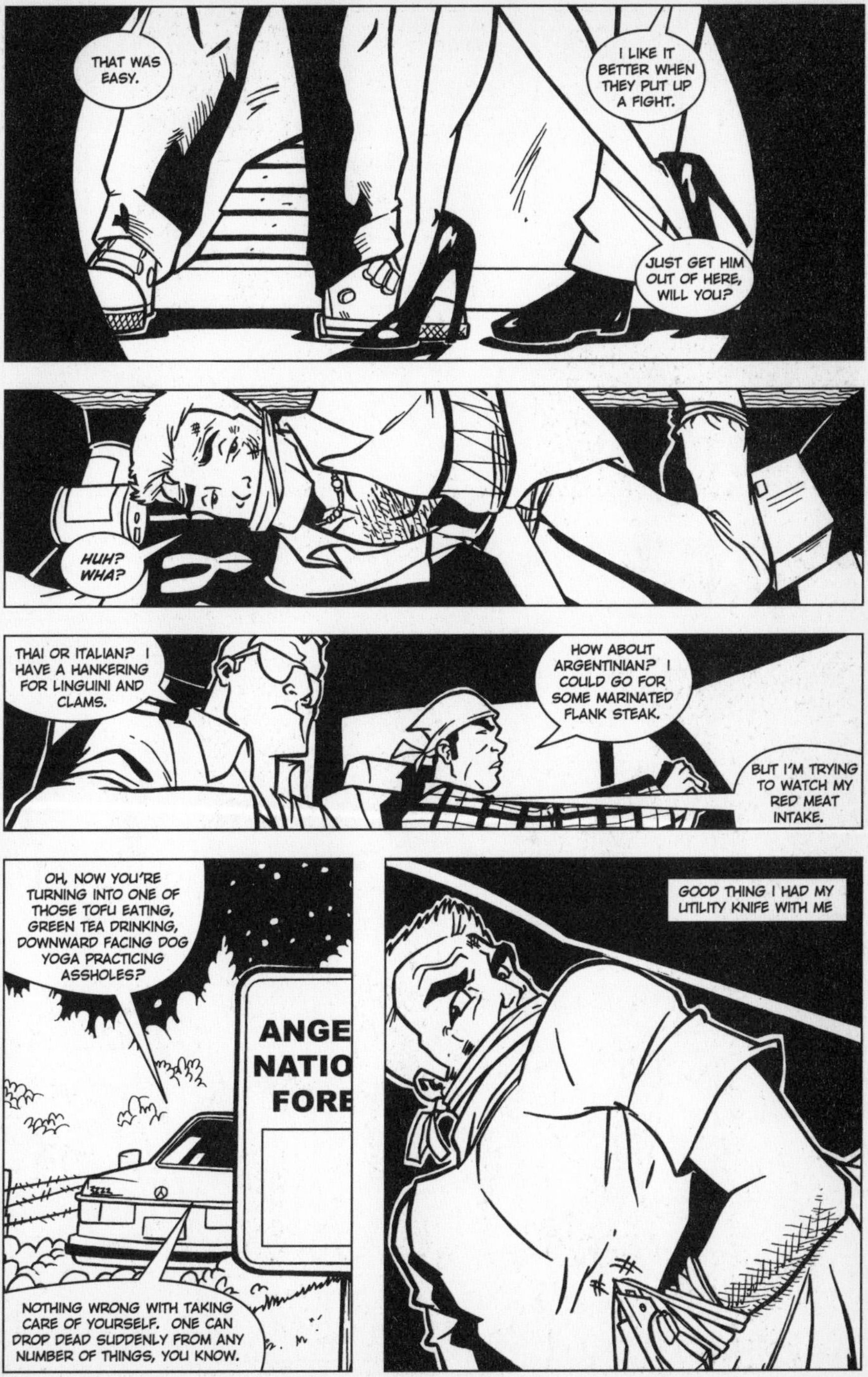
THAT WAS EASY.
I LIKE IT BETTER WHEN THEY PUT UP A FIGHT.
JUST GET HIM OUT OF HERE, WILL YOU?
HUH? WHA?
THAI OR ITALIAN? I HAVE A HANKERING FOR LINGUINI AND CLAMS.
HOW ABOUT ARGENTINIAN? I COULD GO FOR SOME MARINATED FLANK STEAK.
BUT I'M TRYING TO WATCH MY RED MEAT INTAKE.
OH, NOW YOU'RE TURNING INTO ONE OF THOSE TOFU EATING, GREEN TEA DRINKING, DOWNWARD FACING DOG YOGA PRACTICING ASSHOLES?
ANGE
NATIO
FORE
NOTHING WRONG WITH TAKING CARE OF YOURSELF. ONE CAN DROP DEAD SUDDENLY FROM ANY NUMBER OF THINGS, YOU KNOW.
GOOD THING I HAD MY UTILITY KNIFE WITH ME

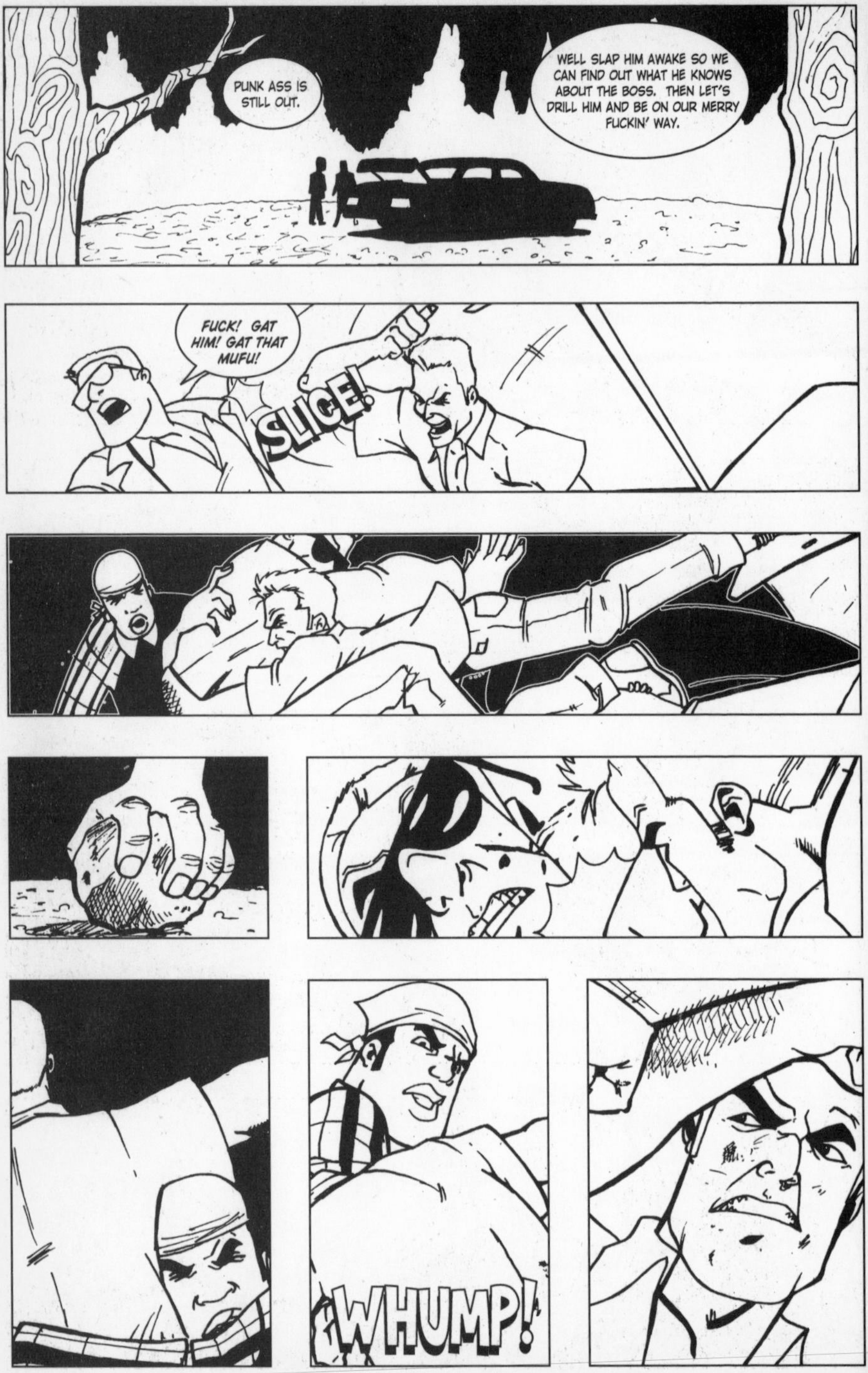
PUNK ASS IS STILL OUT.
WELL SLAP HIM AWAKE SO WE CAN FIND OUT WHAT HE KNOWS ABOUT THE BOSS. THEN LET'S DRILL HIM AND BE ON OUR MERRY FUCKIN' WAY.
FUCK! GAT HIM! GAT THAT MUFU!
SLICE!
WHUMP!

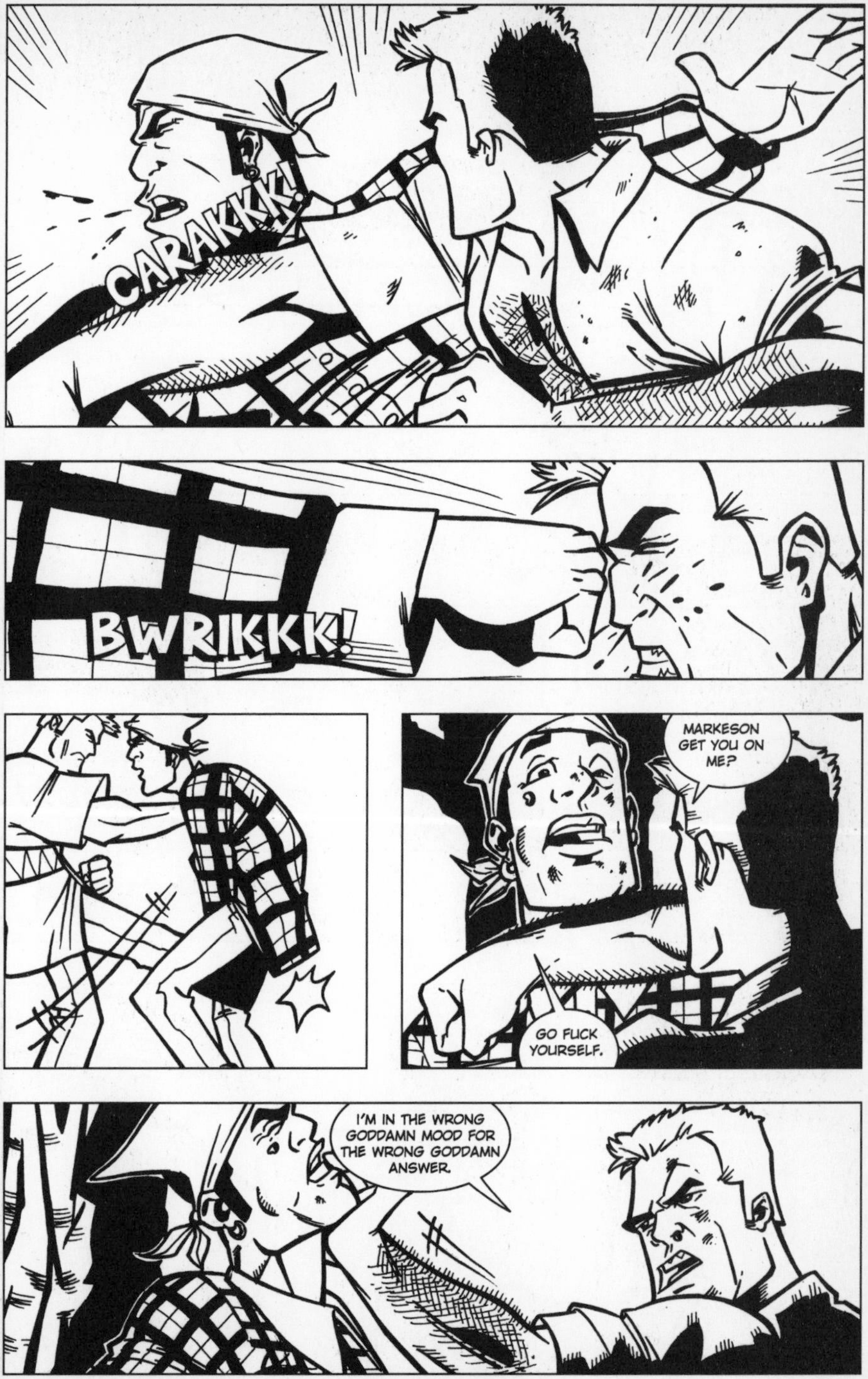

CARAKKK!
BWRIKKK!
MARKESON GET YOU ON ME?
GO FUCK YOURSELF.
I'M IN THE WRONG GODDAMN MOOD FOR THE WRONG GODDAMN ANSWER.

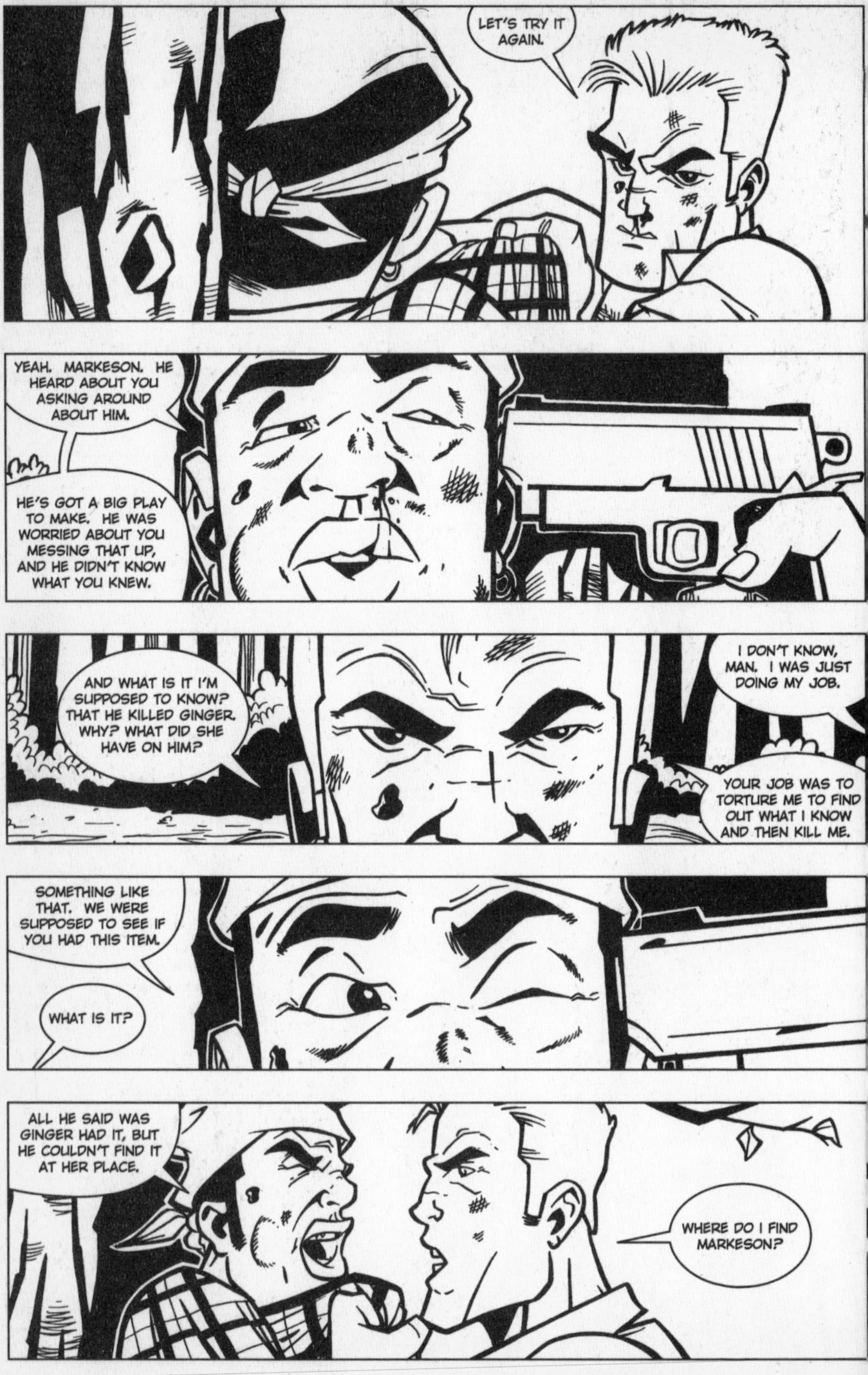
LET'S TRY IT AGAIN.
YEAH. MARKESON. HE HEARD ABOUT YOU ASKING AROUND ABOUT HIM.
HE'S GOT A BIG PLAY TO MAKE. HE WAS WORRIED ABOUT YOU MESSING THAT UP, AND HE DIDN'T KNOW WHAT YOU KNEW.
AND WHAT IS IT I'M SUPPOSED TO KNOW? THAT HE KILLED GINGER. WHY? WHAT DID SHE HAVE ON HIM?
I DON'T KNOW, MAN. I WAS JUST DOING MY JOB.
YOUR JOB WAS TO TORTURE ME TO FIND OUT WHAT I KNOW AND THEN KILL ME.
SOMETHING LIKE THAT. WE WERE SUPPOSED TO SEE IF YOU HAD THIS ITEM.
WHAT IS IT?
ALL HE SAID WAS GINGER HAD IT, BUT HE COULDN'T FIND IT AT HER PLACE.
WHERE DO I FIND MARKESON?

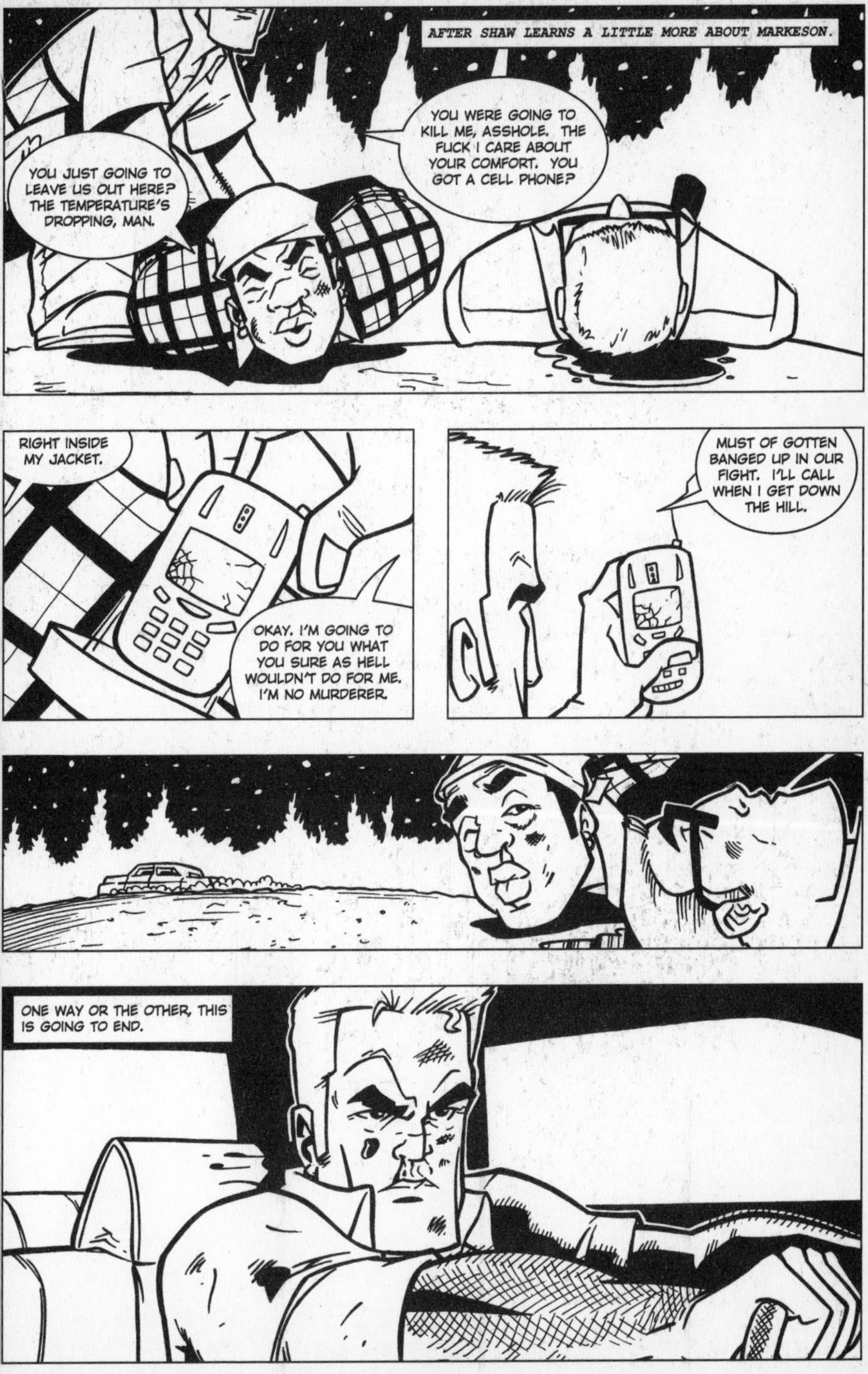
AFTER SHAW LEARNS A LITTLE MORE ABOUT MARKESON.
YOU JUST GOING TO LEAVE US OUT HERE? THE TEMPERATURE'S DROPPING, MAN.
YOU WERE GOING TO KILL ME, ASSHOLE. THE FUCK I CARE ABOUT YOUR COMFORT. YOU GOT A CELL PHONE?
RIGHT INSIDE MY JACKET.
OKAY. I'M GOING TO DO FOR YOU WHAT YOU SURE AS HELL WOULDN'T DO FOR ME. I'M NO MURDERER.
MUST OF GOTTEN BANGED UP IN OUR FIGHT. I'LL CALL WHEN I GET DOWN THE HILL.
ONE WAY OR THE OTHER, THIS IS GOING TO END.

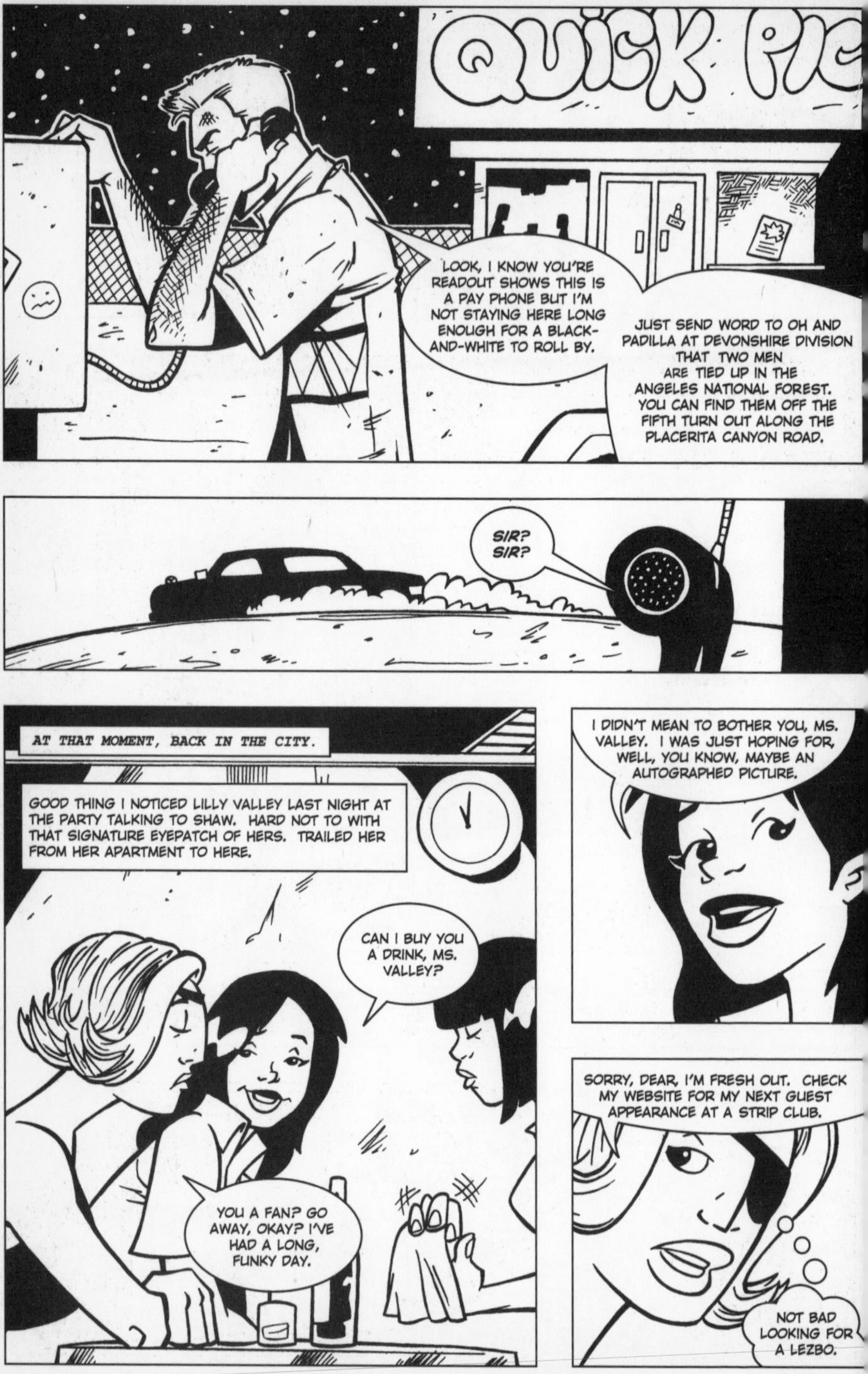
QUICK PIC
LOOK, I KNOW YOU'RE READOUT SHOWS THIS IS A PAY PHONE BUT I'M NOT STAYING HERE LONG ENOUGH FOR A BLACK-AND-WHITE TO ROLL BY.
JUST SEND WORD TO OH AND PADILLA AT DEVONSHIRE DIVISION THAT TWO MEN ARE TIED UP IN THE ANGELES NATIONAL FOREST. YOU CAN FIND THEM OFF THE FIFTH TURN OUT ALONG THE PLACERITA CANYON ROAD.
SIR? SIR?
AT THAT MOMENT, BACK IN THE CITY.
GOOD THING I NOTICED LILLY VALLEY LAST NIGHT AT THE PARTY TALKING TO SHAW. HARD NOT TO WITH THAT SIGNATURE EYEPATCH OF HERS. TRAILED HER FROM HER APARTMENT TO HERE.
CAN I BUY YOU A DRINK, MS. VALLEY?
YOU A FAN? GO AWAY, OKAY? I'VE HAD A LONG, FUNKY DAY.
I DIDN'T MEAN TO BOTHER YOU, MS. VALLEY. I WAS JUST HOPING FOR, WELL, YOU KNOW, MAYBE AN AUTOGRAPHED PICTURE.
SORRY, DEAR, I'M FRESH OUT. CHECK MY WEBSITE FOR MY NEXT GUEST APPEARANCE AT A STRIP CLUB.
NOT BAD LOOKING FOR A LEZBO.

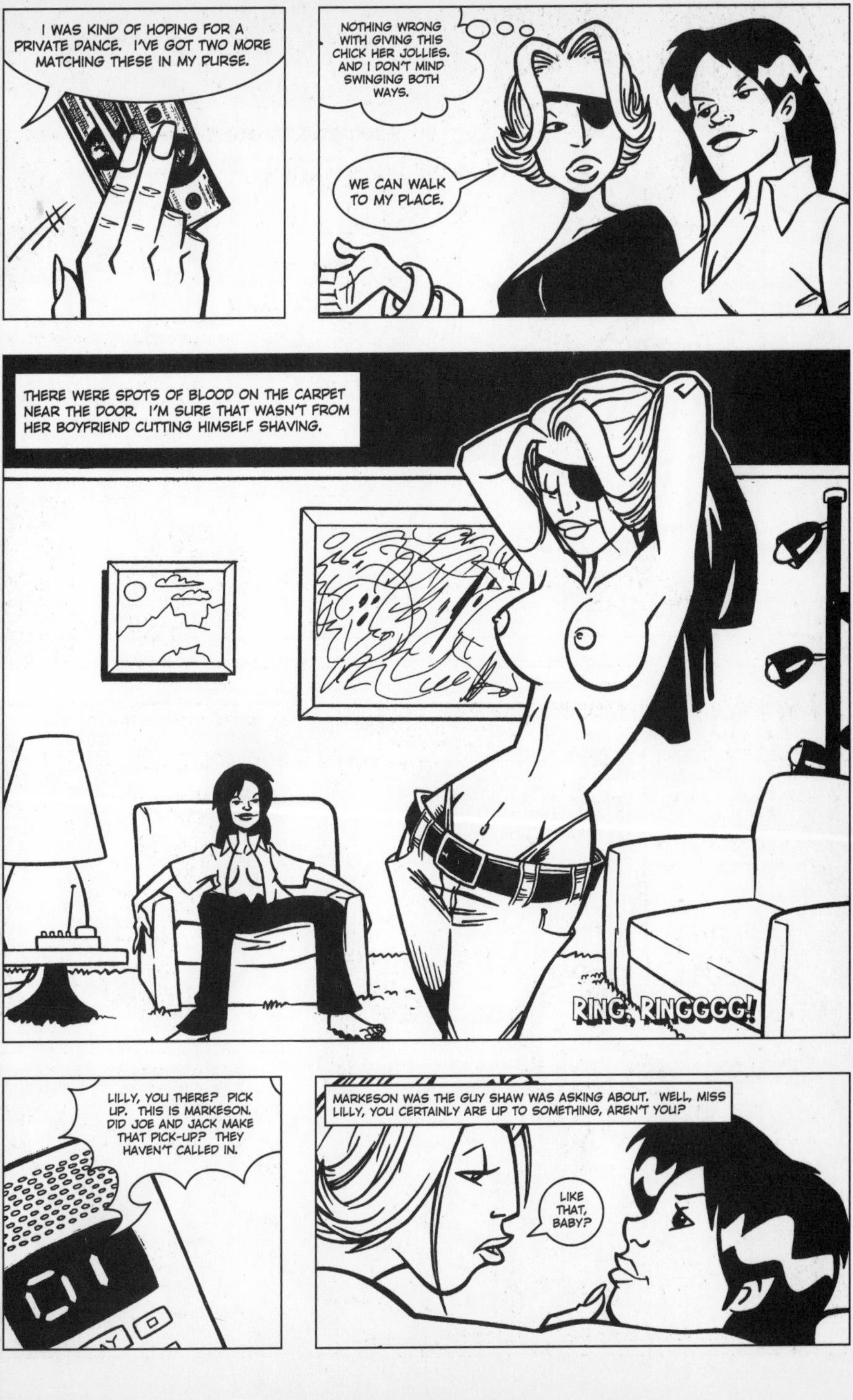
I WAS KIND OF HOPING FOR A PRIVATE DANCE. I'VE GOT TWO MORE MATCHING THESE IN MY PURSE.
NOTHING WRONG WITH GIVING THIS CHICK HER JOLLIES. AND I DON'T MIND SWINGING BOTH WAYS.
WE CAN WALK TO MY PLACE.
THERE WERE SPOTS OF BLOOD ON THE CARPET NEAR THE DOOR. I'M SURE THAT WASN'T FROM HER BOYFRIEND CUTTING HIMSELF SHAVING.
RING, RINGGGG!
LILLY, YOU THERE? PICK UP. THIS IS MARKESON. DID JOE AND JACK MAKE THAT PICK-UP? THEY HAVEN'T CALLED IN.
MARKESON WAS THE GUY SHAW WAS ASKING ABOUT. WELL, MISS LILLY, YOU CERTAINLY ARE UP TO SOMETHING, AREN'T YOU?
LIKE THAT, BABY?

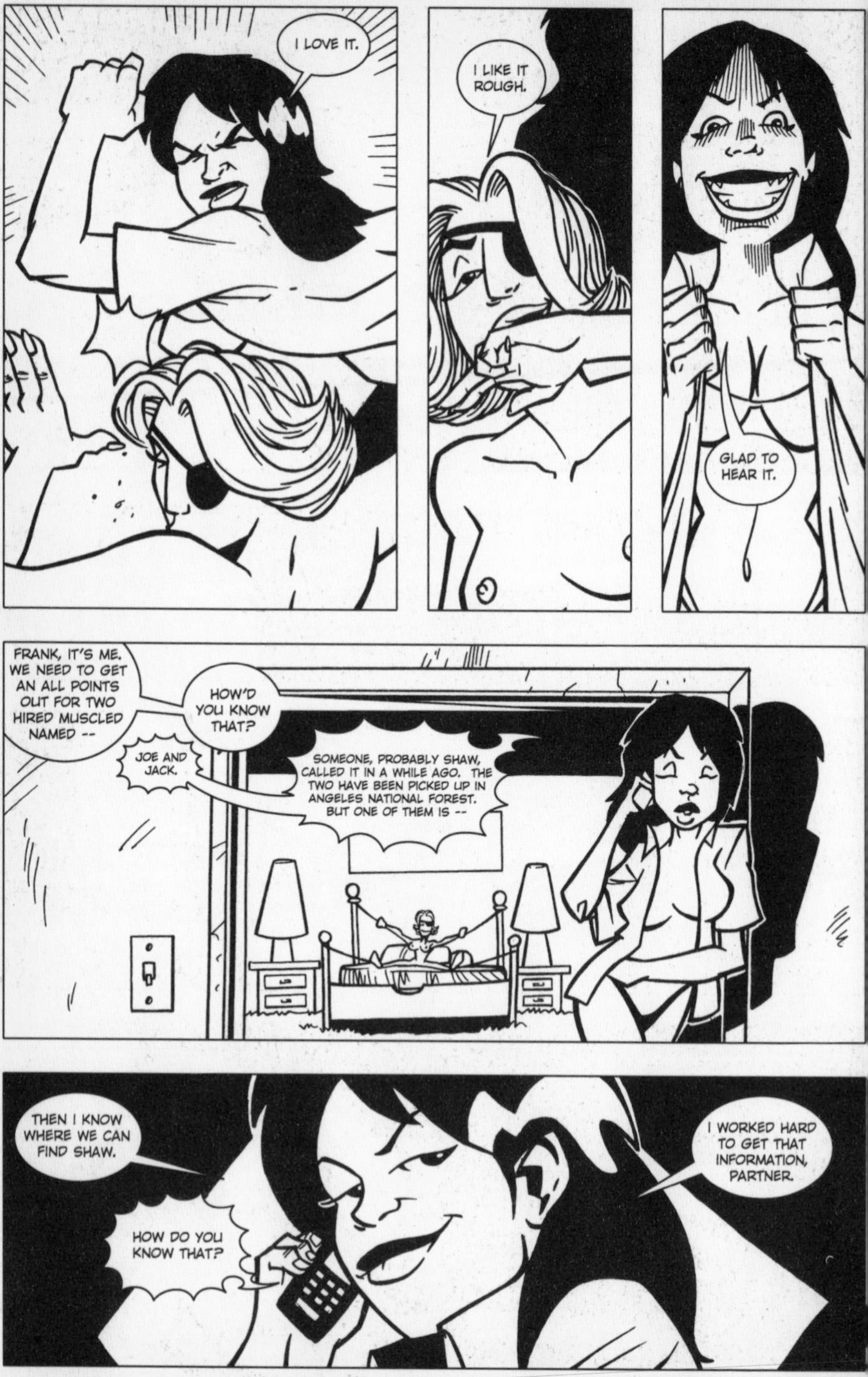

I LOVE IT.
I LIKE IT ROUGH.
GLAD TO HEAR IT.
FRANK, IT'S ME. WE NEED TO GET AN ALL POINTS OUT FOR TWO HIRED MUSCLED NAMED --
HOW'D YOU KNOW THAT?
JOE AND JACK.
SOMEONE, PROBABLY SHAW, CALLED IT IN A WHILE AGO. THE TWO HAVE BEEN PICKED UP IN ANGELES NATIONAL FOREST. BUT ONE OF THEM IS --
THEN I KNOW WHERE WE CAN FIND SHAW.
HOW DO YOU KNOW THAT?
I WORKED HARD TO GET THAT INFORMATION, PARTNER.

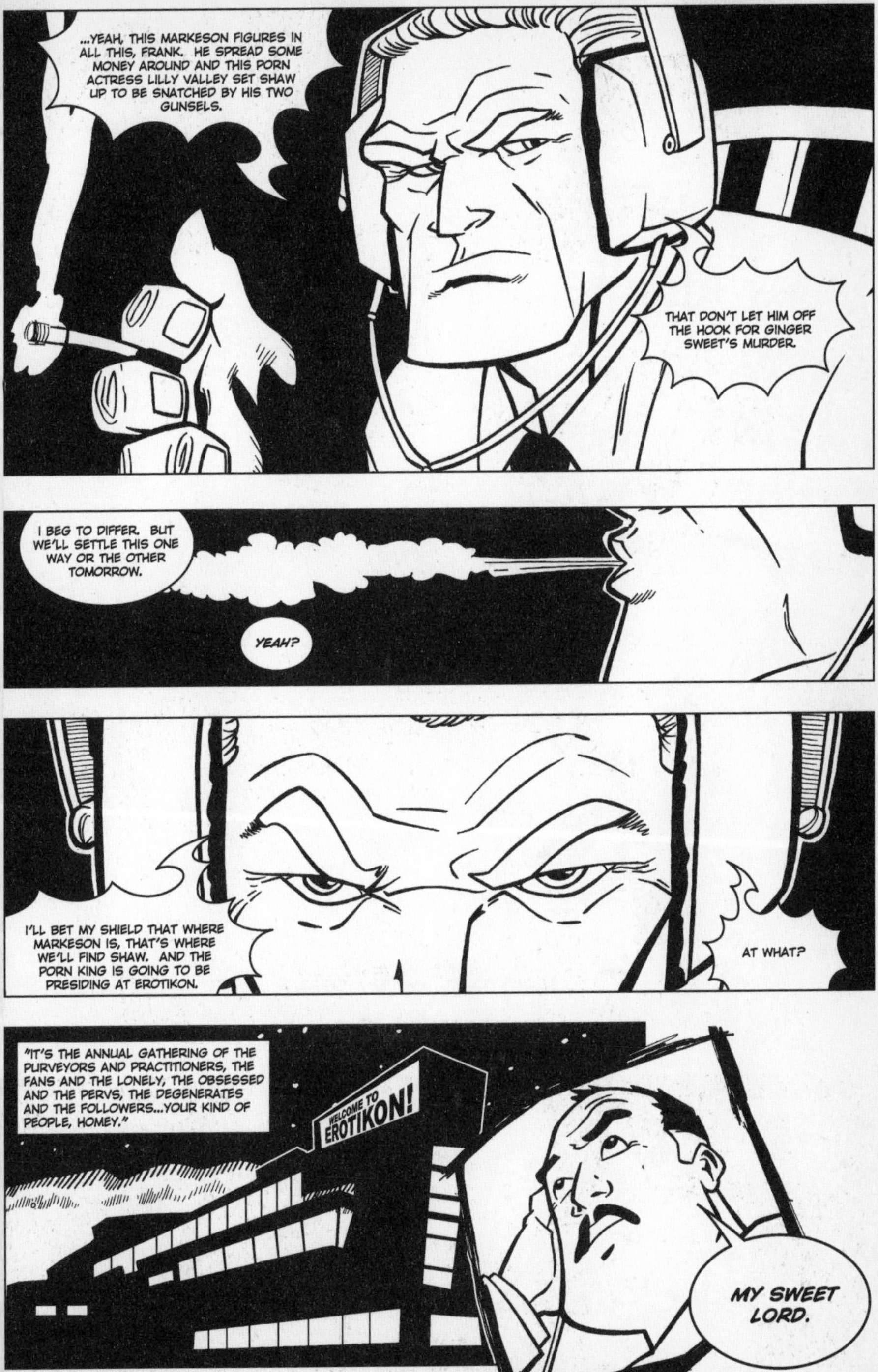
...YEAH, THIS MARKESON FIGURES IN ALL THIS, FRANK. HE SPREAD SOME MONEY AROUND AND THIS PORN ACTRESS LILLY VALLEY SET SHAW UP TO BE SNATCHED BY HIS TWO GUNSELS.
THAT DON'T LET HIM OFF THE HOOK FOR GINGER SWEET'S MURDER.
I BEG TO DIFFER. BUT WE'LL SETTLE THIS ONE WAY OR THE OTHER TOMORROW.
YEAH?
I'LL BET MY SHIELD THAT WHERE MARKESON IS, THAT'S WHERE WE'LL FIND SHAW. AND THE PORN KING IS GOING TO BE PRESIDING AT EROTIKON.
AT WHAT?
"IT'S THE ANNUAL GATHERING OF THE PURVEYORS AND PRACTITIONERS, THE FANS AND THE LONELY, THE OBSESSED AND THE PERVS, THE DEGENERATES AND THE FOLLOWERS...YOUR KIND OF PEOPLE, HOMEY."
WELCOME TO EROTIKON!
MY SWEET LORD.

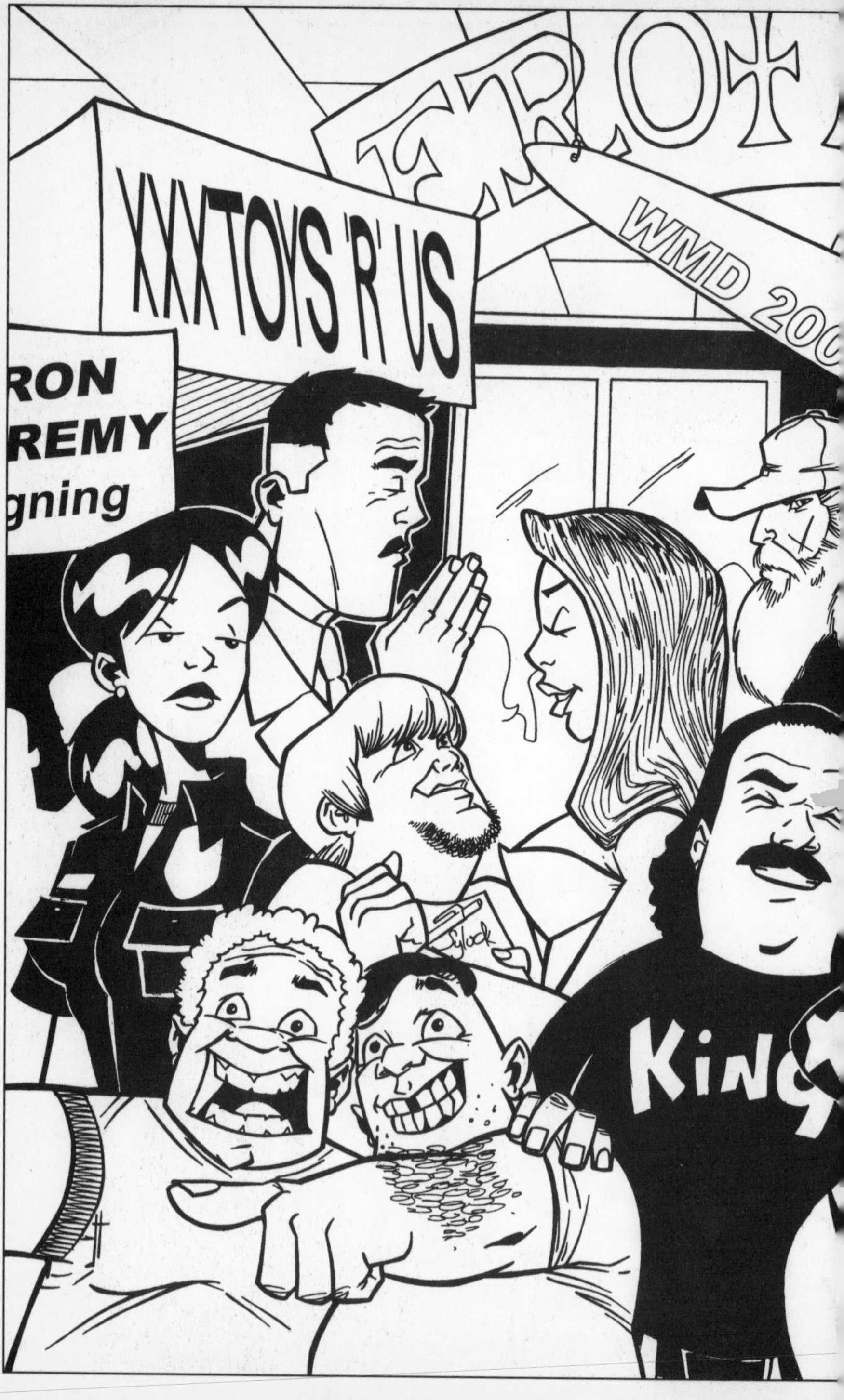
XXXTOYS 'R' US
RON
REMY
gning
WMD 200
Sylock
King

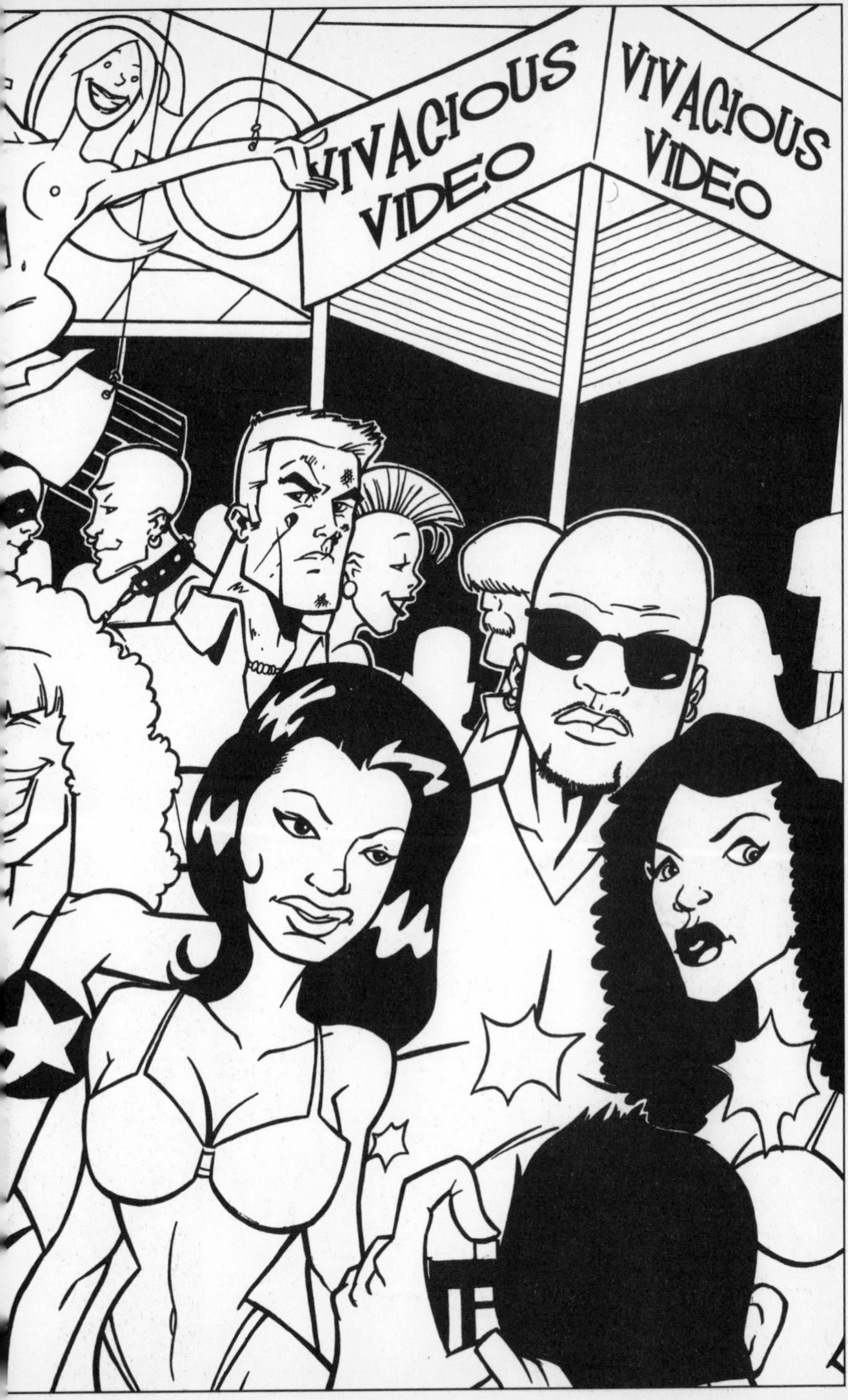
VIVACIOUS VIDEO
VIVACIOUS VIDEO

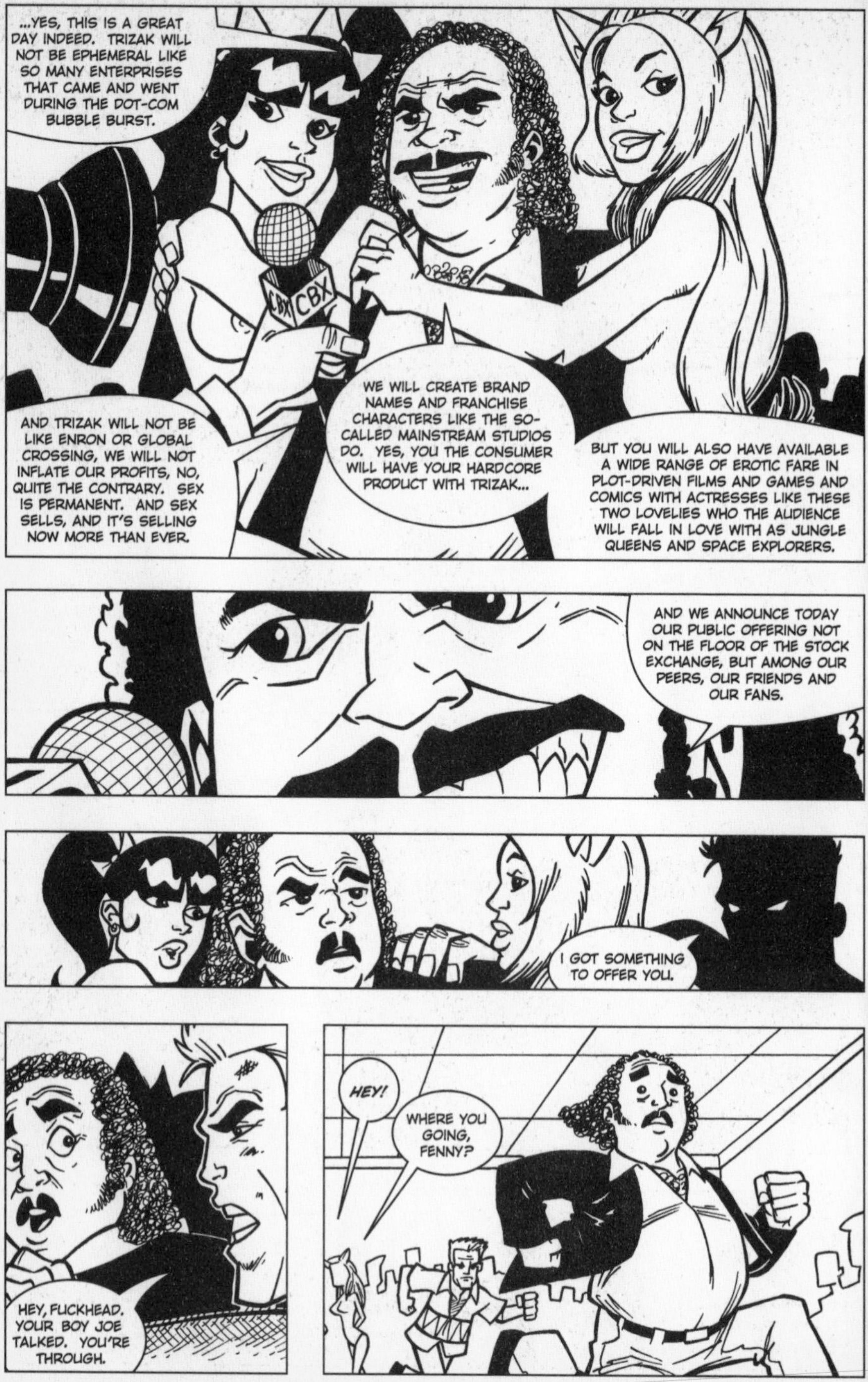
...YES, THIS IS A GREAT DAY INDEED. TRIZAK WILL NOT BE EPHEMERAL LIKE SO MANY ENTERPRISES THAT CAME AND WENT DURING THE DOT-COM BUBBLE BURST.
CBX
WE WILL CREATE BRAND NAMES AND FRANCHISE CHARACTERS LIKE THE SO-CALLED MAINSTREAM STUDIOS DO. YES, YOU THE CONSUMER WILL HAVE YOUR HARDCORE PRODUCT WITH TRIZAK...
AND TRIZAK WILL NOT BE LIKE ENRON OR GLOBAL CROSSING, WE WILL NOT INFLATE OUR PROFITS, NO, QUITE THE CONTRARY. SEX IS PERMANENT. AND SEX SELLS, AND IT'S SELLING NOW MORE THAN EVER.
BUT YOU WILL ALSO HAVE AVAILABLE A WIDE RANGE OF EROTIC FARE IN PLOT-DRIVEN FILMS AND GAMES AND COMICS WITH ACTRESSES LIKE THESE TWO LOVELIES WHO THE AUDIENCE WILL FALL IN LOVE WITH AS JUNGLE QUEENS AND SPACE EXPLORERS.
AND WE ANNOUNCE TODAY OUR PUBLIC OFFERING NOT ON THE FLOOR OF THE STOCK EXCHANGE, BUT AMONG OUR PEERS, OUR FRIENDS AND OUR FANS.
I GOT SOMETHING TO OFFER YOU.
HEY, FUCKHEAD. YOUR BOY JOE TALKED. YOU'RE THROUGH.
HEY!
WHERE YOU GOING, FENNY?

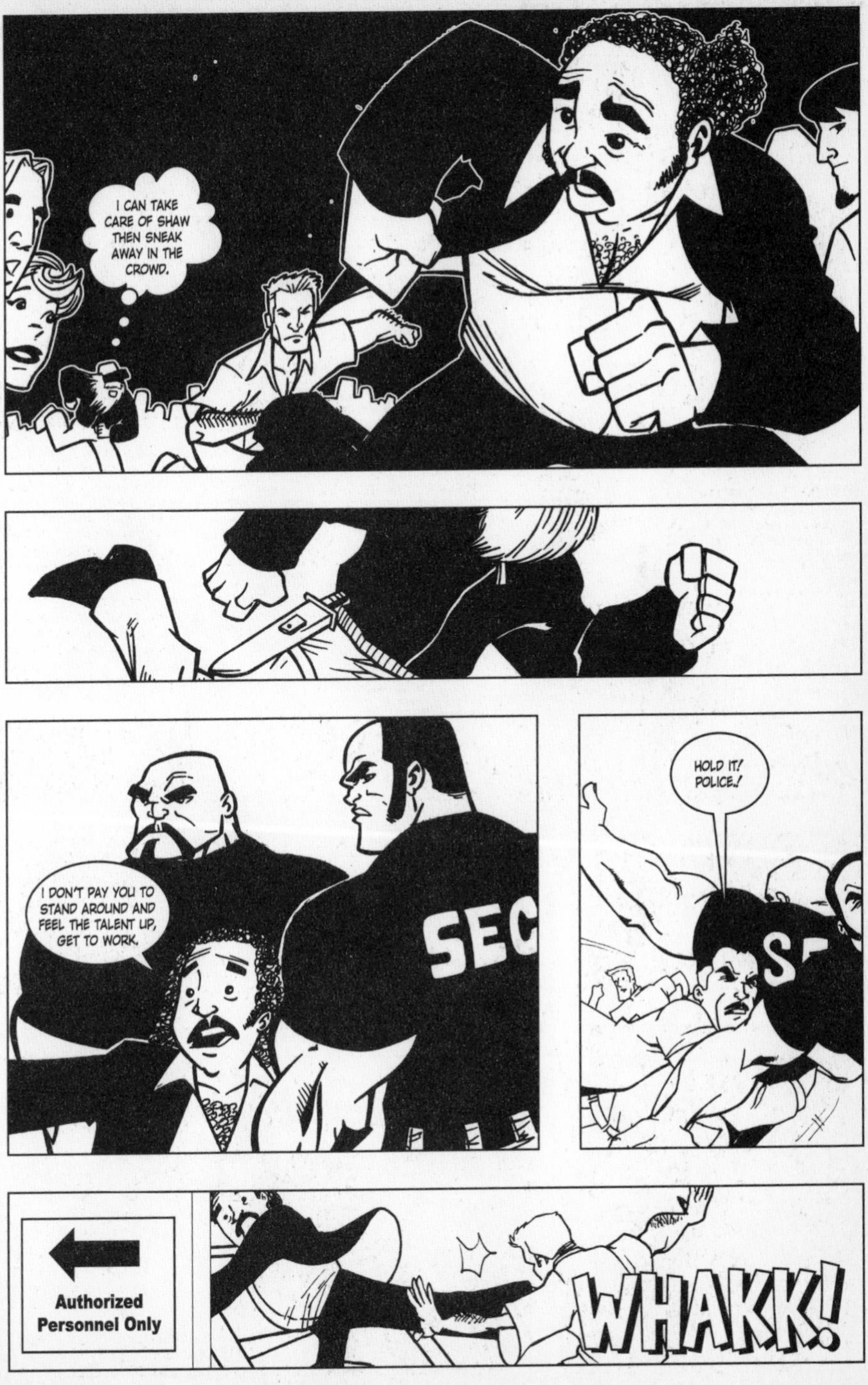
I CAN TAKE CARE OF SHAW THEN SNEAK AWAY IN THE CROWD.
I DON'T PAY YOU TO STAND AROUND AND FEEL THE TALENT UP, GET TO WORK.
SEC
HOLD IT! POLICE.!
Authorized Personnel Only
WHAKK!

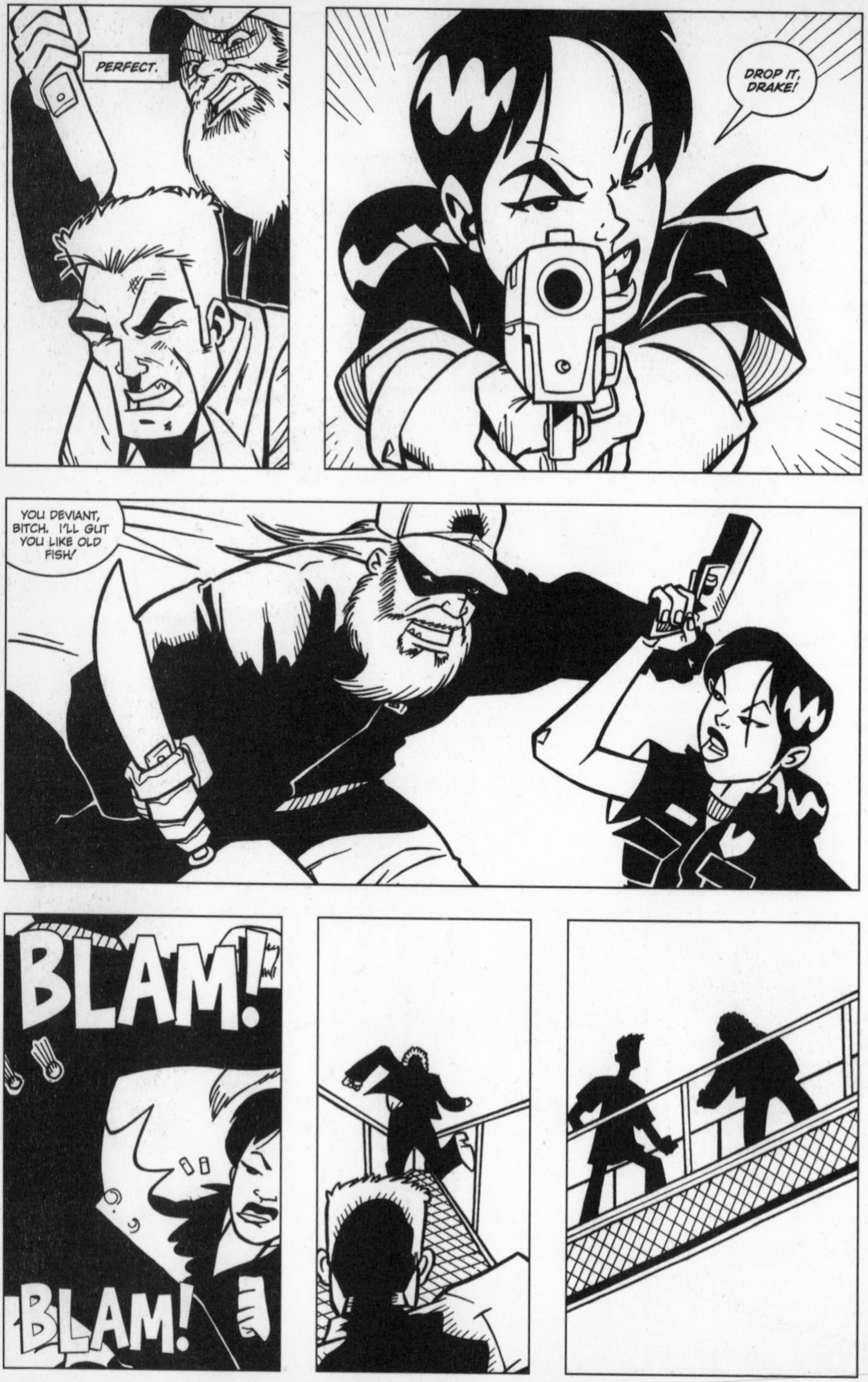
PERFECT.
DROP IT, DRAKE!
YOU DEVIANT, BITCH. I'LL GUT YOU LIKE OLD FISH!
BLAM!
BLAM!

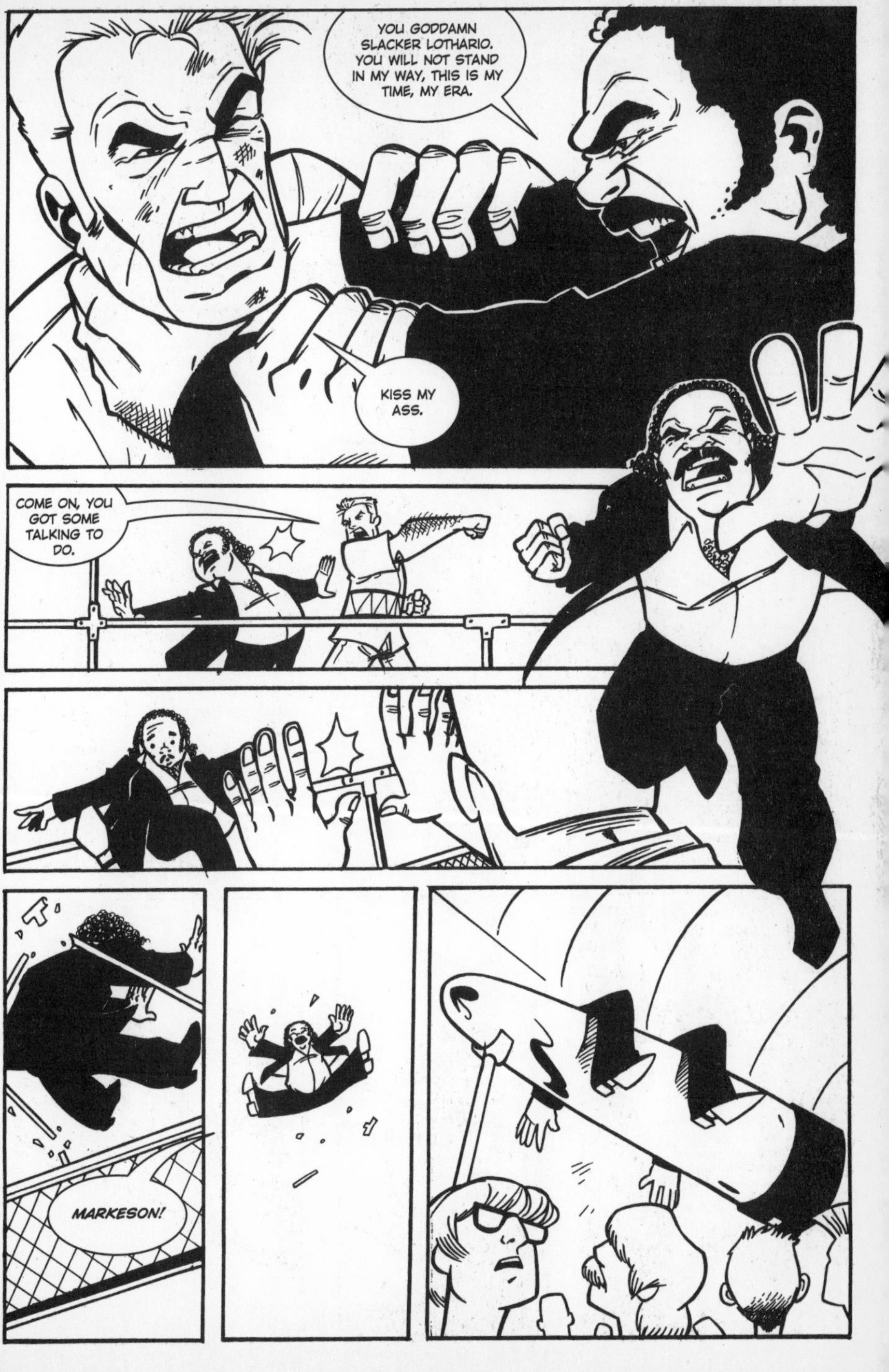
YOU GODDAMN SLACKER LOTHARIO. YOU WILL NOT STAND IN MY WAY, THIS IS MY TIME, MY ERA.
KISS MY ASS.
COME ON, YOU GOT SOME TALKING TO DO.
MARKESON!

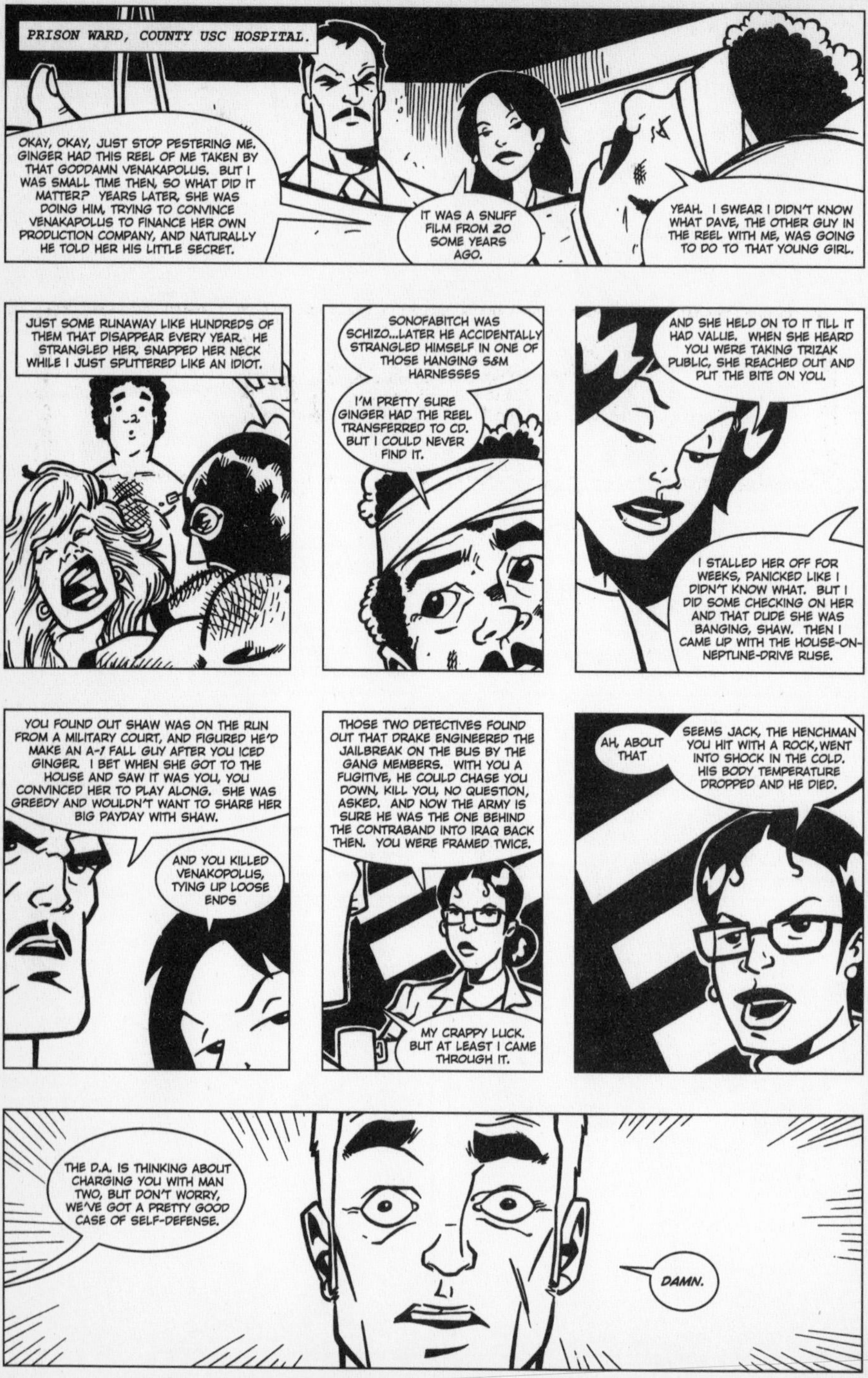
PRISON WARD, COUNTY USC HOSPITAL.
OKAY, OKAY, JUST STOP PESTERING ME. GINGER HAD THIS REEL OF ME TAKEN BY THAT GODDAMN VENAKAPOLUS. BUT I WAS SMALL TIME THEN, SO WHAT DID IT MATTER? YEARS LATER, SHE WAS DOING HIM, TRYING TO CONVINCE VENAKAPOLUS TO FINANCE HER OWN PRODUCTION COMPANY, AND NATURALLY HE TOLD HER HIS LITTLE SECRET.
IT WAS A SNUFF FILM FROM 20 SOME YEARS AGO.
YEAH. I SWEAR I DIDN'T KNOW WHAT DAVE, THE OTHER GUY IN THE REEL WITH ME, WAS GOING TO DO TO THAT YOUNG GIRL.
JUST SOME RUNAWAY LIKE HUNDREDS OF THEM THAT DISAPPEAR EVERY YEAR. HE STRANGLED HER, SNAPPED HER NECK WHILE I JUST SPUTTERED LIKE AN IDIOT.
SONOFABITCH WAS SCHIZO...LATER HE ACCIDENTALLY STRANGLED HIMSELF IN ONE OF THOSE HANGING S&M HARNESSES
I'M PRETTY SURE GINGER HAD THE REEL TRANSFERRED TO CD. BUT I COULD NEVER FIND IT.
AND SHE HELD ON TO IT TILL IT HAD VALUE. WHEN SHE HEARD YOU WERE TAKING TRIZAK PUBLIC, SHE REACHED OUT AND PUT THE BITE ON YOU.
I STALLED HER OFF FOR WEEKS, PANICKED LIKE I DIDN'T KNOW WHAT. BUT I DID SOME CHECKING ON HER AND THAT DUDE SHE WAS BANGING, SHAW. THEN I CAME UP WITH THE HOUSE-ON-NEPTUNE-DRIVE RUSE.
YOU FOUND OUT SHAW WAS ON THE RUN FROM A MILITARY COURT, AND FIGURED HE'D MAKE AN A-1 FALL GUY AFTER YOU ICED GINGER. I BET WHEN SHE GOT TO THE HOUSE AND SAW IT WAS YOU, YOU CONVINCED HER TO PLAY ALONG. SHE WAS GREEDY AND WOULDN'T WANT TO SHARE HER BIG PAYDAY WITH SHAW.
AND YOU KILLED VENAKOPOLUS, TYING UP LOOSE ENDS
THOSE TWO DETECTIVES FOUND OUT THAT DRAKE ENGINEERED THE JAILBREAK ON THE BUS BY THE GANG MEMBERS. WITH YOU A FUGITIVE, HE COULD CHASE YOU DOWN, KILL YOU, NO QUESTION, ASKED. AND NOW THE ARMY IS SURE HE WAS THE ONE BEHIND THE CONTRABAND INTO IRAQ BACK THEN. YOU WERE FRAMED TWICE.
MY CRAPPY LUCK. BUT AT LEAST I CAME THROUGH IT.
AH, ABOUT THAT
SEEMS JACK, THE HENCHMAN YOU HIT WITH A ROCK, WENT INTO SHOCK IN THE COLD. HIS BODY TEMPERATURE DROPPED AND HE DIED.
THE D.A. IS THINKING ABOUT CHARGING YOU WITH MAN TWO, BUT DON'T WORRY, WE'VE GOT A PRETTY GOOD CASE OF SELF-DEFENSE.
DAMN.

the end

GARY PHILLIPS is the author of several novels and short stories in the crime/mystery genre, including four books in the Ivan Monk PI series and two about Vegas showgirl-turned-mob courier Martha Chainey. His prose work has been nominated for the Gold Pen Award from the Black Writers Alliance and the Shamus Award from the Private Eye Writers of America. His recent novella, *The Perpetrators*, features a cover and spot illustrations by comics luminary Paul Pope and his latest novel, *Bangers*, is now available from Kensington Books. His debut graphic novel, *Shot Callerz*, featured art by indy comics sensation Brett Weldele and is still available from Oni Press. Phillips lives with his family in Los Angeles where he's hard at work on new projects for the page and screen.

JEREMY LOVE is the youngest of the creative siblings, the Love Brothers and vice-president of Gettosake Entertainment. Born in Burlington, North Carolina on February 5, 1977, Jeremy grew up enjoying Marvel Comics, classic animation, kung fu flicks and blaxploitation films. Taking an early interest in art, Jeremy pursued a career in the entertainment field directly after high school. After landing many freelance art jobs locally Jeremy and his brothers formed Gettosake Entertainment, now a full-fledged media development powerhouse.

JEFF WASSON is the inker of J. Torres and Tim Levins' fan-favorite *Copybook Tales* comics and the creator of his own independent comic, *Dressed for Success*. He currently lives in Vancouver, British Columbia where he's preparing to start work on his next collaboration with Jeremy Love.

PROSE NOVELS FROM GARY PHILLIPS...

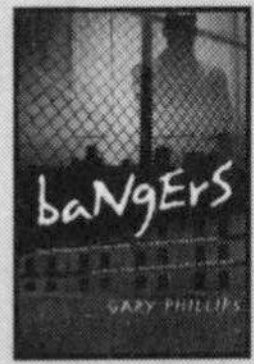
baNgErS
GARY PHILLIPS

BANGERS™
Kensington Publishing
304 pages
paperback
$15.00 US
ISBN 0-758203-82-9

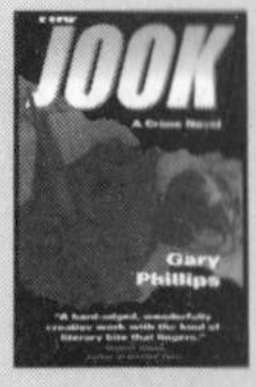
JOOK
A Crime Novel
Gary Phillips

THE JOOK™
Really Great Books
240 pages
paperback
$14.95 US
ISBN 1-893329-04-6

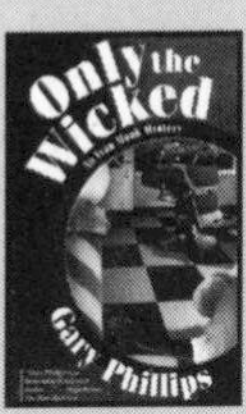
Only the Wicked
Gary Phillips

ONLY THE WICKED™
Write Way Publishing
352 pages
hardcover
$24.95 US
ISBN 1-885173-64-4

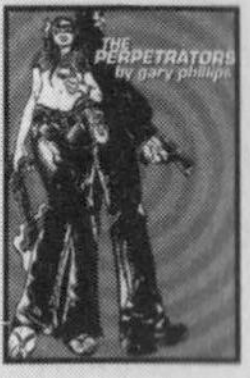
THE PERPETRATORS
by gary phillips

THE PERPETRATORS™
Uglytown Productions
176 pages
paperback
spot illustrations
by Paul Pope
$13.00 US
ISBN 0-966347-37-4

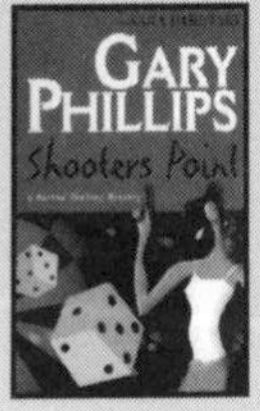
GARY PHILLIPS
Shooters Point

SHOOTER'S POINT: A MARTHA CHAINEY MYSTERY™
Kensington Publishing
256 pages
hardcover
$22.00 US
ISBN 1-575666-82-0

ALSO BY GARY, FROM ONI PRESS...

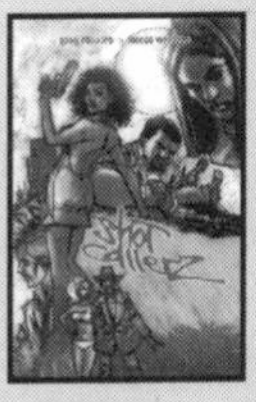

SHOT CALLERZ™
illustrated by Brett Weldele
120 pages
b/w interiors
$14.95 US
ISBN: 1-929998-46-5

For more info on Gary Phillips and his novels, visit www.gdphillips.com